The Blessing

Adrian Caesar was born and educated in England but has lived and worked in Australia for over thirty years. Formerly Associate Professor of English at UNSW@ADFA, since leaving full-time employment in 2004, Adrian has occasionally taught creative writing at ANU. He is the author of three books of literary and cultural criticism and an experimental 'non-fiction novel' *The White* (Picador, 1999) which won the Victorian Premier's Award for non-fiction in 2000 and the A.C.T. Book of the year, 2000. He has also published five books of poetry, the latest of which is *Dark Cupboards New Rooms* (Shoestring Press, 2014).

The Blessing

ADRIAN CAESAR

ARCADIA

First published 2015 by ARCADIA
the general books' imprint of
AUSTRALIAN SCHOLARLY PUBLISHING PTY LTD
7 Lt Lothian St North, North Melbourne, Victoria 3051
Tel: 61+3+9329 6963 / *Fax:* 61+3+9329 5452
Email: aspic@ozemail.com.au / *Web:* www.scholarly.info

ISBN: 978-1-925333-18-3

Cover design Wayne Saunders
Cover illustration Jim Pavlidis
Set in Sabon LT Std 10.7 pt

For Claire

Contents

Part I

The Covenant

Belfast–Manchester
1912–1913

I

Jack Young felt uplifted by a great power. It was as if he were a boy again, being hurled aloft by an unknown uncle's brawny arms, the smell of beer and sweat and cologne sour-sharp in his nostrils, the booming voice in his ear, 'Ay, you're a brave wee laddie'.

The exhilaration of being forcibly propelled into a whirl of new perspectives was on him, and he abandoned himself to the feeling. He didn't want to think. He wanted to lose himself, to surrender to the massive crowd of which he was a miniscule part. He was carried away by the turbulence that filled the imposing Belfast streets leading towards the City Hall.

He'd never seen anything like it—not even the biggest match at Windsor Park or the launch of the *Olympic* could compare to this. The pavements, the roads, the tramways, were filled with thousands of men and women dressed in their Sunday best. Though it was Saturday, many of them had come straight from Church services. Others had come from the pub. The throng seethed with enthusiasm. Union Jacks were everywhere. They flew from the tops of office buildings and were shoved on poles through high windows so they hung like bunting across the way. Men waved them proudly above their heads. Orange sashes added to the colour. The sound of drum and fife bands playing 'The Boyne Water' and 'Protestant Boys' competed with the constant hum of excitement. 'Is that the man himself?' 'Did you see him there, Willie?' 'Ay, that'll be him sure.' 'So it is.' People craned their necks to see what was happening on the steps of the great building, even though they were half a mile away.

Jack stood in the shadows cast by tall buildings, and, straining to see above the crowds in front of him, peered towards Donegall Square. It was a fine autumn day. The over-ripe sunlight of noon accentuated the difference between the white Portland stone of City Hall and the redbrick of the nearby shops and business houses that lined Royal Avenue. The Hall, the distant focus of attention, with its columns and portico looked like a dream of wedding cake grandeur.

He was jostled and tumbled by the sway and press of people on all sides of him. He had to work hard to keep in sight of his friends. But there were no enemies here. All were united in their place and purpose. No matter if you were gentry from one of the great houses, a banker, a butcher, or a riveter from the shipworks, there were ties that bound: all were made equal in this outpouring of passion for the cause.

A cheer went up from the front, and the noise swelled down the street. Broad accents declared it was the 'great man himself'. He was being greeted by the mayor and corporation. Hats were flung into the air. Carson was here. Carson, the author of the Covenant. Carson who would save them from being sold out by the English government. Carson the guardian of their loyalty, Carson the scourge of the Home-Rulers.

There had never been any doubt in Jack's mind that he would come to Covenant Day or that he would sign, pledging himself to oppose Home Rule, 'using all means which may be found necessary'. His Mam and Da, his sisters, his workmates were all in favour; it was about loyalty to your people. But he had not anticipated the thrill of being a part of something so huge. The emotion of the moment surged within him, and he was able to throw his cap in the air and join his voice to the cheers, forgetting in the wild excitement of it all, the troubles in his personal life to which he had no answers.

There was a lull, while Carson and the other dignitaries disappeared inside; they would be the first to sign the Covenant. After half an hour's shuffling, listening to the bands and the craic, there was the hint of further movement. Jack craned his neck to see what was happening. He could just make out ushers in the regalia of the Orange Lodges marshalling a batch of men up the steps and into the City Hall to sign and be presented with their own parchment copy of the Covenant. From half a mile away, standing on tiptoes, it was difficult to see just how many men were let in at a time. Even if there were hundreds, the crowds were so dense it seemed to Jack it would take until after nightfall to have his turn.

The cheers and delirium of midday could not be sustained through an afternoon of waiting, hands in pockets, shuffling forward a few yards at a time. It was not as if you could stare into the windows of the expensive shops that lined the avenue. Too many bodies stood in the way. There was too much time to think. Even the company of his mates, Willie McCullough, Bob Haslam and Herbie Ryan, with their talk of football and the pub couldn't dispel the anxiety that Jack had hoped to shelve for the day. The chances of Distillery beating Celtic that afternoon was much discussed; the fond recollection of previous matches and Guinness celebrations afterwards were lingered over, but all this seemed to Jack like remembrances of an earlier more innocent time, as if they were preoccupations of childhood, rather than the proper concerns of the adulthood he felt pressing upon him in recent times.

Jack's unease was increased when the banter took another unexpected turn.

'Now then, Jack.' It was Herbie Ryan speaking. He was a small wiry man with a beaky nose and quick bird-like eyes. 'My Mammy says she's seen youse out walking the other evenin'.' He paused, glanced at the other fellows, and looked meaningfully at Jack. 'You weren't alone. What do you say to that?'

'I says nothing to your gossip.'

With the declining sun and the onset of shadows, Jack felt the chill beginning, the breath of winter on the air. He shivered involuntarily.

'Hair as black as a raven's wing, titties white as snow.' Herbie chanted the words of a folk rhyme.

'Oh ho,' said Bob Haslam, his eyes alight with mischief.

'Who is she, Jack? Who is she?' Willie chimed in, avid for details.

Jack reddened, uncomfortable, saying nothing, not meeting their eyes. He stared ahead, wishing he could escape the interrogation.

'I seen him, boys, I seen him,' Herbie took up the baiting. 'She's been getting on the Ormeau Road car for weeks. That's her isn't it Jack? The one you have a wee word to as she gets on and another wee word as she gets off. I've seen you.'

Jack and his mates worked on the trams. Herbie was a conductor, Jack a driver. Herbie had used his powers of observation well. Still, Jack said nothing.

Willie and Bob started skylarking, pushing Jack and elbowing him in the ribs. 'Come on, man, tell us the story. Who are you walking out with? Who is she? Have you kissed her?'

'Get away out of it,' Jack shrugged them off. 'I'm saying nothin' to the likes of you.'

But they wouldn't leave him alone. 'Too good for us, is she Jack?' said Willie.

'Is she a toff then, Herbie?' asked Bob.

'That'd be telling.'

They took to jostling Jack again.

'Get away with your bother.' He was becoming impatient now, and frightened that Herbie knew more than he was letting on. There were good reasons for secrecy, and he was determined not to give in. He shrugged off the playful thumps and jabs and jostling.

Herbie began to whistle a familiar tune. Soon Bob and Willie took up the chorus, singing with foolish grins on their faces:

She is handsome, she is pretty
She is the belle of Belfast city
She is courting one, two, three,
Please won't you tell us who is she?

The jingling rhyme was hateful to Jack, but at least Herbie had not said anything else. He decided to get away before there was more trouble. 'You hopeless stumers, goodbye to you,' he said, and risking the wrath of the waiting men in front, he began to push his way forward through the crowd. Ignoring the indignant cries of 'Steady on there,' and 'Easy does it,' he forged ahead. He could hear the shouts of his friends urging him to stay, but he would have none of it. He wanted to be away.

The crowd, though, was too dense to escape entirely. A rattle of drums and trilling of fifes took away the words of the skipping song that still reverberated in his mind. He stood still again, surrounded by strangers now, and thankful to be away from the ribald nudges and winks of his mates who didn't seem to have any understanding of the way he might feel.

Even in this press of bodies, with bands playing and flags flying, with all the babble of talk and laughter, Jack could not free himself as he had wished to; she dwelt in his mind, an ambiguous obsession, beautiful and dangerous. He could not reasonably say what it was in those eyes, green as sea stones, or in that shiny black hair, black as a raven's wing, which had so beguiled him from the start. But from the first 'Good-morning to you' he had heard from her lips in a low voice that seemed to sing, he had been lost. Matters had progressed quickly, from passing a few words with her to meeting her at her tram stop on his day off. 'I hope you don't mind,' he'd said, 'but I wanted a wee chat with you. To see if you might take a walk out with me sometime.' She smiled. At first he thought it was out of pity, but then she said yes.

Walking by the Lagan on long summer nights had soon become kissing in the shadows. And kissing in the shadows had led to the urgent search for quiet places in the meadows and hills around Castlereagh where they would lie down together, and let their passion take its course. No matter that early on she had told him she was a Catholic. No matter that his Mam had always warned him about fast convent girls. No matter that he had promised his mother to remain chaste until his wedding day. Nothing could stop his yearning for Kathleen McCafferty.

He was not at all sure that what he felt for her was love. Rather, there was wonder at her easy ways and laughter. She was less inhibited than the Protestant girls he knew, who always seemed to Jack proud and withheld. They made him feel awkward and turned his usual quietness into tongue-tied shyness. Kathleen was so relaxed herself that it relaxed Jack. She had led him physically, making him wonder at her hunger, her ardent tongue and hands. And when, after their first time, he'd been abashed, worried and guilty at what they'd done, she did up his buttons for him and told him to cheer-up. 'Sure it's only natural, so,' she said. 'If God won't forgive that, he won't forgive anything.'

He asked if she would confess. 'God love you, what a question to be asking a girl.' She shook her head, a glint of gaiety in her eyes. 'I might and I might not. I'll have to see if he's a handsome priest. But there's no need for you to be worryin'. Come here with you and kiss me again.'

Jack could only obey. When he was not with her he tormented himself with recriminations. Perhaps Kathleen was what other people might call 'easy'. But he could not give her up. As soon as he remembered the feel of her breast, the long nipple hardening against his thumb, or thought of her white thighs, he couldn't wait to see her again. He lied to his parents about where and with whom he was spending his time. He kept his secret to himself, yet lived in perpetual fear of someone seeing him and saying something to his parents.

He courted disaster and disaster had befallen him. Kathleen was pregnant. She'd told him last week. He had no idea what to do. She daren't tell her parents; he daren't tell his. They wouldn't have him marrying a Catholic. Kathleen's parents were the same; they didn't believe in mixed marriages. And now Herbie Ryan with his gossip. More to the point, Mrs Ryan with her loose tongue. She'd be leaning into Jack's mother's ear before long, so she would.

The dilemma he was in made him hot with shame and confusion. His only recourse was to dream of running away. But that would be disloyal to Kathleen. Staying with her, though, would mean betraying his family, his heritage, his beliefs. Was he not here now, about to sign a pledge that divided him from Kathleen and her family? Then there was the child to consider. How often had he heard his mother and father inveigh against Fenians with their loose morals and bastard children? He didn't know what to do. He'd been a fool. Kathleen had told him everything would be all right. In his innocence and ignorance he'd presumed she would not fall pregnant. Now he was caught. And there was a doubt in his mind about whether marriage to Kathleen, even if it were possible, was really what he wanted. There was something in her, he told himself, that didn't accord well with his idea of a wife. Or was it his mother's idea of a wife that was the problem? That was nearer the mark.

He'd said to Kathleen that he needed time to think. 'Say and do nothin' yet,' he advised, 'I have to think.'

Thinking hadn't helped. There was no one he could turn to for advice. He'd heard whispers about back street abortionists, the unimaginable horrors of knitting needles and coat hangers, and poisonous potions. It was a world of dark stories that he knew nothing of in reality. He could not think of Kathleen undergoing such tortures. He knew, too, that for many of the poor marriage was a ceremony conducted by themselves without the trappings of priest and Church. A jump over a yard-brush and it was done. But neither his nor Kathleen's family would countenance such behaviour.

Jack made himself tired, revolving the situation in his mind. By the time he was wearily admitted to the long desk-lined corridors of the City Hall, the excitement with which the day had started had dissipated. There was little sense of elation as he signed his name, and took possession of his copy of the Covenant. He was a Loyalist, but he had already betrayed himself. He could not see how he was to regain his honour, his pride. It seemed to Jack, that he was bound to be untruthful, to live in a world of secrets and lies that separated him from his friends and family. There was no alternative.

As he made his way home, Jack thought how easy defending Ulster against Home Rule seemed compared with the complications of his private life. The thought of soldiering appealed to him. A simple game. A man's game. Nothing to do with the women.

But he was besotted with a woman. A Catholic woman. A Fenian. God help him, if his parents ever found out. Kicking the leaves on the greasy pavement, he offered up a prayer that Mrs Ryan had not been blabbing to his mother. He wished he had a place of his own. He wished he didn't have to go home. He wished he was going to Kathleen to lie with her again. Enfolded in her arms, perhaps he could forget for a few moments, the terrible consequences of such moments of bliss.

II

The week after Covenant Day, Jack was on late turn at work. He started his shift in the early afternoon and finished with the last tram at night. Usually, he didn't mind working the unsociable hours. He enjoyed beginning and ending the days alone. In the mornings, he could stay in bed after everyone else had gone to work; his sisters to the mill, his Mam to do her cleaning, and Da to his gardening at the big house. At the end of the day, he relished the long walk through the quiet streets, the feeling of peace and solitude after the business and bustle. He looked forward to getting home, and having the kitchen to himself. There would be a bit of something left for him to eat, some bacon and soda bread perhaps, or mutton with spuds and peas, which he'd warm in the oven. Except at the height of summer, his parents always left the range backed up, so that he could sit in comfort for a while, listening to the creak of the house, smoking a cigarette or a pipe after his meal in luxurious ease, without having to deal with the clamour of his sisters, or the mithering of his Mam.

Tonight, though, as he walked home through the deserted streets, inhaling the smoky tang of autumn, Jack was not easy in his mind. On the quiet, over a cup of tea at the depot, Herbie with a knowing wink and a raised eyebrow had made clear he knew more about Kathleen McCafferty than he'd admitted on Saturday. Without the company of their other mates, Herbie seemed more sympathetic, but still he'd been free with his advice. 'Jack, lad, you should be more careful with the company you keep, so you should. People will think you've forgotten where you belong. I'll say no more, now. But think on, man. Don't let a woman make a fool of you. You should stick with your own people.'

Jack had said nothing in reply, but returned to his work with a terrible heaviness on him. He was worried about losing his friends. He was terrified at the thought of his parents finding out what he'd done. And what defence could he offer? He hardly knew himself what it was that had drawn him to Kathleen. Something about the way she held herself, head up, square shouldered, the pride in her—as if she were ready to take on all comers and beat them. The challenge sparkling in her eyes. But there were mysteries beyond words. All he recognised for certain was the turbulence of feeling that thoughts of her aroused in him.

When he arrived home, all the lights at the front were out as usual. He bent to open the wooden gate that creaked on its rusty hinges. He put his key to the front door as quietly as he could. They lived in a terraced parlour house, which had a tiny paved front garden behind a low wall and an extra small room upstairs and down, thereby distinguishing the dwelling from the two-up-two-down kitchen houses of the poorer workers of Belfast. The front door opened onto a small passage that led past the seldom-used front room and the parlour to the back kitchen, which Jack thought of as the warm heart of the dwelling.

As he stepped inside, he was assaulted by apprehension. A violent sickness threatened his stomach. He swallowed hard. The gas mantles were still lit in the kitchen. He could hear the voices of his parents talking quietly.

He hesitated in the hall, hanging his peaked cap, and fiddling with the buttons of his uniform jacket. It was his habit to arrange this carefully on a hanger, which had pride of place on one of the coat hooks where the rest of the family slung their outdoor gear. Jack was proud of his uniform. Tonight, instinctively, he kept it on, as if to protect him; it was an assertion of his adulthood, his independence.

The kitchen was frowsty with steam from the kettle, which simmered on the hob, and the pungent fumes of his father's pipe. The gas mantles wheezed and popped gently.

'Mam, Da,' Jack nodded by way of greeting.

They looked at him grim faced.

'You'll know what this'll be about then?' His Mam began determinedly. Her broad brow was creased, her thin lips pursed tight. The drawn back hair in its fierce bun, the high-necked blouse, the plain dark skirts, the black woollen shawl—everything about her spoke of severity.

Jack's father, a tall gaunt man, sat in his chair, shoulders slumped. He sucked in his cheeks, which emphasised his bones and made his face seem even thinner than usual.

'I'll be after some supper,' Jack said.

'You'll be getting no supper here, the night,' his Mam replied, lowering. 'Not until you've explained why I've had Missus Ryan gossiping down my ear about your goings on.'

'I've nothing to say. I'm a grown man, so I am. I'm twenty-one years old. I can do as I like.'

'Ay, you can do as you like,' Jack's father butted in, 'but you'll not come back to this house from your Fenian whore.' He removed the pipe from his mouth and spat into the fire. There was a hiss as the phlegm hit the coals.

'Does it mean nothin' to you, to be seen walking out with the likes of her? She isn't decent,' his mother continued.

'Her name's Kathleen McCafferty. I met her on the tram. We got to talking. She's a grand girl.' Even as he spoke, he heard how limp his words sounded.

'Talking. From what I hear there's been a lot more than talking going on.'

'She's a lovely girl,' Jack was at a loss to explain himself.

'Will you listen to the whey-faced fool, father. A lovely girl indeed. Lovely it is to be having kissings and canoodlings down by the river. It doesn't matter to her, what she gets up to. Morals like alley-cats they have, then it's off to confession, a few Hail Mary's and all's right with the world. We'll have none of that sort in this house. Think of your sisters.'

'It's no wonder I've kept quiet about her is it? I couldn't think of bringing her here. But it's all right. I'll find myself somewhere else to live, then you'll not be bothered.'

'That's how it's to be is it? You'd give up your own family to take up with a Fenian?' It was Tom Young again, seething quietly. 'And what of the Covenant you signed Saturday? What of that eh? As sure as there's a Presbyterian God in heaven, the McCaffertys'll be Home Rulers. They want a Papist nation. We've vowed to fight them. You've vowed to fight them.'

Jack was still standing by the door, facing his interrogators. He felt like pacing up and down, but there was nowhere to go. 'I can't see what Kathleen has to do with politics. She's not interested.'

'Have you taken leave of your senses, man? It's all of them we'll be fighting, if it comes to it—has she no Da and brothers? Blood's thicker than water. You need to think on.'

Jack's previous experience of his father was of a man quiet to the point of impenetrability. Now he was taken aback by the vehemence with which his Da expressed himself. He had no reply.

'Your Father's right. You should finish with her before more harm's done. You're thinking of yourself alone. If you won't do the right thing by us, think of what you're doing to her. What sort of a position will she be in, if the fighting starts?'

'It might not come to fighting,' Jack said, lamely. He had no answers to the onslaught. He was perplexed by an impulse to confess the full extent of his dilemma to his parents. His Mam had always helped and advised him. Now, despite her anger, he felt the need of her strength. But he couldn't find the right words. Instead he looked at his feet, the shoes polished to a brilliant shine, his father's work. Every morning Jack was on nights, every night if he was on days, his Da polished his shoes for him. The idea of it choked him now.

'I've been thinking of going over the water,' he said in a low voice, still hanging his head.

There was a pause. Jack glanced up and saw his parents looking at each other, their faces stricken.

'What in God's name would you be wanting to do that for?' It was his mother who broke the silence. 'Surely you won't be flitting with her?'

'I don't know,' he answered truthfully.

'Don't be doing that, son. Finish with this woman and stay here where you belong with your Mammy and Daddy and your sisters.'

'It's not as easy as that.'

'What kind of a man are you?' Jack's old man was up out of his chair now, his pipe aggressively pointed, emphasising each word. 'All you have to do is tell her you'll have no more of her. You found it easy enough to betray your family, your God and your people. How hard can it be to tell this . . . this . . . trollope that it's over between youse?'

'She's going to have a babby.' Jack looked at his father with forlorn eyes. The old man slumped back down on his chair, the wind taken out of him. His mother stared with her mouth open, as if she'd been slapped across the face.

At that moment, the three of them became aware of footsteps thumping downstairs. It was Eileen, the elder of Jack's two sisters. She had on a plaid woollen dressing-gown over her long nightie. Her black hair curled loose in tendrils about her shoulders. 'What in the name of God's the matter?' she enquired as she entered the kitchen. 'There's no rest to be had with all this mithering going on.' She looked from one to the other of them, red in the face, eighteen-year-old eyes blazing.

'Away back to bed. This has nothing to do with you.' Tom Young's gruff voice didn't lack command when necessary, though it was a manner he rarely adopted.

'Are you all right Jack?' Eileen said.

'Ay, I'm all right. Not to worry now. Sorry for the noise. Do as Da says. We'll not be far behind you.'

Eileen searched his face, then looked at each of her parents hesitantly.

'Do as they say.' Mother joined the chorus, her voice more peremptory than the others.

Eileen turned to go. She squeezed Jack's arm as she left. He pressed his lips together, determined not to give way to his feelings.

'We should go to bed too,' he mumbled.

'Not before I've had my say.'

Jack braced himself for more from his mother.

'How dare you?' she said. 'How dare you come into this house fresh from your whorin' and telling us she's a lovely girl. I'm ashamed of you, that I am. After all you promised. After all we've done for you. This is the thanks we get. I have to think of my only son as the father of a Catholic bastard.'

Jack said nothing. He stood, looking at the floor, while his mother stared at him indignantly. After a long pause, he said, 'I'm goin' to bed.'

'Have you nothing at all to say for yourself? At least you might have the decency to let us know what in the name of God has possessed you to act like a fool.'

Jack replied with slow deliberation. 'Kathleen is no whore. She is a lovely girl. And as for bastards, there are plenty of Protestants living o'er the brush.'

'None that are decent.' His mother, red in the face, her voice trembling took a deep breath, as if she were preparing a further tirade. Before she could begin, her husband interrupted.

'Leave it, Nell.' Jack's father rose and tapped his pipe rather more forcefully than usual on the grate. There's nought more to be done or said tonight.' He turned to Jack. 'Leave your shoes for the mornin'.'

'There's no need, Da.'

'Leave them, I said.'

Awkwardly, Jack bent and holding one foot at a time across his knees, he unlaced his boots. He placed them by the hearth. As he straightened to leave the room, his mother came and stood before him. She was a robust woman, but not as tall as Jack. He half expected her to embrace him, as she would do usually, but tonight the gesture was held back. Instead, she looked up at him with fierce eyes. 'Maybe it's best you should go,' she said, her voice low and emphatic. 'But don't take her with you, Jack. Don't you see what she's done? She's seduced you and snared you. The devil's in these Fenian girls. Leave her to her bastard. You can have another life with a decent woman. In a year or two you could come back.' She turned to her husband. 'What d'you say, Tom?'

'If needs must,' he said. 'I've a distant cousin in Manchester. Maybe she could help you out. We'll see. And there's plenty that supports Ulster over there. The Covenant's been signed in Liverpool and Manchester. There's plenty of our own folk there.'

'Thanks,' Jack said, his voice full of misery. 'I'm sorry for the trouble.' He got out of the kitchen as quickly as he could. He was desperate to escape upstairs to the security of the tiny box room in which he slept.

Having gained that sanctuary, he found no rest. He stared out of the window at the deserted street below. A gaslight shone sickly yellow on the pavement, wet now with a miserable drizzle that had just begun. A few leaves, autumn's dirty remnants, scudded along the cobbles. The scene was hollow, desolate. Jack could not reconcile his parents' harsh words with the girl he thought he knew. He didn't feel that he'd been tricked or snared. He had wanted her. But now, what was he to do?

Towards dawn, he fell into an exhausted sleep. Jack Young dreamt he was walking streets that looked familiar, yet he didn't know where he was. The roads all looked the same. Rows and rows of terraced housing. He took a tram, but still he didn't recognise any familiar landmark. When he got off, he knew he was searching for home. But he didn't know where that was.

III

Kathleen McCafferty's father ran a pub in Cromac Street. The family lived in rooms above the bar. Every morning except Sunday, glad to escape the reek of stale beer and cigarette smoke that pervaded her home, Kathleen travelled by tram to her Aunt Mary's house in the Falls Road. She worked there all day, half day Saturdays, hemming and embroidering linen handkerchiefs. It was piece-work. Her aunt's eyesight was failing after years at the needlework, so the family decided that Kathleen should help, giving her an occupation that kept her out of the mills, and out of the pub. Her father would rather hire barmen than have the clientele ogling his daughter, and stitching, though hard and demanding work, was nothing like as punishing as working in the flax mills.

Jack knew Kathleen's routines well. When he awoke late on the morning after the confrontation with his parents, he knew he had to speak with her before he began his shift. Though his head felt thick, as if stuffed with the torn remnants of dream and nightmare, he also had an immediate sense of purpose. He could not bear to go through another working day without talking to Kathleen and putting to her the plan for their future that now seemed so obvious to him. He would go to her aunt's place and wait for her outside. Kathleen often walked out for half an hour at one o' clock to escape the confines of her aunt's company. 'She's a sweet auld soul,' Kathleen would say, 'but dull as a wet weekend.'

Making this resolution, Jack clambered into the day. He went downstairs in his combinations, knowing that he had the house to himself. The lino on the stairs and the kitchen flags were cold to his feet. He was grateful to reach the hearth rug and warm himself at the range. The embers were still glowing. He put some more coal on, giving the fire a poke as he did so, and noticing his polished boots standing ready for him. Soon the kettle was singing on the hob. He made himself some tea, then poured the rest of the water for his wash and shave into the kitchen sink, regarding his face in the small mirror that his Da had nailed to the wall for the purpose.

Jack found the business of shaving satisfying. He loved the idea of the blade providing a daily cleansing and freshening. And there was a chance to indulge in the fascinating business of staring at his face, at first covered in its white beard of soap, then uncovered by the revealing razor. There was always something mysterious about this to Jack. As if the image he uncovered was both himself and not himself at the same time.

He recognised that his broad features and square chin more obviously resembled his mother than his father. He shared her solid build as well. But on certain days, the shadows under his eyes and the shape of his cheek bones made him feel his father's inheritance expressing itself as well. Most of all what fascinated Jack was the feeling that his face was never exactly the same for two days at a time. He often played at making different expressions, amused by the mobility of his features, the way that he could make himself look fierce, or moody, or full of laughter by wilful rearrangements. He didn't consider this vain. On the contrary, he didn't think he was particularly good looking; he found the paleness of his blue eyes and the mouse-brown colour of his hair disappointing. He fancied that the lasses preferred black hair and turquoise eyes.

Yet Kathleen seemed to like him well enough. He remembered her fingers tracing his features like a blind woman feeling her way. She had stared unblinking into his eyes as she explored. It was as if she thought she could learn who he was through touch, absorb him though her fingertips. It was after this, lying together in a daisy-spangled summer meadow, sun-dazed and sleepy she'd said, 'Do you know what I love about you, Jack Young?' He'd felt his heart bounce at the word 'love'. It gave him a waking shock like a cold wave in the sea, breath-taking, exhilarating. 'Go on with you. I've no idea what you see in me. I'm just glad you see something.' She'd put her palms to his face then. 'There's a quietness to you, Jack Young, and a gentleness. You're not full of yourself and forward like the other fellas, always boasting and pawing at me. You have something more about you. I have a feeling you'll make something of yourself.'

It was true he didn't want to be a tram driver all his life. And he'd said so in reply to Kathleen. But he didn't go on to share his dreams with her. It was not only that he was frightened of sounding ridiculous. It was also a superstition that if he voiced his vague ambitions it would make them seem impossible, unattainable. It was better to let his dreams lie dormant like seeds in dark earth waiting for rain. He wanted to cultivate his ideas before he shared them with anybody. Still, Kathleen's words were precious to him. That she believed in him was a grand feeling—one he didn't wish to lose.

As he removed the last of the soap, Jack stared at his face in the mirror and thought of his lunch time encounter with Kathleen. He would be serious, ardent, full of enthusiasm and conviction. He would persuade her of the rightness of his plan. The discussion would be difficult, but his cards would be on the table. The relief would be wonderful. Already, the fact that things were out in the open with his parents had blunted some of the raw edges that had been scraping away at his guts for days. Now, if he could set matters straight with Kathleen, the worst would be over, and he could begin to look forward.

Jack wiped his face on a bit of towel, and slurped his tea. 'Man, that was grand', he thought to himself as he drained the large cup. Warmed by the soothing liquid, he remounted the stairs to dress himself, rehearsing the words he would use with Kathleen to untangle the snarls in his heart and make the crooked straight.

'Good day to you. And what may you be doin' hanging round street corners like some good for nothing layabout?' Kathleen's eyes attempted a smile but her face was creased with care.

Jack appreciated her gesture towards levity, however unconvincing it was. He had waited for her, lounging against the wall of a corner terrace just up the road from her aunt's place, his hands in his pockets. He didn't want to be caught loitering by the auld lady.

'I'm after a word to you, Kathleen. I feel we must get things settled.'

She took his arm and said, 'Let's walk. It's chilly. I'm glad to see you. I can't stop worryin' and I'm feared to death of what my Da will do when he finds out I'm carryin'.'

They began to walk on pavements as dirty grey as the familiar sky. A biting wind blew off the lough like an omen. Jack hated the way the earlier gaiety of their meetings was now replaced by nagging anxieties. He couldn't help being aware of the sway of Kathleen's body next to his; the power of her attraction was undiminished. Yet the sparkle and vivacity of her face seemed dimmed and the music of her low voice was made slow and sombre, every word seeming a burden to her. He longed to make things right between them again.

'I have a plan.' Jack heard the false brightness in his tone. 'I want to see what you think.'

Kathleen glanced up at him, the frown on her face deepening, scepticism in her eyes. 'Go on, then. But saving a miracle, I can't see what's to be done.'

'I think we should go over the water.' Jack paused, aware that he'd been more direct than he'd intended. Before he could go on, Kathleen interrupted.

'How can we up and leave? What would we do in England? We can't get wed can we? Where would we live? Where's the money coming from?'

'Listen a minute. I've been thinking things through. Mebbe it's best if I go first. My Da's got a cousin in Manchester. I could go over, fix myself up with a job and somewhere to live, then you could come and join me.'

'And what then? I'll be showing. My Mam and Da will know. They'll be after marryin' me, so I'll have to explain you're a Prod. If I just flit, there'll be the same trouble in Manchester. You won't want to marry me in a Catholic Church.'

'I might,' said Jack. 'Once I get away from here, and set up on me own. I'd marry for you and the babby. Or I could just buy you a ring. We've had no need of Church so far.' Jack was surprised by his own temerity. He wasn't certain he could go through with such schemes, but that wasn't the point. His main idea was to have Kathleen agree to the principle. He wanted to persuade her they could have a future together in England.

But Kathleen wasn't convinced. She sensed the hesitations in him. 'You're just saying that, Jack Young. Once you're away it'll be goodbye and good luck to you. You're just after running away from me.'

'That's not so,' Jack protested. 'What else can we do? You've said yourself we can't get wed here and we can't live o'er the brush. So what do you suggest?'

Kathleen was silent for a time, walking with her head down, her face set hard. Jack's irritation increased. This wasn't how he'd imagined the encounter. He wanted her to acquiesce so he could leave with a clear conscience, believing that she would join him and they could have a future together. No matter how painful the idea of leaving Belfast, there was an unmistakable allure in the idea of a new life. It would be an escape from the suffocating influence of his parents and a relief from the divided loyalties he couldn't avoid in Belfast. There would be more room to move and breathe in Manchester where nobody knew you, without the nods and winks and knowing handshakes of Belfast—the silent codes that governed whose side you were on.

'Come on,' he goaded her. 'What's your idea?'

Kathleen took her arm from his, and shoved her hands into the pockets of her cheap coat. She spoke in a blank, defeated voice. 'I'll tell me Ma. She'll have me away to the convent—the Little Sisters of Charity that look after fallen girls. But at least I could still see you sometimes. And when the babby's born, you could help me out with a bit of money, and see the child sometimes. It'd be better than nothing, better than being apart.'

'I can't see any future in it. Your parents won't have me near you. My way, there's a chance we could be together. I could send you a ring. You could come over. We wouldn't have to get married. We could say you were my wife. Who's to know the difference?'

'What about your father's auld cousin?'

'I'll soon get clear of her. There's nothing she can do anyway. I'm a grown man.'

Kathleen stopped walking, and turned towards him. She looked into his face. 'I don't know, Jack Young. I don't know. You make it all sound grand, but once you're over there, you'll soon forget me. You won't want to be landed with me and the babby, no matter what you say now.'

Jack held her gaze, trying to persuade her. Trying to persuade himself. 'I want to be with you. I do, honest,' he said. He fumbled in his pocket and drew out a packet of five cigarettes. He struggled to light one, shielding the light against the wind. He didn't usually smoke outside. His Ma said it was 'common' to smoke in the streets. But this was no ordinary occasion. Jack was in need of comfort.

'Are you not after giving me one then?' Kathleen looked at him quizzically, throwing out a challenge.

Jack had forgotten occasionally she'd join him in a smoke. When they were alone in the meadows, it seemed daring and sophisticated. Now, his Mam's words about only fast women smoking haunted his offering.

Kathleen took the cigarette and waited for Jack to light it for her. She inhaled and brandished the thing defiantly, as if she wanted people to notice what she was doing. There was a bravado in her that Jack couldn't help but admire, even if he sometimes felt intimidated by it.

'You'll be doing whatever you want to do anyway,' she said. 'You'll take no notice of me, when all's said and done. It's ever been the same. It's us women who have to bear the consequences of men's pleasures.'

'They were your pleasures as well,' Jack reminded her.

'Ay, they were as well, Jack Young. Now comes the penance. When will you be going?'

Jack drew heavily on his cigarette. 'I haven't made my mind up to go. I wanted to see what you thought.'

'You'll be going. I can tell by your eyes. You might as well be on the boat now. You're not here with me, as once you were. You're already travelling.'

'I'm not at all. Don't you see? I want you to come with me.'

'And haven't I already told you I can't come with you, while we've no money and nowhere to stay?'

'Say, you'll join me. I could go soon, in a week or two, and get set up over there. Mebbe I could send you some money and you could come and have the babby in England?'

'I don't know Jack.' She sounded weary now. 'I expect I'll have the child here at home, where I belong. At least I know I'll be looked after by the nuns. My Mam'll help me as well. She'll have to tell my Da. He'll be after murderin' me. Then he'll be after murderin' you.' She laughed softly. 'So you'd best be on your way out of it.'

Jack threw down the stub of his cigarette and ground it out with his heel. He looked at the pavement not knowing what to feel. An anger unaccountable to himself took hold of him.

'It sounds as if you want me gone. Won't you say you'll come to me when the child's born?'

'I'm promising nothing, Jack. We'll see what happens.' Kathleen stubbed her cigarette. 'We should be getting back.'

They turned together and walked in silence, Jack feeling helpless and miserable. Kathleen with her head in the air.

'How can I persuade you?' Jack muttered.

'How can I persuade you to stay?' Kathleen countered.

'But there's no hope for us here. In Manchester nobody need know we're Catholic and Proddy mixed. Nobody need know anything about us at all. We can just be ourselves. The two of us against the world.'

'Three of us.' Kathleen corrected him, a note of irony in her voice.

'Ay, well, of course. The three of us.'

'I don't know, Jack. A girl needs her Mammy at a time like this.'

They walked on, a silence thick between them like a wall. Jack had run out of energy. He didn't know what else to say. When they came close to the spot where they had to part, Kathleen's arm stole through Jack's and she squeezed his wrist.

'You're a decent man, Jack Young. I'm sorry it's come to this.'

'I'm sorry too, lass. Sorrier than I can say.'

'I don't want you to go.' Kathleen's tone was matter-of-fact. She wasn't pleading or wheedling. Her head was still in the air.

'The only way to make this right is to leave. I don't want to abandon you. I want you to come with me.' He felt a kind of vertigo at the thought of losing her. His stomach dipped as if a black and bottomless pit were opening beneath his feet.

A dizzying emptiness. He sensed her slipping away from him and there was nothing he could do.

They reached the corner where they'd met. Kathleen stopped. 'Best not to come further,' she said. She leaned up and kissed him quickly. He felt the softness of her lips on him, and the subtle intimation of warmth from her body. She stepped away.

'You won't go without seeing me again, will you?'

'Course not.'

She walked off, Jack staring after her, taken aback by the abrupt parting.

'I'll see you soon,' he shouted after her.

She half turned, then hurried away. Jack raised his hand to wave. He thought he might have seen the glassy sheen of tears in her eye. But he wasn't sure. It could have been the unforgiving East wind making her eyes water, just as he told himself that that was his trouble.

IV

Kathleen walked away from Jack Young with her head held high. She would not turn back to look at him. She pressed her tongue against the roof of her mouth and willed herself not to cry. She might not have her man, but she had her pride. She would not give him the satisfaction of seeing her tears. But she knew before she went back for her afternoon's work, she would somehow have to compose herself. An interrogation from her aunt was the last thing she needed. She was not ready to confess her condition to her family. She had to come to terms with the confusion of her own feelings first. Part of her, she now realised, had irrationally hoped Jack would be with her when she told her parents. Despite the fury her father might unleash on him. When Jack said he had a plan, she had felt a flutter of hope, but when she heard his suggestion to leave Belfast something in her instinctively resisted.

Kathleen shoved her hands deeper into the pockets of her raincoat as she pressed on down the Falls Road past her aunt's place. She had no destination in mind. Her only purpose was to delay her return indoors to work. As she walked, she argued with herself, stepping more briskly the more agitated she became. It was surely too much to ask of her—to have her first baby away from home—a stranger in a strange place. However difficult things might be in Belfast, it wasn't a reasonable request. And his suggestion that they should not even travel together struck her as adding insult to injury. She didn't wish to think Jack a coward, but his idea of escaping to England seemed a lot like running away. He didn't want to face the music.

But once she had allowed this thought to form, she immediately began to defend him. The fact that he was a Protestant would be bad enough at the best of times, but in the present circumstances it was a complete disaster. Kathleen's Da was all for Home Rule, a United Ireland, a Republic. He would be livid she was pregnant, but even angrier that the man responsible was a Prod. She could imagine the men coming to violence. Jack was only trying to find a solution, any solution. He wouldn't stand a chance against her father. It was just that she could not accept the necessity to leave everything and everybody she knew behind. No matter how strong her feelings for Jack. She was not sure enough of herself or of him to risk so much. Particularly now she was to be responsible for two. It was not only herself she had to think about.

A shiver went through her, which wasn't induced by the cold wind alone. There was fear and exhilaration mixed in the thought of the secret life she carried deep inside her. When she realised she was pregnant, her first reaction had been panic and a wild rummaging of thoughts about how to undo what had been done. Since then, as she became used to the idea, something had shifted in the depths of her being. Although she was still full of turbulence on the surface, when she thought of the child beginning to grow in her womb, she felt a strange certainty of purpose that nothing and nobody could touch. Though her father might rage and Jack leave for England, the men could not stop or alter the process that had begun inside her. The bond with her unborn child had begun and would grow to fruition and nobody could touch the depth and strength of that however they might try.

Kathleen came to the Church of St Paul's which her family attended every Sunday. It was not a particularly beautiful building but it had the comfort of familiarity. She did not hesitate, but went in through the gate in the railings which led to the side door. Her idea was to get out of the wind and to sit in the quietness, gathering herself and allowing calm to descend. As she entered, the gloom of the interior was only slightly alleviated by the light filtered blue and purple and red from the stained side windows. The bosky light and mingled smell of incense, dust and fading flowers seemed to Kathleen to suggest sanctuary from the workaday world outside. She made her small obeisance towards the distant altar and crossed herself, before she sat on one of the wooden seats towards the back of the Church and far enough along a row to put herself out of the way of other visitors or clergy. She wanted to be alone.

Though she had been encouraged in the faith by her parents and schooling, Kathleen was not devout in any traditional way. There was enough in the words and behaviour of her Mam and Da to make sure that goodness wasn't confused in her mind with either piety or dogma. Her Da, after all, was a publican. A rumbustious bear of a man, who could settle a drunken brawl as quickly as he could instigate a chorus of the rebel songs he loved so well. He was passionate in his opinions and profane in his language. Mean-spiritedness he detested and all mealy-mouthed propriety. Generosity to those he loved was his creed, and as a girl, Kathleen had been left in no doubt as to his love for her. Her Mam, meanwhile, was a woman of small stature and large heart, who had taught Kathleen what she took to be the greatest lessons of her life. As she came to maturity, her mother had warned her that some Church teaching, some men, some priests might try to make her feel ashamed of her body and its functions. 'We women know better,' her Mam had said. 'We bring about God's creation. Pain and suffering there will be but beauty and pleasure are things of God as well. Never forget that. Don't let anybody ever make you feel badly about yourself. And don't let anybody use you.'

Kathleen shuffled on the hard seat as she thought about this and her attraction to Jack Young. Her Da would be furious and her Mam disappointed that she had succumbed to temptation before marriage. They would be even more furious and disappointed that it was with a Protestant. She could not explain it to herself. But from the first moment he spoke to her as she got on the tram, there was something in his eyes, his face, the way he spoke to her that sent a thrill of recognition through her.

After their first encounter, she found herself thinking about him hours later and hoping she would see him again. When she did, she wasn't disappointed. She was assailed by the same intense sensation, a charge of energy which made her feel breathless and giddy. She could rationalise her reaction by saying to herself he was not like other boys she knew. So many of them reminded her of puppies, all bouncing physicality, brash and clumsy and full of self-centred blarney. In Jack's quiet charm, his shyness, she had sensed something powerful, withheld. As she got to know him, she realised it was his masculine pride and passion, which he embodied unselfconsciously. Though he was not a particularly big man, he carried himself upright and square. He seemed to look the world in the eye and say, 'Here I am—who are you?'

In their embraces, Kathleen had experienced a liberation she could not resist. Though all the teaching of her upbringing declared what they were doing to be wrong, all her being was declaring the rightness of it. In the dance of her senses she felt she was joining in the opening of petals to the sun, the whisper of leaves in the trees, the inexorable rhythm of waves to the shore. She was moved beyond the humdrum world of her stitching in a close back room, and the raucous conviviality of the pub at night and brought into touch with deeper realities.

This was why she didn't feel uncomfortable sitting here in the Church thinking of these things. In all her life, coming into this building she had enjoyed the songs and scents and sounds of the ritual, but always felt she missed the meaning. With Jack and in the conception of this child, she intimated an initiation into mysteries she knew her mind couldn't fully grasp but which would nourish her forever. They were the same mysteries she realised now that the Church should stand for—if love and birth and regeneration weren't sacred, what else could be?

That Jack was proposing to leave her seemed a denial of something fundamental between them. Yet she couldn't agree to go with him. Her instinct to resist leaving Belfast was as strong as her affirmation of what she had done with him. She couldn't explain this to herself any further. But she knew it was more than her lack of confidence that was guiding her. There was the pull of home; the sense of rootedness in place. She could not think of the baby being born in England.

Kathleen sighed and rose to leave the Church. She wished she could stay longer but her Aunt Mary would be expecting her. She didn't want to provoke enquiries about her behaviour. Outside, the wind had not abated and now it carried with it a fine but soaking drizzle. At least the little back room where she would spend the afternoon sewing would be cosy.

When she reached her Aunt Mary's the older woman was ironing in the kitchen. The smell of warm linen permeated the house. The women exchanged few words, her aunt clucking at Kathleen's damp hair; Kathleen making light of her discomfort. She entered the workroom and tried not to feel dispirited by the pile of men's handkerchiefs that awaited her attention. She preferred working on tablecloths and women's hankies; embroidering flowers was more interesting and satisfying than working single initials in blue thread into the corners of the plain white squares. Still, it had to be done.

Soon she was absorbed in her task, holding the embroidery hoop and trying to find the rhythm of the needle soothing. Maybe Jack would change his mind. Maybe he wouldn't. She would stitch him a handkerchief with his initials as a monogram. She would have to do it at home in her own time, but she would do it gladly, hoping that in expecting the worst, she might achieve the better result. If he didn't go, she could give it to him for his birthday.

V

To take leave in the imagination is one thing, to suffer the physical act quite another. Jack Young had plenty of time to ponder this truth as he lay sleepless in a strange room in a strange city a few weeks after his departure from Belfast. His stay with his father's cousin, Mrs Donovan, a narrow-eyed woman with a face and temperament to match, like a flat-iron deprived of the flame, thankfully had not lasted long. Jack had wasted no time in finding a job on the Manchester trams, and lodgings in Swinton, close to the depot on Partington Lane.

In this whirl of activity, he attempted to obliterate thoughts of home, of Kathleen, of his Mam and Da and sisters, of his friends Will and Bob and Herbie. It was at night that he could not escape their visitations; memories of his last days and hours in Belfast came back to haunt him with bitter-sweet poignancy. He longed for Kathleen with a raw intensity which surprised him, and he felt the loss of everything and everybody familiar to him like a bodily wound, which only her touch could heal.

At first, Kathleen's refusal to go with him or even commit herself to following him had made Jack hesitant to leave. But his parents had been implacable. They were determined to separate him from Kathleen and the 'shame' they said he'd brought on himself and the family. Jack knew his parents were strong people. Together they were like a force of nature. Arguing against them was like running into granite. They were tough, uncompromising, wilful. All in the name of love.

By the time he booked his passage, he was desperate to be away from them. With the tickets in his hand, he had experienced elation at the prospect of untangling himself from their demands and expectations. He was avid for a taste of freedom. He told himself that all would be well with

Kathleen. He would persuade her to join him. Eventually, they would have a new life together in a new place where nobody knew them. The idea of Manchester attracted him too. It was a bigger city than Belfast, the greatest city in the industrial world. Some men talked of London as the great place, but for Jack brought up on the idea of Belfast's importance through its shipbuilding, its engineering, its linen works and rope works, there was something more appealing about Manchester since it was another industrial centre upon which the wealth of the Empire was built. London and Londoners seemed soft-centred compared with the bracing vigour of the Northern manufacturing centres and their hardy people.

By cultivating this romance in his head of adventuring abroad, Jack had managed to fight down fears of the step he was about to take and to assume an air of swagger with respect to the farewells he dreaded. But when it came to the point, with each successive goodbye, he had felt as if he was being torn like an old sheet into rags, and it was as much as he could do not to give voice to that rending with cries as loud as ripped linen.

Kathleen was brave. They had smoked a last cigarette together on a bridge over the Lagan under a sky pearly-grey like the inside of an oyster shell. They stared at the river, a flowing sheet of indifferent steel, before he walked her home, and they parted. He had held her tight as her tears fell, though all he wanted was for the parting to be over. He could not allow himself to think of the new life that was growing within her; he pushed the thought of his parenthood away, not knowing how to cope with his feelings and telling himself the reassuring story that all would end happily when Kathleen and the child were with him in Manchester. At the last, she pressed a new white handkerchief into his hand. In the corner she had embroidered in an intricate design his entwined initials JWY.

It was just as hard to part from his family. He did not know with any certainty when he would see them again, though he assured them repeatedly in the last few days that he would not be long away. He asked them not to come down to the boat with him. He wished to avoid drawn-out scenes, and was afraid of making a fool of himself in public if he had to stand and wave from the ferry to the quay.

So in the crowded kitchen and hallway he'd embraced them all, one after another. His mother's face crumpled as she pressed her parting gift of a small bible into his hands; his sisters wailing and clinging to each other when they could cling to him no longer; his father with a long face, looking more stooped than ever and offering sombre advice.

Jack allowed his eyes to traverse the kitchen one last time before he left. He was giving up the old warm familiarity of the place and stepping out into the cold. Somehow, every humble thing in the room took on an aspect of rare value, the shabby chairs used by his Mam and Da either side of the range, with their faded floral covers, the hearth rug stained with years of coal dust, the pot-plants in their saucers on the narrow window sill—African Violets, Black-Eyed Susies, and his father's favourites, Campanula, Stars of Bethlehem. How often they had seemed the only colour in a colourless world, bright paint splashes illuminating the drab and grey. He held the handkerchief Kathleen had given him to the corner of his eyes with trembling hands, before he faced his people again.

Herbie, Bob and Willie turned up at the door with the horse and cart to take Jack and his trunk to the boat. Bob's father was in trade, and had offered the transport to save Jack the cost. It was good of him and a relief at last to be engaged in the bustle of loading his things. The presence of the young men with their cheery greetings also lightened the burden of departure. Eileen and his younger sister, Lily, had stopped their weeping in order to make eyes at the young men, and Mam and Da busied themselves supervising the removals.

The next thing he knew he was on the boat. He'd had a last pint of Guinness with the boys at a pub down by the docks while the horse was given its bag and waited patiently outside. 'It won't taste the same in England,' they assured him. They were right. It didn't.

But the parting from his mates was the least desperate. They all vowed to keep in touch. Jack tried not to think of Kathleen as they drank to the Covenant and joined in the toast, 'God Bless King Billy and hell roast the Pope.' After handshakes all round, they were off, telling him to go easy with the English girls.

He would never forget the sailing. The day was blustery with heavy squalls of rain, the light battleship grey. Jack stood by the stern rail, hunched in his coat, his cap jammed tight on his head, watching through narrowed eyes the great cranes and gantries of the shipyards recede. The raucous cry of gulls sounded a strident farewell. It was a portentous moment. He was half-choked with grief, yet aware of an excitement deep within him like the churning water of the ship's wake.

What a year it had been. In April, the loss of the *Titanic* had hit Belfast hard; the pride of the place in building her and the *Olympic*, ships that were said to be unsinkable, was suddenly brought into question. Many of the crew aboard lost to those freezing waters were Irishmen. At the same time, came news of the passing of the first reading of the Home Rule Bill. It seemed as if all the old certainties were being shaken. The frailty of human achievements was emphasised; God or the gods seemed inclined to remind the toilers below that they could never be complacent in their pride or faith.

Jack's own drama only added to his sense that nothing was secure. What had begun in rapturous romance had ended in this parting from all that was familiar. A leap into the unpredictable world alone with no turning back, to fetch up sleepless and hollow with loneliness in this dark room in a lodging house on Partington Lane. The irony of his new address was not lost on Jack, though he consoled himself with the thought that his new room was the largest he'd ever had to himself.

The furniture was heavy and dull, and the wallpaper grimy with its pattern of fading roses, but there was room for his bed and a chair by the narrow grate. He was permitted a fire at night but not in the day time. There was a communal bathroom, where he was allowed his wash and shave each morning, and a bath once a week. There was a dining room downstairs where breakfast and supper were served. If Jack was on the morning shift, he was up before Mrs Morris, his landlady, and was allowed to enter the sanctum of the kitchen to make himself a cup of tea, and find a slice of bread and butter.

It would all have to do until he established himself and got a bit of money behind him. Then he could look about and see what to do next. Much depended on Kathleen. He had written twice to her, passionate letters, spilling his loneliness onto the page, his aching desire to have her in his arms again. He asked after her health and hoped she was getting on all right. He told her of his new job and held out the possibility that he would save enough for her to come and join him by Christmas. He had signed his clumsy messages with all his love, for he felt he had nothing else to give.

He had received only one short reply. Perhaps she didn't take much to writing. Or maybe now he was gone, she couldn't believe in the reality of him anymore. And then there was the possibility of her Mam and Da looking over her shoulder. He'd had no choice but to write to her home address. He could imagine her parents' curiosity at the English stamp. How would she explain it away?

Jack knew he was looking for excuses for her. The letter didn't sound like the Kathleen he thought he knew. There was none of her liveliness and warmth and easy humour. It was constrained. She said she was happy to hear from him and glad that he had settled so quickly in England. She asked how he liked his job and his lodgings and whether the girls in Manchester were prettier than the Belfast lasses. She spoke of the winter nights closing in and the everlasting rain. Her Aunt Mary was no livelier and Kathleen wondered if all her life was to be spent embroidering. There was no mention of her parents and no mention of the baby. More worrying to Jack was the silence about joining him and no mention of missing him. It was as if she didn't trust herself to speak to him with any intimacy. Maybe she was angry with him for leaving. Or the continuing political tension had made her think better of taking up with a Prod. He didn't know. Couldn't know. It made him mad with frustration.

Sometimes he allowed himself to dwell on her Catholicism, and thought with a shiver of all those rituals, medallions and statuettes, beads and bells that he'd been taught to regard with superstitious dread. It was to keep Ulster clear of the influence of Pope and priests and mediaeval mummery that the Protestants were prepared to fight. All his life Jack had been taught to regard the Catholics as backward looking enemies of the industrial modernity which gave Belfast and the North prosperity. And yet Kathleen seemed a thoroughly modern young woman with a mind of her own and the courage of her conviction. Her God seemed more understanding, less judgemental and more forgiving than the Presbyterian God of his father and forefathers. Maybe it was all nonsense in the end. The only theology that mattered was in the sensual ecstasies of love he had shared with Kathleen. He had experienced a bliss with her that made the idea of a heaven beyond earth seem an airy nothing. He thought of his finger tips on the inside of her white thighs, the velvet touch.

A slow tread of heavy shoes making the boards creak disturbed Jack's reverie. Mrs Morris was taking herself to bed. He imagined the earthy and solid figure labouring up the stairs. She was a small, square-shouldered woman, habitually dressed in black from her ankles to throat. Her face was round and fleshy, making her eyes seem too small. The high collared dresses were without decoration, except on Sundays, when Jack noticed a plain silver cross appeared worn on a long chain. Mrs Morris attended the local Church of England. Yet for all the formal severity of her appearance she had treated Jack with some warmth. She was, he thought, motherly towards him, and he had done his best to charm her with his quiet politeness.

The landlady's niece was another proposition altogether. This young woman acted as Mrs Morris' companion. He had been introduced briefly to her when he first arrived and had taken an instant dislike to her. Annie Hargreaves had offered him a cool handshake, her touch light, languid even, her manner haughty. Her mouth had lifted slightly in the suggestion of a superior smile as she bowed her head in acknowledgement of him. It was as if she existed on a plane above the hurly burly of daily existence. She exuded a stoic calm which made Jack feel clumsy and unfinished. Thankfully, Mrs Morris and her niece tended to take their meals separately after Jack and the other lodgers had taken theirs. He hoped he wouldn't have to put up with her airs and graces. The only good thing about Annie Hargreaves was that she reminded Jack of the instant attraction and connection to Kathleen he'd felt—a miracle beyond understanding.

He remembered the first morning he'd noticed Kathleen as she stepped onto the tram. She wore a paisley scarf, green and peacock blue, bright against the grey of her shabby raincoat. Their eyes locked. She seemed to hesitate for a moment. He bid her 'Good Day' and said it was a lovely scarf. For a moment her face bloomed like a flower opening, before she moved down the tram. When he saw her again, there were a few more words between them, then a few more. Always easy. Always relaxed. Never any strain. It was as if everything was ordained between them. Yet it should not have been so. This was the mystery. And now there was her bewildering silence.

Before he tried to settle himself to sleep, Jack Young reached out to his bedside table and, propping himself up, took from the drawer Kathleen's letter to him. Though dulled by the thin curtains, there was enough moonlight entering the room for Jack to read by. But the words were no help to him. Kathleen seemed to disappear in the spaces between them. It was as if she were hiding from him, leading him to search for her, the words a distraction laying false trails, hindering his imagination rather than helping. Try as he might, he could not hear her voice. He put the letter under his pillow and fought for sleep, hoping she would speak to him in his dreams.

VI

Kathleen hurried homewards from the tram stop through a teeming drizzle. Reflections from the street lamps made iridescent patterns, orange and smoky gold, as vehicles splashed along the road. She felt the wet penetrate her shoes, her feet cold in their damp stockings, and thought of her mother's talk about the dark, dreary days before Christmas. Yet, for all her discomfort, it was as if she carried a small flame at the centre of her being, warm and comforting. She placed her hand over her belly as she increased her pace, anxious to get out of the weather. Today, she had felt the baby kick. At first, she thought she was imagining things. The flutter had been so slight. But then she felt it again, and knew. She had been careful not to betray herself to Aunt Mary. Her secret smile was for herself and her baby alone.

The pub in Cromac Street had a side door down a narrow cobbled alley, which ran from the main road to the terraced streets behind. Kathleen bundled inside. As she hurried out of her wet things, she thought of dogs shaking themselves dry. She wished she could do the same. She hung her coat and scarf on one of the pegs and turned to run up the stairs to the family's living quarters. As she did so, she saw on the hall-stand a letter addressed to her from England. It was another from Jack. She grabbed it and whisked upstairs.

Kathleen reached the sanctuary of her bedroom and slammed the door just as she heard her mother call from the sitting room. She did not immediately open the letter. She knew it would disturb her and wanted to be comfortably alone first. She slipped the envelope under her pillow, before taking off her skirt and unrolling her stockings. She opened the door of the old wardrobe that stood in the corner and looked at herself in the mirror. Her eyes travelled down her body to the slight bump that was beginning to show. She lifted her shift the better to see herself and stroked her hand over the rise. 'My little darling,' she murmured, and felt a shiver run through her. If only Jack hadn't left . . . A reflex of tears pooled hot in her eyes. These days, she found herself crying at the slightest thing.

As she blew her nose and sought out fresh clothes, telling herself to dry up, there was a knock on the door. Kathleen had no time to reply before it opened. She turned to see her Mam's head poked round the door.

'Will you come into the warm and have a cup of tea with me?'

A rush of gratitude filled Kathleen. She felt better already. A few cosy moments with her Mam was just what she needed.

'If you give me a minute till I'm decent, I'll be there.'

'I'll fettle the tea.' Her mother glanced round the room, as if looking for something, then let her eyes linger on Kathleen for a moment before she withdrew.

Hastily, Kathleen put on black woollen stockings and a thick plaid skirt which had a bit of room in it. Still, she struggled to fasten the garment, swivelling the back to the front and swearing under her breath as she grappled with the buttons. When she had managed to fasten herself in, she eased the skirt down a little towards her hips and drew her cardigan across the front. She looked again in the mirror, and persuaded herself that nobody could tell. After slipping her feet into the house-slippers her Mam and Da had bought her last Christmas, she hurried to the sitting room, composing a cheerful face as she went.

The sitting room ran along the front of the pub; it was disproportionately long and slender. Two easy chairs and a settee their floral covers stained and faded with age were clustered around the hearth at one end. The only other furniture was an occasional table. The rest of the room was empty. When Kathleen entered, her mother was already seated on the couch in front of a comforting fire. A tray was set on the table with two mugs, milk jug and sugar. Kathleen sat down beside her Mam, who began to pour from the old brown pot.

Kathleen warmed her hands on the proffered mug, then added a spoon of sugar. She only half-listened to her mother's monologue about the state of the weather, the price of vegetables at the market and what Mrs Kennedy said about their Irene's baby's croup. The drone of her Mam's voice together with the hot drink and warmth from the fire were infinitely soothing. There would be enough time to read and worry over Jack's letter later. For now, there was a chance to relax and indulge in the blessed balm of the ordinary. Though the talk moved on to questions about her day, Kathleen was happy to report on Aunt Mary's mood, the number of handkerchiefs monogrammed and table cloths decorated with embroidered flowers.

It was only when a silence fell and Kathleen sensed her Mam looking at her with more than usual attention that her relaxation wavered. She had no time, though, to wonder further what this meant before her mother began.

'I see you have another letter from your friend over the water.'

Kathleen nodded, not meeting her Mam's eye, feeling a hot rush of blood to her face, her stomach lurching queasily.

'She's a fine one for the writing, this auld school friend of yours. What did you say her name was? I can't remember her at all.'

'Jackie Senior,' Kathleen murmured. It had been the best she could do when first put on the spot about the mail from England. Now it seemed the tritest of lies.

'So, how's she going on over there? I've never fancied it myself. Best to stick with your own people through thick and thin is my belief.'

Kathleen didn't reply immediately. A feeling of exhaustion threatened to overcome her. She shrugged her shoulders. 'I don't know. I haven't read the letter. I think she's a bit lonely.'

'Where did you say her people live?'

'I didn't say. I think they've moved away, since we were at school.'

'I can't recall ever knowing anyone of that name round here.'

Kathleen sighed. 'No, well . . .' She breathed deeply trying to force down the tears that threatened to thrust into her eyes. She imagined herself as a stone fountain. She wanted to turn off the tap but the source was like a natural spring. She sipped her tea, trying to dispel the rising hysteria. She glanced at her mother's shrewd and quizzical eyes, and fought off the temptation to cackle like some old harridan.

'Stand up a minute will you? I want to have a look at you now.'

The sudden interruption brought Kathleen back to herself. She knew immediately the game was up. There was no point in fighting. She put down her tea and did as she was asked, standing like a schoolgirl in front of the head-mistress her hands clasped in front.

Her mother's eyes didn't look up but were focused on Kathleen's belly. It was as if she could see straight through her. Kathleen felt the baby move again. She imagined it turning to avoid the grandmother's gaze. Still, there was silence. Kathleen curled her toes, waiting for the storm to break. The tick of the old clock on the mantle and the low seethe and wuther of the fire seemed to grow louder. Thank God her father wasn't here as well.

When, at last, her mother spoke, she did so quietly, looking Kathleen square in the face.

'Have you something to tell me now, our Kathleen? You seem to be putting on weight.' Her mother's eyes dropped again so they were staring at Kathleen's belly.

Kathleen nodded. 'You know, don't you?'

'You are with child.'

'I am, Mammy.' There was relief in the admission as well as shame and guilt. The wave of emotion rushed upwards and flooded her eyes. She took a handkerchief from the cuff of her cardigan and blew her nose.

The older woman pursed her lips. 'Who's the father?'

'You don't need to know.' Kathleen sniffled and continued to mop herself with her hanky.

'I think you owe us that much. Who have you been with and why isn't he here standing beside you, taking responsibility like any decent fella would?'

Her mother's tone provoked Kathleen. She regained a little of her spirit. 'He's a Protestant, if you must know. Are you satisfied now?'

'Jesus, Mary and Joseph. What's your Da going to say?'

'I don't know Mam. That's why I've kept quiet.'

'And does he have a name now, this wee Proddy boy?'

'His name's Jack Young.'

'And would he have anything to do with these letters from England? That's never a woman's hand on the envelope.'

Kathleen nodded. Applied her handkerchief again.

Her mother patted the seat by her. 'Come and sit down with you, and give your auld Mammy a hug. You can tell me all about it, then.'

'What will we do about my Da? How am I going to tell him?'

'You'd better leave that to me. He's going to be fighting furious, sure enough.'

VII

On the third Sunday of his lodging with Mrs Morris, Jack Young was invited to afternoon tea in the front parlour. He didn't know to what he owed this privilege, nor was he aware if the other boarders had been invited. He found it difficult to imagine that Mrs Morris would voluntarily spend more time than she could help with her two other guests, but there was no accounting for taste. Certainly, Jack was glad that his shifts made meetings with Mr Arthur Swailes and Miss Edith Dalrymple mercifully minimal. The former was a salesman from London whose cockney-sparrow cheerfulness and familiarity communicated by a vicious lisp instantly grated on Jack's nerves. There was nothing worse than being greeted for breakfast with, 'All right thquire, 'ow's it goin'? Keeping the trams runnin' on time are yer then?'

Miss Dalrymple, on the other hand, was a spinster well into her forties, Jack guessed, who worked as a school-teacher. She was severe and evidently disappointed in life. She smelt of peppermints and lavender. But Jack thought he had also caught the whiff of strong spirits on her breath on more than one occasion. Medicinal brandy perhaps for the 'heart' she said she suffered from and which she feared would be strained to breaking point by the 'awful urchins' it was her burden to teach.

The notion of sitting over an awkward cup of tea with these two didn't seem likely to enliven Sunday afternoon. Even worse was the thought that Annie Hargreaves might be in attendance. Over the last weeks, there had been occasional sightings. She gave him a nod and a smile when she saw him, and a cool 'Good Morning' or 'Good Evening, Mr Young,' always said with a hint of mockery in her voice, as if she found him an amusing and faintly curious specimen of youthful manhood. Her condescension needled Jack. If she was taking afternoon tea with them, he would have to be careful to hide his feelings. He couldn't afford to upset Mrs Morris. He had worries enough elsewhere. He didn't want to be embroiled in further trouble.

Despite sending another letter, he still hadn't heard a word more from Kathleen. Sometimes he wondered if her silence was a torture she'd designed to punish him and to make him realise how much he cared for her. If it was, it worked. But he couldn't believe she would be so vindictive. He suspected her parents were active in the business, prying into her affairs, intercepting her mail, censoring her response. And behind them he imagined a vengeful God chastising him for his sins. He dreamt of pleading before a higher court: surely a merciful God should sanction love. But the judge looked down with the same thin stern face of his father, pronouncing the sentence. He was doomed to the cell of loneliness for indulging his sensual appetite and abandoning the morality of the righteous. There would be no forgiveness without suffering . . .

Work provided a relief from such gloomy thoughts, and as an antidote to his misery he had tried to make friends at the tram depot. Herbie Ryan had sent him a card early on, telling him to look out for Louis Cockcroft, who, he said was 'one of the boys'—a distant relative of his mother's, who worked on the Manchester trams. Louis turned out to be a driver, and he introduced Jack to all his mates. But as it happened, Jack took to Louis, and they had become good pals. Jack's only regret was that he felt constrained from confiding to anybody the trouble he was in at home or the truth behind his move from Belfast. When asked what brought him over the water, he invariably replied that he'd wanted a change and to see what England had to offer. He'd heard that the money on the trams was better, and he let it be known quietly that he'd wanted to gain some independence from his Mam and Da. This seemed to still most people's curiosity.

Presenting himself for tea with Mrs Morris at four o' clock sharp, dressed in his Sunday suit, Jack was not anticipating either probing enquiries or jovial conversation. He knocked lightly on the living-room door, and Mrs Morris invited him into the stuffy gloom of the 'best' room in the house. It was already darkening outside, so the brown velvet curtains were drawn and the fire reflected bravely off heavy dark wood furniture. An Aspidistra stood on a small table in the bay window, its leaves, newly dusted for the occasion, shone like grotesque giant's tongues, lolling with sinister intent. In the corner a grandfather clock ticked loudly, and on the mantelshelf a display of ornamental plates between two brass Victorian candlesticks, failed to lighten the atmosphere, being either too fussy or dull to attract more than a passing glance. A trolley replete with tea things dominated the middle of the room and was flanked by two armchairs situated either side of the fire. An assortment of straight back dining chairs had been arranged in a semi-circle on the farther side of the trolley, and it was to one of these that Jack was ushered by Mrs Morris.

Annie Hargreaves was already ensconced in one of the armchairs, as was Miss Dalrymple. There was no sign of Smailes. Mrs Morris bustled out of the room, saying that now Jack was here, she would brew the tea. Jack sat with his hands clasped in his lap, looking from one woman to another, smiling but not knowing what to say. The women in turn looked at him like some rare bird. Neither of them spoke. All conversation had ceased when he entered the room. This was the kind of awkwardness Jack dreaded. He was not adept at making chit-chat.

The silence stretched. Jack noticed Miss Dalrymple's face was rather flushed. He wondered if it was the fire warming her or whether she had fortified herself before coming down to tea. Annie's face retained the expression of unruffled confidence and composure that he'd first noticed as her most striking feature. In looking at her now in the firelight, Jack also had to reluctantly admit to himself how handsome she was, rather than pretty.

He could not bear the quietness any longer. 'It's been a raw day, today ladies,' he offered by way of nervous introduction. Miss Dalrymple grimaced and seemed to snort slightly. Jack thought she looked like a horse with her long face and severe fringe cut straight across her brow.

'It certainly has, Mr Young.' Annie Hargreaves took pity on him, a small smile playing at the corner of her mouth. 'But no more so than usual for this time of the year. I can't imagine the weather in Belfast is much better?'

'No, I couldn't say it is.'

The room relapsed into silence. Jack took to staring at the fire, but was worried that the women might think he was eyeing the food on the trolley. He couldn't help noticing the rich cake shining with cherries, the sandwiches and biscuits that awaited them. He longed to hold a plate or a cup and saucer so that he would have something to do with his hands.

At last Mrs Morris reappeared bearing the teapot with her. Effie, the young girl who charred, didn't work on Sundays, so she'd had to make the tea herself.

She handed out plates, while Annie, climbing to her feet, said, 'Sit down Aunt Agnes, I'll do the honours.'

Annie's movement seemed to Jack a further physical embodiment of the unhurried composure he had detected in her face. She was tall, and wore a full gaberdine skirt the colour of forget-me-nots. Jack tried not to imagine her shapely legs beneath, and reddened as she offered him a sandwich.

'There's cheese or ham,' she said. Her voice was well modulated, but not what Jack would call posh. You could hear she'd been brought up in or near Manchester.

'I looked for tomatoes at the market, but couldn't find any,' Mrs Morris said. 'I love a tomato but we must do without.'

'These are grand,' said Jack, acutely aware of his large square fingers, grasping a delicate triangle from the plate proffered by Annie. Her proximity caused his hand to tremble slightly. When he glanced up to her face, he caught the hint of amusement that never seemed to leave her when she was looking at him.

Having distributed food, Annie dispensed milk into cups from a little china jug and then poured the tea. 'Aunt Agnes tells me your father's a gardener,' she said to Jack, as she did so. 'You'll be used to fine fruit and vegetables, I expect.'

Jack's mouth was full. He chewed and swallowed quickly so he could reply. 'Ay, father's a gardener. He's allowed to bring a bit of produce home if he has a good crop.'

'Lovely, to have home grown,' said Mrs Morris. 'It's so hard round here getting decent stuff, and the price you have to pay.'

'It's criminal,' interjected Miss Dalrymple, tossing her head. 'And the next thing you know the farmers and gardeners will be on strike. Everyone else seems to be intent on not working. You'll see,' she offered belligerently, 'we'll have no food on the table next.'

There was a pause as everyone took in Miss Dalrymple's surprising, vehement and dark prognostications.

'I've been thinking of doing a bit of gardening myself,' Jack said to relieve the atmosphere. 'Some of the boys at work were mentioning the allotments to me. I thought I might fix myself up with a plot, and grow some spuds and beans and the like. Mebbe I could get some frames for tomatoes in the summer. You'd be welcome to have some.'

'That would be very kind, Jack,' Mrs Morris beamed benignly, while Annie seemed to confer a more wholehearted, less sly smile upon him.

'I like a nice tomato,' said Miss Dalrymple. 'Daddy used to grow them in the glasshouse when I was a girl. They don't taste the same these days.' She sighed, theatrically as she accepted another sandwich from the plate.

For a moment Jack was transported to the days of his own childhood, when after tea his Da would take him to tend the tomato plants in the greenhouses on the big estate at Donaghadee. The clean antiseptic smell of the plants was in his nostrils and the sight of his father's long fingers under the leaves, inspecting them for greenfly. He heard his Da's voice imparting wisdom, 'the secret to tomatoes, lad, is to starve them till they set fruit, then feed and feed them.'

'Nothing's as it used to be,' continued Miss Dalrymple warming to her mournful theme. 'The old standards count for nothing. You should hear the way some of these children speak to me. No one knows their place any more. All these strikes, and suffragettes and ructions in Ireland. I'm glad Daddy isn't here to see it, God rest his soul. I don't know what the end of it all will be.'

These remarks were uttered towards the fireplace, allowing the others in the room to glance at each other, not knowing how to respond.

'Come, come,' said Mrs Morris, 'we shouldn't have politics or religion over tea. Hand Miss Dalrymple a piece of cake, Annie.'

Annie did as she was bid, while Jack watched in awed fascination as Miss Dalrymple immediately began to devour the cake with avid concentration, while continuing to glower at the fire.

Jack did not refuse a slice of his own, but tried not to be clumsy in the eating of it; he didn't want Mrs Morris or her niece to think him greedy. His homesick recollection of boyhood had given way to a wish that his hosts might think well of him.

He was discomfited, then, when Annie, having resumed her seat said with eyes twinkling, 'I think it's brave of Miss Dalrymple to speak out. We can't stay old fashioned forever, Aunt Agnes. I'd like very much to know what Mr

Young thinks of the suffragettes. Perhaps he thinks that all Manchester women are like the Pankhursts.'

Jack felt three pairs of female eyes upon him, while he tried to rescue an anarchic crumb that threatened to tumble from his lips. It was clear that disapproval of the radicals would be a safe attitude to express as far as Mrs Morris and Miss Dalrymple were concerned, but what was the right answer to escape Annie Hargreaves' ridicule?

'I'd rather stick with tomatoes,' he said.

'Don't be shy, Mr Young, we won't bite you.'

'Annie, really, embarrassing Jack like that.' Mrs Morris mounted a relief expedition. But Jack saw the challenge in Annie's eyes. He would not be put down by her.

'I don't hold with the arson,' he said, 'or the letter-burnings and all the rest of the shenanigans. But when I see my sisters working themselves sick at the mill and they don't get a say, well, I wonder if that's not wrong.'

'Bravo, Mr Young. You see,' Annie turned to the others, 'he believes in the new woman.'

Miss Dalrymple snorted again, and accepted another piece of cake.

Jack remembered Kathleen with a cigarette between her fingers after making love and wondered if she was an example of the new woman. Or if Annie Hargreaves and her seeming independence more closely resembled that daunting figure?

'That's enough now our Annie,' chided Mrs Morris. 'I won't have my guests harassed. Will you have more cake now, Jack, or another cup of tea?' Jack declined the offer of further refreshment.

'If you say so, Aunt Agnes, I'll let Mr Young off the hook for now. But another time I'd like very much to hear his opinion of the state of affairs in Ireland. The newspapers make it sound very bad.'

'I doubt very much if Mr Young wishes to broach any such subject.' Mrs Morris was beginning to sound testy.

‘It’s all the fault of the Fenians.’ Miss Dalrymple’s face went a deeper shade of puce. ‘Home Rule, indeed. It’s a good thing Daddy isn’t alive to hear of it—to think the Empire’s being held to ransom by a band of uncivilised Irishmen.’

‘No more, if you please, Miss Dalrymple. I’ll have no more politics on a Sunday afternoon.’ Mrs Morris’ tone brooked no argument. ‘Let’s hear some more of your plans for a garden, Jack.’

Jack was relieved by this return to safe and familiar ground. He was happy to enlarge upon the procedures that had to be followed in application for an allotment, and the way he would go about preparing the soil for spring planting. Throughout, he felt Annie’s eyes on him, but he refused to meet hers. He directed his remarks to the room in general, and sought to excuse himself as soon as he could without seeming impolite.

He was not allowed to make his escape, though, without a further exchange with Annie Hargreaves.

‘You must keep us informed of the progress of your garden,’ she said. ‘I hope you’ll grow some flowers as well as fruit and vegetables. I do love cut flowers in a room.’

‘I’ll have to see how much space there is, before I promise blooms.’ Jack was anxious not to seem too eager to please her.

‘I hope you’ll allow me to visit your garden, one day,’ she continued, ignoring the warning looks from her aunt.

‘You’d all be welcome to see the garden when I’ve got something to show. If you’d be interested, that is.’

And with that Jack left the room, thanking Mrs Morris for her hospitality. The last glimpse he had of Annie was of her smiling at him, he could not tell if it was in mirth, mockery or a strange attempt at friendship.

That night, in the privacy of his small room with the dreary November weather rattling a grim tattoo on roof tiles and window pane, Jack wrote another letter to Kathleen. He couldn't help himself—in his loneliness he felt compelled by a force too great for his resistance. He wanted to obliterate the unsettling effect of his afternoon encounter with Annie Hargreaves and reassert his feelings for Kathleen. Jack poured his emotion onto the page. He spoke of his love and longing, his wish that she should join him, his desire for her, his realisation that he wanted to be a proper father to their child. He did not speculate on the reason for her silence, but made a rash concession: *If I come home to you, will you have me as your man? Could we not find in Ireland somewhere to be together without the interference of our parents? If we must believe in God, I want him to be yours, the one who forgives us our embraces. Surely He should be pleased with love. And I love you now and always. When I have the money saved, either come to me or let me return to you. You are my heart's darling. I cannot bear the thought of losing you . . .*

VIII

In the days following the confrontation with her Mam, Kathleen lived between numb resignation and unbearable suspense. She stitched through her days at Aunt Mary's trying not to think of the inevitable scene with her father. She wondered if he was delaying a full response or discussion in order to torture her. Since she'd admitted her pregnancy to her Mother, her Da had only spoken to her twice. Once was to tell her to get out of his sight; the second time to swear he would kill the randy wee bastard who had knocked her up. Otherwise, he just glared at her. At home, she had taken to creeping round the place, keeping out of his way. At breakfast she tried to avoid him entirely, and at tea-time she had taken to waiting in her room until she knew he had eaten and was serving in the bar. Then, she would sneak down to the kitchen and take some food back to her room.

Her Mam afforded little comfort. 'You'll have to give him a wee while to get used to the idea,' was all she offered. 'It's only natural, so it is. You can't expect him to be thrilled. He'll come round in his own time. The main thing is to look after yourself.' Kathleen wondered how best to do that. She fantasised about taking her father on, challenging him, shouting at him, telling him it was her life, her body, her child. But when she saw him, caught the look of hurt and disappointment as well as anger in his eyes, she shrank back into silent misery.

Meanwhile another letter arrived from Jack. She snatched it up like all the others. Her Mam said nothing about it. The silence from her Da continued. While at her daily sewing, she had many hours to think of the loving words Jack had sent, his suggestion that he would come back to Ireland and they could run away together. She tried to make him and his plan real in her mind but he existed there like a character in one of the romances she borrowed from the library—appealing and seductive but not quite real. That was the problem with words. You could write anything down and make it seem true. She recognised the desire propelling his pen. She felt it herself especially at nights—the empty ache at the core of her being that longed to be filled. But longings expressed in loneliness had nothing to do with the cold hard circumstances of the real world. Jack had not yet saved enough money to get her to England. So how could he afford to get himself home? And even if he did get back to Belfast, how would he find work elsewhere and how would they afford to move? It was impossible.

Torn between wanting to indulge the fantasy of their love for each other and the impossibility of its attainment, Kathleen couldn't bring herself to reply to Jack's letter. She tried to put words together in her head, but she couldn't make sense of her thoughts and feelings. Coherence was beyond her. So she trudged on from day to day, waiting for her father to speak and wondering if Jack would write again. And all the while trying to hold close the thought of the spark of life she carried, the child she would love beyond all measure and who would love her: an eternal tie that could not be broken.

Sunday came. Kathleen got ready as usual for 10 o'clock Mass. She went with her mother every week. Sometimes her Da would go as well. It depended on his mood and the state of his hangover after a long Saturday night in the pub. She wondered what would happen today. She hoped for an hour or two of peace with her Mam. The thought of losing herself in the ritual hush and soothing light of the Church was delicious to her. But the presence of her father would prevent any such surrender. He would put her on edge. His voice bellowing the responses and the hymns would mortify her as usual but now they would also carry the added threat of his anger, still unexpressed, but surely gathering like thunder clouds casting shadows over the Mountains of Mourne.

Kathleen chastised herself for the fanciful image. Yet the cold stone of her father's face reminded her of those dark granite crags and he had a temper on him like a storm over the Irish Sea. She tied her head scarf beneath her chin and buttoned her coat. For once, she was glad of the season; the bulk of her garments meant there was no chance of curious eyes perusing her thickening waist and stomach. It was nearly time to go, yet she hesitated, listening, trying to guess where her Mam and Dad were. Normally, she would tap on her mother's bedroom door and call out, but this morning with all the tension in the air she didn't know what to do.

If they didn't leave soon they would be late. Kathleen opened her bedroom door quietly and looked down the hall. Her parents' room was at the end. She crept along the passage, talking to herself as she went about the absurdity of behaving like an unwanted guest in her own home. As she approached her parents' door, she could hear voices within. They were arguing, though voices were not raised. The tones were low, intense, unpleasant. Before she could knock, the door burst open and her Da emerged in his Sunday suit, the waistcoat tight over the solid paunch of his gut. Her Mam followed a few paces behind.

'Get away out of it,' he said by way of greeting. 'You will not be going to Church and shaming us before the congregation. You'll stay at home and think of what you've done, bringing this family into disgrace. And with a bastard Orangeman. Some smooth talking young jockey no doubt. He'll do no more riding of you, if I have anything to do with it. Go back to your room. I'll have further words with you later.'

Kathleen didn't speak. She was on the verge of saying she was sorry, but her father's words and their tone stung her so she could not find words. As she turned on her heel and retreated to her room, she caught a glimpse of her Mam's face red and grim with anger and grief, but nodding at Kathleen in a silent warning that to comply was the wisest thing. Resisting the temptation to slam the door behind her, Kathleen closed it quietly and stood listening as her parents went down the stairs and out of the side door onto the street. There were no further words between them. Kathleen could imagine what they'd been rowing about. Her Mam would have defended her daughter's right to go to Church. Her Da would have swept his wife's objections aside.

Wearily, Kathleen took off her scarf and coat and lay on the bed. The one comfort she had was that her Da had promised more words later on. Though it would be bad enough listening to whatever tirade he let loose upon her, at least then it would be done. This everlasting anticipation would be over. She expected he would pack her off to the convent where she would have to work in the laundries with other unmarried pregnant girls. She'd heard tales about it when she was younger. The punishment for loose morals and lack of will-power. A return to Godliness through hard work. Cleaning others' dirty clothes. Cleansing your soul.

There were stories of the brutality of the nuns. But surely they could not all be embittered. Those with a true vocation would have compassion. Staring at the ceiling, which once had been painted white but was now smoke stained from the fireplace that didn't draw properly, Kathleen thought of purity. She didn't believe nuns were necessarily pure. The exquisite sensations she'd felt with Jack, the waves of breathless pleasure their loving had provoked seemed to speak more of God's bounty than any dry and grim pronunciations of 'Thou shalt not'. If there was a God at all. Kathleen was not so sure any more.

She wondered if Jack was at Church in England. She didn't know. She knew he went in Belfast to keep his parents quiet. But left to himself, she didn't know if he was bothered. The only serious conversation they'd had on the subject of religion had ended in an uneasy stalemate. Kathleen had argued that there wasn't much difference: same God, same Jesus, same

Bible, same Christmas and Easter, some of the same hymns even. So what was the problem? Jack said that Pope and priests made a difference. Confession and rituals with bells and incense made a difference. But not that much difference, Kathleen replied.

It wasn't religion that was the problem in Belfast, it was the politics. Kathleen had been brought up listening to the passionate talk of her Da and her uncles in support of Nationalism and the Irish Republican Brotherhood. They were excited about the Home Rule Bill and indignant about the Unionist response and all the shenanigans with their Covenant Day. 'If it comes to a fight we'll give them one', her Da said. 'It's about democracy for Ireland and the Irish. Why should we remain a persecuted minority in this part of the country? It's time the English were out of it.'

Kathleen had not dared to broach this with Jack. She sensed he was a gentle man, much influenced by his family. She suspected he'd been taught to think of Catholics as superstitious and backward, opposed to the spirit of modernity which gave Belfast its jobs and prosperity. She, on the other hand, had been brought up on the railings of her Da, arguing that Belfast's industries should be helping all Ireland, not having the profits drained into English coffers. She knew, too, all the stories about anti-Catholic discrimination here and elsewhere in the North. But she could not believe Jack was bound by such prejudice. He wouldn't have gone with her otherwise, would he? If they could be together, she was sure she could make him see there were not such differences between them. After all, he had shown himself to be a decent man, a good man. She could not believe he was a bigot.

Such thinking wearied her. Kathleen took out his last letter to her and re-read it. It was full of love. But how they could ever be together again, she could not see. She put the letter away, and lay back on the pillow. She placed her hands over her belly and breathed deeply. She wanted to relax, to stop the churn of anxiety. She closed her eyes, and imagined the child inside her, its little heart beating not Catholic or Protestant but neither or both. And surely more important than either.

Kathleen must have fallen into a light doze. She woke with a start when there was a sharp rap on her door. It was her Mam back from Church. 'Your Da will speak to you in a minute in the parlour. He's just making sure everything's all right in the bar.'

No further hint of what was to come was offered. Kathleen swung her legs to the ground as she heard her Mam walk away up the hall. It wasn't clear if her mother would be present at the promised interview or not. Kathleen hoped for some moral support but suspected her parents might not have recovered from their earlier argument. It was possible they were still fighting over her.

Kathleen tidied her hair and went to the sitting room. It was cold and empty. Her Mam must have put a match to the fire, though, for it was just struggling to life, the newspaper and kindling crackling and making the coal smoke. She stood with her back to it, feeling a faint warmth against her calves, listening to the sounds of animated conversation that travelled from the Sunday lunch time drinkers beneath. There was a special joy, her father always said, in taking a drop after Church. The good companionship of the newly shriven. She didn't expect the bonhomie to extend to her plight. It was the men with their beer and whiskey and cigarettes who ruled downstairs, while their womenfolk were at home cooking the dinner.

Kathleen shivered. She turned and poked the fire, as if a warmer room might make her father less frosty towards her. She straightened again and heard him thumping up the stairs. This was it, then. She stood tall and drew her cardigan across her bosom. She was determined not to shrink before him. She would not flinch.

He burst into the room and immediately seemed to fill it.

He was over six feet tall, barrel chested and broad thighed, though light on his feet as some big men are. The whiskey he'd drunk made his face ruddy through his white whiskers. 'Sit down with you,' he said, 'I have something to say.'

There seemed little point in provoking him. She did as she was told, moving to sit on the sofa, while her father took her place by the fire. He warmed his hands for a moment before turning to face her.

'You've disappointed me, Kathleen,' he said. 'I thought you had more about you than to get into this mess. You've let me and your Mammy down. To be seduced and spoiled before a wedding. And by a Protestant at that. After all you've heard said in this house about my beliefs and convictions. I tell you, it's nearly broken my heart. I've been at my wits end these last days wondering what to do. Your Mammy would have you off to the nuns. I don't like the idea myself. In the end, you'd have to bring the babby back here. Everyone would know our disgrace. I have my pride. I won't have it. I tell you.'

He paused and stared at her as if she was arguing with him. Kathleen looked at her feet.

'Have you nothing to say at all? Not a word of apology or regret?'

Kathleen looked up at him and saw the angry bewilderment in his face. She considered what she might say. She was determined not to show weakness. If he had his pride, she would have her dignity.

'I'm sorry you're upset,' she said. 'But I cannot be sorry about the babby and the loving I had with Jack. He's a good man. I already love the child I'm carrying. I can't apologise for that.'

Her reply took the wind out of her father's full-blown sails for a moment. His face was slack with surprise. Kathleen looked down and waited for him to puff himself up again. She didn't have to wait long before he began blustering.

'A good man? Oh yes, a good man? He must be a grand auld lad now, sticking by you the way he has. Off over the water at the first sign of trouble. Not so much as a peep to me. No balls at all. I'd have killed him, mind you. But that's beside the point. He's a coward, a liar, a cheat and a thief. That's how good he is.'

'A thief?' Kathleen couldn't help herself.

'Ay, has he not stolen your virginity and your good name?'

'For God's sake Da. he has stolen nothing. I told him you'd have at him if he came near. He thought it best to go to England. He wanted me to go too. He thought it was the only way we could be together. He thought it was impossible here.'

'Well, at least he got that right. It is impossible. Either here or there.'

'I don't know.' Kathleen looked at her father. 'If I had the money to get there and back, I might go. To see if we could make it work. It would be hard to leave my Mam, though, with a babby on the way.'

Her Da stared at her. 'You're never asking me for money to leave are you? You have some nerve. You can put England and this Jacky boy right out of your mind. Since I'll be paying one way or another, there's no way in God's wide world you're going anywhere without my say so. Do you understand me?'

Kathleen didn't look up. A bitter rage erupted in her, which she daren't give vent to. Everything came back to money in the end. It made her want to join the suffragettes. It wasn't just votes that were needed, but equal pay and equal rights. Then there would be a chance of independence. Not this everlasting subservience to men and their money, or lack of it.

'I asked you a question. Do you understand me?' Her Da raised his voice.

Still, Kathleen didn't speak. She nodded her head but wouldn't look at him.

His tone was softer as he went on. 'I've said I will not have you to the nuns, and I stand by that. I have another idea altogether of how to make things right. Will you listen to me, if I tell you?'

Again she gave her wordless assent, wondering what marvellous solution he could possibly have in mind. When she glanced up at him, he seemed to take a deeper breath before he began, like an actor preparing to deliver a well-rehearsed speech.

'You know Kevin O'Donnell?'

She looked up sharply. Kevin worked in the bar. She'd known him since school days. He was friends with her cousins and lived near them now, in the Catholic enclave of Short Strand.

Her Da answered Kathleen's enquiring gaze with another question of his own. 'Have you ever seen the way he looks at you, now?'

'I have not,' Kathleen shot back. But it wasn't entirely true. Kevin was always quick to have a word with her, and liked to banter, showing his teeth strong and white against the red of his lips and his coal black beard and curly hair. But since she had known him so long and remembered him as a boy, she had never thought much about his carry-on.

'Well, I have,' her Father continued. 'And I've had a wee word to him. And what I want is for you to be nice to him, do you see? He's a fine set-up young man. Many would call him handsome. He'll make you as fine a husband as ever lived. So you're to be nice to him. Do you see?'

It was Kathleen's turn to be taken aback. She struggled to assimilate what she was being told. She had expected all kinds of raving from her Da, but the idea that he might try to arrange a marriage had not appeared even on the furthest horizon of her thoughts.

'I've never been anything else but nice to Kevin. What exactly have you said to him? If he's so interested why hasn't he said a word to me before now?'

'He's after being a bit shy. When I asked if he was sweet on you, he said he was but thought you might be above him, like. He was worried about what I would say. Now, he's keen as mustard. You must write to your man in England and tell him it's over. No more letters. If I see any, I'll burn them. Then, all you have to do is concentrate on a quick courtin' with Kevin. We'll have you married within a month before you're showing too much and then off down south with you to have the babby. Kevin's got some people in Dublin. You can stay with them. Then after a decent time, you can both come home and all's well. Nobody here will be the wiser.'

Her father's enthusiasm for the plan was plain. Kathleen's throat was constricted, as if he were choking the life out of her. She struggled to find words, but there was more that needed to be said. 'You mean he knows I'm pregnant? And you've sorted all this out between you?'

'Ay, we have.'

'And what might have persuaded Kevin to take on another man's child?'

'Like I say, he's keen for you. I told him the other fella had taken advantage, treated you rough like, against your will. And if Kevin became part of the family, you know, I made it clear he'd never be short of a job and all. I told him I'd see you both right. And so I will.'

'What if I refuse?'

'You can't be that stupid. Beggars can't be choosers, Kathleen. You have made your bed. Now you must lie in it. Kevin's a perfectly decent young man. You'll make a handsome couple. If you refuse, which you can't, I'll throw you onto the street with nothing, so I will. I won't be crossed in this. You have done wrong. And if you want to see this as punishment so be it. But it doesn't have to be like that. You can decide to fall in love with Kevin. Then everyone will be happy. There's to be no more argument. I've said what I've got to say. I should be downstairs now, helping out.'

As he moved to go, Kathleen, feeling hope disappear with him, asked one last question. 'What does my Mammy say to all this?'

'She'll come round when she sees what a happy pair you make. You'll come to thank me for what I've done. Be nice to him. That's all you have to do. And all your problems are over.'

Kathleen remained where she was after her father had left the room. She stared into the fire. She placed her hands over her belly. Despite the warmth of the room now, she shivered at the thought of lying down with Kevin O'Donnell. But for the sake of her unborn child, she wondered if she had any choice in the matter.

IX

A fortnight before Christmas, Jack pushed his key into the door of Partington Lane and shoved with his shoulder. He carried an armful of gardening books he'd picked up at the Public Library. He was excited he'd at last made the effort to join and to find so many volumes. He couldn't wait to start reading in pursuit of his interest and ambition. Developing an allotment was only part of what he had in mind. It was the first step in a larger plan. Jack's Da had always discouraged Jack from taking up gardening as a job. 'There's not enough brass in it lad, and too few opportunities', he'd say. 'You need to work at something that will give you a chance to get on.' And so Jack had been apprenticed at Mackies Foundry in Belfast. But he hated the reek and clamour of the engineering works, the drudgery of serving those machines. So when the opportunity came to be taken on the trams he leapt at it. But in his heart he had cultivated this other dream which he had shared with no one. Even now he hardly dared to admit it to himself. He was content to learn step by step. He had an idea that maybe there was money to be made in designing and building gardens. It had come to him one day walking round Ormeau Park. It suddenly occurred to him that someone must have planned and built the space. He was struck by what a grand thing it would be to do. To make such a place from scratch.

He had dismissed the thought as a fantasy beyond the means of someone like him. He hadn't even mentioned it to his Da, for fear the old man would laugh him to scorn and tell him to stick to real life. But the thought of doing something more with his time than driving a tram regularly recurred and the notion of learning how to plan and build gardens niggled at him as if the planted seed had grown to make a burr in his soul—goading him until he had to act. Having braved the library, Jack felt elated. He had faced down the voice of uncertainty and defeat in his mind. He had taken the initiative. Here was something he could tell Kathleen about. Something that might persuade her he was worthy of her.

As he bustled into the hallway, Jack's glance went to the hall-stand where the post was always laid out for collection. There was an envelope for him. Post-marked Belfast. He nearly dropped the books as he juggled to pick the letter up. Kathleen's handwriting. At last. He felt his heart bang in his chest as he turned towards the stairs anxious to reach his room, clutching the letter on top of the books with his thumb.

He was on the second stair when the door to the living room opened and Annie Hargreaves emerged. She looked up at him, a knowing smile that might be a smirk on her face.

'Ah yes,' she said. 'You've got your letter. From your Irish sweetheart no doubt Mr Young.' Her eyes glinted with mischief.

Jack reddened but barely paused in his climb. He felt the fury rise in him and struggled to control his tone. 'I have my letter,' thank you, he said. 'I can't see that who it's from is any business of yours.'

'I meant no offence I'm sure, Mr Young.' The smile, if anything, had grown broader. As if she knew she had scored a point against him. Jack said nothing, kept walking up the stairs. He heard the living room door shut below him.

On gaining his room, he dropped the books on the bed and grabbed the letter. As he tore into the envelope he noticed his hands were trembling. There was a single sheet of white, blue-lined paper inside.

Dear Jack,

I'm sorry I've taken so long to write. Things have been difficult and I don't know how to say what I have to say. My Mam and Da know everything. At first, I kept things quiet and told them the letters from England were from an old school-friend. But then a few weeks ago, Mam looked at me and asked if I had anything to tell her. I looked into her eyes and I knew she knew. She could tell I was pregnant. I told her everything. She told my Da.

He's very angry with me. And with you. It's a good job you're not here. If you were, I don't know what he'd do to you. He has a terrible temper on him. He says I must end everything between us. In return he has promised not to send me to the nuns. He says he won't have the shame of me working in the laundries. He's after marrying me to Kevin O'Donnell—the son of one of his mates. I can't fight my Da, Jack. I haven't any money to run away with. If you sent any now, it would go into his pocket with a smile.

Maybe it's for the best. With things as they are, I can't see how we would make it work between us. My Da will never accept you. He says he won't have me married to a Prod. He won't have his grand-child brought up with someone who is not of the One True Faith. I'm writing this to make a clean break between us. It hurts me, but I can't see any other way. In England I'd be a stranger in a strange place, forever outcast from my family.

I'm sorry to be the cause of pain to you. You are a good man and deserve better. We were foolish to think we could break all the rules and go against our families and communities. But I wish you well, Jack. There will always be a place in my heart for you.

Don't reply to this. My Da will surely open and destroy any letters you send. I absolve you from any responsibility for our child. My Da says he will see me right in that regard.

I wish you all the good things in life, Jack. I'm so sorry. I send you my love for the last time. God bless.

Kathleen xxx

Jack stood with the paper in his hand for a moment, then folded the letter carefully and placed it on the bedside table. He looked at the three gardening books that he'd spilled onto the bed. He bent and one at a time he hurled them against the wall. Breathless, he kneeled and scrabbled for the tin box he kept beneath his bed. He removed a shilling of his savings and clattered down the stairs.

As he went through the front door the last thing he saw before he slammed it shut was Annie Hargreaves appearing again from the living room.

'Whatever's the matter, Mr Young? What's all the commotion about?'

Jack didn't bother to reply. He slammed the door in her face and hurried off.

In the public bar of the Bricklayers Arms, Jack drank his bitter pints alone, shunning the friendly 'how-dos' from the other working men, staring moodily into his glass and wondering at the way his life had gone wrong. For the first few pints, he blamed himself and heard again his parents berating his weakness and immorality. If he'd kept to their ways none of this would have happened. But as he drank on, Jack drowned out their carping and told himself again that what had happened between him and Kathleen was the best thing in his life. How could he accept Kathleen's rejection of him? She was wrong. The pressure of circumstances was to blame. Somehow he would talk her round. Somehow he would find a solution.

By closing time, though, when he chased his last pint with a glass of whiskey, the solution had still not revealed itself to him. He reeled back to his digs through the icy streets, blowing smoke into the frigid air. He felt a pointless rage against life fermenting with the beer inside his belly. It seemed a savage destiny had conspired against him and he had lost everyone dear to him. He was separated from his family. And now from Kathleen. He was alone. And he could see no end to his loneliness.

Trying not to bang the yard door, Jack hurried into the small back garden at Partington Lane. He was desperate for a piss. He undid his buttons under the gnarled old apple tree there. He looked up at the indifferent glitter of the stars as the steam rose off the frost. Befuddled he stood for a moment head-in-air fastening himself again. As he turned towards the back door he looked up and saw a bedroom curtain twitch. He fumbled trying to get his key in the lock. It came as an immense surprise as he did so to find himself imagining what Annie Hargreaves looked like beneath her prim and proper clothes.

X

Christmas came and went. Jack Young stayed in Manchester. After his session in the Bricklayers Arms, he had been tempted to throw everything in and go back to Belfast. He'd thought of seeking Kathleen out, confronting her father. Fighting for her. But when he recovered from his hangover and re-read her letter in the drab light of a rainy Manchester day guaranteed to puncture dreams and enforce reality, he knew it was hopeless. It wasn't what Kathleen wanted. Though she spoke of love, she also told him not to think of coming back for her. She had capitulated to her family, just as he had capitulated to his in coming to Manchester. It seemed their love was not strong enough to defeat the prejudices of their people. He imagined the fussing and fighting with his Mam and Da if he went back to Belfast. The idea sickened him. In a rage with fate, Jack decided to maintain his independence and work his Christmas shifts.

So Jack endured 'Good King Wenceslas' and the Christmas tree in St Anne's Square—their twinkling messages of peace and goodwill a constant goad to his anger and disappointment. As he drove through frost and snow, the cold glitter and dirty slush threw back to him his grief and emptiness. He tortured himself with thoughts of Kathleen with Kevin bloody O'Donnell, and surprised himself that he could nurse murder in his heart. Christ the Saviour was bo-orn, but Jack's only relief appeared in the unlikely form of his landlady, who took pity on him and invited him to Christmas dinner.

In the immediate aftermath of his binge in the pub, Jack had made an abject apology to Mrs Morris for any disturbance he may have caused. He said he had been upset by news from home, but didn't elaborate. Mrs Morris had been stern at first. Reminded him she kept a decent house; told him she didn't want any repetition of disorderly behaviour. But when it came to the point and she realised he was alone for the festive season she extended the hand of friendship. Miss Dalrymple and Mr Swailes went to relatives for the holiday, so Jack felt privileged to join Mrs Morris and her niece at the festive board, though he did so with little expectation of enjoyment.

A small turkey was produced—could they breed turkeys any smaller, Jack wondered—but it was accompanied by a generous helping of spuds, carrots and Brussels sprouts. There was even stuffing and gravy. They gave him a bottle of beer while Mrs Morris and her niece sipped demurely on port and lemonade. As he chewed the dry breast meat and tried to fake some relish, Annie Hargreaves quizzed Jack about his family. She seemed to have forgiven Jack for slamming the door in her face. If she had seen him in the back garden that night, she made no sign. For his part, the corporeal reality of the woman relegated his erotic fantasies of her to the realms of drunken madness. Her immaculate touch-me-not air was very much in place, though the fact that there had been some trouble in his life seemed to have softened her attitude to him. Jack wondered if she had guessed what had happened. There seemed to be less mockery now, less superiority too. Though there was still a faint air of condescension towards him, she seemed to be genuinely concerned for his well-being. Annie listened to his account of his mother and father and sisters so attentively, that he began to believe she was genuinely interested in his situation.

She went on to tell Jack about herself. How her mother and father had run a draper's shop in the city, how they had worked so hard that her father had exhausted himself and died at an early age. Her mother had not long survived her father, dying, Jack was given to understand, of a broken heart. Part of Annie's inheritance had helped to buy the present house, which she had agreed to share with her aunt and run as a boarding house.

Though flattered by these Christmas revelations, Jack was also troubled by them. He was glad of the attention Annie paid him, but wondered at its purpose. Sometimes he allowed the thought to cross his mind that she might be trying to encourage a romantic connection between them. But then he dismissed the idea as both vain and fanciful. Annie clearly came from a wealthier background than he did, and he felt the difference keenly. She was surely too good for him. He persuaded himself to think of her only as a friend. Though her attentions came as a welcome distraction, Jack wanted to remain faithful to his mourning for Kathleen. He resented the confusion Annie caused him, and determined to keep his distance.

In the New Year, as Jack's day-to-day life settled into a routine as predictable as the tram routes he plied through the city, there was no shortage of opportunity to think of these matters. At first, Manchester's streets had held the interest of novelty. Jack had been impressed by Deansgate, Piccadilly, St Anne's Square, the great shopping thoroughfares. But as the place gained familiarity, the novelty waned, and left Jack's mind with time and room to wander.

It was not that he disliked all aspects of the job. He loved the wood and leather smell of the trams and the familiar ritual at the start of each shift as he fitted the brass key into the gears. He liked the feeling of power and importance as he stood in the cab at the front in his uniform, demonstrating his expertise, rattling along as fast as possible between stops, then bringing the car to a halt at exactly the right spot through precision and timing in the play between gears and the steam brakes. There was a satisfaction in knowing you could do the job well. But still, there was not a lot of excitement in the unchanging work and too much time to agonise about Kathleen, their unborn baby, Kathleen's father and Kevin O'Donnell.

The only relief from these toxic meditations was provided by Jack's plans for his allotment. He filled his spare time at the weekends with preparation of the soil for spring planting. Jack took an old sack and a shovel with him through the streets, collecting manure from the road to use on his patch. He'd bought himself a bale or two of straw as well. So he'd been turning the soil over, digging in the manure and covering the whole with straw. Sometimes, on dark mornings before work, he went round to look at his garden, and took satisfaction from the sight of the steam rising from the dung, the frost a silvery icing on the straw under the waning moon. He could imagine the richness in the soil that would enable his vegetables to grow later in the year.

Jack also acquired a window box for his room in which he was cultivating tiny seedlings; he would be able to plant them out in the spring. Though he was primarily interested in growing vegetables, he was busy with a variety of flowers: Aquilegias, Delphiniums, Foxgloves, Pansies, Poppies, Lupins. He imagined presenting Annie with a bouquet, and earning one of those smiles without mockery. Then he mocked himself. For even thoughts of his garden looped back to thoughts of this woman who was, he felt sure, beyond him.

In the long evenings he took up the gardening books again and slowly began to learn about the history of landscape gardening and the development of cottage gardens in the previous century. He dreamt of earning commissions to build gardens for public use or private enjoyment. But he had no idea how to achieve such a goal. He only had a vague notion that the more he learned the better off he would be. When he tired of reading, he enjoyed the pictures in the books and sometimes amused himself by playing with designs for his own kitchen garden, imagining as he did so some old cottage out in the countryside of County Down and what it would be like to live there with Kathleen and their kids.

Lost in such hopeless dreams, he would hear Annie's tread

on the stairs and wonder about her—if she felt as lonely as he did or if she was as self-contained and self-assured as she seemed. Once or twice since Christmas, Jack had agreed to go to Church with Mrs Morris and Annie. Each time he'd been, after Morning-Song, when the congregation were milling in the gloomy churchyard, swapping greetings and gossip, Jack had been disconcerted by the appearance of a middle-aged man with iron hair, dressed smartly in a grey overcoat and bowler hat. Mrs Morris had introduced this gent as Mr Gervais, who worked as a manager in the office at the local colliery. This Gervais took more than a little interest in Annie, and she seemed to treat him with friendly respect, offering him her gloved hand and bestowing upon him her warmest smile. Jack didn't feel he was in a position to enquire how they knew each other, and could only guess at the intentions of this smooth mannered individual. But he felt a tremor of proprietorial jealousy which he knew was entirely inappropriate.

Then his mind would revert to Kathleen. He could not help comparing her with Annie. They were so utterly different from each other. Kathleen with her hair of shining coal cascading with its natural wave, her heart shaped face and teasing eyes. Before she fell pregnant, she'd always been ready with a laugh and a word. There was a liveliness to her, as if she couldn't quite contain all the energy within her. Annie on the other hand was languid. Her long white throat, her oval face, her light brown stylishly sculpted hair all expressed an elegant poise, her sense of serene command of every situation. There was intelligence and wit in the set of her mouth and eyes, but she was not as openly sensual as Kathleen. Indeed, the thought of sexual contact with her was overwhelming. Jack could not imagine having the temerity to touch her, whereas with Kathleen somehow she had made it seem easy and natural to cross the boundary of physical intimacy.

Not even the freezing cold of another shift on the tram could diminish the torment of such thoughts. To think of making love with Kathleen threatened Jack with a delirium which turned whole days to fever and left him aching and exhausted. After one such bout of love-sickness in late January, haunted with frustration and tired of doing nothing about his circumstances, on an impulse Jack decided to send Kathleen a letter with a postal order in it. He knew it was irrational, a cast into the dark, hoping to catch at her feelings, to remind her of him, to assert himself as the father of her child. He wanted to place a mark between her and O'Donnell, to hook her back in his direction. After a couple of pints in the pub, he scribbled to her in a fury. He told her he was determined to help her financially whether she liked it or not and that she couldn't stop him loving her and feeling for the child she carried. He wrote of his loneliness, his desire, his longing for her.

Jack schooled himself in patience, waiting to see if a reply would come. He tried not to feel furiously betrayed when, after a week, nothing had appeared. He told himself stories about Kathleen's parents acting like gaolers, policing their part in the narrow probity of the north.

More days passed and Jack was in battle with himself torn between hopeful images of Kathleen finding a way to defy her parents and despair that she had completely capitulated to them. He remembered how spirited she was, how defiant with her laughter and cigarettes. She never seemed to be afraid. Not even of God. Yet her father seemed to command her. Still, Jack imagined a smuggled letter saying she had changed her mind and that she was coming to join him in Manchester. Every night he peered at the *Evening News*, looking at the 'To Let' pages. He allowed himself to dream about climbing into bed beside her in the privacy of their own room. The luxury of lavender scented sheets. Her dark hair tumbling. And then he would be woken from his reverie by Mrs Morris plonking his tea before him and his visions dissolved like so much coal smoke into the Manchester smog.

He had almost given up hope, when he came home to find a letter from Belfast. But the address was written in an unknown hand. He tore the envelope open with a premonition of foreboding. It contained his postal order ripped in two and a single paragraph written on a scrap of paper, signed by Sean McCafferty: *Leave Kathleen alone. She is married to Kevin O'Donnell and has left Belfast. She wants no more of you. She doesn't need you or your money. Stay clear of us and we'll stay clear of you. If you try to communicate with her or see her, I'll sort you out. I have friends. We know where you are. Be warned. True friends of Ireland can find you.*

Jack climbed the stairs to his room. He felt as if he'd been punched. The old one two. A numb ringing in his head. A hollow heavy pain in his guts. He realised he'd been living in fantasy land. Kathleen was lost to him. So was his unborn child. There was to be no miraculous reprieve, no fairy tale ending. Old man McCafferty had won.

Jack resisted the temptation to destroy the note. He folded it and placed it on the bedside table with an obscure feeling that he needed to keep the evidence of this outrage. He sat on the bed and opened the book he'd been reading with such pleasure. It was Gertrude Jekyll's *Colour Schemes for the Flower Garden*. The book discussed planting for maximum colour effect. Jekyll used plants and flowers as a palette—nature arranged to reproduce the effects of art. Jack had been entranced by the method and the pictures. He had felt the impulse to share his enthusiasm with someone—imagined showing the book to Kathleen. Now it looked like so much decadent indulgence. Pretty frippery for the rich. Not for the likes of him. Suddenly, the future was shorn of promise. The tram lines beckoned all the way to the terminus. It served him right. He had been cultivating his effete dreams of gardening instead of going back to fight for Kathleen. Now he had lost her forever without striking a blow.

In the days that followed, Jack's stomach was acidic with corrosive rage. That he felt powerless made things worse. He longed to know if Kathleen endorsed her father's stand or was she an unwilling victim of the older man's tyranny? Jack couldn't accept that he'd lost her, but he didn't know what to do. He didn't doubt that the threat in McCafferty's note was real. In his darker moments he wondered if violence wasn't endemic to the Catholic Irish and grew indignant at McCafferty's implication that to be a Protestant necessarily meant you couldn't be a 'true friend of Ireland'. It made him feel glad he'd signed the Covenant.

A distraction from these seethings was provided in the second week of February when England woke to the sensational news, announced in black-bordered newspapers with massive headlines, of Captain Scott's death on his return journey from the South Pole. He had been found with two companions, Bowers and Wilson, frozen and starved to death only eleven miles from a depot full of provisions. Scott's other two companions at the Pole, Oates and Evans, had died before the last camp was made. The story was told in Scott's diary, which had been found with the bodies.

It seemed the whole of England was suddenly plunged into mourning. The names of Scott and Oates were on everyone's lips. Scott's message to the public was printed over and over again in the days that followed. No one could have enough of the extraordinary story. That Scott had been beaten to the Pole by the Norwegian Amundsen no longer mattered.

Jack was possessed by the passion of it all, recognising the heroism of defeat: *I do not regret this journey, which has shown that Englishmen can endure hardships, help one another, and meet death with as great a fortitude as ever in the past. We took risks, we knew we took them; things have come out against us, and therefore we have no cause for complaint, but bow to the will of Providence, determined still to do our best to the last . . . Had we lived, I should have had a tale to tell of the hardihood, endurance and courage of my companions which would have stirred the hearts of every Englishman. These rough notes and our dead bodies must tell the tale . . .*

'Isn't it all too thrilling?' Annie Hargreaves had gushed to him as she brandished the *Manchester Evening News* at him as he came downstairs for his tea. Jack could only agree. Scott's words moved Jack beyond the tramlines into a world of heroic sacrifice, which seemed far beyond the mundane realities of life in Manchester. And when, a few days later, he received a postcard from Willie McCullogh, telling him about the drilling he was doing with the newly formed Ulster Volunteer Force, Jack felt he was missing out on the finer possibilities of life. He thought about going back to Belfast to join up. He knew if he did so, he would be accepting the loss of Kathleen forever and the thought of going back to his Mam and Da with his tail between his legs was difficult to contemplate.

But the business with Kathleen's father had made him belligerent. He wanted to fight back. And memories of the rousing of the spirits, the sense of common purpose that he had glimpsed on Covenant Day made him feel less alone with his sense of loss and indignation. The ideas of comradeship, of sharing hardihood, courage and endurance in a noble cause suddenly appealed to Jack in a more intense way than he had experienced before. He thought it would be very fine to die like Scott and his men; a soldier's death. Self-sacrifice would make him honourable again. He would be redeemed.

Such fantasies were often cruelly interrupted as Jack brought the tram to a halt, and watched the stout old women clamber aboard with their shopping bags. They passed the time of day with him in their thick Mancunian accents. 'Ow do, auld cock. How yo doin' today.' 'Ay up. Orrible weather intit. Perishin' cold.' 'Ee thas'll need a brew by the end o't' line.' Jack smiled and nodded and said 'Good day to you, there,' wondering if this was all his life was destined to hold by way of service. It was not the kind of occupation that would make a woman proud of him. He could hardly spend his time boasting of how he tried to make the old dears' days by having a word and a smile.

Somehow everything in his life came back to Kathleen. Thoughts of her and the child she was carrying formed an obsessive loop—another set of miserable tram lines—which he was always attempting to escape and never quite succeeding. So he was glad in early March when he received a mysterious communication, which provided another opportunity of interest outside of his usual routines. Louis Cockcroft was the messenger, sliding an envelope towards Jack one day when they were having a smoke and a cup of tea during a break at the depot.

'My Mam says to give you this. She says it's right that you should go.'

'What is it?'

'I dunno. Open it and see.'

Jack ripped open the envelope. Inside there was a plain postcard. Handwritten in pencilled block letters it said, IF YOU COME TO THE MORNING STAR IN SALFORD WEDNESDAY NEXT WEEK AFTER 8pm, YOU'LL BE WITH THE BOYS. Next to the message, crudely drawn in a circle was the raised right hand: the Red Hand of Ulster.

'What's it say,' asked Louis.

Jack slid the card over to him. Louis raised his eyebrows. 'Some of your Irish pals having some fun?'

'Looks like it.' Jack tried not to betray the full extent of his perturbation. 'Mebbe it's one of my mates, having a laugh.'

'Why send it by my Mam?'

'Perhaps they didn't know how to find me. Herbie Ryan'll have something to do with it for sure.'

'Ay,' said Louis. 'That'll be it. He'll be having you on.'

‘And your Mam said I should go?’

‘That’s the message.’

‘I’d better not disappoint her then.’ Jack put the card away in his pocket, and immediately began to speculate on the possible meanings of this summons to the Morning Star.

XI

Kathleen raised her legs and eased her hips from side to side. She could not get comfortable. The mattress was old and like a poorly filled sack—full of lumps and sags and hollows. It was as comfortless as the room in which she lay. Though she had extinguished the light, still the bare boards, cheap deal furniture and iron bedstead oppressed her. Noise from the bar below made sure there was no peace. In her nostrils mingling with tobacco fumes was the incessant smell of the river. Kevin told her she was imagining things—making things worse than they were. He couldn't smell anything. He put it down to her pregnancy. But she didn't believe him. It didn't matter where she was in the house—upstairs, downstairs, back or front there was the same irritation to her senses. And every time she stepped out of doors onto the cobblestones of the quay the nose wrinkling odour intensified—a gaseous suggestion of swamp which made her want to retch.

It was not what she had expected when Kevin described the pub his cousin kept down by Anna Liffey on Eden Quay. He had made it sound romantic and welcoming. But she was beginning to understand he was full of blarney. He could spin words till he made black sound white. He saw what he wanted to see and believed what he wanted to believe. He had told her a grand story of how cosy they'd be in this billet and how nicely it would do them for a wee while, till she'd had the babby and they could return north. 'You'll be right as rain in Dublin,' he'd assured her, 'there are more people like us than in Belfast.' When she asked him what he meant, he said, 'You know, Irish, Catholic, for the Home Rule and all. Less mithering Proddies.'

But Kathleen missed the accents of home and she was appalled by the poverty and degradation of so many of the people. North of the river leading down to the quays there were streets and streets of houses once grand now converted to dilapidated tenements in which starving families crowded—a family to a room. In the teeming courts and alleyways, she had seen ragged children with no shoes and shawled women gathering by a single stand-pipe queuing for a basin of water. In the city centre, beggars scraped an errant tune from a fiddle or blew faltering notes from an auld tin whistle, while the rich walked past unheeding. Everywhere about the town there was a turbulent atmosphere. At public meetings men shouted militant trade unionism while women with posh accents advocated the rights of women within the Irish nation.

The bar-room arguments that nightly floated up through the boards added to Kathleen's sense of being surrounded by fretting and fighting. Kevin's blunt and voluble enthusiasm didn't help. He was, she recognised, a man who liked to sound big in a cause. She wondered sometimes if he understood half of what he was saying about the great affairs of the day, but there was no denying his rapid and eager mouthing of opinion about Home Rule, the Republic, Irish nationalism, workers' rights and democracy. The only comfort was that he required so little response from her. A nod here and a word there was all he needed by way of encouragement. She wasn't inclined to engage with him, much less to argue. Her only ambition was to make her life as comfortable as it could be in these uncomfortable circumstances. She was learning to manage as best she could.

By day, she had her share of work about the place, cooking, cleaning and ironing. It was part of the arrangement Kevin had made with Brian and Maggie, his older cousin and his cousin's wife. In return for bed and board and a few shillings a week, Kevin would work in the bar and Kathleen was expected to pitch in with domestic labour. Though she did not begrudge the work, as the baby grew it was becoming increasingly onerous, and Maggie seemed or pretended not to notice. One minute she would say in a tone of folkloric wisdom, 'Ay it's a weary weight when ye're carrying,' and the next be directing Kathleen to another pile of ironing. Kathleen carried on and tried not to mind. She deferred to Maggie and Brian and tried to make herself pleasant to them, all the time telling herself this servitude would not last forever and had as its final purpose the safe delivery of her child.

Now, she stroked the smooth taut skin of her rounded belly and murmured to the child, feeling the pact between them, tight and secret, the unbreakable bond. Nothing else mattered. The child was her hope and her redemption. Let Kevin brag and his cousins lord it over her. She could act the necessary part. And sometime in the future, somehow, she would be free. Often and often she stared at the passenger ships tied up at the North Wall and thought of what it would be to board one and sail away. Would she try and reach Jack in England? Would she feel more at home with him there than she did with Kevin here? She didn't know. It was a useless speculation. As her father had said to her before she left Belfast, 'You have made your bed, my girl, now you must lie in it.' And a very uneven auld bed it was at that. 'Never mind my precious one,' Kathleen crooned, 'you and me together will be all right. We'll show them a thing or two, so we will.'

Soon, it would be throwing-out time downstairs. This didn't mean that Kevin would be up to bed immediately. More often than not, if there were regulars in, Brian would see the majority of his patrons on their way, before letting the favoured few remain for a lock-in. On week-nights, this meant the hubbub would subside to a more sedate hum of voices—friends and neighbours enjoying a last 'small one' together. On Friday and Saturday nights, though, the noise level would increase as the singing began, the clapping and stamping and laughter. She could always hear Kevin's voice belting out 'Boolavogue' or 'The Rising of the Moon' and would understand why her Da approved him so. Tonight being Thursday, Kathleen hoped for a gentler end to the day, and willed herself to sleep. She felt exhausted a lot of the time and wondered if she was getting enough rest. She didn't like to complain to Maggie. She had too much pride. She would not appear weak before the older woman.

Kathleen must have fallen into a light doze. She woke to Kevin banging into the room, cursing because there was no light. She feigned sleep but he would not have it.

'I saw you, Katie-belle, you're not asleep at all. I saw your eyes open, and lovely they were too. I'll soon be in beside you, then we'll have some warming. There's been some rare good craic with the boys tonight. There are moves afoot your Da will be proud of. There's to be some organising. We won't stand by and do nothing while the Prods are busy drilling to fight. There are leaders who know what's what down here and they'll be calling for volunteers soon enough and I'll be first in line, so I will. I tell you, I don't mind if it comes to a fight. We'll put them in their place once and for all.'

Kathleen lay still and said nothing. She tried to breathe evenly as she heard the stages of his undressing punctuate his monologue. The clunk of his shoes falling on the floorboards was followed by the rasp of leather against metal as he undid his belt. The rustle of trousers off and then a pause and a muffle to his voice as the jumper went over his head and he undid his shirt buttons. And all the time his voice droned on about drilling and rifles and what a grand thing it would be to be a part of it all.

And then with a bounce and roll, still with his combinations on, he was in next to her. She smelled the sweat of him and the stale sweet whiskey and tobacco breath. Instinctively, she rolled onto her side away from him, knowing he would bring himself close to her.

'Ay, you like the spooning don't you?' He curled himself into her. She felt his knees beneath her buttocks and the rasp of his stubble against her neck as he nuzzled her. Though his hands were cold on her, she registered the animal warmth of him as he pressed himself to her. She clasped her hands round her belly as if to keep the baby safe from his marauding.

'Will you leave off, now, Kevin. It's late and I'm tired.'

'You know you love it. You're so beautiful and you're all mine.' His hands, warming now, continued to explore and she felt his cock stiffen against her backside. She had hoped that once her pregnancy began to show, he would leave her alone, but if anything he had become even more importunate. It was as if he thought the more he had her, the more she and the baby would belong to him. On the wedding night, after their first time together, he had whispered breathlessly, 'Now the babby's mine and so are you.' Since then, it had become a repeated refrain. As if the more he said it, the more it would be so. An act of persuasion and self-persuasion. Kathleen said nothing to his ardent claims. She recognised the uncertainty in him. She knew he was all bluster. There was no point in making him feel small. The other truth she reluctantly admitted to herself was the way in coupling with him her body betrayed her. He was, as her father had said, a good looking man, handsome, well-made and muscular. If she was in the mood, she could forget the particularity of Kevin O'Donnell and lose herself in physical sensation. But recently she had felt less and less in the mood. Now, she was determined.

'Will you give over, Kevin, and have some respect. You can see how I'm fixed with the babby and all and I'm so tired. It's time to stop till after the child is born. It is surely.'

'I cannot help myself, you are so lovely. Please Kathleen, I'm aching for you. Just lift your leg a little now.'

Kathleen felt his fingers searching for her tender places. For a moment, she wondered if it was easier to give in. But his wheedling together with the rough insistence of his hands decided her. She timed the roll towards him onto her back precisely. Kevin cried out in pain as she bent his wrist back under her.

'What are you at you stupid bitch, you've nearly broke my hand.'

'Didn't I tell you I wasn't for having any? I've had enough with you mithering me. It's not decent with me in this state.'

'You are my wife aren't you? You should be more friendly. What happened to your vows, now? You promised to love, honour and obey. And this is the way you treat me when I'm after a bit of loving.'

'What was said in Church doesn't mean you can have your way with me whenever you feel like it. If you don't learn to behave like a proper man, you'll have no more of me at all.'

'I'll give you proper man, so I will.' He turned to grasp her shoulder, but she shrugged him off.

'That's your idea of being a man, is it? To handle me roughly? I won't have it, Kevin. Do you hear me? It does you no credit. And to think you speak of loving me.'

'I do,' he said. 'Haven't I married you, while you're carrying another man's child? Isn't that enough for you? To show how much I love you?'

Kathleen felt the anger spark inside her, flint on flint. She recognised she was going to hear this tune for the rest of her life. But she couldn't afford to go too far now and burn her bridges. She needed to coax him. Talk him down. She didn't want their row to escalate. And she didn't want him harbouring grudges. She looked up at him, still sitting there, rubbing at his wrist. He looked like a little boy torn between anger and grief, but uncertain of his ground and puzzled to know what to do.

'It's more than enough, Kevin.' She was careful to keep irony from her voice.

'I didn't mean anything by it. You're a good man. Come on with you. Lie down here beside me why don't you and we can be friends. Let's get some sleep, or we'll have your auld cousin after us.' She reached her hand out to him and touched his arm. 'I can't be expected to be hungry for loving when I'm heavy with child now can I? You know I can't.'

Grudgingly, he lay down, and rolled so that his back was to her. She didn't care if he was inclined to sulk. She had got her way. That was the main thing. It was only a little victory but at least it was one. Soon he would be snoring. If she knew anything about him at all, he would wake tomorrow and behave as if nothing had happened. He'd be bright and breezy, garrulous and full of bravado as ever. The most she could hope was that in the future she managed as well to have her way. For in the exchange she had not only encountered his petulance, but felt an intimation of the violence in him. She saw her life with Kevin would be spent in endless negotiation and manipulation. It was an exhausting prospect.

But at least for now she could relax. She rolled away from him to her side of the bed and curled up with her hands on her baby. As she stroked her belly, she felt a responsive kick. The touch of her child comforted her. As the silence settled and the old pub creaked and groaned itself to sleep, she could hear the faint ring and tinkle of the ships' rigging at their moorings, and her thoughts took flight. She fell asleep wondering how Jack was getting on and whether he still thought of her.

XII

On the appointed Wednesday just after eight o'clock, when Jack Young pushed open the heavy door leading to the public bar of the Morning Star, he didn't know what to expect. The door revealed a long narrow room with sawdust on the floor and a few square tables and chairs. The place stank of stale beer. Swirls of smoke eddied in the dirty yellow light, and the hum of conversation seemed to pause as Jack stood uncertainly, peering to see if he could see anyone he knew. Paint the colour of rancid cream peeled from walls that were trimmed in a brown that reminded Jack of cow shite. Nothing so far suggested it had been a good idea to accept this invitation.

The strange communication that had summoned him could be a practical joke. Still, Jack wondered why the invitation hadn't been made more directly. It would have been easy for anyone in Belfast to find his address through his mates; he could see no need for an intermediary. Jack made towards the bar. The pub wasn't particularly full. There were one or two men lounging at the counter, and a couple of the tables were occupied. A game of dominoes was underway at one of them.

As he ordered a pint of bitter, a voice he recognised with a Belfast accent called out, 'Jack. Jack Young. Over here with you.'

Jack turned and saw the burly figure of Bob Haslam twisting round in his chair, waving him over to a corner table. He was seated with two other men, whom Jack didn't know.

'Bob Haslam. What the hell are you doing here? Why didn't you say you were for visiting.'

'Bring your pint over, man. I've some friends to introduce you to.'

Jack approached the table. Bob rose to his feet. He was over six foot tall and well-built with a round, fleshy face crowned with a mass of brown curly hair. He had an oddly youthful appearance, as if the child's face had not been entirely erased by the years; you could still detect traces of the little bruiser who'd terrorised his Elementary School teachers. Jack shook hands. He glanced at Bob's companions, one of whom seemed too well dressed for the establishment they were frequenting.

This was a middle-aged man, whom Bob introduced as Mr Johnstone. He wore a smart blue suit and tie, with a gold collar-pin. His sparse brown hair was slick with brilliantine and centre parted. His complexion was pock-marked, as if he had suffered from severe acne as an adolescent, or else had been the victim of some horrid complaint in later life. It gave him a faintly sinister air. The other occupant of the table was a thin weasel faced individual with shifty eyes, who barely looked at Jack as he was introduced as Frank Lynch. Johnstone spoke with an Ulster accent. Lynch sounded like a Liverpudlian.

They settled to their chairs and drinks. Bob handed round cigarettes. They lit up. Jack wanted to bombard Bob with questions but felt inhibited by the presence of the two strangers.

'How's Manchester treating you?' Bob grinned like a foolish puppy. 'Herbie and Willie said to say hello and they hope you've not been terrorisin' the English girls.'

'I'm fine.' Jack drew on his cigarette. 'The English girls are too stuck-up. How's things in the auld country?'

Bob glanced at Mr Johnstone before replying. 'Struggling on,' he said. 'Struggling on.'

'I had a card from Willie. He was tellin' me about drilling with the volunteers.'

'Whisht, man, not so loud,' Mr Johnstone interjected, glancing nervously about him.

Jack reddened under the rebuke.

'The landlord's orright,' said Frankie Lynch with his nasal

twang, 'but you never know who else is about.'

Jack bristled a little, but said nothing. He thought it was hard that you had to be careful in England about proclaiming loyalty to the Unionist cause. The whole point was to be true to England and the Empire.

The men sipped their beer. The atmosphere was strained. No one spoke for a moment. It was Bob Haslam who broke the silence. He talked about how similar the weather was in Belfast and Manchester and how he missed the sight of the lough every day. He said he'd seen Jack's parents and sisters; they were well and sent their love.

The glasses were empty by the end of this monologue, and Mr Johnstone rose, saying what will you have?'

Jack asked for the same again. Frank said he'd give Mr Johnstone a hand with the drinks. While they were at the bar, Jack hissed in an undertone, 'What's all this about? Why the hugger-mugger with the postcard. What's going on?'

'My Da's sent me over to help Mr Johnstone with a little business venture.' As he said this, Bob winked and nodded his head conspiratorially. 'It's after being a bit sensitive, so we don't want too many people knowing what's what or who's involved, if you take my meaning.' He paused, and winked again.

Johnstone and Lynch plonked the beers down on the table. Lynch spilled a little of Jack's pint and wiped it dexterously from the table with the sleeve of his raincoat.

Jack muttered his thanks. The men settled themselves again. Jack glanced from one to another then said to Bob, 'So what's this business venture got to do with me?'

As Bob made to reply, Mr Johnstone laid a restraining hand upon his arm. 'Allow me to explain,' he said in a low voice. 'I need a few good men to help me out with a little export trade I'm trying to arrange. Bob here thought you might be interested.'

'But I've already got a job.'

'Ay. Of course you have. This would be more in the way of casual work, on your day off, once every few weeks. Tell me, have you ever driven a motor-car or a truck?'

'I have not,' said Jack, his interest pricked now. He had always fancied learning how to drive a motor. The idea of being in complete control appealed to him. Not like the trams, where you were tied to the rails and the trolley wires.

'A pity. But Frank here could teach you. There's nothing much to it. You'd pick it up quick enough, I'm sure.'

'So it's a driver you want?'

'Yes. I need to have a few truck drivers I can call on to make an occasional run to Birmingham or Liverpool and back.'

'Birmingham? That's a long way isn't it?'

'It's a twelve hour round trip. You'd start at five in the morning, and be back by five at night.'

'And what would I be carrying?'

'Well now, there's the thing. Before we go into that I need to know we can trust you.' Johnstone paused. He dropped his voice, so that Jack had to strain to catch what he was saying. 'Bob, here, tells me you signed the Covenant?'

'I did.'

'Ay, but did you mean what you promised?'

Jack shifted in his chair, his hand clutching his glass of beer. It was a question that discomfited him. He didn't want to think too closely about protecting Ulster by 'any means possible'. The possibility of civil war. Instead, he allowed Sean McCafferty and Kevin O'Donnell into his mind and felt the familiar rage rise in him, an acid reflux.

'I did,' he said.

'Then you're willing to do something for the cause?'

Jack glanced round the table. Three pairs of eyes intent upon him. It wasn't the moment for hesitation or weakness. The idea of heroic action beckoned.

'I am.'

'You need to think carefully now. Before we go any further. You don't need to make a final decision about the job yet, but if we take another step, take you into our confidence then you're pledged to secrecy. If you're caught betraying us, there will be consequences.'

Frank Lynch nodded as he ground a cigarette butt out in the cheap blue tin ash-tray.

'I'll not betray you,' Jack said, 'but neither will I say yes to a job without knowing properly what it's about.'

'Fair enough. If you're sure now. I thought if you had an hour to spare, I'd show you. I've a place not far from here where we could discuss my proposition a little further, and you could see what you think, in private like, without having to be worried about the company. What do you say?' With this he looked round the pub meaningfully. Bob nodded and smiled at Jack encouragingly.

'All right, then. I'll have a look.'

'Good man. Before we do let's have a whiskey for the road. I'll get us a drop of the auld Bushmills.'

The whiskey was bought and drunk. They raised their glasses as Mr Johnstone toasted 'the auld country'. Then they ventured into the weather.

The night was dark and blustery with scudding clouds obscuring a thin moon. It was not a long walk, but they soon left the main road and entered a warren of dimly lit side streets where cramped terraces of the meanest kind lay cheek by jowl with factories, mills and warehouses. The air smelt sulphurous. There seemed no hint of spring.

They came to some large wooden gates set into a brick wall, which was surmounted by broken shards of glass to deter any would-be thieves. Faded paint across the doors declared this to be the domain of W. Johnstone and Sons Ltd.

The proprietor was busy removing the padlocks and shoving open the gates, which fetched onto a courtyard around which were several buildings of different sizes. One looked like an office. Another was clearly a warehouse. Yet another huge edifice made of brick looked as if it housed some sort of manufacturing plant.

'This is my bleach works,' Johnstone said to Jack, as he led the men across the cobbles toward the warehouse. There was more fiddling with padlocks, before the great doors could be rolled aside. Frank Lynch produced a torch from somewhere and led the way forward into the cavernous space.

As Jack's eyes grew accustomed to the gloom, he made out hundreds of barrels stacked in neat rows. On the concrete floor beneath them, he could see a white powdery substance gleaming in the torch light. The nose-tickling smell reminded him of laundry day in his Mam's back kitchen. Bleach, he presumed.

'Come this way,' Johnstone said leading them down an aisle towards the far corner of the building. 'I want to show you the most interesting bleach you've ever seen in your life.'

Bob kept catching Jack's eyes, grinning and winking, reassuring that all was well. Jack didn't know what to think. They reached a batch of barrels that looked just the same as all the rest. 'Do the honours, Frankie,' said Johnstone with a grin.

'Here, give us a hand, lads.' Bob and Jack helped him to manhandle a barrel to the floor. It was heavy, and Jack almost groaned aloud with the weight of it, sucking in his breath as he took the strain. As it hit the floor, a dusting of white powder escaped from the seams. Mr Johnstone toed it with his fine leather shoes, his eyes smiling with a complacent gleam. 'Bleach,' he said. 'Nothing but bleach.' He laughed aloud. 'Open her up, Frankie.'

Frank took a crowbar that had been leaning against the wall, and levered the top off the barrel.

'Look at this lovely stuff.' Johnstone invited Jack to see.

Jack peered in. He looked up and saw the others were focused on his reaction. He'd half guessed it would be something like this, but still it was a shock to find himself staring at the shining grey-blue metal of rifle barrels. The guns were neatly packed with an outer circle of thick corrugated cardboard. Between this and the outer wall of the barrel was a white powdery substance.

'Open another Frankie. Show him the range.'

Frankie obediently prised the lid off another barrel. This one was packed with boxes of .303 ammunition. The spaces between the boxes and the barrel were filled with the same white powder.

'Clever, isn't it?' said Johnstone. 'That stuff looks just like bleaching powder. It's farina—finely ground starch. The barrels leak a bit, the customs officers are reassured. They're full of bleach for the linen works as they're supposed to be. If it really were bleach, it would ruin the ammo.'

'So what's the game?' asked Jack, still not sure exactly what he was being asked to get into.

'It's for the boys back home,' blurted Bob.

'Ay, so it is,' agreed Johnstone. 'The Volunteers haven't enough guns or ammunition. Our job is to arm them. They're drilling with wooden dummies at the moment.'

'Will it come to a fight, do you think?' Jack was aware of his heart emphatic in his chest. He felt his breathing was slightly constricted, as if he'd been running. There was something deeply disturbing about the sight of the guns, yet he was excited as well.

'It's looking that way, right enough. Here's your chance to do something for the cause.'

'What exactly would I be doing?'

'Simple delivery driving. Are you interested?'

'I don't know. What are the risks?'

'It's not illegal, unless you get caught,' Bob said and laughed at his own joke.

Johnstone gave him a withering look. 'You could start on the Birmingham run,' he said, addressing Jack again.

'There's hardly any risk there. The guns and ammo have been bought fair and square in the name of a gun-dealer in Manchester. They're stored in a warehouse down there. We have paperwork covering all that. The only possible problem would be if you were picked up dropping the stuff off here. The Liverpool job's a bit more risky. By then the stuff's been packed into the barrels, and it's shipped as bleach. If the Customs got hold of the job at the port, we'd be in trouble. But if everyone keeps their mouth shut, the chances of getting caught are slim.'

'I don't know. I don't want to end up in clink.'

'You won't. You could always say you'd been hired as a delivery driver, and you were following orders. You didn't know what you were carrying.'

'With this accent, I doubt if anyone would believe that.'

'It's not about belief, it's about proof. But it won't come to that. Come on, have an adventure. Help out the boys back home.'

Jack searched Bob's face, looking for the reassurance of familiarity. He was uncertain of his ground. It had seemed easy to sign the Covenant with thousands of others. There was a feeling of belonging and solidarity. Here, in the cold warehouse with the two men he didn't know, he was lost.

Yet Bob was nodding his encouragement. 'Help us out, Jack. If the lads are armed, the government will think twice about trying to force Home Rule on the North.'

There was an appeal to Jack's idea of romance in the scheme. It was a damn sight more exciting than driving a tram. It seemed poor spirited, and cowardly to say no.

'I'll give it a go,' he said.

'Good man.' Johnstone was business-like now. Get the lids back on those barrels, Frankie. Let's get out of here. Jack, you'll not see me again, and it would be best if you and Bob didn't mix too much. Best not to make the connections between us obvious. Frankie will be your contact, and he'll get you going with the driving. You'll only need a few outings, and you'll be right as rain. And here's the bonus. When you do a trip to Brummie, we'll slip you a few quid for your trouble.' The men shook hands, and soon they were away.

On the long walk home alone, Jack had plenty of time to wonder if he was doing the right thing.

XIII

The canteen at the depot was loud with men's voices. Great white mugs of tea were banged onto trestle tables, ash-trays were fought over, and the air was blue with tobacco wreaths and profanity. Occasionally, the shriek of one of the floral-aproned women serving behind the counter would rise above the din, telling some brave spark not to get fresh with her. The hiss of steam from the urns was only slightly less vicious.

Jack sipped his brew and lit a smoke. Louis would be along soon and would want to know about the meeting at the Morning Star. Jack wasn't looking forward to the interrogation.

' 'Ere Jack. Give us a fag.' The speaker who plonked himself down on the bench opposite was a pasty faced youngster from the slums of Hanky Park who'd just started as a trolley boy. His name was Charlie Shuttleworth and he was a royal pain in the arse. Always on the scrounge, he had a loud and dirty mouth on him to boot. It was all bravado of course but he'd already earned the nickname 'Cocky'. When he wasn't being irritated by the boy, Jack felt sorry for him, sensing the uncertainty behind the mask. Now, since the lad's presence might save him from Louis' curiosity, Jack decided to put up with the interruption to his tea-break with a good grace.

'I dunno, Cocky,' he said. 'What would your Mammy say? Smoking at your age. It'll stunt your growth, lad.'

'Never mind me Mam. I'm old enough to work, I'm old enough to smoke. And I'm old enough to 'ave a jump as well.'

'Holy God, you're barely out of nappies.'

'I'd take me nappy off for that Sally Hardcastle and give her a seeing to, I'm telling yer. I would that. Come on, give us a ciggy. I'm dying for one.'

Jack reluctantly offered him a smoke. 'I hope I won't have your Mammy after me.'

'Forget me Mam. That Sally reminds me of my big sister. Lovely tits on her. I could introduce you if you like. To my sister, I mean. I reckon she might be a real goer.'

Before Jack could reply, Louis arrived with his cup of tea and an iced bun. 'Who's a real goer and how would you know, nipper?'

'He's talking about his sister,' Jack said.

'Lovely.' Louis rolled his eyes and took a bite out of his bun.

'Are you going to eat all o' that?' Cocky enquired.

Louis ignored the boy and looked at Jack as he chewed. 'How did you get on at the Morning Star then?' he said between bites.

'Ooo. Has he bin out with a tart?' The boy addressed Louis with a prurient leer.

'Shut it.' Jack advised.

'What was it all about?' Louis ignored the youngster.

'What's it always about,' Cocky said, puffing on his fag like a seasoned smoker and making an obscene gesture.

Louis Cockcroft leaned forward across the table confidentially and said to the boy, 'Listen, sonny, shouldn't you shove off and play with someone your own age?'

'They're all mardy bastards. I'd rather 'ave a smoke with you blokes.'

'You've got one then?'

'One what?'

'A smoke.'

'No. Jack's holding.'

Jack reached for his packet of Players and offered one to Louis. Louis took a cigarette and tamped it on the table top. He bent forward as Jack struck a match and offered the light before extinguishing the flame with a deft flick of the wrist.

'Come on,' Louis urged, as he leaned back and exhaled, 'What went on?' He blew smoke rings as he waited for Jack's reply.

'Nothing much,' Jack said. 'Just a bit of business.'

'Business,' Cocky hooted. 'Was she a prossie, then?'

'For Christ's sake, I wasn't with a woman.'

'What are you talking about then?'

'We're not talking to you about anything.' Louis intervened. 'Scarper before I clip you round the ear.'

The kid didn't move and was inclined to sulk.

'We'll all have to go in a minute,' Jack said.

'Not before you've told me the tale,' Louis insisted. He turned on the boy again, raising his voice this time, 'Go on, get lost before I lose my temper.'

'You're a miserable pair of fuckers,' Cocky complained as he extricated himself from the bench. 'I only want to be mates. I don't know why you 'ave to 'ave secrets. I'm old enough to know there'll be a tart or brass behind most stories.'

Louis showed the boy his fist. 'Bugger off, before I sing yer a nursery-rhyme.'

Cocky Shuttleworth slouched off, showing them two fingers as he departed.

Jack felt sorry for the lad and even sorrier that he was now alone with Louis' curiosity.

'Come on now. Out with it.' Louis urged.

'There's nothing to it. The message was from a Mr Johnstone, who has a bleach works. He comes from Belfast, but lives here. He wanted to know if I could do some casual work, driving a truck.'

Louis looked disappointed. 'Old Johnstone. Is that all?'

'You know him?'

'Mam used to work for him.'

'That explains the message then.'

Louis frowned and considered Jack, blowing a stream of smoke into the air, forgetting now to make rings. 'But why's me Mam so secretive about it all. And why aren't I invited to do casual work?'

'Because your Ma doesn't want you to kill yourself trying

to drive.'

'I've always fancied trying to drive.'

'But your Ma doesn't fancy it, I reckon. And then, maybe she understands I need the extra cash to send home to my folks.'

'So you're going to do it?'

'Ay, I thought I'd give it a try.'

'Well you're a lucky bugger, that's all I've got to say.'

'Mebbe. But it'll mean I've not much free time.'

'I'm goin' to give me Mam some stick over this.'

'You're a brave wee man now. If your Mammy's anything like mine, I bet you don't.'

Louis looked stung for a moment, as he ground his cigarette out. Then he brightened a little. 'So are you on for the match on Saturday?'

'I'm sorry. It's my first lesson on the truck.'

'T'hell with yer then. It's your loss.' Louis drained his mug, and made to move from the table.

'Don't be like that. Tell you what. I'll meet you for a pint afterwards.'

They took their mugs back to the counter as they were leaving and shouted their thanks to the girls. Louis fancied himself with the lasses and he winked at the prettiest as he loitered for a word.

Jack said his cheerios and entered the tram-sheds relieved that he'd negotiated the conversation with Louis. He hoped that telling half-truths wouldn't get him into bother. It seemed the only thing to do and it was a comforting story anyway. Jack didn't want to dwell too much on the implications of gun-running.

When he reached his tram, Cocky Shuttleworth was busy changing the sign-board ready for departure. He seemed to have recovered from the sulks.

' 'Ere Jack,' he said before Jack drove off. 'Next time yer go t'the Morning Star yer should take me sister. She'd show yer some business, I'm telling you. There'd be no need for secrets with her.'

'No thanks, lad.' Jack replied. 'I've got enough trouble as it is. I don't need any more.'

Jack didn't relish the petty deceits he had to practice in order to protect himself and the enterprise he'd embarked on. He told himself the untruths were for the good of everyone concerned. It wouldn't do to implicate Louis in illegal matters, much less Mrs Morris or Annie Hargreaves. Yet it had been a disturbing moment when over a cup of tea on Friday afternoon, after he'd finished his shift, Annie had casually enquired if Jack was going to the match as usual with Louis the following afternoon.

Since Christmas, such little chats in the company of Annie and Mrs Morris had become more frequent. Depending on what shift he was working, he might be invited to morning or afternoon tea or even a late supper with his landlady and her niece. Jack took their invitations as a kindness. He thought they sensed his unhappiness, and imagined him to be homesick. There had even been a walk or two on a Saturday or Sunday afternoon after Church, sedate promenades through Victoria Park, polite conversations about the progress of his allotment, the well-being of his family in Belfast.

Now, in reply to Annie's question, Jack's first unthinking impulse was to tell the truth. 'No,' he said, 'I'm not going to the match,' and only when he saw the surprise on Annie's face realised the difficulties his denial would cause.

'That's not like you,' she said, enquiry lingering in her voice.

Jack told her that he had to go and see his father's cousin, Mrs Donovan, the one who had looked after him when he first arrived from Belfast. He'd heard she wasn't well.

'That's very kind, Jack,' she said, tea cup poised before her mouth. Then, with her little upturned smile of mockery, 'We'll have to wait for our next walk out together, then?'

'I'm afraid so.'

Annie put her head to one side and considered him thoughtfully. Jack looked back at her, meeting the challenge in her eyes, trying to give nothing away, wondering what it was she really wanted from him. At least he knew what the game was with Johnstone and the truck driving. With Annie he had no idea. He was equally uncertain about his feelings for her. He knew that he admired her in some ways and was flattered by her attentions. But he could not rid himself of his initial feeling that she considered herself superior to him. Though he was glad of her kindness to him, her knowing glances and mocking smile knocked him off balance, made him feel vulnerable. He was always a step behind her somehow. There might be a potential for making a fool of himself while learning to drive, but he reckoned it would be a more straightforward transaction than any of his dealings with Annie Hargreaves.

Saturday afternoon, the kind of raw blustery day in late March when the few daffodils and jonquils that had dared to peep in the allotments and public gardens were flayed by vigorous gusts of Easterly cold air. If his mother had been there, she would have complained of the wind being fit to take the face of you.

Having had an uncomfortable morning on the trams, Jack approached Johnstone's bleach works in a mixed humour. He was anxious to try his hand at the driving, but the weather made him think that sitting with one of his gardening books by the fire might have been a preferable alternative. He would have foregone the football and persuaded Annie it was too cold for walking.

Jack entered the cobbled yard and looked about him. The scope of the place looked even bigger and more impressive than it had done in the dark. He looked round, trying to identify the main office. After a moment, Frank Lynch appeared from a low red brick building on his right where two steps led to a double glassed door.

'Orright,' Frankie said, a typical scouse greeting.

'Ay, Ay,' Jack replied, eyeing the man coolly.

'I 'ope you're goin' to shape better than some of the other fuckers I've been tryin' to teach. Come 'ed, let's get on with it.' Frank hawked and spat in a familiar kind of way as he led Jack across the yard. They turned left down the side of the warehouse where Jack had been shown the guns and presently came to a wooden lock-up with a corrugated iron roof at the end of the road.

Frankie undid the padlocks and swung back the doors to reveal two wagons, the olive paint still bright on the mahogany coachwork. W. Johnstone and Co. was emblazoned in white down the sides. The brass on the lamps gleamed. Jack thought they looked magnificent machines. He stood staring while Frank launched himself into the driver's seat.

'Stand on the running board so's you can see what I'm doin',' he said.

Jack did as he was told. The driver's seat was protected by a windscreen and a canvas hood that was an extension of the canopy which covered the back tray. Otherwise it was open to the weather.

'Orright. First things first.' Frankie introduced Jack to the various controls. There were three foot-pedals: one each for the forward and reverse transmission and one brake. A hand-lever on the right-hand side of the steering wheel had a double function. Pulled right back, it worked as a brake on the back wheels; otherwise, it was used to hold the clutch in neutral. Below the steering wheel, projecting forward from the floor were two further hand-levers. One was the throttle and the other was the spark lever.

This information delivered so quickly bewildered Jack. It was nothing like a tram.

'Now then. Starting. You with me?'

'Yes.'

'Orright. First pull this back to put her in neutral. Then turn this switch ' 'ere on to Magneto. Open the throttle five notches like this.' Frankie pressed the hand lever on the throttle stick and shifted it the required distance. 'Then,' he continued, 'move the spark lever three notches, like that. You with me?'

'Yes.'

'Shove out the way, then.' Frankie jumped down and moved to the front of the truck. 'Yer prime her by pulling this wire 'ere.' He bent down and tugged on a wire under the radiator. 'Then we give her a turn with the starting handle. Y'ave to be careful with this so you don't put your shoulder out.'

Frankie gave the handle a couple of turns, and the engine coughed, then roared into life. A plume of exhaust rose blue and pungent, behind the truck. Frank raced back to his seat and revved the engine just as it sounded as if it might die.

'There y'are. Nothin' to it. Engage forward gear by pressing the forward pedal, keep your foot on the brake, release the handbrake, now foot off the brake and away we go. The wagon juddered into motion, obliging Jack to jump from the running board. Frankie drove the wagon out of the garage and came to a neat halt outside.

'Orright. Now it's your turn.' He switched the engine off and jumped down. 'Come 'ed. Don't hang about.'

Jack, anxious not to betray his nervousness, did as he was told. He sat in the driver's seat, inhaling leather and petrol, gripping the wheel for the first time, as if he was about to drive off; it felt great. Frankie tested him on the controls. When Jack confused the forward and reverse transmission pedals, Frankie shouted, 'No, no, no, you hopeless tosser. Other way round.'

Jack eyeballed the smaller man. Frankie grinned at him, showing his yellow teeth in a supercilious leer. 'Go on,' he said, 'let's see what you can do.'

Jack tried to contain his temper while he concentrated on the starting sequence. Magneto. Neutral. Throttle. He grasped the lever. It was stiff and he felt clumsy as he pulled it through the notches. Then the spark lever.

'Where have you got them?' Frankie asked.

'Throttle on four. Spark on five.'

'Wrong.' Frankie sounded pleased. 'Throttle on five. Spark on three. Get it?'

Jack didn't reply. He made the adjustments, and stepped down from the wagon. He applied himself to the crank handle giving it an almighty wrench and jarring his shoulder in the process. The engine turned heavily, without the faintest hint of starting.

'Wrong again.' Frankie stood hand rolling a smoke, the paper attached to his upper lip as he teased a wad of tobacco out of an old leather pouch. 'You've not much of a memory 'ave yer?'

Jack cursed himself for a simpleton, and remembered the carburettor needed to be primed. He found the wire under the radiator and gave it a good tug.

'Not too much or you'll flood her.' Frankie removed a stray strand of tobacco from his tongue with fastidious fingers and spat contentedly.

Jack thought how good it would be to plant his fist into the weasel's face and punch the smug smile off it. He cranked the engine again. Nothing happened. He could feel the sweat breaking out on his forehead, despite the scathing wind. He cranked again. Again, the engine gave a limp cough but refused to fire.

'What have you got for biceps? Knots on cotton? Give it

a good heave.' A stream of blue smoke followed this advice issued through pursed lips.

He'd laugh if I did my shoulder in, thought Jack, staving off the humiliation that was beginning to prick him and trying to concentrate on the job. Taking a deep breath, he swung again. This time he felt the engine turn and splutter into life.

'Quick now. Before it dies.'

Jack rushed round and hauled himself into the driver's seat. He put the crank-handle aside and set about engaging first gear. This time he got everything right, and the truck began to lumber forward. Jack experimented with the transmission and was soon in second gear.

'Ay up,' Frankie shouted, as Jack drove past him, leaving him in a cloud of exhaust fumes.

Jack deliberately swung off down the road and round the corner into the main yard. He could hear Frankie running after him yelling for him to stop.

'I haven't taught you 'ow to change gear. If you smash that truck, I'll smash you.'

Jack laughed aloud. This was grand. There was nothing to it, once you got going.

'I'll burst youse when I get hold of yer.' Frank paused to step on his fag end.

'You and whose army?' Jack shouted back. He drove the wagon round and round in a circle in the yard. Frankie tried to stand in his way to make him stop, but Jack was enjoying himself too much. Deliberately, he drove at the spindly figure, now fairly dancing with rage.

'You cunting bastard.' Frankie stood aside, breathless, hands on hips.

Jack drove the wagon back the way he had come, towards the garage, and brought the vehicle to a neat halt. He applied the hand brake, and waited for Frankie to catch up.

'I'll 'ave you,' Frankie threatened as he approached the vehicle. He jumped on the running board and made to grab

Jack. Jack pushed him away.

'Don't be so daft,' he said.

Jack jumped down from the truck to where Frankie was standing fists clenched, hands by his side.

Frankie came at him again, trying to catch Jack by the scruff of his collar. Again Jack shoved him away and told him to calm down.

'Arrogant Irish fucker.' Frankie stared at him, fuming.

'I thought we were supposed to be on the same side,' said Jack.

'I'm not on anyone's side but my own. And you'd do well to remember it.'

'What are you helping for then?'

'Johnstone pays me. That's the point. The only point. I couldn't give a fuck about Ireland.'

'I see.'

'Do yer? Do yer really? Do yer see 'ow much damage I could do? A little word here. A little word there. And you're finished. In the nick. So it'd pay you to pay me some respect. Orright?'

Jack regarded Frankie Lynch with a look which he hoped conveyed his contempt. Then putting his hand to his cap brim, he mimed the tugging of a forelock. 'Yes, sir, Mr Lynch,' he said. 'Whatever you say.'

Frankie brushed past him, and climbed into the truck. He said nothing as he turned the vehicle round and backed it into the garage. Jack stood aside, watching.

'That's your lot for this afternoon,' Frankie shouted, as he turned the Magneto to off, and the engine died. 'I'll see you next week. If you behave yourself, I'll show you the gears properly.'

'Thanks very much to you,' Jack said, and turned on his heel. He walked away, half in a mind to try and get in touch with Bob to tell Johnstone where he could shove his driving.

XIV

By the time Jack reached the pub where he had arranged to meet Louis, he had calmed down and he began to see the funny side of what had happened. Thinking about the wee man dancing out of the way in a perfect rage as he drove the wagon in circles brought a smile to Jack's face.

The pub was full of blokes coming from the match. United had won, so there was a loud and cheerful crowd standing shoulder to shoulder in groups, talking enthusiastically about this corner and that free-kick and did you see Pemberton elbow our Harry in the face?

Jack edged his way towards the bar, looking out for Louis. Wedged in the three-deep scrum for drink, watching the pints being poured thick and fast, Jack caught sight of his mate standing to his right, just about to be served.

'Louis,' he shouted above the din. 'Mine's a pint of Guinness.'

'No Guinness on tap here mate,' Louis shouted back.

'Get us a bottle, then, man.'

Jack was relieved to extricate himself from the crush, and find a narrow spot by a wooden pillar, which had shelves all round to take the ash-trays and glasses. Louis, bearing the glasses high in his hands to avoid the arms and shoulders of the throng, pushed his way through. He plonked the glasses down, and took Jack's bottle of Guinness with the top off out of his coat pocket. 'There y'are, lad,' he said. 'Get that into yer.'

Jack poured the rich black liquid slowly, creating the perfect glass with a creamy white head. He took a sip. Not as good as Belfast. But it would do for now. 'Grand,' he said, savouring the taste. He took a cigarette from Lou's proffered packet. They lit up. Jack took another sip of his beer. He loved a cigarette with Guinness. The sweet tobacco and the bitter ale. A great combination. He loved, too, the craic that went with the situation. Louis told him all about the game, asked him how the driving had gone. They had a laugh as Jack described Frankie the scouser. Soon it was his turn to go to the bar.

With drinks replenished and smokes on the go, their talk became more confidential. Louis wanted to share with Jack his plans for the bright blonde-haired beauty of the canteen, Ethel Hazelhurst.

'She's just my type,' Louis said. 'Not stuck up, and will 'ave a laugh. A looker too. There's something to get hold of there. I don't like 'em too scrawny.'

'Lovely,' Jack nodded.

'I'm goin' to save up me pay and invite her to the pictures. Just think, sitting there in the dark together.' Louis' eyes took on a far-away look as he imagined the possibilities opened up by plush seats, a box of chocolates and a pretty lass in the intimate flickering light of the screen. 'I'll have to get the right kind of show,' he continued, almost as if he was speaking to himself. 'Something romantic. Something that might put ideas in her head.'

'What kind of ideas would they be then?' Jack enquired, his eyes giving the lie to the naivety of his tone.

'Why don't you come too? Ask one of the other girls. What about that Hardcastle woman, Sally isn't it? She's a bit of all right.'

'I'll not be botherin' Sally. They're nought but trouble the women.' Jack drained his glass decisively.

'I knew it,' Louis said, thumping his fist on the shelf and making it shake. 'A man of experience. I knew tha' would be. It's always the quiet ones who con the skirts. Same again?' He grabbed Jack's glass. 'Then you can tell me all about them.'

Before Jack could protest, Louis had disappeared again towards the bar. The crowds were thinning now, but there were still enough customers to make the trip to and from the bar a fairly lengthy expedition.

Jack lit another cigarette and wondered how he was going to deal with what looked to be an inevitable quizzing from Louis. The loneliness of not confiding had to be weighed against the dangers of disclosure. Not that he didn't trust Louis, but he hadn't known him long. And you never knew what gossip might go on. If someone like Cocky Shuttleworth got wind of a tale, it would be all round the depot in no time.

It was hot in the room. Jack suddenly felt uncomfortable. He undid the button of his donkey jacket and considered taking it off. But there was nowhere to put it. He wiped his brow with the palm of his hand, inventing a story that would satisfy his mate.

'Now then,' said Louis, as he delivered the beers, spilling his own a little in his enthusiasm. 'What about these Belfast girls then? What 'ave they been doin' to you and what 'ave you been doin' to them?'

'Ay, well, wouldn't you like to know?'

'That's why I'm askin. You might have some tips, like.'

'Leave 'em alone, that's my tip.'

'So you had a girl in Belfast?'

'Ay.'

'Dark, blonde, brunette?'

Jack held his glass of Guinness up to the light. Her hair was black and shiny as that. Her skin was white as the froth on top.'

'Bloody 'ell, a poet.' Louis paused while he took a long draught of ale. 'So what happened? Are you still in touch?'

Louis' innocent remark together with the beer brought back vivid memories. Touching. The feel of her breast against his palm. The search of his finger-tips against the moist lips between her legs. He banished the thought as he felt the familiar disturbance in his loins.

'No, not in touch.' He had not meant to betray so much sadness and anger in his voice. Louis looked at him, his face softened now, the laughter gone, replaced by concern.

Jack appreciated the response. As the silence lengthened, the loss of Kathleen and his unborn child threatened to overwhelm him. He felt the spaces blossoming in him which longed to be filled with love. Instead there was only beer and cigarettes.

For now, Louis was not asking any more questions. They drank some more. Pint after pint. Each one seemed to go down quicker than the previous one. Louis, under the influence, having reiterated his plans for the conquest of Ethel Hazelhurst, began to urge Jack to reconsider his rejection of Sally Hardcastle. And if he wasn't interested in Sally, there were plenty of other girls to choose from.

Jack tried to make clear his feelings were already tangled enough without encouraging further complication. He listened with half an ear to Louis' enthusiasm for the chase, and thought about Kathleen, wondering where she was now and what she was doing. To think of her in O'Donnell's arms was an exquisite torture that he couldn't bear for long. Instead, he thought about Annie Hargreaves. She seemed to exist in a different world from the one he'd been in all day and the one that Louis was inviting him to participate in now. In his drink befuddled mind she beckoned as a shining quandary.

The question was could he ever hope to enter Annie's life in any other way than as an impoverished supplicant, begging to feast at her table? Though they had walked out together under the watchful eye of Mrs Morris, Jack was uncertain as to the significance of these passionless meanderings through the public gardens. Was he just convenient and friendly company, a kind of strangely accented curiosity for Annie to amuse herself with for half an hour when she felt like it while she waited for Mr Gervais to propose? Or was there something more. He didn't know whether to hope for the latter or not.

They left the pub later than either had intended and when the sharp air hit his lungs, Jack felt dizzy making his farewells to Louis. He sucked peppermints all the way home, and on the short walk between the tram stop and the front door in Partington Lane, he concentrated on walking in a straight line by aligning his steps to the edges of the paving stones.

What he definitely wished to avoid was any encounter with either Mrs Morris or Annie. Even though he didn't consider himself to be drunk, he knew he was not entirely sober. Any hint of this condition might prove disastrous to both his continuing residence with Mrs Morris and any interest in her niece.

Application was required in fitting his key to the lock on the front door. He took a deep breath and watched his hand intently, holding the key out, trying to steady the shaking. With infinite care he edged the key towards the keyhole. He wanted to make sure there was no unseemly scrabbling. With a sigh of relief he felt the key engage the lock. He'd done it. No problem.

The hall light was on, illuminating the hall-stand with its pegs and mirror. The other doors were closed. All was silent. Jack made for the stairs. As he took the first step, he heard the parlour door open, and Annie came out.

'Ah, Jack,' she said. 'We thought that might be you. You're awfully late. Is everything all right?'

'Thank you, fine,' he replied, trying to make sure his words didn't slur. 'Mrs Donovan is poorly, though. I stayed to make her tea.' The lie slipped from his tongue, as he stood there one hand on the banister rail, one foot resting on the first step.

'I'm sorry to hear that,' said Annie, appraising Jack's face.

'I'll say good night, then,' he said, anxious for the inquisition to be over, and making to continue his ascent.

'Yes goodnight,' she said, frowning. Then, 'can you smell peppermint?'

'Ay, perhaps I can a little.'

'Mrs Dalrymple must have been overdoing it again. She loves her mints.'

'Ay, she does that. Well, goodnight then.'

'Good night, Jack.'

Jack thought she gave him a rather knowing smile as she retreated into the parlour. But in his confused state he wasn't sure. He wasn't sure of anything.

He clambered between cold sheets, remembering the humiliations of his driving lesson, thinking about the potential for humiliation in his dealings with Annie. There seemed no certainty in the world. Even when he made his thoughts turn to the consolations of his allotment, he knew there were no guarantees of crop and flower. You could work hard and still lose everything. But you were supposed to believe that the value was in the work. That's what his father had taught him. 'Sufficient unto the day is the labour thereof.' His father had also warned him many times about the evil of strong drink.

Jack tried to sleep, dizzily wondering about his day's work and what it might mean. But sleep eluded him. The booze seemed to make his mind speed and his body restless. First he felt cold, then as he thought of the gun-running and the lies he'd told he felt himself break out in a sweat. The sheets and blankets seemed to constrict him. He wrestled with them, as he wrestled with his conscience. Was he letting his anger over Kathleen and her father lead him into a life of secrets and violence? He had lied to Louis. He had lied to Annie. What place did she have in his life? How could you build friendship on lies? Much less love?

It was some small consolation to know he hadn't lied to Kathleen. If she had come to England he wouldn't have got mixed up in the gun-running. He would have put her first. But she hadn't. And she had given up on him. Apparently she accepted her father's view of things. In those circumstances, he didn't have to answer to her or his memories of her. He was a free man. But he wasn't free of feelings for Kathleen. He loved her, didn't he? Or was it now only the idea of her he loved? He couldn't tell and hated himself for allowing the distinction into his mind.

The room waltzed before Jack's eyes as the ideas turned like a sinister carousel up and down, round and round with nothing solid to hang on to. She loves me, she loves me not, danced on his tongue, the backstreet game, blowing dandelion seed to the wind, came back to taunt him with answers as fickle as a random breath. What Kathleen and Annie felt for him were mysteries that consumed him and kept him awake until he heard bird song herald the first grey light peeping through the curtains. It was only then that he fell into an exhausted slumber.

XV

Kathleen trod the creaking floor boards by the bed in her old blue dressing gown with the baby on her shoulder. The fire had burnt low and though spring was coming on, the air was chill. Outside, beyond the curtains, the night was a wall of darkness. No stars penetrated the cloudy gloom. Kathleen reckoned it must be beyond three o'clock by now. And still the infant wouldn't sleep, but wriggled and squirmed and gave vent to bursts of wailing, heart-rending in their intensity. The child had fed well more than an hour ago, the little lips and tongue pulling and lapping from her cracked nipples hungrily, causing Kathleen an intake of breath at first until spittle and milk lubricated the chapped skin. Watching the tiny mouth working reminded her of goldfish nibbling, and made her smile. But those pleasures seemed a long time ago now.

Her failure to pacify the child began to whittle away her fragile confidence. A tight ball of panic began to form in Kathleen's gut. She wished her mother was still with her. It had been a great comfort to Kathleen to have her Mam there for the birth and for a full week afterwards. The older woman had a magic touch with the baby. It was only since Kathleen had been alone that Niamh seemed more unsettled.

The situation was made worse by the heavy presence of Kevin, who lay in bed with the covers over his head. She feared he wasn't asleep. Every so often he would groan theatrically and roll over. Maybe he was just dreaming. As long as he was quiet, Kathleen didn't care. She dreaded his interventions. When Niamh was first born he had made a brief pretence of interest and concern, cooing over the infant and chucking her under the chin. But when he realised work and responsibility were involved, his manner had become that of a sulking school boy, fluctuating between indifference and whining aggression. It was plain he resented the baby and Kathleen's absorption in caring for her.

Kathleen crooned a lullaby as much to comfort herself as the child. As she sang, in an effort to bolster her flagging morale she recalled the strength she'd felt at the birth. At the height of her labour, with her Mam and the local mid-wife encouraging her, when the contractions were close together and the pain pure and bright as a cloudless sky, Kathleen had experienced a moment of euphoric empowerment; there came a moment when her fear was overtaken by a feeling that she was indestructible and could do and achieve anything. Why then, she wondered, could she not console the little bundle in her arms, who shuddered now with the effort of her bawling? It was as if the child were already experiencing the limitations of love to provide comfort and the way the world stood against the fulfilment of human desires.

Such reflections weren't useful. The ball of panic wound tighter. A weight of weariness descended. Kathleen found herself praying for respite. She raised her voice louder in response to the infant's cries, astonished at the stamina of the tiny creature. Already there seemed to be a battle of wills between mother and daughter. Kathleen was determined to respond with love and more love. She raised her voice further, then realised, too late, her mistake. Kevin's tousled head emerged from the blankets. He roared at her, his eyes wild.

'For fuck's sake can't you hush the squalling brat? How's a man to sleep with all this din? I'm exhausted, so I am. Don't I have to be up in an hour or two for work? I'll be good for nothing. What in the name of Sweet Jesus is wrong with her?'

'Shouting won't help.' Kathleen turned her back and walked again. Kevin's voice seemed to have startled Niamh, who hushed for a breath, before resuming a plaintive rhythmical wail. It was not a sound designed to placate an angry man. Moments passed. Kathleen felt Kevin's eyes on her as she struggled to quiet the child. She found herself praying for silence. Still, Niamh wouldn't settle. The ball of panic began to spin.

'For the love of God, can't you do something woman?' Kevin held a pillow over his head, covering his ears. Kathleen ignored him. Instead, she began to sing. In a quavering voice, trying to beat down the rising hysteria she felt, she intoned one of her Mam's auld favourites:

Where Lagan Streams sing lullaby
There blows a lily fair,
The twilight gleam is in her eye
The night is on her hair . . .

Kevin sat up and let fly again. 'Can't you stick the mewling thing back on the tit or put a dummy in or something? The whole house will be awake. At least when your Mammy was here we didn't have this palaver every night. I was glad to see the back of the auld witch. But at least she could keep the little whelp quiet.'

Kathleen cradled the baby's head, feeling the silky tresses she'd been born with soft and warm against her palm. Niamh's eyes and hair were the exact colour of Jack's. In that moment, not for the first time, she was glad. She didn't answer Kevin but sang on, willing strength into her pure contralto.

And like a love sick leannan si,
She hath my heart in thrall
No life have I, no liberty,
For love is lord of all.

The next moment, Kevin was out of bed and standing over her in his yellowing combinations. She felt the yeasty stink of his breath on her, sour from beer and tobacco.

'You mean to ignore me do you? I'll make you pay me mind, so I will.' He grabbed at her arm. The baby shrieked louder as Kathleen evaded his grasp.

'You're a fine brave man, so you are. What are you at? Get

back into bed with you. Can't you see you're making things worse?'

He stood there, his arms straight and hands clenched, fairly bursting with indignation. Despite her fear, Kathleen was aware of how ridiculous he looked. She thought him pathetic.

He shook his fist at her. 'I will not be ruled by you and the child. I will not. How am I expected to work, if I have no sleep? Tell me that will you?'

'If you came to bed early and sober for once, it might help. It's drinking till all hours that makes you tired. It was after midnight again when you came in. Where were you till then, I'd like to know. You need to learn some sense.'

'I'll give you sense.' He took a step towards her.

Kathleen held the child tight to her. She stared him down. 'Get away out of it back to bed with you,' she said. 'The babby won't be quiet while you're fussing so.'

'I told you where I was going last night and I told you to keep your trap shut about it. I was with the bhoys. And what if we had a few drinks afterwards. We'd earned it. Marching up and down half the night we were.'

It was true that he had not been able to keep his activities from her. He was so proud. There were moves afoot to counter the UVF. Drilling had begun in secret. Kevin's face shone whenever he spoke of it. He held himself taller and more square. It was as if it made him feel special. His life had taken on an importance and meaning which had been missing when all he could say of himself was that he was a barman. Kathleen had seen it before with her father and uncles. As soon as the politics were mentioned, the Republic and the Brotherhood, the talk took on an air of self-importance entirely missing from chatter about football and the races. There was a mystique that flattered and seduced.

Though she was tempted to make some withering remark about playing at soldiers, Kathleen restrained herself. Her first concern was with the child. She needed to wheedle Kevin back to bed and restore some peace.

'Ay well,' she said, 'all the more reason you should be back in bed. I have no chance of quietening her till you lie down.'

She saw him hesitate. There was still fury in him. He leaned forward from the waist, bringing his face close to hers. She could see the bloodshot flecks in his eyes.

'Do you know what I hope?' he demanded.

She felt the spittle hit her cheek, nearly gagged at the smell of him. She shook her head, her lips a grim line. She didn't want to provoke him further.

'I hope there is a fight. I hope the Proddy fuckers up North bring it on, so we get the chance to sort them out once and for all. Then we'll have Ireland for the Irish.'

Kathleen gave a little shrug, as if to say, I've heard it all before. She could think of no words that might smoothe the fighting cock's puffed up feathers.

Kevin narrowed his eyes. 'I know I don't count now you have the babby. I know you couldn't care less about me. You don't care what I say or do. But I haven't finished yet. Mebbe you'll care about this. Do you know what else I hope? I hope your man comes back and I hope he joins the UVF. Nothing, do you hear me? Nothing would give me greater pleasure than to kill Jack Young.'

Kathleen patted the baby's back, while purposefully looking into Kevin's eyes. The child was nearly exhausted, gulping and shuddering after the last outburst. There was silence for a moment. Deadlock. It was Kathleen who spoke first.

'You're talking foolishness now. You should be ashamed of yourself to speak of killing in front of this innocent wee thing. Get back to bed with you. Jack's in England. He won't come back. You knew what you were doing when you agreed to marry me. There's no point in resenting the child now. If you pay her some attention and treat her right, she'll be your daughter, sure enough. It's up to you. Now get into bed, for God's sake and let's have some peace at last.'

Kevin didn't answer at once. He scowled at her, then flung himself onto the bed. But as he gathered the bedclothes about him, he couldn't resist having the last word, a parting shot.

'If you were a decent mother and could keep the wean quiet, there'd be no problem.'

He rolled over so that his back was to her and pulled the covers over his head. Kathleen took another turn about the room with Niamh. The baby was exhausted, the little body had trembled into stillness, but Kathleen didn't want to relinquish her yet. She wanted to cling on to the little bundle of living warmth, her precious daughter, feeling the strength of the bond between them in the gathering calm after the storm. She wanted to forget Kevin's wounding words and let the tension drain from her. Most of all, she wanted to dismiss the queasy stirrings of guilt that threatened her following such ructions with Kevin.

It was true that he had entered into the marriage freely. It wasn't her fault. He had even persuaded himself through her pregnancy that the child would be his. But neither of them had been prepared for the reality of Niamh's arrival and the indisputable fact that she looked nothing like Kevin. It was as if the child were stamped with the die of Kathleen and Jack's passion, and Kevin read the imprint there. Kathleen knew that her boundless love for her daughter would only serve to increase Kevin's sense of grievance. But there was nothing to be done. She had to struggle through as best she could.

After a few moments, when she was sure that Niamh was properly asleep, she bent and placed the child in the wooden cradle Kevin had bought for her before the birth. She tucked the infant in, and kissed her brow, inhaling the milky, musky scent of her skin. Kathleen walked to the window and stared out. She gathered her dressing gown to her at the neck. The darkness was beginning to lift. Soon it would be dawn. She could see the grey swathe of the river and the shape of ships, barges and tenders beginning to emerge.

Kevin snored and shifted in his sleep. She turned to look at him, lying on his back now, his mouth open. Despite his brutal blustering, she could still feel sorry for him. Sorry that she could not love him; sorry that he was determined to ensure his lovelessness by rejecting the child. Only a few weeks before the birth, he had arrived home with the cradle and had a straight back nursing chair delivered for her comfort. He had tried to impress and win her. She had been grateful and full of hope that things might work out. They might learn to rub along together. But Niamh's birth had come between them. Never mind that she had agreed on the Irish name to please Kevin. The more he saw of the child, the more aggressive he seemed. It was a relief when he was at work or out with his cronies.

Kathleen stood staring out over the water until she could bear the cold no longer. The light was silver within the room before she got into bed, easing herself in gently so as not to wake Kevin. She kept her dressing gown on and lay rigid on the edge, away from the snores and ripe farts of the sleeping man. She couldn't relax enough to contemplate sleep. She heard the cry of a gull and the melancholy wail of a siren—some steamship preparing to sail on the morning tide. She thought about Jack Young over the water and all she had lost in losing him. Maybe she should have gone with him. Maybe she should have fought harder against her Da. But his solution had seemed to make sense. It was only now she realised she had been a fool to think that things could work with Kevin. She saw now, she had traded love for social acceptance.

She kept wondering whether to write to Jack. It was easy to begin letters in her head, telling him about Niamh. But then she couldn't find the words to go on. She worried about bringing trouble on them both. Suppose she told him how unhappy she was with Kevin? What then? She was married to the man. Kevin had rights; she had obligations. Any solution with Jack would mean subterfuge or an outright fight. And then supposing they were together, they would be bound to live as outcasts from society. What would that mean for Niamh?

Kathleen made herself stop the wearying speculations. She was over-tired and overwrought. Her task, her only task, was to make sure Niamh was looked after. That was all that mattered. Kathleen was determined there would be an unshakeable bond between them that no men's fooling could spoil. This was her purpose and her consolation. Nothing would deflect her from this sacred path. Thinking so, reminded her she needed to look after herself. It would not be long before it was time for the next feed. She reached to the bed-side table where she had discarded two cabbage leaves hours ago. Now, she took them and slipped them inside her nightdress, their cool moistness a balm against her sore nipples. The physical comfort she gained from this simple remedy seemed also to ease the stings of heart and mind.

She fell to sleep at last, imagining she was cradled in the arms of her baby's Protestant Da.

XVI

Jack Young stood in his shirt-sleeves, leaning on his hoe. He surveyed his allotment with great satisfaction while breathing in the glass-clear air of a perfect May morning. His spuds, peas and cabbages were coming on. There were enough broad beans to pick and take home for Mrs Morris to boil with the Sunday roast. Lupins, delphiniums, pansies and poppies splashed their vibrant colours across his small flower-bed. In a minute he would see how his tomato seedlings were doing in their frames. He could even hear birds singing, which made him grin to himself. Louis' old joke about the Manchester air being so bad it made the sparrows cough didn't apply in the pale lemon light of a spring morning under a sky patched blue with frothy cloud.

Though the gardens were adjacent to a railway embankment, Sunday mornings were mercifully quiet. There were not many trains, and when Jack did detect the rumbling approach that grew into a clanking roar, he felt a sense of exhilaration as the steaming monster roared past, an awesome image of speed and power, laying its sooty trail across the land. Jack would watch and dream and wonder about the faces at the carriage windows. Where were all those people going? How long were their journeys, and when would they be home again?

Jack's thoughts went back to Belfast. Here he was, surrounded by the marvellous growths of spring, not knowing if he was a father. The babby must surely have been born by now, but he hadn't heard a word. And didn't expect he would, though he couldn't help hoping that Kathleen might think of him and get word to him. She was slowly slipping from him. He fought to conjure her to his mind, where she existed as a series of images, sounds and sensations that seemed as shifting and insubstantial as the disappearing vapour left in the wake of the speeding express. He told himself she and the baby were real. But all he experienced was a gaping sense of absence and loss.

Work was the antidote. Jack began hoeing between the rows of vegetables. He relished this labour of weeding and making neat; he wished he were capable of creating such order in his life, so there was only good cultivation with no wild growth. But he recognised the difficulties of achieving this, given the chaotic and competing clamourings of human desires and deceptions. The world of his working life was the epitome of order, yet in part it bored him. Learning to drive and doing his first run to Birmingham and back had given his life an element of risk. He could think of himself as more than just a tram driver. He was an undercover agent; a soldier for the cause; an independent adventurer.

And what would the routine order and frustration of his bachelor existence add up to, if it were not for that excitement, and the occasional interest provided by Annie Hargreaves? His friendship with Louis was a consolation. But he found it difficult to bear the more general company of men. Their constant ribald talk of women with its undersong of desire and desperation reminded Jack too much of his own dilemmas and made him wish for gentler company. He looked forward to his Sunday afternoon teas with Annie which had become a regular occurrence and there had been more walks out together in Victoria Park. Mrs Morris was always in attendance, but lately she had taken to making excuses to loiter behind so the two of them could talk in confidence.

Through all of this, Jack hardly knew what to hope for. He recognised Annie bestowed on him that flawless full smile more often now than the little mocking upturn of the lips with which she'd first favoured him. But he had also seen her react to Gervais in similar fashion on more than one Sunday at church. He suspected it was just friendship she sought from him, a little companionship of her own age to brighten her days. He persuaded himself this was a good thing and all he wanted from the relationship.

Still, Jack thought Annie showed a genuine interest in his past, asking him many questions about his life in Belfast. On one occasion out walking she suddenly asked him if he had loved and lost a sweetheart there. Jack recalled his flustered over-anxious denials with hot shame. She had laughed at him, said she didn't believe him. 'Methinks he doth protest too much', she said. And to make matters worse, he'd asked her to explain what she meant by that.

Another time, she wanted to know about his attitude to Home Rule. He tried to explain how the Protestants of Northern Ireland wished to remain loyal to their heritage, and that they didn't want to be ruled by Pope and priests. He also proudly told her how Belfast was the only industrial city in Ireland and that the Protestants were frightened of Catholics taking their jobs and gaining an interest in the industries they'd developed.

Annie, frowning, suggested that tolerance was a virtue and that surely the Protestant interest could be represented in a Home Rule parliament. She feared the idea of civil violence. 'Surely,' she said, 'you couldn't contemplate killing your fellow countrymen.'

Jack remained silent. Worried and perplexed himself. It was so difficult to explain to someone from outside. The fear was of being overrun by people who did not share your values and your way of life. 'They are different,' he'd said in another conversation, as he tried to explain his position. But even as he said it, he thought of Kathleen and wondered if he really believed what he was saying. Annie looked sceptical.

What once seemed obvious to him was no longer clear. Yet he was helping to arm the UVF. It was easy to tell himself the guns were for defence, to protect Belfast from the onset of Home Rule. But when Annie said she couldn't understand why men seemed only to be able to settle an argument with guns, he experienced doubt. Doubt about what it meant to fight for what was right. Doubt about himself. Doubt in relation to Annie. Doubt about his lingering feelings for Kathleen.

The more he learnt about Annie the more it confirmed in his mind she belonged to a different world from his. One of her paternal uncles had even been to a university and was an engineer. The other was an Inspector of police in Lancaster. Her father, John Hargreaves, the eldest, had inherited the family business: Hargreaves & Son: Drapers. They were all middle-class. The family thought John Hargreaves had married beneath him, but he didn't care. Annie's mother had been an assistant in the shop, before she married the proprietor. But she came from a respectable family of miners steeped in Methodism and ideas of working-class decency. Though John was Church of England, according to Annie, her father had recognised in her mother a woman who would help him in the business, working hard and practising thrift. She had needed no fripperies or cosseting. She was a hard-worker who kept a home as immaculate as the accounts, which she wrote into a ledger in a minute but scrupulous hand every Sunday afternoon.

It was a far cry from his or Kathleen's background. He remembered Kathleen telling him about her family—the raucous parties in the pub, the beer and smokes and card nights. The singing and dancing to fiddle and tabor. Fierce loving and fierce fighting. Everyone wearing their emotion on their sleeve. Sean McCafferty was one of eight children, her mother one of five. The place was always full of aunts and uncles and cousins. Kathleen was the first and only child, a Saturday night accident, she called herself with a giggle. The result of too much whiskey and gin. But her Mam could have no more kids, so she was the apple of her Da's eye, a fact which obviously had worked against Jack in the recent ructions. But it was the easy expression of passion that Jack was attracted to—it wasn't like the stitched up emotional life of his own parents.

Jack reached the end of another row, and took another breather. In spite of all his confusions, he felt glad to be alive doing this physical work. He loved growing his own produce; he loved the sweet smell of the straw and the dried dung he'd spread as manure. He shoved the hoe into the soil and bent down on one knee, taking a handful of the black Lancashire soil into his hand and holding it to his nose as it trickled from his palm. The loamy richness of it was wonderful. It smelt of leaf mould, liquorice and coal; the distillation of decay and growth over many years. You could tell that it would grow great stuff.

It was while he was still in this attitude of praise, thinking how much closer to God he felt in his garden than in any church, when he became aware of a movement behind him. Before he could scramble to his feet, he heard her voice.

'Jack Young, Young Jack,' she said, 'a vision of a kneeling knight.'

Then there was the throaty sound of her laughter. 'Here's a lady on an errand for fruit and flowers. Will you serve her?'

Jack blushed, surprised to see Annie alone, dressed in her Sunday best, looking radiant as the day. He stood there speechless, gazing. She wore a skirt the deep mauve of Victoria Plums. Her blouse was white with flounced sleeves. She carried a wicker basket over her arm, and on her head was a straw hat with a wide brim decorated by a ribbon that matched her skirt.

Annie squinted gaily at him in the sunlight, her head on one side, 'Are you not pleased to see me,' she enquired. 'Have I trespassed on your privacy?' Still there was a smile in her voice, but she sounded less certain now.

'You're welcome here,' he said. 'You startled me, that's all.'

They stood in silence, looking at each other. Jack noticed

her fine leather boots beneath her skirts. They were pointed and fastened up the sides with little buttons. Unaccountably, he thought of undoing them and disclosing the delicate foot and ankle beneath. He glanced up again, and saw that she'd seen him looking.

'I was just worrying you'd get your fine shoes dirty,' he said.

'I wasn't,' she replied, smiling at him again.

'I could clean them for you.'

'There's no need.'

'I could though.'

'Would you?'

'Yes.'

Annie turned away. 'I want you to show me everything. What have you got for my basket?'

'The broad beans are for picking, over there.' Jack pointed. 'And there might be an onion or two that's ready.'

'Your flowers are gorgeous,' Annie said, passing the flower-bed.

'I'll cut you some, when we've finished the vegetables.'

Jack and Annie stood side by side at the bean-poles, wrestling the long curly pods from their stalks and throwing them into the basket Annie had placed on the floor. Jack tried to concentrate on the task at hand, but his eyes kept sliding to watch Annie's fingers, less dextrous than his own, struggling to detach the beans without damaging them. She had long slender fingers, pointed and delicate. He imagined her long slender legs.

'These should be grand with the dinner,' he said to break the silence.

'Aunt Agnes says to ask if you'll join us. She'll serve Swailes and Miss Dalrymple in the dining room first. I think we'll keep the beans to ourselves.'

'Thank you,' said Jack. 'I'd like that.'

When they'd picked all the beans that were ready, Jack

showed the way to the onions. Annie admired the neat rows of spuds and cabbages, which were doing well.

For the second time that morning Jack knelt. This time he was purposeful, plunging his hands into the dark earth, feeling for the globe of each onion and easing them out of their beds, dark purple, shining treasure.

'My father used to say an onion was like love,' Annie ventured as she watched him. 'It's sweet, but makes you cry.'

Jack looked over his shoulder at her, uncertain what to say. He felt the hot blush rise to his face, and turned back to his scrabbling, anxious not to give himself away in case she was mocking him.

'These need to stand for a day, and then hang to dry.' Jack tried to keep his voice matter-of-fact.

'I didn't know the process was so complicated.' A wry arch of her eyebrows accompanied this remark, as she looked Jack straight in the eye.

'I'll cut some flowers,' he said.

As they came to the flower bed, Jack took his penknife out of his pocket. He bent to the task, cutting some delphiniums first. Self-consciously he laid them in the basket on Annie's arm. She touched the deep blue petals gently between her thumb and finger. 'Do you like me, Jack?' she said.

'I like you.' Jack was gruff as he stooped to cut the short stems of some pansies. His hands shook slightly as he fiddled to make a posy with the variegated flowers, red and blue, black and yellow. He thought of Gertrude Jeckyll's colour principles. He felt a kind of panic in the pit of his stomach.

'What do you want from your life?'

Jack was taken off guard. At first, he didn't know how to reply. He thought of his life so far. The apprenticeship at Mackies, the tram driving. All those rails. His dreams of making gardens. Kathleen.

'I want my life to mean something. I want it to make sense.'

He placed the flowers beside the Delphiniums, frowning

still as he wondered at her question and his sudden answer. She laid a hand lightly upon his arm for a moment then withdrew it. Jack stared at the spot as if some exotic butterfly had landed there for a moment.

'I know what I want,' she said. 'I want a man to love, a family and a home of my own. That's all I've wanted, since my parents died. There's so much trouble in the world. People tearing at each other. I want to live in quietness.'

He turned again to the flowers. The Lupins now, pink and white, frilled cones, a variety called The Chatelaine.

'That's why I like it here in the allotment,' he said. 'The quietness.'

'And the solitude,' Annie murmured, as if completing his remark. 'I'm intruding, aren't I?'

Jack didn't reply. She was intruding. He didn't know if he was glad or not. Her presence was bewildering. It was as if he was invited to play a game but the rules were written in a foreign language. He was floundering while she played on.

'You're very quiet. So many men are loud and coarse. That awful Mr Swailes.' She paused. 'All right thquire.' She chuckled as she mimicked the salesman, her eyes alight with the momentary wickedness she'd allowed herself.

'What about Mr Gervais? He seems a proper gentleman.' Jack faced her with the flowers in his hand.

'A family friend. He used to help my father and mother with the accounts. I always think of him like that, ruling his life with columns of figures.'

The bouquet in the basket was nearly complete. He saw her fingers trail lightly against the spikey petals of the lupins, caressing the shaft of the flower. Jack felt as if he might suffocate. He turned to the last of the blooms. Bold poppies, their red faces turned towards the sun. He cut them clumsily in his agitation, half-wishing she had not come to the garden, wondering if she was toying with him.

As he came close to her again, setting down his final

offering, Annie held the basket towards him with one hand and with the other laid her palm against his cheek and let it rest there for a moment. He felt a tremor in his body as if he'd been scorched.

'Jack,' she said, as if savouring the word for the first time. 'Jack. All straight and square. Straight back, square chin, square hands.'

The drop of her voice gave her speech an intimacy that shook Jack. As she took her hand from his face, instinctively he reached to touch the place where it had been, feeling he might be marked there forever.

'Could you learn to love me, Jack? Surely you've guessed it's what I dream of?'

Jack shook his head, bewildered. 'I thought you were just being kind to me. We were friends. I can't believe, you know, someone like you . . .'

She put the basket down and held out her arms. He embraced her, a little awkwardly at first, self-conscious about the sudden surprise of it all. But the press of her arms against his back eased him, until in the distance he heard the approaching rumble of a train.

As the noise gathered strength, Annie moved back so that she could look into his face, holding his upper arms. She smiled her radiant smile, as the express roared past in a pother of clanking pistons, rattling carriages and drifting steam.

'So much for quiet,' she said as the diminuendo began.

'You can have too much of a good thing.'

'I can't have enough of you.' Annie disengaged herself frowning and took up her basket. 'It's what I dream of,' she repeated.

Jack didn't know how to respond. It was all too much, too soon. He felt as if he'd been ambushed. He could hardly credit her words. Yet he felt in her presence and her embrace an appeal to his manhood. Still, he said nothing.

Annie brushed a stray hair from her face and looked at him doubtfully. You don't want me then,' she ventured, her eyes straying away from him, the colour rising in her face. 'We can forget this ever happened if you prefer.'

Jack shook his head again. 'I'm just trying to understand. I mean, I never thought . . .'

They gazed at each other. She standing with the basket on her arm; he awkward, his arms dangling at his side.

'I should be going back. Aunt Agnes will be anxious.'

'Does she know?'

'About what?'

'How you feel.'

'No.'

'What should we do?'

'Do? I think that's up to you.' The old mocking smile was back on her face, daring him, hinting at superior knowledge.

'Well, will we walk out together, or not?' Jack's exasperation made him speak in tones he would never have dreamt of using with Annie previously.

'That's up to you, Jack Young. If you're prepared to make your intentions known to Aunt Agnes. Or not . . .'

She shrugged and began to walk away. Jack watched the sway of her hips, the graceful movement of her limbs beneath her skirts. After a few steps, she turned and waved. 'Thanks for the flowers. See you at dinner time.'

Then she was gone, and he was left alone with his unruly heart and a determination growing within him to woo and win her. Kathleen and her father had defeated him. They had robbed him of his child and now Kathleen was with O'Donnell. Here was a way of fighting back. Though he was still left with a lingering sense of disbelief, he was flattered. Annie Hargreaves presented herself to him as quite a catch.

XVII

When Frankie Lynch passed on the message that Mr Johnstone wanted Jack to do a run to Liverpool, he was placed in a quandary. The request came at a delicate moment. Three months had passed since Jack, full of trepidation, had sought an audience with Mrs Morris to make known to her that he and Annie wished to walk out together and that his intentions were entirely honourable. Mrs Morris had pursed her lips and looked Jack up and down before relenting. 'I've no doubt you'll do as you wish, without my say-so,' she said. 'You're a decent lad, Jack Youg, and the only thing I could wish for is that you were worth a bit more brass.'

Jack, only too aware of his shortcomings in this regard, had assured his landlady that he would always work hard and take whatever opportunities arose to improve himself. 'In fact,' he said, 'there may be a chance to do a bit of truck driving on my days off and you never know where that might lead.' Mrs Morris had raised her eyebrows and looked sceptical, as if she thought driving a motor could not possibly lead to anything worthwhile.

Afterwards, Jack couldn't explain to himself why he had mentioned truck driving to Mrs Morris. He still hadn't told Annie about his infrequent trips to Birmingham, always saying he was working extra shifts as an excuse for his long absences on what should have been his days off. He felt there was little risk involved in the Birmingham run. There was nothing necessarily wrong in transporting weapons within the country; it was their export to Ireland that had been made illegal. So there had seemed no reason to tell Annie anything.

Hence Jack's worries now about an excursion to Liverpool. Taking guns to the docks seemed to him a risky business. Yet it would earn him more money and he was beginning to worry about buying Annie an engagement ring. He had not formally proposed to her, and she had begun to tease him about his purposes in a way that made him anxious to make his future certain. He hoped if he made a decisive move his doubts would disappear. For in the dark silent nights when he woke alone and thought of Kathleen he wondered what he was doing. Who he was becoming. Sometimes it seemed his only talent was for betrayal. Once he was married to Annie, he hoped he would feel certainty and find himself again.

Such were Jack's preoccupations as he drew heavily on a moody cigarette in the unsalubrious surroundings of the Morning Star while Frankie Lynch regarded him with hostile eyes.

'Come 'ed,' Frankie said at last, 'Are yer goin' to do it, or what?'

'I'm thinking about it,' Jack replied. 'I need a minute or two.'

'I can't see why. Brummie or Liverpool. I can't see the difference meself.'

'There's a difference. You know there's a difference.'

'Can't see it. You're just chicken.' Frankie sniffled loudly, and wiped his nose on the back of his shirt-sleeve.

'What's it to you, anyway?' Jack fired up. 'You're just the errand boy. You couldn't give a toss about anything 'cept getting paid.'

'You're wrong there. Not that it's any of your business. Apart from the money, I don't want the bother of havin' to teach any other fucker how to drive.' Frankie stared belligerently at Jack.

'Why don't you take the truck to Liverpool, then? You'd know the way.' Jack ground out his cigarette violently.

'Because I've got better things to do with me time. And because Mr Johnstone wants you to do it.'

'Ay, so that I can take the fall if anything goes wrong.'

'I knew it. Yellow. That's the trouble. Yer've got no guts.'

Jack didn't trust himself to reply immediately. He drained his pint and banged it down on the table. He imagined what it would be like to smash it into Frankie Lynch's ferret face. It was the feeling of powerlessness he resented most. Whatever he did, he'd be wrong somehow.

'I'll do it,' he said, staring Lynch in the eyes.

'Next Wednesday.'

'I'll have to change my shifts.'

'Fuck yer shifts. Tell them yer sick or something. Pick up the truck at the yard 5.30. The paperwork will be there ready. Between then and now, you'd better have a look at a map.'

'You can tell Johnstone this is the last run I'm doin'.'

'We'll see. Yer an easy touch, Jack Young. All I've got to do is call yer a sissy, an' you'll do anything.' Frank laughed showing his yellow teeth.

'Think on,' Jack replied. He clenched his teeth hard and stared at the little jockey of a man. 'This is it. I'm doin' no more driving for Johnstone. You can call me what you like.'

He got up from the table and walked out. The air outside felt fresh and clean. Whenever he'd been in the company of Lynch, Jack felt he needed a long hot tub afterwards.

'Why must you work extra shifts on your day off? It's as if you don't want to spend time with me.'

In the grey half-light of a summer's evening, Jack and Annie were sitting in the parlour. Mrs Morris had left them together on the pretext of helping Effie tidy the kitchen, giving the young people a chance to speak with each other. It had been a warm day. There was no fire in the grate, yet Jack stared at it as intently as a man fascinated by the dance of flame.

'You know I'd rather be with you than anything. But it's the money. I need the money.'

'We don't need the money. I've got plenty for both of us.'

'That's not what your Aunt Agnes says.'

'Aunt Agnes wants to protect me, that's all.'

'I'm not so sure. If I had more brass, it'd make everything easier.'

'What would be easier?'

'You know what,' he said, sulky now.

'No, I don't. Come on tell me. What's so important that you'd give up time with me?' Annie's almond shaped eyes crinkled in amusement as she challenged him. She laid aside the sewing she'd been doing, then leant forward, her hands clasped in her lap.

Jack rose from his chair and stood by the mantelpiece with his back towards the non-existent fire. He took his pipe out of his pocket and clamped it between his teeth. He didn't attempt to light it—Mrs Morris didn't approve of smoking in the living-room.

Annie regarded his discomfiture with a smiling frown. 'Sometimes,' she said, 'I wonder what's going on inside you, Jack Young. Sometimes you have this broad, honest open face and eyes like a baby, but then you get this closed in look about you and have such silences, as if you're shutting yourself away. Why can't you just tell me, Jack?'

He took the pipe out of his mouth. 'I should have thought it was obvious, that's all.'

'Well, it isn't.'

'Don't you think a man might be ashamed of not having enough money?'

'So that's it. Pride.'

'If you say so.'

'Jack, Jack, love.' Her voice softened. 'You've got to accept that I don't care about the money. I was just lucky to inherit a bit from my parents.'

'I won't be inheriting any from mine,' Jack said and relapsed into glum silence.

'I've told you, it doesn't matter.'

'It matters to me. Don't you see? I can't provide the things I want for you.'

'If I've got you, I've got all I want.'

Jack felt a pressure well up inside him. He suddenly felt trapped by the armchairs, the ornaments, the aspidistra. He wanted to pace up and down, or fling something against the wall. Instead he gripped the bowl of his pipe hard in his trouser pocket as if to crush it.

'I'm not good enough for you. That's it . . . that's it.'

'But you are.' Annie, perceiving his distress was on her feet now. She came to him with arms outstretched and took his hands in hers. 'You're being silly, Jack, lad. You're the man I want. I don't care about money.'

'I can't even afford an engagement ring,' he said staring into her eyes, mesmerised by her.

She smiled. That radiant, dazzling smile. 'Are you proposing to me then?'

'I can't. I can't bear it if you say no. And if you said yes, I couldn't believe it.'

'But why not, Jack. I don't understand at all.'

'What can somebody like you see in someone like me? I'm a tram driver. That's all, a tram driver.'

'I'm not having this.' Annie withdrew her hands, and stared at him, a wicked merriment in her eyes. 'I'll explain how I feel, if you propose to me. Otherwise, I'm saying nothing more. I'm not betraying myself, if you're not prepared to speak out.' She sat down again, just as she'd been before, leaning forward on the edge of the chair, hands clasped in front of her.

Jack looked at her in the darkening room. Light from the window played on her hair, illuminating individual strands, turning tawny to gold, while her face was increasingly obscured by shadow. Dust motes could be seen, the minute particles making their way from light into the dark. Somewhere a fly buzzed. The ticking of the grandfather clock amplified the silence.

Annie bent her head and looked at the floor. Although her face held its customary tranquillity, there was a seriousness to her eyes, the set of her mouth, as if she contemplated for the first time the possibility of her own humiliation.

Still the silence stretched.

Then Jack made a move. He stepped forward, offering Annie his hands. She looked into his eyes and took them. He raised her up so she was facing him. Jack stumbled for words, 'Shall we, then,' he said 'Shall we wed? Will you be my bride?'

Annie's face relaxed, though her expression was serious still. 'Jack, my man. Yes we shall. You should know I will.'

They embraced and Jack felt the touch of her lips against his. As he did so an image of Kathleen came to him, holding a baby, and he thought of Judas Iscariot.

'I'll be true to you, always,' he said to Annie.

'I know you will. That's why I love you. Because you're good and square and straight and true. You never boast or bluster. I love your gardening hands, Jack Young, and your open face.'

They stood together silent in each other's arms for a moment, Jack wanting to believe her words, silently making a determination to become worthy of them. Only too aware of his shortcomings.

'And you don't mind about the ring?'

'I only want a wedding band.'

'After this week, I won't do any extra shifts unless you want me to.'

'I don't want you to. I want you here with me as much as possible. And when we're wed we can make ourselves comfortable here. As long as you don't mind Aunt Agnes. Maybe with your income in time we can afford to do without the other lodgers.'

'I just wish I had enough so we could buy a place of our

own.'

'It doesn't matter, Jack. Can't you be happy with me here?'

'I can be happy with you anywhere.'

'That's settled, then. Let me go and tell Aunt Agnes. She might give us a drink of sherry.'

Smiling broadly, she left the room. Jack gazed after her, wondering at what he'd done.

The drive to Liverpool came as a relief. It was better to be doing it than thinking about it, and action was a fine antidote to the confusions of his love-life. There had always been an element of uncertainty before his previous trips, a tingle of fear about setting off alone along unknown roads towards an unpredictable destination. This time there was the added pressure of the freight he was carrying and the possibility of a Customs and Excise check as he drove the truck onto the docks.

But the day was warm, and there was an exhilaration about being his own boss for the day, in charge of the three-ton truck, bearing responsibilities, playing his part in an historic struggle. So he romanced to himself as he drove through the outskirts of Manchester, past the mills and the factories, their steam and soot staining the blue, past the countless little shops with their awnings and goods displayed on the pavement and the ragged urchins on the street, staring after his impressive vehicle as he would have done not so many years before.

He emerged from the city into a day that seemed even brighter than before. The darkness of so much brick, the obscuring haze of the industrial chimneys gave way to stretches of more varied landscape where hedged fields with crops of wheat and barley were punctuated by huge black wheels which dotted the vista, the devil's bicycles at each of the many pit-heads that stretched from Walkden down towards the industrial towns of Wigan and St Helens, where the coal that fuelled the wealth of England was hacked out of the ground by the sweat and blood of thousands upon thousands of men, labouring for a few shillings a week, mole-black in the dark.

Jack didn't like to dwell on the life of the miners' miles beneath the surface. It made him feel lucky to be alive and breathing in the summer, tainted though the air was by the occasional gust of exhaust or the sweet inhalation of horse dung and straw from the road.

Towards midday Jack pulled in at the side of the road to stretch his legs and eat the bread and cheese that Annie had prepared for him the night before. She had taken to doing little things like that for him, and he would find in his snap-tin a cake wrapped in a serviette or some biscuits that she'd made. He also had a flask of cold tea with him, which was welcome in the heat of the day.

Jack ate his lunch ravenously and too fast. His hunger was fuelled by the proximity of his ordeal with the Customs. If they opened a barrel and found the weapons, he would have to feign ignorance and surprise. He had imagined this over and over again. He had even taken to practicing such reactions in his shaving mirror of a morning. The worst thing was his accent. Its unmistakable Belfast burr and lilt would be immediately suspicious if anything went wrong. He had tried to cultivate Mancunian, practicing his 'thee' and 'thou' for fun with Annie, concealing from her the serious purpose of his attempts. But he had never got the hang of it. She said he sounded like a Mancunian from Belfast.

As he continued his journey and came to the Liverpool suburbs, the roads became more crowded again and the fields were left behind. The air was not so smoky as Manchester, but it was bad enough, and the rows of workers' cottages round Garston docks looked poorer than anything he'd ever seen before.

The dock road was alive with traffic, and the pavements crowded with life. There seemed to be a pub on every corner, and groups of sailors intent on progressing from one to another in various stages of intoxication. Small children with no shoes stood singing or dancing outside each hostelry, trying to con a coin from the paid-off merchantmen before it all went in beer and women.

As he crawled along, the interest of his surroundings began to be tempered by apprehension. He saw a pub called The Baltic Fleet on his right hand side, and knew that soon he would pass the Albert Dock and come towards the Landing Stage. From there on he would have to keep his eyes open for Trafalgar Dock, his destination.

The traffic became worse the closer he progressed towards the hive of activity at the Pier Head. Jack remembered his bewilderment on arrival from Belfast. He'd never seen anything like the bustle of people and vehicles of all descriptions when he'd first stepped ashore. Now, he was bolstered by a sense of having travelled far since that day, less than a year ago. Here he was in charge of one of the same vehicles he had stared at with a sense of boyish enthusiasm and awe not so long ago. He was part of this great hub of world trade; he was a part of momentous events. He hoped it was not a part that would end in shame and humiliation.

Until this moment, Jack had hardly allowed himself to think of the full consequences if he was caught, arrested and charged. It would certainly mean the end of his proposed marriage. Mrs Morris and Annie would not have anything to do with any criminal activity. Jack rehearsed his script again in his mind, and thought about the faces of surprise and indignation he had practised in his shaving mirror. The question was, if it came to it, would he be cool enough to act the part, or would he, like some amateur at the Music Hall, become stage-struck, dumb with fright, and give himself away completely.

Well, that was the test. He'd soon know if he was to pass or fail. He was beyond Princes Dock now. Not far to go. He searched anxiously to his left hand side, waiting for the solid brick walls to give way to the gated entrances to the docks. The truck juddered against the cobbles, and he was aware that his backside was sore from the constant vibration through the poorly protected seat. He saw the Princes half-tide dock go past, then the East Waterloo Dock. He glimpsed a pub called The Neptune on his right hand side, which had a figurehead of the watery King complete with Trident as its sign.

Jack was taut with apprehension. He felt constricted in his guts and chest, as if the breath were being squeezed in and out. He wanted to find the right place to make his delivery, yet simultaneously shrank from the ordeal. His hands were damp on the steering wheel. He wiped them one at a time on his trousered thighs. Victoria Dock. He read the lettering and let out a little gasp. Trafalgar Dock was next. Yes. Here it was. He swung the wheel. He was suddenly acting automatically as if entering another dimension, another heightened reality.

Just past the gates, he was stopped at a small brick office. A bloke in collar-less short sleeves leaned out of the window. 'Warrer youse for?'

Jack hesitated for a moment, translating the thick Scouse accent. Just like Frankie Lynch's. 'Bleach for Belfast,' Jack shouted back.

'Wait there.' The man emerged. ' 'Ave youse got papers?'

Jack waved them.

'On you go then. Report to the Dockmaster's Office. The round building with the clock down there by the transit sheds.' He pointed the way. Jack drove on, across the cobbles, down one side of the dock the way that he'd been shown.

He drew to a halt at the office, a circular domed building surmounted with a clock and a bell. Jack jumped down from the truck. By the adjacent wharf he could see some large barges being loaded, and there was a small coastal steamer also alongside.

On entering, he was met by another clerk at a desk. 'G'day to you,' Jack said. 'I've a load of bleach for Belfast.' He brandished the papers. The clerk nodded and took them from him. He scrutinised the documents through narrowed eyes.

'Orright,' he said, looking up. 'Just turn right here, and drive along to number two shed. We'll have a gang along presently to unload.'

Jack did as he was told. There followed an agonising twenty minutes in which nothing happened. Jack smoked and drained the dregs from his bottle of cold tea to relieve his parched mouth and throat. It didn't help much. The inside of his mouth felt as if he'd been sucking glue. He wondered if there was anywhere he could get a drink of water.

Jack was still contemplating this option when he saw two men approaching from the direction of the Dock-Master's office. One wore a uniform peak cap, white shirt and tie, blue trousers: the Customs Officer. The other wore a flat cap and a long white overall coat. Jack jumped down to greet them. He felt his heart buffeting his ribs.

Before he could greet the two officials, another gang of men approached from the other direction, having emerged from one of the sheds further along the wharf. These all had flat caps, despite the heat, and heavy canvas dungarees, collarless shirts with knotted kerchiefs that acted as sweat rags round their throats. One or two of them also wore long, heavy leather aprons.

'Customs and Excise,' the man in the uniform cap said to Jack as he approached. 'Let's have your papers please.' Jack handed them over.

'I'm Fred Quinn, Wharfinger here.' The man in the white overall offered his hand. 'I'll be counting the barrels off.'

Jack greeted the officials as cordially as he could. He tried not to sound over eager. Nice and casual. Hands in pockets now.

'Open her up, then.' It was the Customs Official. Jack went to the back of the truck and with trembling fingers began to untie the lashings of the canvas protecting the barrels. He was clumsy and suddenly felt very tired. He made an effort to concentrate and to steady his hands. After what seemed like a long effort the rope obeyed him and he had the load uncovered. The Customs Officer scrutinised it. There was some fine white powder on the wooden boards near the last barrels. 'Thank God,' thought Jack.

The Customs Officer put his finger to the powder and rubbed it against his thumb. 'Pretty fine stuff, for bleach,' he said.

'Ay, it's top grade,' said Jack. 'You can't use anything but, with fine linen.'

'Hmm.' The Customs Officer scrutinised Jack carefully. 'That's a Northern Irish accent isn't it?'

'It is.'

'How long have you been in England?'

'About ten months.'

'Did you sign the Covenant?'

'Is it any of your business?'

'I could make it my business. If you want to avoid the trouble of opening these barrels, you'll answer the questions.'

'All right. I signed the Covenant.'

'And then left the country? Seems a bit odd.'

Jack said nothing. Waited for the next question. The anger he felt towards the Customs Officer gave him a brittle defiance.

'So what can you tell me about W. Johnstone, bleach manufacturer?'

'Nothing.'

The Wharfinger, standing at the front of the wagon, watching proceedings, coughed as he lit a cigarette. He looked embarrassed by the interrogation.

'So who hired you?'

'A bloke I met in a pub. Asked if I wanted to make a few extra bob by doing some driving.'

'A bloke in a pub.' The Officer repeated the words with a supercilious smirk. 'I wonder where I've 'eard that one before? So does this bloke in the pub have a name?'

'What's all this about? I'm just here to do a job. Open the bloody barrels, if you've got a problem. I just want to get unloaded and on my way home.'

'Things will go much quicker if you answer the questions. The bloke in the pub—his name?'

'Lynch. Frank Lynch.'

'How long have you known him?'

'Four or five months.'

'You didn't know him before you came to England?'

'No.'

'Know anything about gun-running?'

'No.' Jack brought to bear the innocent indignation he'd practiced before his shaving mirror.

'Are you sure?'

'Of course I'm sure. What would people want to be doing with running guns? I don't understand you, man.'

'You don't understand?' The superciliousness had returned.

'No, I don't. I don't know what you're talking about. And I'd like to get on with the job.'

'All right. All right. Keep your hair on. We have to make sure, don't we?' The Customs Officer nodded to the Wharfinger. 'All right, Fred, they can unload it now.' Turning again to Jack, he said, 'Don't forget. If there's anything found in them barrels any time, I'll remember you. I'll remember this little chat we've had.'

'There's bleach in the barrels. From Johnstone's bleach works. I picked the load up from there this morning.'

The Customs Officer turned on his heel. As he passed the

Wharfinger he said in a barely disguised undertone, 'God save us from quick-witted Irishmen.'

Jack took out a cigarette as he moved aside to let the dockers get on with the job of unloading. He inhaled deeply, concentrating on keeping the elation he felt from his face. He'd survived. He'd be on his way home soon. He'd never do another run again.

'I'll give you a lift in a minute lads, when I've had my smoke.'

'Bloody 'ell, these are 'eavy,' one of the dockers grunted as he helped to manhandle a barrel off the truck and onto a trolley. 'Does yer bleach have lead in it?'

XVIII

Summer days, salad days, straw boater days with Annie on his arm and the whole world a green park, the birds singing, the pigeons ruffling their plumage, children with ice-creamed faces and blessings on their golden heads. So Jack Young would remember the first few days after his adventure in Liverpool. Shadows cast by thoughts of Kathleen and the baby were banished by the sunshine of relief. He drove his tram with a perpetual smile on his face, and he bent to check the leaves of his tomato plants with a whistle on his lips. He wrote to his parents and sister to tell them of his betrothal. His Mam and Da gave their muted approval. They were sorry Annie was neither Irish nor Presbyterian and his father wrote, 'Are you sure she's not too fine for the likes of us?' But Eileen's response was all excitement and how was she going to manage to get to the wedding? Her postcard was also full of the UVF and how she had volunteered as a nurse. 'You'll think me a great auld Orange Woman,' she wrote.

Jack was unperturbed. Surviving the Liverpool run had given him a new confidence. He was free. Free of parents. Free of Ulster. He'd done his bit. Now he was looking forward to a new life in Manchester with Annie. Perhaps one day they would go back to live in Ireland. But for now he was happy with his lot. He shut away the possibility of violence breaking out in Ulster and how he might feel obliged to go and fight if it did. Rather he denied the possibility, and said to himself that something would happen to prevent civil war. The guns he'd helped to run would mean that everyone knew the UVF meant business. They would act as a deterrent to the English government forcing Home Rule on people who did not want it.

Thus, every day Jack Young stepped forth as if he was entering a new world. He had risked and survived. And that had given everything an extraordinary savour. When he tasted the first new potatoes from his garden, and had them boiled with salt and pepper and butter and a little fresh mint, he felt as if he had never tasted spuds before. Nothing could be finer. All was new in the world. He even shared with Annie his dreams about designing gardens and she had promised to help him in any way she could. He cherished a sense that at last his life was going to come right and happiness awaited him.

Jack knew in the back of his mind such euphoria couldn't last. But he was utterly unprepared for the manner of its disappearance. Walking to the depot one early morning, thinking anxiously about the nuptial delights of his forthcoming marriage, which inevitably brought back memories of Kathleen, he passed as he always did the local corner shop. Old Higginbottom, the proprietor, was just putting out the news hoardings for the day. Jack said 'Good day' as he passed and happened to glance at the bold black letters on the sign under the masthead of the *Daily Express*: *Rifles and Ammunition from Manchester Seized in Belfast. Special Branch to Investigate Gun-Runners.*

A day of torment followed. The newspaper report was not specific enough to make clear whether the load opened in Belfast was the one Jack had transported to the docks. The report merely said that a consignment of freight from Manchester had been seized by Customs Officers and had been found to contain rifles and ammunition. '*It is thought the munitions were intended to help arm the Ulster Volunteer Force.*'

There was nothing Jack could do to still his nerves. He went through the day, forcing himself to concentrate on his driving, trying to numb himself to the awful possibilities of investigation and detection.

On his tea-break, Louis Cockcroft noticed the change in Jack's mood. 'What's up, lad?' he asked. 'Tha' looks as if tha's lost a five pound note.'

'I've never seen a five pound note,' was Jack's glum reply.

Jack had to stave off Louis' further concerned enquiries, blaming his preoccupation on a headache induced by the heat and the rattling tram.

It was the same when he got home at the end of his shift. Both Annie and her aunt asked Jack what was wrong with him. He hated appearing weak by using the headache excuse, but he could think of nothing better to say. He was packed off to bed early with two aspirin and a jug of water.

Three days passed in this state of suspension, and the strain of having to act as if nothing was wrong began to paint dark shadows under Jack's eyes. Annie had begun to pester him to see a doctor. He told her to stop fussing. He was just a bit tired. He'd be right as rain in a day or so. And he believed what he was saying. The more time that passed, the more he persuaded himself he was safe. There were no further reports in the paper. The whole issue seemed dead.

On the evening of the fourth day since the report, Jack was sitting over his tea with Annie in the dining room. They were eating a salad with tinned salmon and tomatoes from the allotment. Aunt Agnes had made some of her special mayonnaise to go with it. Jack always flattered her about her mayonnaise. 'Grand,' he said, 'the best I've ever tasted.'

Jack had assured Annie that he was feeling much better today. He was pleased that she had stopped pestering him about the doctors. They were eating in a companionable silence when there was a loud knock on the front door. Jack and Annie looked at each other. Jack tried to keep his face steady, neutral, though his body was suddenly tense and his heart seemed to riot against his chest. He took a deep breath, to try and calm himself. He could hear Aunt Agnes' steps, then voices in the hall.

'I can't think who that could be,' Annie said.

Jack forced himself to keep eating, though the salmon in his mouth now seemed to be made of cardboard.

The front door shut and the living room door opened and closed. Aunt Agnes was taking whoever it was into the parlour. Jack strained to hear. There seemed to be more than one strange voice. He continued to chew mechanically, feeling the food might choke him. He swilled tea into his mouth to help him swallow.

'The Wedding Invitations came from the stationers today,' Annie said. 'They're lovely. We can start writing them together later on.'

Jack nodded his assent.

'You're very quiet again, Jack,' she continued. 'Are you sure you're feeling all right.'

'Right as rain. I've told you. I'm grand.'

'You just don't seem yourself. You keep getting that old closed-in look.'

'I'm sure you're imagining it, I'm fine so I am.'

Their conversation was interrupted as they heard Aunt Agnes come out of the living room. Jack and Annie's eyes met as she opened the door.

'Jack,' Mrs Morris said, 'there's two men here to see you. Policemen.' She looked and sounded grim, worried.

Jack didn't need to act in order to appear startled. 'What are they after?'

'Come on. They want to see you now.'

'What's happening? What's going on, Jack?' Annie's face was a picture of concern.

'I dunno. Don't fret, lass.' He hauled himself to his feet. As he left the room, following Aunt Agnes, he looked back at Annie. 'Don't worry, love,' he said. 'Everything's all right.'

Now the ordeal was upon him, Jack felt the onset of an icy calm. It was the same feeling he'd had on the wharf in Liverpool. Somehow the confrontation with authority angered him, injured his pride. He wasn't going to show them he was afraid of anything.

Aunt Agnes held the door open for him, and made to follow him into the room.

'If you don't mind Mrs Morris. We'd like to talk to Mr Young alone.' The speaker was a heavy set man in middle-age, wearing a blue pin-stripe summer suit. He had luxurious moustaches and small dark eyes set deep into his fleshy jowled face. He and his sidekick were standing together, backs towards the fire place.

'I'm Inspector Reith,' he said as Aunt Agnes left the room. 'Special Branch. This 'ere is Constable Givens.'

Jack held out his hand as he crossed the room towards them. They ignored his gesture.

'This ain't a social call, Mr Young.' It was the younger man, Givens, who spoke. He was long and lean and bony with greasy black hair. Clean-shaven and pale-skinned, he looked a great deal less prosperous than his superior, and spoke with a distinct cockney twang.

'Mr Young, we're investigating a most serious matter and we believe you may be able to help with our enquiries.' Reith's tone was neutral, his eyes watchful.

'I'll help in any way I can,' Jack replied.

'Nice to 'ave a co-operative subject, gov,' Givens remarked, taking a notebook from his inside pocket.

Reith ignored him. 'You come from Belfast, don't you?'

'Yes.'

'How long have you lived here?'

'In this house, you mean?'

Reith sighed. 'No, here in England.'

'I've been here since last October.'

'Like it here, do you?'

'Yes.'

'What do you know about gun-running?'

Jack practised his surprised and indignant look. 'I know nothing about it.'

'Nothing at all?'

'No.'

'He's as innocent as a lamb,' Constable Givens sneered. Reith silenced him with a glare.

'So why did you leave Belfast? You've got family there, haven't you?'

Jack licked his lips. 'I fancied a change.'

'But you'd just signed the Covenant. You were going to defend Ulster by any means possible. It seems an odd time to leave?'

Jack remained silent. The clock's heavy tick seemed to echo the thump of his heart beat.

'It couldn't possibly be that you left in order to help the cause by running guns for the UVF?'

'I've told you already. I know nothin' about guns.'

'That's odd, because we have reason to believe that on the 16th of this month you delivered a truck full to the Trafalgar Dock in Liverpool.'

'Bleach, I delivered. Barrels of bleach. I had papers.'

'Dear, oh dear, Constable Givens. Can you hear the man? He had papers.' Reith's voice raised now. 'Of course you bloody-well had papers. False papers. Forged papers. Lying bloody papers. Just like you're lying to us now.'

'I'm not.'

'Yes you bloody well are,' Reith roared.

Jack said nothing. He worried that Annie would hear the shouting and swearing through the wall.

Reith took out a cigarette and tamped it on the packet. He lit it with a silver lighter, and inhaled theatrically. He regarded Jack with hostile eyes.

'All right,' he said quietly. 'Let's start again. Let's go back to why you left Belfast. Help me to understand.'

Jack couldn't prevent himself from blushing. 'That's

private,' he said, staring at the floor.

'So private it makes you red in the face?'

Givens gave a sickly smile. 'Gun-running is fairly private.'

'It had nothing to do with gun-running. I know nothing about gun-running. I was earning a few extra shillings by doing a bit of driving that's all.'

Reith sighed. 'I'm asking you again. Why did you leave Belfast?'

Jack glanced behind him, as if he was afraid that Mrs Morris might be listening by the door. 'If I tell you, it must remain between us.'

'I can't promise that, lad. It depends what you have to say. I can promise this, though. If you don't give me a satisfactory explanation, you can come down the station until you do.'

Jack bit his lip. 'I was running away from a girl.' He looked up and stared at the two men.

'Got some tart up the duff, did you?' Givens sneered pruriently.

'Mrs Morris mentioned you were engaged to be married to her niece. Bit of a Lothario are we?' Reith eyed Jack with evident distaste.

'Has she got a bun in the oven as well?' Givens showed his mis-shapen teeth and gums in an ugly grin. Jack clenched his fists and moved a step forward.

'Leave Annie out of this. I'm going to marry her. That's why I was doing the extra work. To make a few bob for the wedding.'

Reith grunted. 'Steady lads. We'll not have fisticuffs. Let's talk about how you came across this job then.'

Jack told them about meeting Lynch in the pub, and how the Scouser offered him some work on behalf of Johnstone's bleach works. The interrogation went on and on. Which pub? Had he ever visited the bleach works? How well did he know Johnstone? What kind of a person was this Lynch? Did Lynch have any connections to Northern Ireland?

Jack countered each question as best he could. He even began to believe his own story and became more and more vehement in the telling of it. Eventually, the policeman tired of the game. The interview came to a close with Reith warning Jack.

'I can't prove you knew what was in those barrels. But you'd better be careful from now on. We'll be watching you. Watching who you drink with, who your pals are. If I get the slightest excuse, I'll have you. Understand?'

Sensing he had survived the ordeal, Jack responded by mixing his lies with a little of the truth. 'I've done nothing wrong,' he said. 'But I'll be doing no more driving for Johnstone or anybody else. It's too much trouble with my accent. As soon as I open my mouth, I'm a suspect.'

Reith pursed his lips. Givens said, 'It's no bloody wonder. Bloody mad bastards you Irishmen. I reckon you're guilty as hell.'

'We'll see ourselves out.' Reith moved past Jack, followed by Givens who allowed his sleeve to brush against Jack's. 'I'll be seeing you,' he said.

Jack said nothing. He heard them open and bang shut the front door. He collapsed into one of the armchairs, and wiped his brow with the back of his hand. He was aware of the sweat beading his hairline. He was given little time to recover, though, before he heard the stirrings of his landlady and Annie.

Jack rose to his feet as they entered the room. He didn't wish to give them the impression that he had been overly disconcerted by the interview. As soon as he saw their faces, though, he realised that a worse interrogation was to come. His landlady's face was puce and Annie, though maintaining the customary dignity of her demeanour, was clearly in a state of considerable agitation. They faced him, Mrs Morris's hands clasped in front of her, Annie, with her hands clenched into fists by her side.

'How dare you,' Mrs Morris began, 'bring disrepute on this house? I've never once had a policeman knocking at my door before, much less been questioned in my own home. They asked me, if I knew you'd driven a truck to Liverpool. I told them. I told them.' She paused breathless with indignation.

'What did you tell them?' Jack asked. But before Aunt Agnes could reply, Annie started up.

'Why didn't you tell me you'd been to Liverpool?' Annie was accusative, indignant. 'What have you been doing?'

'I've not done anything wrong,' Jack pleaded. 'It was just a way of making a bit more brass. A man in a pub offered me a bit of work. That's all. It's over now.'

'But why keep secrets from me, Jack?' Annie was insistent now. 'How am I to trust you?' Her fingers played nervously with the silver locket she wore round her neck.

'Annie, love, I was doing it for us. I've told you before how shamed I am not to be worth much money. But I only did one run. I'm finished with it now.'

'There. You've as good as admitted it.' Mrs Morris interjected. 'Gun-running. That's what the Inspector said. Gun-running.' She uttered the words as if their enunciation might taint her.

'You told me you were doing extra shifts on the trams.' Annie said bitterly.

'I only did one drive. It had nothing to do with gun-running. I didn't tell you because I didn't want you to fret. And I've promised not to do anymore. No extra shifts. No driving.'

'Why lie to us, if everything is so innocent? Tell me that. Why lie?' It was Aunt Agnes again, fairly shaking with indignation. 'The policeman reckons you did it sure enough, but he can't prove it.'

'I've had nothing to do with gun-running. I'm being picked on because of my accent.'

'You expect us to believe that? This is a decent house this is, and I won't have my niece involved in any thuggery.'

'Please. You have to believe me.' Jack looked from one woman to the other. He knew he was losing ground. 'I'm not going to be involved in thuggery. I've never been involved in thuggery. All I want is to be wed and to settle down.'

'There will be no wedding.' Annie spoke abruptly with glacial calm. She put her arm round her aunt and led her to a chair. She straightened then and faced Jack a look of cool disgust on her features. 'I will not marry a liar. I will not marry a cheat. I will not marry a common criminal. And to think I thought you were straight and square.'

Jack said nothing. He stood looking at Annie Hargreaves feeling sick to his stomach.

'I'm sorry,' he said at last.

'I think you'd better pack your bags,' Mrs Morris said from the chair. I won't have Annie upset any further.'

'But I haven't done anything.' Jack made one last protest. 'It's not as if I've been arrested.'

'Goodbye Jack,' Annie said and walked out of the room, a stricken expression on her face.

Jack turned to Mrs Morris, but she wouldn't let him speak.

'Go on. Get out. I don't want to see your face again. After all we've done for you. All the kindness we've shown you. This is how you repay us. You've broken Annie's heart. I hope you're satisfied. I don't want any more words. Please leave. Now.'

Jack did as he was told. With weary steps he climbed the stairs and began to pack, poisoned to the core by shame and bitterness.

Part 2

Another Covenant

Ypres–Belfast
1919–1920

I

On an autumn day with dark clouds sagging like wet army blankets and the air sharp enough to shave the face off you, Jack Young drove his truck through the ruins of Ypres. The damp and cold made his shoulder ache, but he was used to its churlish reminders and did his best to ignore them. Work would warm and loosen the muscles later in the day. He steered with his good left arm and propped the right on the sill with his fag between his fingers. His woollen half-gloves just about keeping the circulation going. Grand. The two lads next to him, Harry Dawson and Fred Hardaker, were younger than him and silent. They were familiar with Jack's frame of mind—they knew better than to chatter first thing on a Monday morning.

It was nearly a year since the armistice and two since Jack's fighting had come to an end in the fetid mud and shell-holes near Gheluvelt. Though he tried not to think of the horrors he'd encountered in the desperate last days of the battle, Jack felt the filth he'd been coated with had somehow penetrated more deeply than the shell fragment that had sliced his shoulder. He felt besmirched from the inside out. It would take a long while yet before he felt clean again. Sometimes he wondered if he ever would. His only hope was that his work would help. As soon as he'd heard they wanted gardeners to help build the cemeteries for the fallen boys, he knew it was what he must do. It was a deep instinct in him. No matter that it took him back to the battlefields. The idea of transforming the places of desolation seemed like an atonement.

The truck was laden with gear—picks, shovels, axes, rope, gravel, soil—everything needed for the initial heavy labour of clearing spaces, levelling and making paths. The work was in its early stages. Next spring and summer would come the prettier tasks of sowing and planting. By then, perhaps, some of the graveyards would have their full complement, laid out in rows like battalions on parade. As it was, the Graves Concentration Units were still at their grisly task, of finding, disinterring and re-locating bodies from the shattered fields of France and Flanders, bringing together Officers and Men of all the allied nations, gathering them into the great democracy of the dead.

In the back of the truck, too, Jack and his workmates had their camping gear. They would be out for the week, living under canvas until Friday afternoon when they would return to their wooden pre-fab billet for a weekend of thin beer, rough wine and oeuf et frittes just like the fare they'd enjoyed as soldiers in the local estaminets. Jack preferred the working days. He liked to be out in the air and away from anything that might speak to him of domesticity and the loneliness that harrowed his soul. To labour until exhausted, then take a rough meal round the campfire, have a pull or two of rum and slide into unconsciousness in his sleeping bag with the scent of wood-smoke and leaves in his nostrils was his only idea of satisfaction. The younger boys were full of the charms of the local girls who were coming back to Ypres as the re-building got underway. But Jack kept to himself. He had given up hope of happiness with a woman. He nursed his disappointments in love, recalling with shame his humiliation with Annie Hargreaves and yearning for what might have been with Kathleen McCafferty.

Now, as they approached the eastern boundary of the town, Jack had to take both hands to the wheel to avoid the many pot holes that still scarred the road. Repairs and renovations had begun in the north and western parts of Ypres where the damage from shell-fire had not been so great. Here on the eastern fringe, the few buildings still standing were faceless and blind like broken dolls' houses, their interiors exposed to the elements, their masonry cracked and tumbled. Ragged stripes of wallpaper still blew in the remains of a child's bedroom; stairs with no banisters led towards the sky, then stopped in space where an upper-storey had collapsed. The famous Cloth Hall, had one smashed tower still standing. It looked like the remains of a ravaged wedding cake surrounded by great crumbs of stone.

They chugged on, out of Ypres and along the old familiar Menin Road, past Hellfire Corner where the ammunition wagons used to time their run between the shell bursts. The landscape all about them was doleful still. From the churned sea of mud on either side of the road a few splines of stricken timber could be seen—the only perpendicular relief to the monotonous undulations of the shell-holes. But the wounded countryside no longer had the power to frighten Jack or his companions. The great work of restoration had begun. The corpses of men and beasts that used to line this road of sorrows had been long cleared off and fresh gales were brisking away the smells of death and decay. No matter if Jack occasionally thought he could catch a whiff of poison gas on the air, or the faint suggestion of decaying flesh. He knew the worst was over and in time men working with nature rather than against her would re-claim the land. One day farms would flourish here again. Only last week out towards the remains of Passchendaele village, Jack had seen two men and a boy out with a team of horses trying to plough. It was an amazing sight. Jack had stood and stared for a good while, mesmerised by the unfamiliarity in this place of destruction.

Today's destination was a cemetery south east of the flattened remains of Gheluvelt, not far from the site of Jack's last action in the war. He tried not to let this bother him. He'd worked there once before and seen no names he recognised. Not that he'd looked very closely. The dead were the dead. He'd seen enough to know. He didn't need to look for reminders. In his gardening he sought to honour his fallen comrades, but he tried to keep a distance from those who lay beneath the troubled earth. Keep things impersonal.

The ghosts rose up to haunt him often enough in nightmare. He didn't need their company by day.

When Jack and his companions arrived at the graveyard, the first thing they did was arrange their camp-site. They pitched their tent on a piece of level ground just beyond the cemetery entrance. There was an unspoken agreement to keep the land of the living separate from the fields of the dead. They laid out their sleeping gear nice and comfortable in a neat row at a respectable distance from the ranks of those whose rest was permanent. Next, they put up the lean-to, which would shelter their kitchen area. Later, they would build an open fire, but for now they got the little Tommy cooker going for a brew, before they started work.

Jack threw a handful of tea into the seething water, then straightened and lit a cigarette. Harry and Fred stood talking quietly between themselves, waiting for their morning brew. Gossiping about their adventures with various Mademoiselles no doubt. Or comparing the prices of different cafes or wondering at the Belgian propensity to eat horse meat. Jack didn't care. He didn't begrudge them whatever fun they could find. Like him, they were survivors. Like him, they had their awful stories to tell. But they refrained. For much of the time, thankfully, they were quiet and inward, finding their solace in the open air and the seasons and most of all in their dream to make beautiful the places where the dead soldiers lay.

The cha was good and strong, leaves and all going into the enamel mugs as Jack poured. There was sugar and powdered milk and the luxury of a sweet biscuit. Peak Freen's assortment, shipped out to them by their employers. They stood munching Custard Creams and Jammy Dodgers, relishing the warmth and comfort afforded by the hot drink and sweet treat. It wasn't like the old days in the trenches when the tea tasted of coal tar and the only biscuits they had were hard tack you wouldn't feed to a mongrel. Jack knew the war was over right enough, however much it might have stained him.

'We'd best make a start, then, lads,' Jack addressed his companions, as he tossed the dregs of his tea aside.

'Right-oh.' Harry and Fred shouldered their tools and marched into the cemetery, while Jack flung his spade and rake into the wheelbarrow and trundled behind them.

Soon they were hard at it. Their work was to level the graves and the broad avenues between the rows. They took a row each, doing the rough work first, shovelling off the obvious mounds, filling in holes, removing debris. Later they would mark the avenues with string and pegs, and dress them with top soil, ready for planting grass seed in spring. At the foot of each gravestone there would be a small bed in which roses and flowers would be grown. But they were a long way off that stage yet. The graves were still marked by rough wooden crosses. There were rumours that the first stones would begin to arrive from England soon.

Jack bent to his task, levelling a grave mound. He spaded the heavy clay-bound Flanders mud with which he was richly familiar. He heaved the excess soil into his wheelbarrow. He would use it later to fill in any potholes in the avenue. As he shovelled, he tried to concentrate on the job at hand. He hoped the corpse was buried deep enough. He had a horror of uncovering body parts. Involuntary memories came to him, vivid and sickening, of digging in the same mud before they went into action in 1917. In a grim parody of gardening, they had tried to fashion trenches out of the running slime. Every time the entrenching tool went in, the grey water would swirl and all manner of filth would be stirred. Blood and bone. The brute reality of fertiliser. The remains of the generations of soldiers who had passed that way before. The smell had been beyond description; a noxious cocktail of human and animal excrement, gas, and rotting flesh.

Jack took a deep breath and shook his head as if to dislodge the memories and let them drain away. He could feel the beginning of a sweat beneath the layers of his clothes. A few more shovel-fulls and this one would be done. He was only after a rough job today. He would follow up later with the spirit level.

Once he had made the grave-site flat and neat, Jack hefted the wheelbarrow with his gear in it. He trundled along the row. His shoulder twinged. There was something about the slight stoop and the straight lift needed to push the thing that aggravated the depleted muscle round his shoulder blade. It was a petty annoyance he did his best to ignore. But before he started work on the next grave, he paused and did some shoulder rotations before lighting a smoke. He stood enjoying a moment of peace as the sun squeezed some watery citrus from behind a leaden cloud. He thought with pleasure of the dinner he would cook later over the campfire and the rum he would drink with his pals.

After this grateful interlude, Jack turned back to his work. It was only as he was poised to shift the first spade-full of earth that he happened to glance at the name on the tall wooden cross. Usually he didn't take much notice. But now he stopped and stared before he completed the action with his shovel. He felt stunned. As if somebody had slapped him in the face. He plunged his spade upright into the earth and began to roll another smoke. Charles Shuttleworth. 'Cocky' to his mates. Aged 16 years. The lad had come to the battalion with the last lot of reinforcements before the action at Gheluvelt. He'd lied about his age to the recruiting bloke, just as he'd lied to be taken on as a trolley-boy at the tram depot. It seemed a miracle that his body had been found. Jack had not thought to find any of his former comrades from that terrible ordeal. Most of them had been shelled to shit or sunk in the glue. They would have the dubious honour of a name on some memorial to the missing. They would have no known grave.

But here was the pimply youngster with jug ears from the

Salford slums. He'd been so proud of the nickname they'd given him at the depot that he'd introduced himself to the battalion as 'Cocky'. The night before the attack, Jack had caught the lad sleeping with his thumb in his mouth. The boy had wept and cried out for his Mam before they went over. In the name of Christ, it was a shame.

The whole show had been a shambles. The front line was nothing but a series of loosely connected shell-holes full of mud and water. They'd endured two nights huddled in the mud under the assault of driving wind and rain with neither hot food nor rum ration. Then they were sent into the attack. The gelatinous swamp over which they were supposed to advance clung to their boots, making each step forward a matter of struggle under the roof of shells. Jack saw men stumble and fall beneath the metal storm. He saw Cocky crawling forward on all fours his rifle nowhere to be seen. They had not moved far before they were enfiladed by machine guns housed in concrete bunkers. The mud was so bad there was no chance of attacking these strong points. The men were scythed down or staggered on.

Jack survived for the first few hundred yards of the advance and then found a shell hole full of blokes where an officer gave him a message to take back to Headquarters. It was on that journey back to his own lines he'd stumbled across Cocky, blind and dying, moaning for a priest. Jack hadn't known till that moment the kid was Catholic.

Now, Jack took up his spade and began to level the boy's grave. He did the work with a tender reverence. He thought of all that had passed between them before Cocky died. The strangeness of it. 'Tell me Mammy' were the last words the boy spoke. Jack had done his best to fulfil that commission. He shivered despite the sweat on him when he remembered banging on the shabby wooden door of the two-up, two down terrace in Hanky Park.

A woman had answered the door with a baby whining on

her hip. Jack could see her standing there staring at him now. He guessed Mrs Shuttleworth was in her thirties, but she looked older. Her hair was lank and greying, her face worn and seamed. Her body sagged shapeless with child-bearing. The only light left in her shone from defiant eyes. When he had stated his purpose she'd invited him into the frowsty back kitchen. It reeked of coal smoke, unwashed bodies and dirty nappies. Damp laundry hung from a rack suspended from the ceiling. A thin girl maybe ten years old stirred a pot on the range listlessly, while two toddlers fought on a threadbare rug in the middle of the floor. A wooden crucifix was nailed to the smoke stained wall above the kitchen table.

The interview that followed was harrowing. When he had planned the visit, he had reckoned without the children. Tears had leaked from the ten-year-old's eyes as she made him a cup of tea and listened to his tale. A pall of misery lay over the household. It seemed that when they had heard about Cocky's death the father had gone out on a drunk and never come home. Mrs Shuttleworth didn't know and didn't seem to care where her husband had gone. Whether he'd joined up or taken off with another woman or come to a bad end seemed a matter of indifference. Two older girls working at the mill were all that stood between the family and complete destitution. 'What do I care about the Germans,' she'd asked. 'I'd be no worse off if they won the bloody war.'

Jack had found himself lying about the kid's painless death and how a priest had done things properly administering the last rites and all. Sometimes the truth wouldn't do. What was the point of making things worse? When he left, Jack had given the woman a few shillings—all he could afford. At first she'd been reluctant to take it. When he pressed, she'd looked him in the eye and said, 'God bless you.'

Now, as he finished making the grave flat and neat, it was as if he were tucking the boy in for Mrs Shuttleworth. He knew she would never see her son's grave, not having the money. She had lamented the fact in front of him. It seemed a peculiar providence that he should be given the task of tending Cocky's resting place. There seemed a significance in it, which Jack reached for and couldn't quite fathom. Part of the mystery of things. Part of the puzzle of his survival. Jack recalled in startling flashback the desperate faces of the men he'd left in the shell-hole before he traipsed back over No Man's Land. Staring eyes under tin-helmets. Dry tongues licking nervous lips as they prepared to go forward. None of them were ever seen again. Not a trace. Nothing at all. Napoo. Finis.

Jack flung his spade into the wheel barrow and prepared to move on. Before he did so he stood in front of the cross bearing Cocky's name. He took off his cap. He considered saluting, but the gesture seemed false and futile. Instead, he replaced his cap, stepped up to the marker and placed his palm on the painted name. He remembered the boy's profane and boisterous cheek, and Mrs Shuttleworth's words, 'If he could have harnessed that energy, he could have made something of himself. Too late now. He was only a lad.'

He was only a lad. Jack stepped back and continued with his work.

After a break for some bread and cheese, Jack and his mates worked on through the afternoon until the light began to fade. They gathered wood and built a decent fire against the gathering cold. When it came on to drizzle, they sat under their tarpaulin on their camp chairs nursing a tot of rum each, while they prepared a corned-beef hash with spuds and carrots and onions.

Harry Dawson handed round his fags and said, 'Will we have a song, now, while we're waiting for our grub?' He was a small, thin-faced man from Cumberland with eyes shiny brown like conkers.

'Off you go then,' said Fred, laconic behind his black beard, his lips shining a weird red in the firelight.

Harry glanced at Jack. Jack gave a little nod, as he exhaled a stream of sweet tobacco smoke. He trusted them not to sing any of the old songs from the war. It was an unwritten rule of their camp fire. They sang anything and everything but. One of the old hymn tunes, maybe. Or something from the Music Halls. Most often a song they'd learned from their Mam or Da or Grandma from the days before the world went mad.

In a light tenor with a nasal edge to it, Harry gave vent with one of his favourites 'Down by Kirkby Stephen, I happened for to be,' the story of the 'Lish young buy-a-broom' they'd all become familiar with. Jack had no idea where Kirkby Stephen was but presumed it was somewhere up in those lakes Harry was always on about. Anyway, it was a lively tune, and when they reached the part of joy, they all joined in with a will,

And I rolled her in my arms my boys
And wouldn't you do too . . .

Jack saw in the eager faces of his companions young men's dreams of a lightsome encounter. Never mind. It was the stuff of harmless fantasy. The song finished. He rose and stirred the pot, savouring the smells. For some unaccountable reason, he remembered Cocky Shuttleworth recommending his sister's favours. Now she was just another one of the bereaved. Jack found himself hoping she'd maybe met a decent fellow. Then chided himself for a sentimental fool. He turned his attention back to the grub.

'Not long now and we'll be right,' he said.

'Another song, then?' Harry enquired.

'Here's one for Jack.' Fred gave Harry a sly glance before he began.

I'll tell me Ma when I get home,
The boys won't leave the girls alone

'Oh no. Not that.' Jack's voice wasn't loud enough to stop the boys, who entered the chorus with gusto.

She is handsome, she is pretty,
She is the belle of Belfast city.
She is courtin' one two three.
Please won't you tell me who is she?

'I hate this bloody auld song,' Jack muttered. But he was talking to himself. The lads were well and away. *Albert Mooney* and all the rest of it.

There were too many memories there for Jack. Of Kathleen and his Belfast mates. Herbie Ryan and Bob Haslam killed with all the other Ulster lads on the first day of the Somme. Willie McCullough surviving, only to die in the Irish splendour at Messines Ridge when the Northern boys of the 36th Division went in next to the Southern Irish of the 16th. He could hear their voices taunting him across the years and see Kathleen, hear her voice too, and feel the sweet breath of her on him. It was enough to make him weep.

Jack fumbled for a cigarette and lit it with a trembling hand. Harry and Fred didn't spare him. Every verse and every chorus. Jack recalled the last time he'd seen her. It was towards the end of winter, 1918, when at last he was free of hospital and convalescent home and they had given him leave. He'd spent a week mooning about Belfast, uncomfortable with the suffocating solicitude of his family, and threatened by a sense of terrible dislocation between the man he had once been and the man he was now. In his solitary wanderings around old haunts, he had taken himself past the McCafferty pub in Cromac Street more than once. It was not that he expected to see Kathleen. Last he'd heard she was in Dublin. It was more a morbid form of self-punishment, an idle and luxurious dwelling on all he had lost that took his steps that way. He had gleaned his just rewards for self-indulgence.

On his last day, he'd taken the tram into town to have his photo taken—his Mam wanted him to have them done in his uniform—and he couldn't see why not. Afterwards, he'd decided to walk home, the day being fine and having nothing better to do. And he knew his way would take him past the McCafferty pub. It was late lunch time. He slowed his pace when he came by there, knowing that he couldn't see in through the frosted glass of the windows, hoping he might catch a glimpse inside through the open door. He wasn't inclined to enter the place, not fancying an encounter with the old man, and wearing the King's uniform, after all.

It happened as he approached that a man was leaving the pub and another entering. One held the door open for the other, allowing Jack to see the gloomy interior and Kathleen behind the bar, her raven hair piled and pinned on top of her head. She was pulling a pint. A man's meaty hand lay on her shoulder. Kevin O'Donnell, Jack presumed, standing right beside her. The door threatened to swing shut. Jack, still gawping, caught it for a moment, until she looked up from the glass, and he thought she looked his way. He had hurried off then, his heart drumming fiercely and his legs feeling suddenly boneless, aware only of a seething chaos inside of him.

He did not know yet if he had recovered entirely. As he rose now, and lifted the billy of stew off its hook over the fire, and began to dish up the grub onto the waiting enamel plates, he could see her there in his mind's eye, that bastard's hand on her shoulder, and maybe a flash of recognition in her eyes as she looked towards him. Should he have gone in and said hello and risked a fight with her man there and maybe her father as well. He didn't know. He'd been so surprised to see her, though it was what he had been hoping for.

'You all right, Jack?' Harry asked as he took the proffered plate.

'I thought you'd like one of the old Irish songs,' Fred said. 'Make you feel at home.'

'Who says I want to be at home?' Jack took his seat with

his plate hot on his knee.

With a drop of rum inside him and a belly full of food on the way, Fred wasn't to be cowed by Jack's surly rejoinder. 'Still, I bet those Belfast girls are a bit of all right.'

'You leave the Belfast girls out of it,' Jack said. 'If you take my advice you're better off with the Mademoiselles from Armentieres. Or at least from Ypres.'

The boys chuckled at that and all three of them were silenced by the stew.

Later, tucked into his sleeping bag, Jack considered the peculiar intensities of the day. First Cocky Shuttleworth's grave, then the memories of Kathleen sparked by the skipping song. It seemed a strange conspiracy of events that must have some meaning. He thought of the leave he would have at Christmas time. And if he dared to seek out Kathleen and speak to her again. There was his child to consider too. That he had a son or a daughter whom he'd never met seemed a pressing matter. He'd seen so much of death that this spark of life, flesh of his flesh, took on an aspect of wonder. He wanted at least to set eyes on the child. It came to him that he had spent his time since the end of the war in a torpor of defeat. Maybe it was time to rouse himself. The way Cocky had died had taught him that Catholic and Protestant didn't matter. He recalled the crucifix nailed to Mrs Shuttleworth's kitchen wall. There had to be a meaning in it all. Love and redemption. Was there a possibility of such hope in his life?

An owl hooted in the distance. Jack wondered where it could be. He decided it must be in Sanctuary Wood. Regeneration of the copses had begun. It was a comforting thought to send him to sleep, adjacent to all the young men who would never wake again and who lay beneath their white crosses, which shone in the uncertain light of a cloud-veiled moon.

II

Kathleen perched halfway up an old paint-stained pair of step-ladders. She leaned and stretched reminding herself of some long-necked craning bird. The ladders wobbled on the uneven flags of the bar-room floor. Her calf muscles felt the strain. She was attempting to pin-up the Christmas tinsel on the wooden pelmet above the bar. It was half an hour before lunch-time opening and she would need to look sharp to have the job done in time. Once she had this end in place, there would have to be repeated shifts, ascents and descents of the ladder as she fixed the loops of the tired glitter above the full-length of the counter. Still, it was work she was happy to do. Anything to bring a bit of cheer to the old place. She had already draped some paper-chains in the sitting-room upstairs and was after buying a tree from the markets as well. She wanted to give Niamh the best Christmas possible.

It was awkward to wind the end of the tinsel round the drawing pin and push the thing in. On the third attempt, precarious on one leg, she felt the satisfying give in the wood as the point penetrated, neatly trapping the tinsel. Kathleen let go to make sure it held. She paused for a moment, re-establishing her balance before climbing down the ladder. To her intense irritation, she heard someone knocking on the glass at the top of the front door. It was an ill-mannered, peremptory kind of a sound—some drunk perhaps desperate for the first sip of the day. She looked over but couldn't see through the green-painted glass. The knock came again, more insistent than ever.

'All right. All right.' Kathleen climbed down. Of course her Da wasn't going to be shifted from his wrestle with the accounts in the back office. Ever since she'd come home in 1916, her father had increasingly relied on her. The war meant there were not enough young men to do the bar-work, so it had been a simple solution to let Kathleen earn her keep. From starting with a few shifts, she was now working more or less full-time. When she wasn't serving, she was cleaning, and when she wasn't cleaning she was re-stocking and when her Da had finished counting, she was trotting off to the bank with the takings. It was hard work on her feet all day and half the night, but it was more sociable and more varied than stitching. She had come to enjoy the rhythms of the trade, which left her free to walk Niamh to and from school each day and to spend time with her before the evening stint behind the bar.

Kathleen hurried over and shot the bolts on the door. She struggled with the key, which was stiff in the lock. The rapping on the door continued.

'Will you have a bit of patience,' she shouted, as she hauled open the door.

'Would you hurry up with you. The whole of Belfast will see me standing on the pavement.'

The voice fell on her like a blow. She felt a hollow pain in her gut, as if she'd been thumped. Kevin glanced nervously up and down the street before he thrust past her into the pub. He wore a flat cap low over his eyes, a donkey jacket and thick cord trousers. His beard was trimmed back to a thick stubble. A canvas holdall weighed heavily from one arm.

'Well say hello, why don't you? Aren't you delighted to see me? I can't wait to get my hands on you.' Kevin gave a lascivious smirk and dropped the bag which fell with a metallic thud.

Kathleen locked and bolted the door. She turned back into the room. He stood facing her with open arms. 'Will you not give me a kiss then?'

'I will not.'

He stepped towards her and pulled her to him. She resisted stiffening her body against him, her arms determinedly at her side. He kissed her roughly on the face and mouth but she refused to meet his eyes, staring past and through him to the drooping tinsel hanging from the pelmet.

He let go of her. 'Ah you're a cold bitch, so you are, but I'll warm you later. Mark my words.'

'You have no right.'

'I have every right. I'm your wedded husband aren't I?'

'You're no husband to me. I haven't seen hide nor hair of you these six months or more.' She didn't add what a blessed relief his absences were.

'I'm not for wrangling with you, Katie belle. You know I have business that keeps me on the move.' He glanced at the bag on the floor. 'Talking of which I could do with getting that out of the way. Is your father in?'

She gave a little nod. 'He's in the office.'

'I'll go and say hello. You'll keep till later.' He showed his teeth again in an ugly grin, before hoisting up his bag. He lifted the hinged section at the far end of the counter as if he owned the place and walked behind the bar, through into the back office.

Kathleen moved back to her task with the tinsel. She wiped her nose on the back of her hand and spoke sternly to herself. She climbed the ladder with shaking legs and tacked the decoration, wishing she had a hammer so she could strike the pins in. If only Kevin would leave her and Niamh alone. Every time he disappeared she hoped it was for good. Every time he turned up again he was more boastful and complacent than ever. It was as if someone polished the bad penny to a brassy shine before rolling it back into her life.

Kevin saw himself as a hero. There were plenty of others willing to endorse the idea— men and women for whom violence had become a sacred rite. It didn't seem to matter that the rising in 1916 had been a hopeless failure. Kathleen remembered the shattered streets, the dead civilians with cold dread. A fourteen year old boy had been shot in the early exchanges. Yet the leaders had been made into martyrs and the foot-soldiers like Kevin, who'd been interned in England, had been welcomed home as great Irish patriots. That her father treated him as such filled Kathleen with bitterness.

As she savagely tacked the Christmas tinsel her thoughts sped to Niamh. Protecting her daughter from Kevin's mood swings and uncertain temper was her priority. He was an unsettling presence to say the least. He either tried to drown the little girl in over-exuberant affection or more often treated her with brutal indifference. The child was patently frightened of him. It had been a blessing when Kevin was deported to prison in England. It had given Kathleen the excuse to leave Dublin and bring Niamh home. The relief had been wonderful. It was like the lifting of a siege. She no longer had to spend all her energy negotiating Kevin's unruly presence. Though in Belfast she was dependent on her Da for the roof over her head, the sense of liberation had been profound.

But since Kevin's release and return to Ireland, he had brought back the shadow of the prison house to haunt her. At first, when he didn't come to find her in Belfast, she thought she might be rid of him for good. But then he'd turned up, establishing a pattern that had been repeated several times in the last two years. Each time he was away for months and then arrived on her doorstep, unpredictable as ever, bullying and demanding, telling her the cause he was pledged to was more important than life. She did not ask him what he did or where he'd been. She didn't want to know. She shuddered at the thought. The newspapers were full of the shootings in the south—policemen and soldiers mostly, characterised as enemies in the struggle for independence. With his love of guns and his self-aggrandizing talk of fighting for his country it was all too easy to imagine what he was up to. Making up stories to explain Kevin's comings and goings to Niamh was more difficult and needed greater powers of invention.

Kathleen hurled herself up and down the step-ladders

in a manic flurry. She was bruising her thumb on the last drawing pin, when her father came out of the office and stood underneath her, looking up.

'You'd better come in here and have a wee word,' he said. His voice and face were troubled.

'What about opening up?'

'Leave it be for a minute or two.' He turned and went back towards the office without waiting for her.

Kathleen hated the idea that her father no less than herself seemed to be at the beck and call of Kevin. As she climbed down, she considered disobeying the summons and opening the pub as usual. But that might only make things worse. Despite herself, she was curious to know what was up.

The office was a small space tucked between the main bar and the snug round the back. It contained a couple of filing cabinets, a small safe, two chairs, one either side of a small desk. The desk was covered in papers—bills, invoices, receipts—and the large bound ledgers in which the accounts were kept. When she entered, the men were seated either side of the desk. A whiskey bottle stood between them. Her Da's glass was empty in front of him. Kevin cradled his, slouched low in his chair with his legs wide apart, one of them jiggling up and down on the ball of a nervous foot. His holdall was on the floor next to him. Since there was nowhere for her to sit, Kathleen was obliged to stand awkwardly at the end of the desk between the two men.

Kathleen looked from one to the other of them. They eyed each other as if deciding who might speak first.

'Well?' Kathleen demanded, irritated by the ongoing silence.

Her father cleared his throat. 'The thing is,' he began, looking down and scratching the back of his hand, 'Kevin's situation is after being a bit sensitive, and the upshot is the fewer people who know he's here, the better. He needs to lie low for a week or two.'

'I bet he does. And we're to shelter him, I suppose.'

'I am your fucking husband,' Kevin muttered.

'Steady.' Kathleen's Da fixed his son-in-law with a silencing glance. He looked at Kathleen and pulled on his ear lobe. 'Kevin is family. We'll do our best to help. We're on the same side.'

'Are we?' Kathleen felt the fury rise like bile from her stomach. 'I'm not sure I hold with the murderin' of people to get your own way.'

'The Dail is the rightful government of Ireland. British forces are a legitimate target.' Kevin had his lines down pat.

'It's Irish policemen being killed,' Kathleen protested.

'They can't be Irish if they're working for the British crown.'

'What does Irish mean to you? Were not all those soldiers who died in France Irish, though they wore the King's uniform?'

'Enough.' Kathleen's Da slapped the table. 'I'm not after a debate. It's practical matters we need to look to and quickly. I'm losing money while we're sitting here.'

'What do you want of me?' Kathleen challenged the two men, defiance in her eyes.

'You've to keep your mouth shut, obviously.' Kevin swigged the whiskey in his glass and reached for the bottle. 'And I need to keep out of sight. Nobody's to know I'm here.'

'What about Niamh?'

'We're worried about that.' Her father said less belligerently. 'We don't want her saying anything at school.'

Kathleen stared at Kevin before she spoke. 'Well get away out of it and there'll be no problem.'

Her father continued, his tone reasonable. 'We were thinking perhaps you should take the wean to Mary's place after school.'

'Oh were you now. I don't think so. What kind of a tale am I to tell the child? And what am I to do? Abandon her there?

What excuse could I have for leaving her there with Aunt Mary? I can't move in with her. I'd have to traipse half way across the city every night after I've finished here.'

'You could think of some story, if you tried.' Kevin said.

'I've a better idea. You go and live at Aunt Mary's. If you want to be private, it's a better bet than the pub and it'll keep you clear of Niamh.'

Kevin looked at Sean McCafferty.

'It's an option,' Kathleen's Da said. 'Mary will see you right. She's hot for Cumann na mBan and all the rest of it.'

Kevin's brow furrowed under his cap. His leg was still bouncing. There was obviously something on his mind, but he was having difficulty finding the words.

'What about . . . being with you?' Kevin looked up at Kathleen, his eyes intense. She knew what he was after, but she would make him play a long game to get there.

'What about being with me?'

Kevin reddened. 'You know what I mean. Spending time together. Alone.'

'I can't see how it's to be managed. What with the secrecy and all.'

Kevin raised his voice, despite the presence of her Da. 'You can't deny me my rights.'

'I can't see you have any rights. You're never here.'

'I'm a soldier for fuck's sake.'

'You don't look like a soldier to me.'

'I'm fighting for Ireland's freedom.'

'You're after murdering Irish policemen. What about their freedom?'

'Right. That's it.' Kathleen's Da struck the table again. 'You can work out your differences in your own time. The pub needs opening Kathleen. I'll walk round to Mary's with you, Kevin, at half-three or so, when the light's beginning to go and before Kathleen brings Niamh in from school. All right?'

'Lovely,' Kathleen said and made to leave the room. Kevin

caught her by the wrist as she went past, and held her fast.

'I will see you,' he said. 'One way or another.'

Kathleen tried to wrench her arm away from him. He held her for another moment, staring into her face, showing his teeth in a threatening leer. Then he let her go.

'I'll be seeing you,' he said again.

Kathleen freed herself. There were customers knocking on the door. She shouted to them to hold on, while she got the ladders out of the way. Then she unlocked the doors, placated the grumbles and set about serving the pints and whiskeys.

It was good for her. It meant she didn't have to think too hard about Kevin and what had passed between them. There was relief in the work and in the thought he would be staying in the Falls with Aunt Mary. She fervently hoped he wouldn't be bothering Niamh. The other determination in her mind as she flexed her muscle on the beer pump was to deny Kevin the satisfaction of sleeping with her. She would not have his paws on her again, if she could help it.

III

When Jack Young arrived in Belfast a few days before Christmas, he found himself surprised by familiarity. With his eyes accustomed to the wreckage and building sites of Ypres and the grave-marked landscape of the battlefields, he expected to find his home town somehow strange. But it wasn't. The rows and rows of red-brick terraced houses were just the same as they always had been. The monumental buildings in the town centre were still monumental. And over all, the rearing gantries of the shipyards stood remote and massive, towering over the lives of men as inspiration or threat depending on how the mood took you. It was only behind the curtains, behind the hard facades there lurked caverns of loss. All those homes with missing sons and brothers, fathers and husbands, all given to the loam of France and Flanders. Blood and bone. Something must have changed. But the change seemed hidden.

At home, round the kitchen table, though his younger sister, Lily, had grown into a fine young woman, and Eileen's fella, Hughie McCullough, was often present, nothing much else had shifted. Jack's father was more taciturn than ever and his mother still veered between smothering affection and lemon-lipped judgement. She was as quick to anger as she was to sentimental tears. The fate of the Ulster boys in the war gave her plenty of scope for emotional ventilation, as did the current actions of traitorous Fenians and Sinn Feiners. She had made it clear she would brook no mention of Kathleen McCafferty. It seemed to Jack that, if anything, the war had hardened his parents' attitudes. As far as they were concerned the Catholics were still the enemy and the local boys had died to keep Ulster British and Protestant. Hughie McCullough's belligerent support of the same views while Eileen looked on with starry eyes didn't help.

Jack kept his mouth shut and nursed his secret purpose. He suffered the claustrophobic family atmosphere as best he could. The more he heard the prejudice frothing from the mouths of his parents, the more determined he was to see Kathleen again. He had not suffered the war for nothing. He was seared by its bitter and brutal lessons. He nerved himself for action.

On the day before Christmas Eve, he decided it was time to make a move. But first he had to suffer at the hands of his Mam. She insisted on feeding him a cooked breakfast. She reckoned he looked too thin. After his Da and sisters had left for work, Jack was treated to sausages and bacon, eggs and soda bread. The small goods, Jack was told as he tucked in, were from Hughie, whose father owned a pig-farm out Antrim way and a shop that sold the products in Belfast town. The information didn't improve the taste to Jack's mind. He hadn't taken to Hughie. But he didn't say so. He concentrated on getting the grub into him. He didn't want to betray the tension that twisted his guts and made each mouthful painful. His Mam had an uncanny ability to sniff out untoward behaviour. Awkward interrogations were the last thing he needed. He thought of the times he had forced himself to eat before going into action in the war. Last suppers full of portent forced down because you never knew when you would eat again. This was different, but still . . .

He escaped as soon as he decently could, telling his Mam he was going into town to scout for Christmas presents.

'Keep your money in your pocket is my advice,' his Mam said as she kissed him goodbye. 'Think on don't be buying anything daft. Hughie has promised us a turkey so there's nothing much else we'll be needing for a feast.'

'He's a grand auld lad that Hughie,' Jack replied as he swung out of the door.

Jack took the tram to the top of Cromac Street. He had time to kill before the pubs opened, so he walked down to the St

George's markets for a look around. His plan was simple: he intended to walk into the McCafferty pub at lunch-time and speak to Kathleen. If that meant a confrontation with either Kevin O'Donnell or her father, then so be it. He had given up too easily in 1913. He could see it plainly in retrospect. The war had shown him what was important. The things that had driven him and Kathleen apart were lies and delusions. He wanted a chance to persuade her that this was so; to tell her that they should be together because they always should have been together. His temptation to marry Annie Hargreaves had been about loneliness, ambition, thwarted desire. Though he wasn't proud of the part he'd played in the gun-running, there was a blessing in the way it had saved him from a false move. He knew Annie was wrong for him, because faced with death, it wasn't Annie he had thought of, but Kathleen and their child. And on the one and only occasion he'd been tempted to go with a French prostitute in the upstairs room of an estaminet in Arras, it had been Kathleen he thought of as he closed his eyes and tried to imagine he was making love and not indulging in a drunken fuck for a few lousy francs.

Such were Jack's thoughts as he approached the redbrick and sandstone façade of the markets under a lowering sky the colour of a dust-bin lid. It was cold, but not the sharp cold of frost. This was the dark bitter weather that promised soaking rain and damp spirits. He refused to see a portent in it, and passed under the arched entrance with its inscription in Irish: *Lamh Dhearg Uladh*. He remembered when he was a boy asking his Da what it meant and the way his Da had raised his chin and squared his shoulders as he delivered the proud reply: 'The Red Hand of Ulster'. It was only now as he entered the yellowish-grey light of the covered market's interior that he saw the irony. It was Irish. And yet his father wanted to be British. Jack tried to apply the test to himself. Was he British or Irish or both? What did these words mean?

As he walked the concrete floors of the market staring at the fruit and vegetables, the butcher's stalls with chicken and geese and turkeys hanging, the bright yellow butter and cheese displayed, he reached deep inside himself for the answer. But he found none. He realised he didn't know and he didn't care. As he said this to himself, the image that came to his mind was of Cocky Shuttleworth dying in his arms on the battlefield, the rosary beads twisted between the boy's fingers.

It didn't do to go back there too often. Jack tried instead to concentrate on the sights and smells and festive atmosphere around him. There were holly wreaths and mistletoe and somewhere a boy's voice unfurled, 'Once in Royal David's City', in a treble pure as a chiming bell. Suddenly Jack was threatened by the hot spring of tears to his eyes. He stopped and looked up at the dangling carcasses of some ducks and geese still feathered, their poor heads drooping over a counter full of butchered meats—fine looking pork and lamb and beef. Breathing in through his nose, he inhaled the close scents of the place, the raw made clean and the processed tangy, both of them provoking human hunger. Despite himself Jack felt the saliva in his mouth.

He collected himself and walked on. With Christmas not far away, there were lots of people shopping, despite the difficult times and the unemployment. There were plenty in Belfast who'd done well in the war. The place had been a hub for manufacturing and the export of farm produce. Men like Hughie's Da had made fortunes. Doubtless the fortune would be Hughie's one day. Certainly, McCullough Senior had done his best to make sure his son survived to enjoy it. The word was Hughie had been forbidden to join up. His Da put it out that his boy was working on the farm—essential war-work—to save the lad from white feathers and scorn. In fact, according to Lily, Hughie spent most of the war working in his father's shop with his apron and boater on, sporting the badge that advertised his military exemption. All of which Jack could just about stomach. What stuck in his craw was the fighting-cock bravado of the brash young man. A few days in the trenches would have cured that. Or not. There were some poor bastards who'd enjoyed it—couldn't get enough of the fighting. But they were few and far between. Like Jack, most regretted the discovery they could kill. It was only the conquest of fear that let pride back in.

Remembering the desperate passion of fighting made Jack stop for a moment. He took off his cap and ran his fingers over his forehead and into what was left of his hair. He realised he was sweating, though the air was cold. Suddenly the idea of what he was about to do—the possible confrontation with Kevin O'Donnell or Kathleen's father seemed exhausting. But the thought of being cowed by these men was worse. If Kathleen didn't want to see him or let him meet his child, then let her say so to his face. That was the point. To know for sure that she concurred with their wishes. Then, perhaps, he could get on with the rest of his life without the torment of 'what if' or 'what-might-have-been.'

He jammed his cap back on and continued to meander round the market. The fruit and veg merchants had their stalls decorated with holly wreaths and mistletoe for sale, while their mountains of spuds and pyramids of carrots enticed the eye with the colours of earth and sun. There were apples, too, their waxy skins polished green, yellow, red. Oranges and lemons gave out their scents of exotic places and blazed their colours like beacons from a brighter world than grey Belfast.

Jack's eyes roved as the market traders shouted their wares and the women stopped to buy. It was then he saw her. She was at a stall twenty yards away, with an orange in her hand, leaning forward to inhale its scent. He stared to make sure he was not hallucinating. It was as if his thoughts had conjured her. He slowed his pace, his eyes fixed on her, as she put the orange back on the display and stood looking, a small frown on her features, lost in decision making. As he continued towards her, Jack became aware of his raised heart-beat. Light-headed and breathless, the concrete floor felt like cotton wool. The sounds of the market continued but they seemed to come to him from a long way off. All his senses were directed towards her.

She was talking to the market-trader now—a fat round-faced man whose beady eyes played on her as he put two oranges in a brown paper bag. She held out her hand with the money in it. The man took her cash, gave her some change. She put the oranges in a string bag and turned to walk away.

Jack picked up his pace to follow her. Though she looked more prosperous than when he'd last seen her, he was sure it was Kathleen. She wore a black woollen top-coat over an olive skirt, which dropped to her ankle boots in the latest fashion. Her hair was pinned up at the back and she wore a neat little hat to match her skirt. But these trappings didn't matter to Jack. It was the markers of her beauty that made him know her: the milky complexion against her crow black hair, the wide forehead and straight nose, the generous delicate arch of her eyebrows, the gentle inverted v-shape of her full upper-lip, the way her cheek-bones suggested themselves without insisting.

He hurried anxious not to lose her in the busy precinct. At the end of the aisle, she turned right and disappeared from view. When Jack got there and turned, he couldn't see her. A flutter of panic breezed through him as he stood, eyes darting through the stream of shoppers. Then he saw her again at a stall contemplating some bacon. There were others in front of her to be served. Jack didn't pause to consider any further. He walked up behind her, touched her arm and said, 'I'm told McCullough's in town have grand rashers.'

Kathleen jumped and turned to him, ready to be affronted. She stared at him, frowning. He knew he was thinner in the face, worn looking, but he saw her eyes widen as the recognition dawned. A smile fit to light the world replaced her frown.

'Jesus, Mary and Joseph. Jack Young. Is it really you?'

'I'm glad to be mentioned with the Holy Family.' He looked into her eyes, green and deep as the Irish Sea off Donaghadee. 'How are you? You look fine, so you do.'

She nodded, still mute, still with the daft smile splashed across her features.

Jack tried to find something to say. He felt giddy, breathless, off balance. Banality was all he could manage. He asked a needless question: 'You're back in Belfast? I heard you'd been in Dublin.'

'I've been back since 1916.'

'At your Mam and Da's?'

'Yes.'

'And . . .' Jack wanted to ask about the child, but didn't know how.

'We don't shop at McCullough's. My Da's not keen.' Kathleen was still looking at him as if he were an apparition.

'Why doesn't that surprise me? You'd best get on and buy your auld bacon then. Mebbe we can have a stroll once you're done?'

Jack's suggestion galvanised Kathleen. She resumed her place in the queue. Jack stood behind her. They waited in awkward silence until she was served. When her bacon was being wrapped, Kathleen half-turned and said, 'I can't believe it's you. Jack Young. After all these years. How long have you been in Belfast?'

'Only a couple of days.'

'Are you in Manchester still? I expect you're wed.'

'No,' Jack said as Kathleen took possession of her parcel. 'Neither in Manchester nor wed. Not that I was short of offers, you understand.'

Kathleen looked quizzical, not knowing if he was serious. 'It wasn't that the English girls didn't take to you then?'

'They took to me all right. But I only had thoughts for you.'

Kathleen blushed. 'Still full of Blarney. And you're back in Belfast for good?'

Jack thought he heard a note of hope in Kathleen's voice, but wasn't sure. He knew he must tell the truth, but was reluctant. To describe his work in Flanders was a matter of delicacy to him. And he didn't want immediately to seem a fly-by-night presence in her life again. Already, he was mesmerised by her. His imagination over the years had not played him false. She was as beautiful to him as his mind had suggested on countless nights of lonely recollection.

'I'll tell you about me in a minute. First, I want to hear about you and . . .'

'There's not much to tell you don't know already.'

Suddenly, she was on the defensive, protecting herself. They stood there in the market scrutinising each other. Jack wanted to reach out and touch her, reassure her, hold her. But he knew it was too soon. The throngs of people brushing past didn't help. He wished he could take her for a walk by the Lagan as they'd done in the old days. He felt the risk of words and remembered climbing the ladders to go over the top. He mustered his courage.

'I was on my way to see you. Killing time before I walked into the pub. I saw you there a few months ago. Behind the bar. I've been thinking of nothing else since. I want to talk to you Kathleen. To see how you are and to ask about the wean. I have your letters still. I keep them by me after all this time.'

'You saw me?'

'I did.'

A look of recognition dawned on Kathleen's face. 'I remember. There was a day. I thought I saw you looking in. I told myself it couldn't be.'

'It was me.'

'I can't believe it. I can't believe I'm standing here talking to you.'

Jack touched her arm. 'We should take a turn. Get out of the crowd.'

Kathleen glanced about her nervously, as if suddenly aware and frightened of her surroundings. 'I don't know,' she said. 'I want to talk to you. Of course I do. But . . . I wouldn't want Kevin or my Da getting wind you're about.'

Jack shrugged. 'What can they do to me?'

'Kevin's a dangerous man.'

'The German army was dangerous but I'm alive and kicking.'

'I'm serious Jack. He's said more than once he'd like to kill you.'

Jack placed his hand under her elbow. 'Come on with you. We'll walk round the market. There's less chance we'll be seen in the crowd. I'm not for letting you run off when I haven't spoken to you all these years. I want to hear about the babby.'

'She's a babby no longer. She's a real little girl, our Niamh.'

Jack tried to speak but found he couldn't. A gale of emotion overwhelmed him and snatched his words. Wonder at the idea of a daughter, his daughter vied with sudden fury at the thought of Kevin's place in the little girl's life. He remembered that proprietorial hand on Kathleen's shoulder. Imagined Niamh calling Kevin, Da. Considered the long years of absence from his daughter's life. And all the time Kevin had spent with her . . .

'Our Niamh,' he said at last, aware of Kathleen's scrutiny. He steered her into the stream of shoppers.

'She's lovely Jack. She has your hair and eyes and chin.' Kathleen sounded nervous now, as if she was trying to placate him.

Jack knew he had no right to be angry. He had forfeited everything when he left her alone and pregnant to face her parents. Yet he struggled to keep his voice even.

'You say Kevin's dangerous. What kind of father is he to

the wean?'

Kathleen didn't reply immediately. She looked troubled. 'I don't know how much I should say.'

'For Christ's sake it's a simple enough question.'

'Don't be angry with me, Jack. I don't want you to be angry.' She looked about her again, as if frightened they might be drawing attention to themselves.

'I'm sorry. I'm trying not to be. It's just the thought of you and the child with him, when it should be me.'

'But you left Jack. What could I do? I didn't know it was going to turn out like this.'

'Like what?'

'I don't know where to begin. I'm not supposed to say anything.'

'You're not happy with him?'

Kathleen's mouth twisted in a bitter grimace before she replied. 'I am not.'

'But you stick with him?'

'What choice have I got? Once married, always married. And besides, Kevin and my Da are thick as thieves. I rely on my Da for a roof over our heads and a bit of brass.'

'Does Kevin work for your Da?'

Kathleen shook her head. 'He used to but not anymore.' She looked and sounded agitated now. She lowered her voice as she went on. 'I can't go into it, Jack. It's too complicated. Kevin's often not here. He comes and goes as he pleases. I'm not supposed to say anything. It's more than my life's worth. He says he's fighting for Ireland. Like I've told you. He's a dangerous man.'

'And a father to our child? He must set a fine example.'

'He's not here most of the time.'

'A kid needs a Da, don't you think?'

Kathleen stopped and turned to him, a note of irritation in her voice. 'I do my best. It's not been easy.' She paused. Her face changed. She looked panic- stricken, as if someone had made an appalling suggestion to her. She searched Jack's face anxiously, her face creased with concern.

Jack reached to put his hand on her arm. 'What's wrong?' She flinched away.

'Don't think for a minute you can take her. That's not what you're after is it? You can't take her from me. You can't.'

Jack raised his hands palms upwards. 'That's not what I'm about. I don't want to hurt you any more than I have already.'

Kathleen nodded. Her face relaxed as she puffed out her lips and released an audible breath of relief. Jack tried to imagine the little girl. He'd love to see her but he didn't know how to ask.

They embarked on another circuit of the market. The aisles seemed busier than ever, sometimes making it difficult for Jack and Kathleen to walk comfortably side by side. All the while Kathleen surveyed the faces in the crowd, clearly on edge in case she was spotted by someone who knew Kevin or her Da.

'I should never have left when you were pregnant. I regret it every day of my life.' Jack blurted the words he'd dreamt of saying for years.

Kathleen pressed her lips together as she looked at him as if trying to contain her emotion. It took her a moment before she replied.

'It wasn't your fault. We were young. I should have come with you. It seemed impossible somehow. I've often thought of you, Jack, and our times together. Our walks and loving in the meadows. We were grand together weren't we? I keep your letters still. But I won't lie to you. Since my Da persuaded me to marry Kevin, my first concern has always been Niamh.' Kathleen's eyes filled with tears. 'I've done my very best for her. I've tried to shield and protect her.'

'You mean Kevin hurts her?' Jack was alarmed now.

'Not physically. He fawns all over her one minute; he's sharp and cold with her the next. Then he leaves again. It's no good, but what can I do? At least this time he's not staying with us. I'm trying to keep him away from her.'

'Not staying with you?'

'Don't ask Jack. Please.'

'It sounds a fine auld carry on.'

They were silent again for a few paces. Kathleen blew her nose. She gave a little laugh. 'It's the cold you know.' When she had composed herself, she said, 'You still haven't told me about yourself. I'm to believe in all this time you've never been wed or had a lady friend?'

'I had an escape before the war. There's been nobody since. But I've held you close in my heart, so I have. That's why I decided I must do something. See how you were fixed. Ask after the child.'

'I'm glad, Jack. Glad to see you. I often wondered about you during the war. There were so many killed. You said you were in France?'

'France and Belgium. I volunteered in 1914 with all the others. Fought at the Somme and Ypres. Last year, I put my hand up again. I work as a gardener for the War Graves Commission. Helping to build the cemeteries in Flanders.'

'Mother of God. I would have thought you'd be glad to get out of it, away from the war and everything to do with it.'

'It's hard to explain. I have such memories of the boys I knew. And such memories of the ugliness. The way they died in the filth. You've never seen anything like it, Kathleen. It was as if the earth was turned inside out. It's the thought of putting everything to rights I like. The idea of making somewhere beautiful for those lads to lie. I remember when I was wounded, I was out in the mud and rain trying to crawl back to our lines through the filth and the debris. I was praying to God to help me. I imagined Him not as the God of Battle that our officer bloke talked about, but as the Great Cleanser. And it's like that, do you see? I'm helping to clean it all up.'

Kathleen's eyes shone as if she was moved. 'You were

wounded, then?'

'Ay, but it was nothing much. I'm right as rain, now.'

'I'm glad, Jack. Glad you got out of it all right. I've often thought about you . . . I'm glad to see you, so I am.' That smile again.

'And I, you.'

'Meeting here. It's like fate.'

It was all Jack could do to restrain himself from clasping her to him there and then. But he knew he mustn't make a scene. Draw attention. They walked on in silence for a few minutes. They were on their third circuit of the market by now.

When they came near the entrance she said, 'I'll have to go, Jack. I have to be at the pub for opening time.'

Jack had been dreading this moment. The idea of seeing her walk away was already painful to him.

'Can I not walk with you?'

'Better not. I'd love you to. I'd love to keep talking to you. I've had nobody I could really talk to all these long years. But I have to go.'

'We must see each other again.'

'Yes.'

'I'd like to meet Niamh.'

'I'd like you to meet her. It might be difficult, but I'll see what I can do. As long as you promise not to let on who you are to her. I'll not have her upset or unsettled. You'll promise me won't you, Jack? You'll just be an auld friend of her Mammy?'

'An auld friend indeed,' Jack said. 'I'll practice that.'

They stood there in the crowded market place facing each other with eyes that spoke their gladness, uncertainty and hope. When they had made a tentative plan to meet again, Kathleen took Jack's hand, leaned forward and kissed him briefly. He felt the warmth of her on him, the sweet soft touch of her lips. She turned and walked quickly away.

IV

Early on Boxing Day morning, Jack's breath made clouds as he walked briskly towards Ormeau Park. The air was blade bright; the pavement beneath his feet frost spangled. It looked as if some celestial confectioner had decided to decorate the drab streets with festive icing sugar. No one else was about. There was no traffic. Jack relished the energising cold, the freedom from the stifling warmth of the family kitchen. The sound of his footsteps was the sound of liberation. At the thought of the momentous meeting in prospect, he quickened his steps. He felt like running to expend the energy wound tight inside him, but restrained himself. He didn't want to be taken as some kind of imbecile by peepers behind lace curtains. He didn't want to be noticed at all.

He had spent Christmas in a welter of impatience, his mind full of unholy thoughts. His Mam had been on his back for being quiet and having a face like a fiddle. She accused him of spoiling the party. Jack felt sorry for her now he was out of it. There hadn't been much of a party, after all. Hughie and Eileen carrying on, making themselves the centre of attention, while Lily goaded them and his Mam did her best to join in the raillery. His Da hadn't helped. Stern faced, silent and heavy as a boulder, the old man remained unmoved by all that went on around him. Jack had sensed his Mam's anxiety as she tried to jolly everyone along and generate the happy family Christmas that was the product of her imagination and the focus of her desire. Though Jack did his best as he was chivvied and harassed in search of the elusive Christmas spirit, his thoughts had only been for Kathleen and Niamh and the hope of meeting them. More darkly, the idea of having a wee word in a significant ear about the presence of Kevin O'Donnell in Belfast had tip-toed across his mind more than once. Or better still an anonymous tip-off. An easy way, perhaps, to remove his rival from the scene.

But there was something hateful in the idea. He wanted to win Kathleen and the child fair and square. He didn't want his love sullied any more than it had to be by subterfuge. Yet the rendezvous Kathleen had tentatively suggested for this morning was by necessity a hole-in-the corner affair. It couldn't be helped. What else could they do? If she could get away from her family without arousing suspicion, Kathleen would bring Niamh for a breath of fresh air in the park. With a bit of luck they would bump into each other by the bandstand. Then Jack had a little surprise planned for his daughter. He didn't know if she would like it.

As he hurried along, he tried not to get ahead of himself. Maybe Kathleen wouldn't show up at all. Seeing her again and meeting his daughter seemed too good to be true. Yet the bright day and the exhilaration of escape from the claustrophobic proximity of his family made him tingle with hope. He felt intensely alive, acutely aware of his body moving through space. The sensation reminded him of going over the top for the first time, but then the predominating emotion had been dread; now, it was anticipation.

Jack shook his head as he approached the elaborate brick and ironwork of the park gates. Something in their formality made him think of cemeteries. He couldn't help himself. Wherever he was, no matter what he was doing, it seemed he couldn't escape the war for long. Even the leafless trees, the black tracery of their branches making charcoal patterns against the sky, reminded him of the woods and copses on the Somme that first winter in the trenches. As he walked into the park and along the broad avenue, he attempted to dispel the melancholy turn his mind had taken.

He clutched the large canvas shopping bag he carried tighter. He'd had a hell of a job smuggling the thing out of the house. Not wanting awkward questions, he'd held the bag to his chest under his coat as he popped his head round the kitchen door and delivered a cheery farewell. 'Just popping out for a breath of fresh,' he'd said. Then made his hasty get away. If Kathleen and Niamh showed up, there was a chance he could begin to redeem the past and make some sense of his survival.

So many dead. So many maimed. He'd been to see Louis Cockcroft in the Sanitorium back in 1918. Grey haired, a blanket draped over the remains of his legs, he'd sat in his wheelchair fidgeting and twitching. There was no conversation. Dull-eyed, Louis had stared, as if he'd never seen Jack before. Jack attempted to exchange words. But random streams of filth issued from Louis' mouth in a muttered monologue of manic intensity. The spittle gathered and frothed then dribbled down his chin. Blasted in mind and body, the blithe, kind and confident young charmer Jack had known had gone for good. This wasn't Louis any more. Jack hadn't had the heart to visit again. He'd assuaged his guilt by fulfilling a promise and going to see Cocky Shuttleworth's Mam. What an ordeal that turned into . . .

Jack saw his destination in the distance. A shaft of pale sunlight pierced the high grey cloud, making the rotunda shine. The beauty of the morning distracted him and though the frigid air made him wheeze, he experienced the cold as purifying. He kept to the path as long as he could. Then, when he was adjacent, he struck off across the grass towards the bandstand, his feet making the frost crackle and leaving green prints against the sparkling white.

There was nobody about. An empty park bench was covered in rime. Jack stopped and looked about him. A reconnoitre. He was uncertain which way to walk. Instead, he gingerly mounted the steps into the bandstand. The wooden boards were treacherous with ice. Yet Jack persisted. If he walked the perimeter it would give him a 360 degrees view. If anybody approached he would see them. It was a vantage point. The sunlight on the grass. Fields of fire. His mind made leaps he didn't like.

He saw them when they were still a long way off. They were coming from the same direction he'd travelled in. They must have caught the tram from Cromac Street down the Ormeau Road. He could tell it was them by the way she walked—head up, square shouldered, her free hand making a funny little flapping gesture as her arm swung backwards and forwards, as if it might give her extra traction. There was something defiant in her stride that Jack loved. The little girl in a red coat and woollen bonnet, who held Kathleen's other hand, was struggling to keep up. Every few steps, she took a little run and skip, looking up at her mother, not, it seemed to complain, but more to question the need for this hurry.

There was a tense luxury in watching them move towards him not knowing they were observed. Soon he would show himself, but for a moment he wanted to savour the sight of them and the elation their appearance provoked in him. He felt a wild relief and a curious recklessness, as if something long locked up in him had been let go. A dizzying liberation. He wanted to preserve the scene somehow. If only he could draw or paint. It wasn't a photograph he was after. It was something more than that. This frosty scene. The young woman and girl walking towards him, not knowing they were observed. The sun struggling against the grey and white. The contrast between the red coat and Kathleen's black. They came nearer and Jack moved to meet them. Kathleen stepped gingerly over the grass as if worried the frost might spoil her leather boots. The child seemed less fussy and stared towards him as he waved.

'This is my friend Jack, I've been telling you about,' Kathleen said to Niamh as they came up.

Jack and Kathleen exchanged an ardent look by way of greeting. He saw at once she was as glad to be there as he was.

'Hello there. Is this the little darling?'

'It is. This is Niamh.'

Jack squatted on his haunches to make himself the same size as his daughter. The little girl clutched and leant into her mother's leg. With her head to one side she regarded Jack with solemn eyes. They were blue, but it seemed to Jack they had a purity and intensity of colour altogether finer than his own. She had the same heart-shaped face as her mother; the rosebud mouth seemed to belong to neither of them. From beneath the knitted bonnet with its variegated zig-zag of stripes there peeped a strand of brown hair. Though it was closer to his colouring than Kathleen's, it looked darker, more lustrous than his—Niamh was immediately beautiful to him. He felt the lurch of love and the attendant anxiety. He wanted to reach out and make a lasting connection with this small unknown person. He was afraid he would be clumsy or over-eager.

'Hello Niamh. That's a pretty coat you have on.'

'Say hello to Jack,' her mother encouraged.

The little girl turned her face into her Mam's leg and twined closer in a paroxysm of shyness.

Jack glanced up at Kathleen's face. Her pale skin was reddened by the cold. Her eyes glittered. Perhaps that was the cold as well. Jack couldn't tell. She gave him a little nod of reassurance, as if to say, go on. He registered the awkwardness of the moment acutely. He had no idea how to make conversation with a six year old. He remembered the inwardness of his own childhood—the way he would retreat into the imaginary worlds of his solitary games.

'Look, Niamh,' Jack ventured. 'I thought we might have some fun with this.' He straightened in order to take from the bag the kite he'd bought on Christmas Eve. It was only a piece of thin cotton stretched over a dowelling frame. Cheap as chips. He could have made something better himself, but he hadn't wanted to cause a stir at home.

The little girl stared as Jack held it up. Its tail of red and yellow bows unravelled.

'What is it?' Niamh asked.

'It's a kite. Isn't that grand,' Kathleen coaxed.

'Come on, I'll show you.' Jack was all energy now. 'We'll go down here where there's a bit of room.' He led the way onto the lawns below the band stand. He gave Niamh the kite to hold and her instructions—how she was to toss it into the air when he said 'go'.

He walked backwards unravelling the string. It wasn't a windy day, but he reckoned there was enough breeze. Kathleen stood by her daughter, arms folded across her chest, hugging herself. At his signal, Niamh launched the kite, jumping with both arms flung in the air. Jack tugged the string. Kathleen and Niamh cheered and clapped as the fragile bird dipped and soared. Once the kite gained height, it began to catch air currents that couldn't be felt on the ground. Jack had to work hard as it bucked and swooped. Niamh shrieked and ran under it, her hands lifted aloft as if to reach into the sky and push the coloured red and yellow triangle back towards the clouds.

Jack's feelings were like the violent swoop and swing and dive of the kite. Niamh was obviously enjoying herself. To see the little girl, his little girl running up and down with such a smile on her face filled him with giddy joy. The miracle of her small being was astonishing to him.

'Come over here with you,' he shouted to her. 'Help me out.'

Niamh looked to her Mam. 'Go on,' Kathleen urged.

'In front of me here.' Jack ushered his daughter so she was standing directly in front of him. 'Take the bobbin in your left hand and pull with the right. See, like this.'

Niamh nodded solemnly, apprehensive. He passed the bobbin over. The little girl gave a cry and staggered as she felt the pull of the kite. Jack kept one hand higher up the string to steady the flight.

'Look, Mammy, look. I'm flying.' Niamh's face was alive

with delight.

Kathleen applauded and shouted her encouragement. For a few moments Jack and Niamh flew the kite together. But the fragile harmony didn't last. A sudden gust buffeted the kite sideways. Jack tugged violently trying to keep it airborne. But the kite was moving too fast and despite his best efforts it plummeted to the ground. Niamh stood still, looking at it in horror, frightened it was broken.

'Here, give me the bobbin. Run and pick it up,' Jack said. 'Follow the string.'

She did as she was told. Kathleen and Jack exchanged a comic grimace of alarm. Niamh reached the fallen kite. Jack reeled in the string towards her. 'Hold it up above your head,' he shouted. 'Now run away from me and when I say so, let go.'

The little girl obeyed him her legs working overtime, gangly and wayward as a newly born lamb. On his signal, she released the kite. Jack tugged it into the air, and he laughed with glee as it caught the wind and he let it soar, the string reeling off the bobbin. Niamh stood craning her neck upwards.

Jack felt the presence of Kathleen by his side. She slipped her arm through his. Though he was working hard to keep the kite aloft, he looked at her for a moment and their eyes met. There was no need for words. Jack remembered the times when their bodies danced together in passionate fields of summer. Kathleen leant up so that he could feel the warm breath of her on his face just before she kissed him.

He had no time to dwell on the lush promise of her lips. The kite was suddenly caught in a violent down draught. Jack fought as hard as he could, but the kite was too small and light for the conditions and it veered in a sudden arc and hurtled towards the ground at considerable speed. Jack heard an ominous crack as it hit and crumpled. He knew at once it was broken. His elation turned to anxiety as he watched Niamh run to the broken thing. He reeled in the string. His daughter crouched to examine the wreckage, as if she were tending a live and wounded creature. Jack looked at Kathleen ruefully, before he hurried towards Niamh.

'Never mind,' he said. 'Don't fret. I'll fix it.'

Niamh looked at him wonderingly. 'How will you fix it?'

'With some tape and a bit of glue.'

She looked at him. 'You've no glue and tape here, though,' she said.

'No it will have to wait for another day. The breeze up there was too strong.'

She smiled at him, her blue eyes shining, as if she felt his disappointment and wanted to reassure him.

'It's all right,' she said. 'It was fun when it flew.'

'It was as well,' Jack said.

They gathered up the kite. As they walked back towards Kathleen, Niamh slipped her hand into Jack's.

'We're going to be grand friends you and me, aren't we?' Jack said.

'Yes,' said Niamh. 'I like you. When can we fly the kite again?'

'We'll have to ask your Mammy.'

Niamh ran towards her mother, shouting, 'The kite's broken but Jack will mend it. When can we come again? When can we Mam?'

'I don't know darlin'. Maybe at the weekend, if you're good.' Kathleen bent to embrace the child.

'I'm always good,' the little girl said, arching back and turning her head to make sure Jack was hearing the exchange.

The sight of the two of them together made Jack feel the world was a beautiful place. All his desire was focused on them. He wanted to make love to Kathleen. He wanted to be a father to his child. He wanted to make them his family and protect them and provide for them. He wanted to live in peace with them for the rest of his days.

'I'd best get her home now, Jack, out of the cold.'

Kathleen's words deflated him and reminded him of the difficulties that stood between them.

'Will I see you at the weekend then?'

'Please Mammy. Say yes. We want to fly the kite don't we Jack? Please Mam.'

'If we can,' Kathleen said.

When they parted at the park gates, Jack bent and kissed the top of the child's head through her bonnet, not wanting to encroach on her with any over-familiarity. He took Kathleen's hand for a moment. She kissed him briefly, the merest brush of the lips, but in the look she gave him as she did so he wanted to read the promise of a future.

As he made his solitary way back, walking slowly to delay his return to the cramped intimacies of home, he wondered at his capacity for hope. Maybe it was the Christmas season that had him considering miracles. How else was he to free Kathleen from the bonds that tied her to her family, Belfast, and Kevin O'Donnell?

V

Some weeks later, Kathleen sat up in bed holding a cheap writing pad against her raised knees. She wore a shawl over her thick nightdress to ward off the February cold. A plain white candle stuck in a saucer by her bed-side cast a soft confiding light. She had extinguished the gas lamps to encourage the intimacy of this time she loved, when the pub was shut and everyone else asleep. There was a deep quiet about the place broken only by the stretch and groan of timber and brick as the old building cooled and settled for the night. She stared ahead lost in dreams. There was so much to say and so much unsayable. She did not know how to begin her letter to Jack Young.

The time she'd spent with Jack at Christmas had spun her into a giddy confusion. Having reconciled herself to making-do in order to focus on Niamh's welfare, suddenly she felt alive again. In Jack's company, she had felt the spring of desire so long dormant well up inside her and she was glad. When she first saw him at the markets, she was overwhelmed. By the time they parted that first day, she was responding to the new reality of him. Though he looked older and his face was more careworn than the young man she'd known in 1912, there was an increased confidence about him. He was more certain of who he was. She felt the old spark between them blow rosy and threaten flame. Whatever the risks, it had been easy to agree to see him again . . . and again.

When he was with Niamh, the way he played with the little girl won Kathleen over, suggested another step down a forbidden path. She found she didn't want to resist. She had lived to regret not going to England with him in the first place. Though the obstacles were formidable, now she wondered if she was to be offered a second chance. Her parents and Kevin stood in her way. But to see her daughter, their daughter, happily playing with her Da was something worth dreaming about, maybe fighting for.

Jack had mended the kite and it flew again in Ormeau Park. At parting, Jack gave it to Niamh for safe-keeping. He had held the child and kissed her and told her he would come back in the summer. The little girl promised to remember him and look after the kite. That night, as Kathleen tucked her up in bed Niamh said, 'I like Jack. He's funny.' Pleased yet perturbed, Kathleen replied, 'I'm so glad my darling girl. You have to remember, though, you mustn't let on to Nan or Grand Da. I can't explain. But it's important. If we want to see Jack again, he must be our secret. Do you understand?' The little girl nodded solemnly. Kathleen hated the necessity of conspiracy and deception but she saw no alternative. Prejudice and hatred squeezed her into lies. Yet she wanted her love to be true.

Before Jack took the boat, they had risked a last meeting, just the two of them at the markets. It was the most difficult of their encounters. Having just found each other again, they now had to say goodbye. Both of them were on edge, tense and somehow shy. Every bump of their hips and brush of their arms as they walked close together, every touch of their eyes, made their yearning for each other palpable. Yet they knew they would have to wait many months for any fulfilment of their longing. A brief embrace, a touch of the lips was all she had to remember their parting by. That and the fervent words he'd spoken to her. 'We have to be patient,' he said. 'Like gardening. Preparation can't be hurried. Then you wait for flower and fruit and crop. That's what we must do.' Breathless with choked desire she had whispered, 'There will be fruit and flower.'

It was then he put his plan to her. 'I'll come back in the summer. For you and Niamh. We'll get out of it over the water to Ypres. I'll have enough money. We can get set up in a little place there. We'll say you're my wife. There's nobody will know any different. I'll tell my bosses a tale if I have to . . . Will you do it? Will you come with me this time?'

She had been so surprised by the audacity of the suggestion that she hardly knew how to respond. The speed with which he had made such a determination knocked her off balance. In her mind she had been imagining a future in which Jack returned to Ireland permanently. It made her reply less than enthusiastic. She couldn't now remember exactly what she'd said though she knew she had questioned what it would be like for Niamh living amongst those graveyards. How the idea made her shiver. She saw the way his face twisted in pain at her words. But she had to be honest.

Despite his subsequent urgings, she couldn't bring herself to commit to the plan. Instead she prevaricated, saying she would think about it and putting to him her alternative idea of a future together in Ireland, though in truth she had no idea how that was to be managed either.

Thus they parted with everything unsettled between them. The only thing certain was his promise to write. He had learned he could write to her by way of the post office so her family would not suspect. He was true to his word. He had been gone from Belfast over a month. Today she had received her third letter since his leaving. In every one he reiterated his scheme for their future, elaborating on the details. His latest idea was to suggest to his colleagues and bosses that he was coming back to Belfast in the summer to be wed and that his bride-to-be had a child by another man who had been killed in the war.

It was a plausible story. But Kathleen found it difficult to accept as her story. Despite Jack's attempts at description, which dwelt upon the re-building, she couldn't imagine what life would be like in the ruined city of Ypres. She couldn't even pronounce the name of the place. She only knew it from the newspapers and returned soldiers in the pub as 'Wipers'—not a word that conjured hopeful visions. And the graveyards where Jack had found his vocation filled her mind with nameless dread. No matter how hard she tried, she couldn't fathom his enthusiasm for his work. She understood he had a deep sense of obligation but she couldn't quite see why. It was not as if he hadn't done his bit. He had served and been wounded in the cause. Why he felt he had to do more was dark to her. On the other hand, with all the difficulties they would face in Belfast, she appreciated his impulse to forge a future elsewhere.

For now, the task at hand was to reply to Jack's letter. She was nerving herself to be honest and express again her uncertainty while still giving voice to her feelings for him and her hopes. To get away from Kevin was a dream to savour, but leaving her Mam and Da and taking their granddaughter away from them was another matter. And what if in this slender re-acquaintance she had mis-judged Jack Young? She went over their meetings again in her mind, reassuring herself, remembering how good he'd been with Niamh, how much she'd longed for his arms. It was hard to believe in it all with him not here; it reminded her of when he had disappeared to Manchester those years ago. Still, she had to make a start somehow.

> *Dear Jack,*
>
> *How I wish you were in Belfast, and I could set eyes on you again. It seems a long time since you were here and even longer till I see you again. I received your letter today. It was good to know you are well and that your thoughts and feelings towards me haven't changed as the time and miles between us have grown.*

Kathleen paused. What to say next? Writing made the complications of her life press in upon her. For years she had subsisted by focusing on the daily routines necessary to raise Niamh in love and security. Jack's appearance in her life again, exciting though it was, threatened her with chaos.

Her mind drifted. She remembered their first loving in the meadows. How she had allowed herself to give way to passion without thinking she might be setting a trap for herself. It was, she recognised now, the opposite impulse that had led her: it was freedom she was after all those years ago. She and Jack had shed prejudice and stricture with the same alacrity they had shed their clothes. For a few blissful moments they had experienced liberation as well as love. With a smile to herself, Kathleen remembered how quick Jack had been to unbutton himself, how slow afterwards to do himself up once more. She saw again his slow and trembling fingers, his face troubled with the enormity of what they had done, and how she had chivvied him and made light of it all, still intoxicated in the aftermath of their abandoned coupling.

And then the pregnancy and all that followed from that. She could not and never had regretted Niamh. But the circumstances and the decisions she'd made subsequently constituted the bonds that now entwined her. She wanted to rebel but did not know how. Her confidence as well as her gaiety had been leeched away. She thought about love as triumph or love as tragedy and the thin line between the two.

Her deliberations were interrupted by an odd noise. She sat poised, listening, resentful of the disturbance. There it was again. Like a dash and rattle of hail against her window. But the night had been dry and cold with frost when she'd come to bed, the moon a white scimitar. A third volley had Kathleen out of bed and anxiously peering down to the back yard of the pub below. There was a figure out there but she couldn't make out who it was because the frost was already forming on the outside of the pane. She shoved the window up and shuddered as the frigid air hit her like a splash of the sea. Though his cap was pulled down low, and the collar of his donkey-jacket was up-turned, she knew at once it was Kevin.

'Will you let me in for fuck's sake? I'm freezing my bollocks off down here. I need to have a word to you.'

Kathleen pulled the window shut. She stood breathing deeply, willing him to go away. She knew he was unlikely to budge. But maybe if he was drunk he would stumble off into the night. Another percussive splatter on the window. If she didn't open up it might be a brick next. She heaved the window open again and stuck her head out in time to see him bending to scoop another handful of freezing soil from one of the tubs where her mother grew herbs.

'What are you at?' she hissed down. 'It's one o'clock in the morning. Get away home with you.'

'This is my fucking home. Let me in or I'll wake the whole household, so I will.'

Kathleen thought of Niamh. 'All right. Be quiet with you, and I'll be down.' She hastened to put on her slippers, and scurried downstairs to the back door. She slid the bolts as quietly as she could. He brushed past her as she opened the door.

'By Christ I'm cold,' he said. 'Let's get upstairs.'

There wasn't much Kathleen could do to stop him. She put a finger to her lips, to urge him to be quiet, then followed him to her room. Once inside, she realised her mistake. The writing pad was still where she'd left it abandoned on the bed covers. In her agitation and anxiety she had forgotten to hide it. She felt sick at her own stupidity. She tried not to look at it, to keep Kevin's gaze from falling there. He, meanwhile, had flung off his cap and was unbuttoning his jacket. He turned to her, his eyes traversing her body and lingering at the swell of her breasts beneath nightgown and shawl. 'It's time you warmed me Kathleen,' he said. 'I won't be denied.'

'Why now? You've not been near me in weeks.'

'I've had business to attend to. I'll have to be away south soon. By Jesus, you look fine with your hair down so. Come here with you.' Shrugging off his top-coat, he took steps towards her.

Kathleen stood mute and passive her hands by her side. A gust of sour breath hit her. She was torn between revulsion and fear. If she gave in to him, maybe she could distract him, whisk the writing pad away. But the idea of suffering under his brutal touch was horrible to her. One arm was round her now. He pressed his face to hers. She felt the prickle of his beard. His other hand groped for her breast. She smelt the familiar stale breath on him as he pressed his tongue hard against her lips trying to force open her mouth.

'Come on you frigid bitch.' He grasped her by the throat now. 'I will have you,' he hissed. She felt the spittle against her face, as she tried to push him away. He was too strong for her and he forced her back onto the bed. He stood over her, unbuckling and unbuttoning his trousers. Still, Kathleen didn't know whether to fight or surrender. She didn't want to cry out and waken Niamh or her parents. She just wanted him to be gone.

Kevin had his head down now, pulling at his trousers with one hand and groping for the hem of her nightdress with the other. Kathleen felt for the writing tablet with her left hand thinking to either push it under the pillow or knock it off the bed onto the floor. Kevin was forcing her legs apart with his knees as he raised her nightgown. Then he was on top of her, trying to force his way inside her. As he butted against her, a self-protective instinct took hold.

'Slow and gentle now with you, Kevin. Don't hurt me. Please. Don't be rough. Let me help you to it.' She eased herself under him and with her right hand reached for his cock trying to arrest his frenzy and show her co-operation, while with her left hand she groped for the writing pad.

It was then, looking up at her for a moment he noticed what she was at. Propping himself on one arm he reached up and snatched the thing out of her grasp. Seeing he was momentarily off-balance, Kathleen pushed at his supporting arm and shoulder with all her might. He fell off her and landed with a thump in an ungainly heap on the floor. Kathleen rolled the other way and stood up so the bed was between them. He was on his feet in a moment and hauling his trousers up, red in the face and full of rage, waving the beginning of her letter to Jack in the air.

'You're a fucking whore, you know that? Jack fucking Young. A wee bird told me they'd seen you talking to some fella at the markets. I thought nothing of it. I should have known better. I should have known what an evil sneaking ungrateful slut you are. I'll give you Jack Young so I will.'

He advanced towards her, seething low and intense. 'I'm going to make you eat this.' He waved the piece of paper in the air. 'I am going to shove it down your throat, so I am. And when I've finished with you, I'm going to hunt down Jack Young and I'm going to kill him. Do you understand? I will kill him. You don't even understand who he is, what he is, do you?'

Kathleen was backed against the wall, with Kevin, hands loosely by his side, feet apart, right in front of her. She was terrified and bewildered, but preparing to fight. She had for now escaped violation. If he attacked her, she would have at him. Tense and preparing herself for physical confrontation it took a moment for Kathleen to take in Kevin's words. In reply, she could only stammer, 'I don't know what you mean.'

'Don't you now? Well, let me tell you. Jack Young was a gun-runner for the UVF. I don't suppose he's let on about that, has he? Helping to smuggle arms in to kill your people, so he was. And you want to be carrying on with him. You're a fucking disgrace.'

'I don't understand. I don't know what you're saying.'

'I'm telling you that in 1913 he was helping smuggle guns from Manchester. I don't need you for an excuse. He's a legitimate target. I'll have him so I will. But first I'm going to have you.'

He moved to grab her by the arm. She took a step forward and kneed him hard in the balls. He let go of her and doubled over for a moment. She tried to thrust past him to get round the bed and to the door. But he stood up and swiped her across the face with his open hand. It caught her cheek and then her nose. It sent her reeling against the wall. She cried out in pain and slumped to the floor. She was stunned. There was a buzzing in her ear and her nose was bleeding. He bent over her and took hold of her jaw. He forced her mouth open and attempted to shove the screwed up letter to Jack into her mouth. She felt the paper, its woody taste against her tongue. She tried to bring her top teeth down to bite him, but his hold on her bottom jaw was too strong. He was forcing the paper back against her throat and she began to gag and choke. She thought he was going to kill her. She roared as loud as she could, but all she could manage was a hoarse bark.

Kathleen felt the world begin to revolve and blacken at the edges. She was on the point of losing consciousness, when she became aware of a further commotion. Her father burst into the room and was on Kevin in a flash.

'What in Christ's good name are you at?' He hauled Kevin away from her. She felt the world steady and right itself.

The two men faced each other. 'Have you lost your senses?' Old man McCafferty demanded. 'Have you seen the state of her?'

Kevin stared at his father-in-law, full of belligerence. 'Have you heard what she's up to? I've caught her writing sweetheart stuff to Jack Young. She's been meeting him and carrying on.'

'Is this true, Kathleen?' her father demanded.

'Yes. No. I haven't been carrying on. He isn't here anymore. He's back over the water.'

Kathleen's mother bustled into the room. 'Jesus Mary and Joseph, what's all the commotion about now? Can't a body get some rest?' Her eyes let upon Kathleen, blood still dripping from her nose. 'My God, what's happened here?'

'Come and help her get cleaned up mother,' Sean McCafferty commanded. He turned to Kevin. 'You,' he said. 'Get out. Now. I don't care what's she's done, there's no call to take your fists to her. I won't have it. Go on, before I give you a smack myself.'

'To hell with you all, then. You have short memories. I've made a decent woman out of this slag. Don't you forget it.'

Sean McCafferty clenched his fists. 'Get out, I said. You will not stand and insult my daughter in front of me. On your way.'

Kevin looked at Kathleen as her mother helped her to her feet. 'Think on,' he said. 'If I see Jack Young, I'll kill him. No problem at all.'

Kathleen's Da made to get hold of the younger man. Kevin shrugged him off. He gathered his coat and cap and left the room without another word.

'I'll speak to you in the morning,' Kathleen's Da said to her, as her mother helped her towards the bathroom.

As they made their way down the corridor, Niamh emerged from her room and cried out at the sight of her mother.

'Go back to bed, love,' she said. 'I'm all right. I've just had a bit of a fall. Your Gran is helping me out. Everything's fine, so it is. Everything is fine.'

The little girl, half asleep still, did as she was told. In the bathroom, Kathleen splashed clean water onto her face, while her mother clucked round her. Despite the pain and shock, she felt a seed of hope lodge deep inside her: perhaps the rift between Kevin and her father meant she would never have to see her husband again.

VI

Jack Young knelt to his task, planting roses in the fields of the dead. It was a beautiful morning in early June, with pale lemon sunlight, the sky milky blue, and a light occasional breeze. It reminded him of the days before the Somme battles in 1916 when the troops had been full of hope, and the rolling green of the French countryside acted like a balm for minds made anxious by the ordeal to come. The woods and copses, near and far, had provided a glitter of leaves and a promise of cool reflection. Then the artillery took over. Trees and men were blown to ragged splinters by the shelling of both sides. Now, as he inhaled the air, fresh and cool as spring water, it made him feel that anything and everything could be made new. Just as Sanctuary Wood was putting on new flutters of green, Jack liked to think of the oaks and beeches, the hazels and hornbeams in Mametz Wood re-generating and shading the ground where so many had died in agony.

The job today was one he relished. With his heavily gloved hands, he placed the root bole firmly into the soil, dark chocolate with potting mix, and bedded it in with his trowel, tamping the earth down to make all secure. The old wooden crosses had been replaced by uniform grave markers in Portland stone. Earlier in the spring, they had sown grass seed in the avenues, which was now beginning to show. Then, they had augmented the wild flowers, poppies, cornflowers, white camomile and yellow charlock, which they had encouraged at the foot of the graves, with dwarf lupins, alyssum, nasturtiums and candytuft. They were all low-growing plants that would provide bright bursts of colour and help prevent the soil splashing up when it rained, so the headstones remained as clean as possible. Now came the finishing touch: a white or red rose bush for every two stones, so that eventually a bloom would nod over every name regardless of rank, colour, creed or nationality.

It was Gertrude Jekyll's notion that the English country garden should be the model for the appearance of the cemeteries. Jack had felt a small proprietorial thrill when her name was mentioned at a briefing for the gardeners. It made him feel in the know and proud of his pre-war reading. He liked to think he was helping to put her ideas into practice. He liked, too, that idealism had prevailed to make sure there were no distinctions made in the ranks of the dead. Battles had been fought in parliament, but for once, a generous idea had prevailed. The bodies were buried together as they had fallen. Officers and men rubbed shoulders, as did Catholics and Protestants. Men of England, Ireland, Scotland and Wales mingled with their brothers from Australia, Canada, New Zealand, India and the West Indies. Often, there were a few German burials included in a cemetery, if such graves were there already when the plot began.

The news from Ireland just now was filled with stories of murder and mayhem in the south and gathering tensions in the north. Jack wondered at the propensity of his countrymen to kill each other. Here in France and Flanders, Irishmen from north and south of all denominations had fought and died together side by side. They lay here under rows and rows of gravestones side by side. It didn't make sense to Jack. But then he guessed most of the Irish boys engaged in guerrilla warfare had avoided the killing fields of Europe. Though maybe there were some so embittered by their experience of fighting for England they now wanted to fight against the country that had sent them to the slaughter. For his part, Jack preferred the advice whispered by the dead. He'd seen bereaved relatives searching out their loved ones, and witnessed their grief as they stood staring at a name engraved in stone. It spoke to him of love abiding. All that mattered.

Jack couldn't write of such things in his letters to Kathleen. It was beyond him. Instead, he directed all his energy into persuading her that the plan he had conceived was a practical possibility. He was unashamed by reiteration. On the contrary, he felt the more he spoke his desire to be with Kathleen and Niamh, the more often he imagined their escape from Belfast and the more he tried to create in words their future life together, the more real it became. He would not let things drift. The months that separated them had been long and he was desperate not to let time and distance dilute Kathleen's feelings for him. He was anxious, too, not to lose the connection he'd begun to forge with Niamh. So he enclosed post-cards to her in which he told her about the re-building in Ypres and the boys and girls he saw coming back into the town and going to school. He told her about the creatures and birds that were returning to the shattered woodlands and meadows around Ypres. He never failed to recall their fun with the kite and to anticipate further adventures when he returned for his next visit in July.

As he moved his planter-boxes and gear on to the next pair of gravestones and spread his old piece of sackcloth for a kneeler, Jack's mind moved to the letter he intended to write that evening. He was worried about Kathleen. When she'd first written in February about her fight with Kevin, and her Da's furious reaction, it seemed she was being pushed closer into his arms. Though outraged by the violence towards her, Jack recognised what he stood to gain from Kathleen's disaffection towards these men. Since then, she had written impassioned letters about her dreams of setting up a home with him and Niamh. But she was clearly not convinced by the prospect of Ypres. And there was an even deeper shadow-side to her hope which seemed to be growing as her situation calmed. In recent letters it seemed that Kevin and her Da had managed to sow a seed of doubt in her mind. It was clear they had tried to spread poison about him. She did not tell him exactly. *They say you are a bad man and have done bad things. I don't want to believe it Jack. I can't believe it. Tell me it's rumour and gossip, Jack. I need to be sure you are a good man. I'm so afraid of what Kevin's at . . .*

Jack was afraid too. And not just of Kevin. He was scared his past was going to undo him. Somehow Kathleen's men knew about the gun-running. He was sure of it. Not that surprising after all. Both sides had their networks of watchers, spies, informers. The nudge and wink men, the money under the table men, the men in the shadows prepared to sell themselves and their knowledge. The men who did violence at one remove.

He remembered the awful time in 1913 after he was thrown out of Partington Lane. He had been haunted by the gaunt figure of Constable Givens and the little weasel, Frankie Lynch. Everywhere he went, he thought he was being followed. Perhaps he had imagined Givens. He never actually saw him. It was more a feeling, an intimation. Jack would whirl round in the street and see a coat tail disappearing, or a figure would step into a doorway, leaving a trail of tobacco smoke behind. Lynch, though, was an all too palpable presence emerging from the shadows and collaring Jack after work, threatening what would happen if he breathed a word more to the coppers. The outbreak of the war had come as a blessed relief. In putting on the uniform and fighting for England, Jack had thought to find redemption. God help him. How naïve could you be?

It was difficult to assuage Kathleen's doubts by protesting his own virtue. He didn't want to lie to her. But he could not bring himself to broach the gun-running by letter. If he had to admit to it, he'd rather do it face to face. Instead, his only tactic was to reiterate his love, his commitment to their future. Though Kathleen continued to write warmly to him, she could not conceal her hesitations. Phrases like *Do I really know you?* and *Is it really possible for this to work?* punctuated her protestations of love and affection. In her last letter she wrote, *Could we ever be happy—a Proddy and a*

Catholic mixed?

Jack finished bedding in another rose. He moved his gear again. He was in row D. He knew where he was. He stood for a moment looking at Cocky Shuttleworth's grave before spreading his piece of sacking. He didn't know if the boy would have appreciated the white rose that would blossom above his name. The kid had lived his life a long way from flowers. And he had died in the fetid dirt of the battlefield. Of course, there was nothing here to distinguish his life and death from any of the others. Except maybe his age. Only Jack knew his story. He hadn't told it all to the boy's mother. He hadn't told it to anybody. He had kept the meaning to himself.

He knelt to his task with a sense that it was a sacred trust. Though he was doubtful about God, he could not put it to himself any other way. As he trowelled the hole and scattered the potting mix before placing the rose, it came to him that maybe it was time to share Cocky Shuttleworth's last moments and what had followed from them.

After supper, in the long twilight of the late spring evening, Jack took himself off to write to Kathleen. He left his companions to their rum and tobacco. They had tried to josh him about his romance, but he had soon made it clear it was no laughing matter. He wanted none of their ribald jokes or innuendo. He had said so in no uncertain terms. They made no comment when he took himself off a little way from their camp site and seated on a tree stump, lit up a cigarette and took out his pencil and paper.

My Darling Kathleen,

Thank you for your letter. I cherish them, though it's hard not to worry about your doubts and fears. I know they are only natural, but it is hard at this distance to reassure you. You say you don't know who I really am. I'm hoping we are going to have many years together to find out. We don't have knowledge. We have love and faith. I'm asking you to believe in me, Kathleen, as I believe in you. I am sure I have much to learn about you. I hope so. It is love and faith that leads me, not knowledge. It's only a few weeks now before I'm back in Belfast and then I hope I will be able to convince you where our future lies. I think I've found the perfect place for us. Walking about the town last weekend, I saw a terraced row of cottages, which had been damaged by shellfire, but has nearly been repaired. They are prettier than Belfast houses. The brick is lighter and they have bright red tiled rooves and the windows are tricked out in white paint. They are not big or grand, but they are pretty and the street is wide and quiet. I am going to make enquiries about taking a lease on one of them. I want to have it ready, so you can see the possibility of stepping into a home not a hostel. Of course, if you came, you would want to improve what I've done. Can you imagine the joy of making our own home together?

If you and Niamh were to join me here, my life would be complete. With all the difficulties now in Ireland, and the history between us, you must know how hard things would be for us in Belfast. Here, I have been out all day in the fine weather, planting roses. Can you imagine? What a lovely thing. So far from the bustle of cities and the chaos of men. Here all is calm and order to which in time will be added the beauty of our plantings. Already the grass seed is growing and it's possible to imagine wide avenues of lawn, emerald against the graves, and then the bursts of colour from the flowers, scarlet and yellow and blue. The rose blooms will be a glory, purer white than the stones, blood red for their love and sacrifice. It is grand to feel a small part of making this memorial.

Can a Catholic and Protestant live together? I want to tell you a story. I haven't told anybody else. It's about a boy, Charlie Shuttleworth, who started at the depot in Swinton in 1913. He was always trying to play the big man, though he was only 13 and looked younger. So we called him 'Cocky'. Anyway, he came to the battalion in 1917, before that last action when I was wounded. He cottoned on to me because he remembered me from the depot. He was a nuisance of a lad, but I tried my best to look out for him. We shared a shelter at night with a couple of other blokes, and he was always giving me a fag so I'd listen to him go on about the French girls and the drink he'd had and all the rest of his nonsense.

It was a cruel thing to see him facing battle. He was only a boy. I had to be hard with him, Kathleen, and tell him to play the man's part. Once we were over the top, there was nothing more I could do. It was every man for himself. It was a rare struggle through the mud—you've never seen anything like it. We'd only managed a hundred yards or so before an officer gave me a message to take back to our line. As I staggered back I heard a voice crying out. At first I couldn't tell where it was coming from. I stopped and listened and saw an arm raised. I went over to see what I could do to help. It was Cocky Shuttleworth. There wasn't a mark on him I could see apart from the dirt. But he was blinded. He must have been caught in a shell burst.

He didn't recognise my voice. He said 'help me.' I put my arm round his shoulders and tried to raise him up, but he couldn't stand. He begged me to find a priest. I noticed then in his hands rosary beads. I had no idea he was a Catholic. I said I would go and get help, but he begged me to stay. Then he said 'say the words. I need the words.' Over and over again he pleaded with me. I knew the Catholic priests were often in the front line to help the dying but I didn't know what was said. I did my best. I recited the Lord's Prayer. Then I asked for forgiveness of his sins. And then I blessed him as best I knew how. It seemed to quieten him for a while. I thought he might be drifting off, but he came to again and said 'Did you make the sign? Make the sign.' I made the sign of the cross over him and, God forgive me, the words Jack, Queen, King, Ace went through my mind. It seemed though to lead to a moment of inspiration. I wet my finger and made the sign of the cross on his forehead. He said, 'Tell my Mammy', then gave a queer little shudder, and there was a croaking rattle in his throat, and he was gone. He's buried in the cemetery I'm working in now. I planted roses by his grave today.

That's enough for now. This letter is long and the light is going. The point is it taught me Catholic and Protestant doesn't matter. If there is a God, a Great Creator, He doesn't care about such differences. If there is anything I know. I know that.

So yes we can be together. You and Niamh could go to the Catholic Church here. I will save my praying for the gardens. I can't pretend to be any better than another man. But what I can say is I only want what's good for you and Niamh. And all I want is a chance to show and share my love.

If we believe, all things are possible.

All my love, darling girl.

Jack folded the letter up and stuck it in his shirt pocket. He would post it as usual on Friday afternoon when they returned to Ypres. He stood and stretched and decided to have a last stroll in the purple light. The evening star was showing. A lark fluted notes of evensong. Jack walked into the cemetery. He saw Harry and Fred by the campfire pause in their conversation as they lifted their heads to watch him. They made no further sign of interest. Jack was glad. He wanted to be solitary. He made his way to Row D and stood bare headed before Cocky Shuttleworth's grave. Since the end of the war, the boy's death had remained with Jack as a symbol of all the senseless slaughter. In writing his letter this evening though, Jack had revealed to himself that at least there was some meaning in what had happened. It was no comfort to young Cocky Shuttleworth or his bereaved family. But Jack made a pledge there and then to assuage the guilt of his own survival and honour the sacrifice of the boy by doing everything he could to bring about the wedding, unofficial though it might be, between a Catholic and Protestant.

VII

'Come on now, love. Time to rise and shine.' Kathleen bent to shake Niamh awake. It was a Saturday morning, pale sunlight filtering through the thin curtains making the light soft and warm, the dust motes dancing. She paused, looking down fondly at her sleeping daughter, who didn't stir. It was close in the room and Kathleen was aware of the little girl's small-creaturely smell, overlaid with the faint remains of Pears soap from the previous night's bath.

As she laid a gentle hand on Niamh's shoulder, she noticed the little girl's arm was tucked above her head under the pillow as she slept. She was holding something in her hand. Niamh stirred and her eyelids fluttered. She stretched, but still her arm remained hidden. Kathleen lifted the edge of the pillow. Niamh was too sleepy to realise what was happening. In her hand, she was holding a post-card. With a lurch of emotion, Kathleen recognised it as one of Jack's sent recently to the little girl.

Kathleen struggled to contain the wave of anger that rose and curled within her. Over and over again she had lectured Niamh on the need to keep their letters and post-cards secret and safe from prying eyes. Kathleen kept them in her needlework box, which had a natty false bottom, concealing a storage area where she placed her precious keepsakes. Niamh had helped herself without permission. Kathleen couldn't imagine the ructions if her Mam or Da caught their grand-daughter in possession of such a thing.

Kathleen snatched the post-card from her daughter's grasp.

'You've been in the sewing basket without asking,' Kathleen began. 'How many times have I to tell you, we must leave the letters and cards from Jack safe in there? If you want to see him again, you must do as I say.'

Niamh sat up in bed rubbing her eyes and looking

miserable. 'It's my card. I like to have it. It says, "Lots of love from Jack" on it.'

'I know, I know. But I can't seem to get through to you if your Nan and Grand-Da find out there'll be hell to pay.'

'I don't understand why Nan and Grand-Da don't like Jack. We like him. He's nice. Why can't they?'

'Holy Mother of God, Niamh, have I not told you over and over again why not. It's not about who he is but what he is. My Mam and Da think belonging to a different Church makes you a different person because you have different beliefs. And they think Proddies want to do us harm.'

'Do they want to harm us?'

'Some of them do. Not Jack.'

'Is that why Grand-Da calls them Proddy bastards?'

'Niamh, I've told you before, you mustn't use words like that.'

'Grand-Da does.'

'Well Grand-Da shouldn't. And neither should you. I want you to promise me never to use those words again and to leave my sewing basket alone.'

The little girl sat on the side of her bed, looking at her toes. 'But it's my post-card.'

Kathleen rubbed her brow with her fingers and fought for calm. She did not want to lose control and let the wave of anger break. If she began shouting, she might never stop. As the time for Jack's arrival in Belfast drew near, she was aware of a terrible edginess. What had been a comforting dream was about to become a hurtling reality that would test her. Every day was a tight-rope walk. It was as much as she could do to keep herself on the high-wire without dealing with Niamh's difficulties as well.

Before she replied to the little girl, she began to busy herself folding away some of Niamh's clean clothes. She found the process steadied her and she was able to speak reasonably. She was, after all, glad about Niamh's affection for Jack. She didn't want to discourage such feelings.

'It is your post-card. But you must let me look after it for you. You've been so good all these months. In a week or two he'll be here and we can have a fine time together. But only if you're a good girl. All right? Now get on with you and get dressed.'

'Sorry.' The tone was unapologetic. The face sulky. Niamh stood and pulled her nightgown over her head, then, as if exhausted, sat back down on the side of the bed.

'Will we fly the kite again when Jack comes?'

'That's what he promises every time he writes to you, isn't it?'

'When will he be here?'

'I've just told you. A couple of weeks. But you mustn't breathe a word to your Nan or Grand-Da, darling girl. If you want to see Jack again and be with him, you have to trust me on this.'

Niamh nodded her assent though her eyes were still troubled. She tugged her vest over her head. Kathleen went back to her task folding clothes away in the drawers, hoping the child was mollified for now. It made her feel sick with anxiety trying to navigate this territory. It tested her certainty. In the wake of the bust up with Kevin, she'd been dismayed when her Da repeated the accusations Kevin had made about Jack. She thought it was spiteful nonsense. The idea of Jack as a gun-runner didn't seem right. He was always quiet and gentle with her. Yet a seed of doubt lingered. What if he had not told her the truth? What if he was still involved somehow with the UVF? She knew he couldn't be. It didn't make sense. And yet. And yet . . . It made her long to see him and talk to him and have his reassurance. His letters were all well and good, but she wanted to look into his eyes and see the loving kindness there.

Kathleen put away the last of the clothes. The Saturday morning was set fair to be spoilt. Niamh had given up on getting dressed and was playing with a rag doll, muttering to it in an inaudible undertone, a look of sulky concentration on her face. Sharing her troubles, Kathleen guessed.

'I tell you what,' Kathleen said. 'Let's go to the park. We haven't been for a while.' Since their winter visits with Jack, Ormeau Park had become a special place for Kathleen and Niamh. It was where they went to escape the pub and be alone together. 'Going to the park' had become a code between them. It was the antidote to troubles and the place of fun. It was where conversations both serious and silly could be enjoyed. It was where they could relax together and share their secrets.

In response, Niamh said something to her doll, then stood and regarded her mother with solemn eyes her head on one side, as if considering. After a moment she said, 'That would be . . .' She paused for dramatic effect, looking coy and lifting one leg, bending it at the knee—a physical containment before delivering the verdict: 'grand.' On the pronouncement she threw her doll aside and ran and hugged Kathleen's legs. 'Thank you, Mammy.'

'Let's get a move on then. Maybe I can persuade your Grand-Da he doesn't need me and we'll take some sandwiches for lunch.'

'Grand, grand, grand. Can Rosie come as well?'

Rosie was Niamh's rag-doll. 'Of course she can. But you'll have to look after her mind. I've got enough to think about with you, little darling.'

A few minutes later, Niamh was dressed and they clattered down the stairs together to have some breakfast and plead for a holiday from the pub. The old man was in a good humour. Permission was granted.

They took the tram then walked through the sunshine into the park. On the lawns below the rotunda, Kathleen spread a blanket for their picnic. They played 'catch' with a rubber ball until it was time for lunch. Flopping onto the blanket sweating and breathless, Kathleen poured out glasses of home-made lemonade which they drank thirstily before unwrapping egg and lettuce sandwiches from their grease proof paper. They ate in silence for a while, watching other people strolling, or playing or just lying in the sun.

'It will be grand when Jack comes back won't it Mammy?' Niamh looked at Kathleen earnestly.

The question came out of the blue. The little girl must have been sitting thinking about him. After all these months away, Kathleen wondered at her daughter's bond with Jack. She had never exhibited anything like the same attachment to Kevin. Maybe that wasn't so surprising given her husband's unpredictability and his prolonged disappearances which had now become permanent absence. But there was something in the quality of Jack's response to the little girl that had made an instant connection. Perhaps Niamh sensed his love for her, his gentleness.

'It will. Of course, it will.' As Kathleen spoke, a little thrill of nerves down her spine made her shiver, despite the sunshine. Someone treading on her grave. She hoped nothing would happen to spoil everything. The political future made everything seem uncertain. The shootings in the south in defence of the self-proclaimed Nationalist government made the atmosphere in Belfast tense and uneasy. There was a sense of trouble brewing, though what form it might take wasn't clear. Kathleen heard the gossip in the tap-room as well as her father's commentary on the situation. All of it suggested that in Belfast two communities were living side-by-side hoping for different futures.

How could you explain such things to a child? The idea of living in peace and not having to explain seemed wonderful to Kathleen. Yet it meant moving away from everybody and everything she loved. It made her feel restless thinking this way. She wanted him here so she could talk to Jack, hold him and feel his goodness. Convince herself a future with him was possible. Unaccountably, as she considered these things, she had a recollection of his eye-lashes. She noticed them the very first time he said 'Good-day' to her on the tram. He had long curling eye-lashes and his eyes seemed to hold something deep and mysterious. Passion perhaps. She remembered feeling defenceless against his gaze.

'What are you thinking about Mammy?'

'I was thinking maybe we should have brought the kite today and flown it.'

'The little girl looked stricken and shook her head. 'We can't do that. We can only fly the kite when Jack's here. Those are the rules. It's not fair to fly it without him.' Niamh spoke with solemn conviction.

'Would you like Jack to be your Daddy?' Kathleen uttered the words before she'd thought about them. Surprised herself. It was as if finding Niamh with Jack's postcard had thrown her. The enormity of the words seemed to hang in the air like a threat. She had a queasy intimation that things were slipping from her control.

Niamh considered her mother with serious eyes. 'You mean Jack could be my new Da?'

Kathleen struggled to keep her voice from wavering. 'That's what I'm thinking.'

The little girl looked puzzled. 'What about my auld Father. And Nan and Grand-Da?' She began pulling at blades of grass fretfully with one hand and scattering them to the wind.

'I've told you before haven't I? Me and your Da had a falling out. Like sometimes at school you have a quarrel with your friends. With me and your Da it was serious. We found we didn't like each other anymore. He hit me. Which people should never do. And so we have been separate ever since. Don't you think you and me have been happier?'

Niamh thought about this for a while and then said, 'I like Jack.'

'Ay, I know you do, And so do I. And so would your Nan

and Grand-da if only they'd let themselves.'

'So how can Jack be my Daddy?'

'Don't you worry about that now. Just as long as I know you wouldn't mind. That's the important thing. We have to wait till he comes back, and then see.'

Niamh nodded. She seemed satisfied by this. She finished her egg sandwich and Kathleen gave her a homemade iced bun. There was a relief to both of them in the end of the awkward conversation. But still, Kathleen felt anxious and wondered if she'd done the right thing by asking Niamh. If it didn't work out, what damage might she have done?

After lunch, Kathleen suggested they should play ball again. They left their things on the blanket and played on the grass nearby. As they tossed the ball between them, Kathleen watched the trajectory. Sometimes Niamh caught it, other times she lost concentration and she dropped it. The arc of the ball through the air, the uneven rhythm of catch and spill made Kathleen think of her life's decisions. The way everyone must act without knowledge of the consequences. You made decisions in faith and hoped the arc would come home to safe hands, whatever the risks involved. As she threw the ball to her daughter again, she prayed that what she had begun with Jack would lead to a secure ending for her and her little girl. To be wrapped in safe hands seemed something worth praying for. As long as that enclosure didn't become another trap; as long as spill did not spell disaster.

VIII

On Jack's first night home in July, his Mam made a fuss as usual. There was a special tea with ham and tongue and cold chicken—the small goods all courtesy of Hughie McCullough. There were boiled new potatoes and a nice salad, too, with lettuce, tomatoes and cucumber and home-made mayonnaise. There were bottles of Guinness for Jack and Hughie, while the girls had lemonade. Jack's Mam stood by her chair at one end of the table, sawing slices of new-baked bread from the loaf under her arm, while singing 'You're as welcome as the flowers in May to dear old Donegal.' Judging by her wide smile, the geographical slippage didn't seem to bother her. Jack hated it all. He could feel the indigestion beginning before he'd started eating. He would have been uncomfortable under any circumstances, but the knowledge that his purpose in Belfast was to persuade Kathleen and Niamh to leave with him and thus betray his family made it ten times worse.

Jack was sitting next to Lily and opposite Eileen and Hughie. His parents were at either end of the table. His Mam dished out the bread, and the family helped themselves from the other plates and bowls crowded on the festive table. Hughie was in the position of Mr Bountiful the Benefactor, which made him even more intolerable than usual in Jack's eyes. He was over-confident and over-familiar. There was something in his manner which seemed to suggest it was only natural that women should adore him and men admire. He called Jack's Mam 'Mrs Y' and she responded to the young man with a flirtatious anxiety to please. Hugh passed the plates of meat with a proprietorial air, which made Jack sick and reminded him of the Christmas turkey, which had been similarly donated.

Once plates were loaded, Jack's Da uttered a grim and

minimalist Grace. His Mam then raised her glass in a toast. 'Welcome Home, son,' she said. 'I wish we saw more of you. But we must make the most of it while you're here.' The others raised their glasses. His father, stone-faced, sipped water.

There was silence for a few moments punctuated only by the light tinkle of knives and forks on crockery.

It came as no surprise that it was Hughie who spoke first. His theme took up where Jack's Mam had left off, bringing a sly smile to the auld woman's face as if they had rehearsed the gambit.

'Do you not think of coming home for good, Jack? Back where you belong.'

'I don't.' Jack hoped his curt reply would be enough to silence Hughie. No such luck.

'Your Mammy and sisters miss you and we'll be needing all the good men we can find soon enough.'

The women murmured their assent. Jack's Da gave Hughie a narrow look but said nothing. Jack felt the acid stir in his guts.

'I've a good job and a good life where I am, thanks.'

'But it's not home is it?' Eileen chipped in.

'It's home to a lot of lads I knew and fought with.'

Jack's Da, usually taciturn on these occasions, spoke in a low growl. 'Let the dead bury their dead. There's troubles enough amongst the living to look to. The Sinn Feiners are everywhere and if we don't look to it we'll be part of a Papist nation before you can blink. I would have thought you might want to play a part in protecting your birthright.'

Hughie didn't allow Jack time to reply. 'Ay,' he said. 'There are exciting times ahead. Did you hear what Carson said at Finaghy just now Jack? He's still the man he was in 1912. I was there. The crowd were wild for him. He says what we all think. He spoke out against Home Rule. Said we wouldn't tolerate Sinn Fein. "We will re-organise," he says, and everyone was cheering and shouting. And it's beginning, Jack, we are re-organising.'

'I won't be joining you. I'm only here for a wee holiday.' Jack had deliberately left his visit until after July 12th, thinking to miss the Orange parades with their Lambeg drums and military enthusiasm. But it seemed he couldn't avoid the incendiary consequences.

Still, Hughie refused to back off. He carried on, his tone all innocence. 'You surprise me Jack. Your sister tells me you were a grand auld Orangeman once upon a time. Signed the Covenant and all.'

'That was then, this is now.'

'A promise is a promise, Jack. Isn't that right?'

'Circumstances change.'

'A wee bird told me you helped the boys out with a little import and export trade in 1913.'

Jack's Mam and Da exchanged a glance. His Mam said, 'We're proud of what you did son. It was the Haslam's told our Eileen about it.'

Jack looked at Eileen's smiling face. He wasn't enjoying this.

'There's nothing much to be proud of. It was a long time ago.'

'But it's the same fight we have on again now.' Hughie was indefatigable. 'We have to stand strong against the Republicans. There's moves afoot to throw the Fenians out of the shipyards and mills. That will be a start.'

'Not before time,' Jack's Da interjected. 'They had no right coming up here and taking our boys' jobs while they were at the war.'

Jack couldn't help himself. 'That sounds like ripe auld nonsense to me. There were plenty of Catholics fought and died in the war.'

'That's beside the point.' His Da gestured with a belligerent fork. 'It's what's going on here that matters. We must get rid of the enemy within.'

'Now then, Father,' Jack's Mam sounded nervous. 'There's no need to get worked up. We're for having a nice tea for Jack. Mebbe we should leave the auld politics for a bit and keep things sociable.'

'Don't be so soft, woman. Hughie's right. Jack should come home where he belongs. Get his job back on the trams and help out the boys.'

Jack said nothing. He continued to eat but it was an effort to get anything down. He concentrated on chewing. He felt as if the food might choke him. The silence round the table grew taut, the tension palpable.

'You have nothing to say to me?' Jack's Da was not for letting go. 'You sit at our table, filling your face, yet you want nothing to do with us. I can't understand what kind of a man you've become. I brought you up decent to respect your God and your country. But you don't seem to care about home or family or faith anymore. I don't understand you living in foreign parts. I don't. Isn't Belgium a Catholic country?'

'I fought side-by-side with Catholics in the war. Can't you see how that might make a difference?'

'I cannot. It has nothing to do with the situation here. That's what I'm talking about. Your loyalty here.'

Jack couldn't stomach anymore. 'If you'll excuse me. I've had enough,' he said. 'Thank you, Mammy.'

He got up from the table and was out of the back door before anyone could say anything more. He fumbled for his cigarettes with shaking fingers. He thought he might be sick. He didn't want to risk any of them following him, so he let himself out the backyard door into the cobbled alleyway that ran between the backs of the houses. He stood and lit his cigarette, then walked on, trying to calm down and already wondering how he could face going back inside.

He had not walked far when he heard the clatter of a door being banged to on its latch. He turned and saw Lily running after him. He was surprised. He thought she was cowed by her Mam and Da. She never said 'boo' at the table. Sat with her head down, silent and thoughtful. It had been the same at Christmas. Now, she came up to him a nervous lop-sided grin on her face. Breathless, she stood in front of him in her cheap cotton dress. It was white with a pattern of purple flowers.

'I thought I'd keep you company. I could do with a cigarette,' she said.

'Since when have you smoked?'

'Since I was wee. Come on, be quick and give me one.'

'I bet Mam and Da don't know. They'd kill me if they saw me giving you a fag.'

'There's a lot Mam and Da don't know.' Lily took the proffered cigarette and waited while Jack struck a match for her. She took a puff and exhaled theatrically. 'I don't believe you're scared of them.'

'You can't argue with them. It's like banging your head on granite.'

'That's why I don't bother,' Lily said. 'I keep my thoughts to myself.'

'Chasing after me won't do you any favours with them.'

'I'm sick of their mithering.'

'Ay, well. You have to live with them. I don't.'

They walked along the backs, smoking their cigarettes, Jack wondering at his sister's vehemence. Suddenly, she seemed all grown up.

'I wish I didn't.'

'Didn't what?'

'Have to live with them. It's not so easy for a girl, Jack. Getting out of it. I have this friend, Bridget. She wants me to go to evening classes with her. I want an education, Jack. I want to understand why people are always at each other's throats. I want a different kind of life.'

Jack gazed at the brick walls of the house backs, rust

coloured and uniform. They seemed to close in, mean and forbidding, as if to press everyone who came from round here into their allotted place. A narrow alley between the shit-houses. Catholic or Protestant. He thought of tram rails. He thought of planting roses in the gardens of the dead. He thought of his own hopes of escape with Kathleen which involved the betrayal of his family. He looked down at the cobblestones and wondered if his heart had become as hard. He should try to be kind to Lily.

'You don't agree with yon man Hughie and Eileen, then?'

'I do not. Mam and Da, Eileen and Hughie are full of the auld bitterness. I've no time for it. I keep my eyes and ears open about this town. You can find fear and hatred pure and simple or you can find the kindest, grandest people on earth. The best and the worst. Protestant and Catholic has nothing to do with it.'

Jack gave her a wry grin. 'You're very wise all of a sudden.'

'It isn't sudden.' Lily sounded stung. 'I've had all my life to think about it.'

'I didn't mean to offend you.'

'I know you agree with me. And I know why.'

Jack gave Lily a sharp glance. 'Like I said in there. I fought beside Catholics during the war. I saw there was no difference between us.'

They reached the end of the alleyway. Lily stopped. Jack guessed she didn't want to be seen on the road with a fag on. She stood with one arm under her breasts, her hand cupping the other elbow as she smoked, waving the cigarette around as if smoking it was a defiant rebellion. It was a warm evening. Jack could see a glisten of sweat at her hairline.

'That's not the whole story, though, is it Jack?'

'I don't know what you mean.'

'I mean,' Lily said, looking him straight in the eye, 'Kathleen McCafferty.'

Jack was jabbed off-balance. He tried not to sound too

anxious. 'What would you know about Kathleen McCafferty?'

'Quite a lot, as it happens.' It was Lily's turn for a knowing smile. 'I know she's a Catholic and the mother of your child. I know she's married to Kevin O'Donell but she's had some kind of a bust up with him. I know she lives and works in a pub in Cromac Street. So I'm wondering if you might not be looking out for her.'

'Holy God, is there no end to the gossip in this town? How do you come by all of this?'

'It was Eileen who put me on to it first. We were going into town on the tram one day last year and 'Leen suddenly shouts out, "Look there, look there, it's Jack's auld flame." I only got a glimpse of her. The tram was moving that fast. And then 'Leen told me the tale. And how she hadn't seen Kathleen for a long time. Thought mebbe she'd left Belfast. "Not a word to Mam and Da" she says to me, and I swore not to tell. After that I kept my eyes and ears open. I seen her a time or two in Cromac Street, but no sign of a man. 'Leen says the same. She thinks O'Donnell might not be about anymore. Hughie reckons the police are after him. Says he's an IRA man.'

'I might have known Hughie would have something to say about it.' Jack walked on round the corner into the street. Lily ground out her cigarette beneath her heel and hurried to catch up.

'You're not mad at me for mentioning it, are you Jack? I'm on your side. I wanted you to know . . .'

'You have a nerve poking your nose into a man's business.'

'I'm not poking my nose. I'm trying to help. Can't you see, I'm not like the others? If it's about love we're talking, I don't think Catholic or Protestant has anything to do with it.'

'Who said anything about love?'

'I'm guessing.' Lily was trotting beside him, trying to keep up with Jack's angry stride. 'Will you slow down and listen to me a minute. You remember I spoke about my friend Bridget at the mill. She's Catholic. Her Mammy knows Kathleen's.

They go to the same Church. Bridget had some gossip from her Mammy how there'd been trouble just after Christmas between Kathleen and Kevin O'Donell and how it was all on account of you meeting with her. So it set me wondering. . .'

Jack felt as if someone had punched the breath out of him. He was dizzy with violent implications. It seemed as if half of Belfast knew his business. He had thought all was secret between him and Kathleen; they would elope and be gone before anyone knew a thing. The question was if Lily knew so much, who else did? And how much dare he say to Lily?

'Come on, Jack. Say something, why don't you? I didn't mean to upset you. You don't need to worry. I've not said anything. Not even to Eileen. She doesn't approve of Bridget.'

'I bet she doesn't. How did you become pals?'

'I don't know. We just took a fancy to each other. I saw her reading a book on the tram. It made me curious. I looked out for her at the mill, said hello one lunch time. We just clicked. She's clever and bright and funny and kind and . . . I don't know what. She's a true friend, Jack. We've become close.'

Something in the intensity of Lily's words moved Jack. He thought about what she'd said—the mysteries of human connection. The way Lily had confided in him made him feel he could trust her with his story.

'It was like that with Kathleen,' he said. 'I didn't mean to betray anybody or anything. I fell in love with her those years ago. I tried to deny it and run away. But now the only thing that makes my life make sense is to be with her. You mustn't breathe a word. Not to anybody. Specially not to Bridget. Or Eileen. This O'Donnell is a dangerous man. I don't want him or Hughie getting wind. And there's no point trying to persuade Mam and Dad. You have to keep this to yourself.'

'I will, of course, Jack. This is why I wanted to talk to you, private like. To let you know I was on your side. There's troubles coming soon. Lots of rumours about evicting Catholics from the yards and mills. I heard a whisper it might start tomorrow.

I reckon it's as well for you to know what's what.'

'It's good of you. You've a wise auld head on those young shoulders.'

Lily gave him a bright-eyed smile, obviously pleased to be praised.

They walked on in silence now, round the block until they were back in the alleyway behind the house.

'I'm not looking forward to going back in,' Jack said.

'It'll be fine. We'll get round the Mammy. Eileen and Hughie will be off courting, and Da will be at the hearth with his cup of tea and his newspaper. Act like nothing's happened. Trust me.'

'You're a grand girl, Lily. Come here with you.' The evening was cooling. Velvet air giving way to cool cotton sheets of breeze. Jack held her to him and rested his chin on the top of her head. They stood there for some moments in each other's arms, brother and sister, with the first stars peeping fitful through high cloud and the purple summer sky throwing a mysterious robe over the relentless brick of the terraced houses and the alleyways.

IX

The following day, Jack took the tram up the Ormeau Road towards Cromac Street and the markets. He was jittery with anticipation. He fidgeted with his ticket, rolling and unrolling it; his leg bounced; his eyes were restless; his thoughts unfocused. Fixing a rendezvous with Kathleen had been difficult. Her days were busy. Between taking Niamh to and from school and her shifts in the pub, there were few moments for leisure. In their last exchange of letters they had settled on the markets as the best option. Kathleen went there regularly to shop before the pub opened at lunch time. Though there was always the possibility of being seen by unfriendly eyes, the same was true anywhere in the city. There were no places where privacy was guaranteed. At least here they could pretend their meeting was an accident—two old friends bumping into each other and having a chat.

The thought of seeing her again after six months was both thrilling and daunting. All his hopes for the future were focused on Kathleen and Niamh. They had become his compass, providing a direction and purpose beyond his work. He lived his life within the cycles of nature and within earshot of the dead. All of his experience from blood and bone to seed and flower, from decay to fertiliser once more illustrated the truth he heard in the voices of his slaughtered comrades. No soldier he'd ever served with had ever spoken of hatred for the Hun. They spoke of friends and family and home. They served and died for love. And as they marched forward to kill and be killed, Jack had learnt the meaning of love thine enemy. All he wanted was to love Kathleen and Niamh. It seemed simple but it wasn't so. The perversity of human beings made sure of that.

When he alighted from the tram, Jack experienced the warmth of the day as an oppression. His shirt was already sticking to his back. The air seemed thick and heavy, as if a thunderstorm might be coming. Yet there was no sign of cloud. The light was clotted with ripe sunshine which fell against pavement and brick without fully illuminating either. It was as if the urban landscape sucked the brightness from the day, absorbing the heat and radiating it back into the streets stale and shop-worn.

He arrived at the markets early. Of course he was early. How could he not be early? All he wanted was to see her, hear her, be with her. He wanted to erase the doubts that had arisen in their correspondence. In the spaces between words, in the gaps between the lines, Jack imagined threats thriving like weeds between the ordered rows of a flower bed. He wanted to make all well in their garden. He had a sudden memory of his encounter with Annie Hargreaves in his allotment in Manchester. He shivered in the sunlight as he recalled the way that had ended. The shame and humiliation of being thrown out of the house. The sneering detectives. Annie's face with the hurt and anger of betrayal written across it, making her eyes hard as shining stones.

Jack took a turn round the market. He thought he would be less conspicuous that way rather than standing by the entrance. The place was brighter than at Christmas. The scent of cut flowers and vivid strawberries mingled with the heavier odour from the cheese stalls. Tomatoes, lettuce and spring onions were also abundant signalling the season of salad with mayonnaise for tea. The atmosphere, though, was strangely at odds with the celebration of seasonal produce. Jack wondered if it was his paranoia. Everywhere he looked he sensed tension and expectation. Both stall-holders and shoppers had watchful eyes, and closed-in faces, the exaggerated carefulness of the fearful trying to second-guess attitudes and allegiances. Where conversations were in progress, they seemed to be withdrawn, clandestine affairs; heads together, low-voiced exchanges with glances darting everywhere on the look-out for eavesdroppers or intruders.

Towards the end of his second circuit, Jack saw Kathleen walk into the market and stand for a moment, uncertain. Without thinking, he waved and hurried towards her. She was wearing a frock to match the strawberries and a green cardigan for their leaves. He felt his throat constrict and his heart battering with the beauty of her. He felt like a man running into the sea bracing for the exhilaration of the waves, his body tense and tingling as he came up to her.

She turned and saw him and gave a tentative smile of relief, before she looked round to see if anyone was observing them. Jack had forgotten all his forebodings in the excitement of seeing her. He clasped her to him, because he couldn't help himself. Because he must. He held her there in his arms, while she gasped, 'Jack, Jack you shouldn't. Not here.' Then, 'Let me look at you. Is it really you?'

'It is me, as sure as life,' he said. 'My God, you're beautiful.'

She pushed him away gently. 'We should walk.'

'Ay, all right.' He didn't want to let go, but knew he must. For the first few steps they took together, he felt shaky as if his passion had fevered him, as if his body was made unfamiliar to him. He heard her speaking but couldn't assimilate her words. He saw her soft inviting lips moving, glimpsed her teeth and tongue. He wanted to stroke her face and trace her eyebrows with his finger. He wanted to stop her mouth with kissing and breathe his love into her. He didn't want words. He wanted to move into the delirium beyond words in which people are changed by the dance of intimacy. But he could not. And now she was saying, 'You're not listening Jack, you're not with me.'

'I am, I am,' he protested. 'I'm that glad to see you. You haven't changed your mind about me, about us? If you'd only agree, we could go as soon as you like. I have the money for the tickets. I have rented the cottage. I have bought new sheets and blankets. Everything is ready. It's up to you now, to decide.'

'You make it sound easy Jack.'

'It is.'

'There are troubles coming here.'

'All the more reason to get out of it. Is O'Donnell about?'

'I don't know. He's not been near me. After that time he showed violence to me, my Da said he'd keep him away. But he could be in Belfast for all I know. My Da plays his cards close sometimes. And with all the fighting in the south and the wild talk up here, God knows what's going on. What I do know is they both say the same about you.' She glanced at him and pressed her lips together as if nerving herself to speak further.

'Go on with you, then. What do they say about me?'

'I don't want to believe anything bad about you, Jack. I want to believe in us. In a future. But I have to be sure. For Niamh's sake. You must see that. And before I even think of leaving my home and people. I can't do that unless I feel certain. No doubts. No hesitations.'

'Will you get on with it, for the love of God?'

She lowered her voice, so he had to lean in to hear her. 'They say you were a gun-runner. For the UVF in 1913. They say it makes you a legitimate target. I don't want to believe them. Honestly, I don't. I just want to hear you say it's not true.'

Jack looked about him. 'I wish we could have this talk somewhere else.'

'I'm not hearing you deny it, Jack.'

'A bit of privacy would go a long way.'

'You know that's not possible. We agreed this was the best place. You're frightening me, Jack. Just tell me it isn't true.'

Jack suddenly felt claustrophobic as if every eye in the place were following them. A butcher in a blue and white striped apron behind his counter sharpening a knife seemed to take an inordinate interest in them. Two old dears having a gossip paused in their talk as they passed. A group of blokes at the coffee stall, market traders maybe, with their fags on gave them a once over. Sweat prickled at the back of Jack's neck and above his top lip. He took hold of Kathleen's elbow and attempted to steer her the quickest way out of the place. She shrugged him off, her indignation beginning to show.

'You must let me explain,' Jack said. 'I will not lose you over this. I can't speak surrounded by other folk. Come onto the street with me here.' He propelled her out of the main entrance and walked by the outside wall a little way. There were still people about but it was less crowded; he felt less hemmed in. He stopped and reached for his cigarettes.

'I'm not liking this, Jack. I'm not for jumping out of the frying pan with Kevin into the fire with you. I won't do it, do you hear me? It's hard enough running off with a Prod, never mind one who's a bloody auld Orangeman.'

'Will you listen to me, for Christ's sake, Kathleen? I did some driving for a bloke in Manchester, carrying the guns. I was young and stupid and I'd just heard you were wed to O'Donnell and your Da was threatening what he would do if I tried to get in touch with you. I was angry. It was a way of getting my own back. It was stupid. I've regretted it ever since. I thought it would be clear to you—what with me working in Belgium and all. I've had my fill of the politics and the violence. I've seen enough killing to last me. And like I've told you seeing young Cocky Shuttleworth dying with the beads in his fingers changed me. You have to believe me Kathleen. I'm not the silly young fool I was in Manchester.'

Kathleen looked angry. She stood staring at her feet.

'Don't give up on me. I have to tell you the rest of the story Kathleen. I'm a changed man since the war. I won't have anything to do with the fighting here again. Never. Listen to me, will you? This is important. You remember what I wrote to you about Cocky. The way he died?'

Kathleen nodded her assent.

'Well, there's more. After he died, I was hit trying to get back to our lines. I was unconscious for a while and then came to. Night was falling. I managed to stagger on for a while but I was exhausted and couldn't go any further. I collapsed, lying there in the mud surrounded by the filth and debris of the battle. The next thing I knew I was being lifted. Some stretcher bearers found me. It took six of them wading through the sludge to get me out. They took me to a Casualty Clearing Station. There were rows and rows of us lying on stretchers waiting to be seen. I had the handkerchief you gave me when I left Belfast in my pocket. I held it clenched in my fist and I thought of you Kathleen. And I thought of the child and wondered if it was a boy or a girl. And I prayed Kathleen, like I've never prayed before that I would be able to get back and be with you and make everything right between us. Because I knew as I lay there, gazing at the stars that it was you I loved and no other. You were in my mind, see, and I was praying and this priest came along to one of the Jocks who was lying there. I watched and heard him murmuring the prayers over this bloke, saying the words properly. I felt bad because Cocky hadn't had it done right. I began to feel guilty. As if I'd done wrong somehow by praying over him. Anyway, when the priest came by, I stopped him. Said I wanted to speak with him. "You're one of ours," he said. I told him I wasn't a Catholic. He said he meant Irish from Belfast. He gave me a cigarette and lit it for me. I told him about Cocky and what had happened and asked if I'd done wrong. Do you know what he said to me Kathleen? Do you? He said, "Bless you, son. You've done a wonderful thing. We're all God's creatures to be sure. You have done no wrong." And before he left, he blessed me again and he said, "May God go with you, all the days of your life." And since then Kathleen I've felt blessed. And I feel as if my prayers are about to be answered. So I'm not going to be getting mixed up in any auld politics or violence or shenanigans. Do you see? Do you understand what I'm saying? I was blessed by a Catholic priest.'

Kathleen stood silent her hands by her side. Jack searched her face like a man trying to read a map of unknown territory. He could see the contours but he didn't know what they meant. She looked blank, stunned, as if she didn't understand at all. He looked into her eyes. She raised her arms and took a step towards him. As she clasped him, he put his hands to her face, letting them explore, making her known and familiar to him once again.

'Jack, Jack,' she said. 'I'm sorry I doubted you. You can understand surely. They wanted to make me hate you. Instead they've made me love you the more. Why haven't you told me that story before?'

'I don't know. It was never the right time until now.'

They stood there in the street holding on to one another heedless of the passers-by. Jack felt the warmth of her, the inviting softness. She smelt of lavender. Then she was whispering to him.

'I want to be with you Jack. You'll give me the courage, won't you? God knows I'll miss my Mammy and Da and the auld place, but I want to be free with you and I want our Niamh to grow up in peace and without hatred. I just wish it didn't have to be in Belgium.'

'Once you see the place, the re-building, you'll feel differently. And there's a whole community of English-speakers there—all the blokes and their families working like me for the War-Graves Commission.'

She shivered in the sunlight. 'I hate the thought of those cemeteries.'

'You wouldn't have to go near them, if they upset you. You could maybe get a job in one of the cafés or take up the needlework again, or just concentrate on looking after Niamh and the house. It doesn't matter. The only thing that matters is that you come with me. We'll give each other courage won't we? Isn't that what love means?'

She looked at him doubtfully. He stepped towards her. 'Come here with you.' He kissed her. There in broad daylight on the Belfast Street. She was compliant in his arms. It was as if they were daring anyone to object. After a minute or two Jack said, 'We should do your shopping.'

'Ay, we should. You can tell me some more about Wipers as we go.'

X

That evening, Kathleen was busier than usual behind the bar. From the moment the doors opened she had been rushed off her feet. So much so that her Da had been obliged to come and help her serve. Her arms ached already from pulling pints and many of the men who crowded into the place talking volubly were taking whiskey chasers. The atmosphere was crackling with aggressive energy. Tensions in the city had come to a head. As she worked, Kathleen gleaned news of what had gone on earlier in the day at the shipyards. It seemed the Prods had held a lunch-time meeting and resolved to throw any Catholic workers out. Violence had followed. Men had been viciously attacked. Some in the pub bore scars and blood-stains. Others had their shirts and overalls ripped at the neck where angry Prods had torn at their clothing, seeking the tell-tale medallions, the sign of their faith. There were tales of men jumping into the lough and swimming for it; there were others who'd been carted to hospital. Kathleen listened to the seethings about reprisals with fear in her heart. Apparently trams carrying Protestant workers home had been stoned. Some had been boarded and beatings administered. Kathleen's Da engaged in heated conversation with several of his customers, asking for details and trying to get a sense of developments. Kathleen could see he was keeping a weather eye on the open doors. There was every chance that trouble could erupt nearby, living as they did in a largely Catholic area abutting the mainly Protestant enclave further down the Ormeau Road.

Kathleen tried to concentrate on her work, serving the drinks, handing back the change. In a rare lull she walked round and collected empty glasses. Her mind felt as crowded as the pub. Her earlier elation at resolving her doubts about Jack and the excitement of their plans was draining away into fear and anxiety. The sense of solidarity between the men in the pub, their shared identity forged by their sense of unity against a common enemy made Kathleen feel like a traitor. If Jack walked in now and they knew he was a Protestant, he would be lynched. Her Da's enthusiastic identification with his customers didn't help her. For the moment though there was nothing she could do, but carry on with her work under her father's instruction. And hope for the best.

Back behind the bar now, she was pulling pints again. As more drink was taken the noise levels rose and a fevered atmosphere of expectation began to foment. Then, a shout went up from the boys nearest the door. 'The Prods are marching from Donegall Pass. Our bhoys are coming down from the markets. Let's be ready for them. We'll show the bastards this time.'

Kathleen felt fear—a cold stone in the pit of her stomach.

'What will we do, Da?' Kathleen asked.

By way of reply, he raised his voice to the assembled company. 'Steady lads. I don't want any fighting in the house. If there's to be fisticuffs let it be on the street. I have my wife and daughter here and my livelihood to protect. Think-on. The first sign of trouble in here and it's out with all of you.'

'Don't be a spoil-sport, Sean. You used to like a good fight. Don't worry, we'll be out of here mob-handed if the Prods come by. Won't we boys? We'll send the fuckers back down the road so we will.'

'I'm all for giving them a hiding, just not in my pub.' Kathleen's Da winked at her. 'We'll be all right, trust me,' he said to her.

'I think we should stop serving.'

'I don't think it's come to that yet. We're making a good few bob extra. It's handy money. You just keep the beer and whiskey flowing. Let me look after the rest.'

Kathleen did as she was told. Another rowdy surge of men entered the pub, making the place more crowded than ever.

There was a crush at the bar. They seemed intent on getting as much drink into them as quick as they could. Kathleen hated the fevered atmosphere but there was nothing she could do. She continued to work as fast as she could. Her father was doing the same. He looked and sounded as if he was enjoying himself. Encouraging the enthusiasm.

A shout from the door. 'They're coming on now. Let's be having you. We'll stand and fight them, so we will.'

A great cheer went up. Sean McCafferty bellowed at the top of his voice. 'All right lads, those of you for fighting outside with you. I'm locking up now. I won't have my pub wrecked. We'll keep the fighting outside if you don't mind.'

There were some shouts of disappointment from those still queuing to be served. Others started to spill out onto the street. Kathleen's Da moved from behind the bar and forced his way through to the door. He opened it wide and shouted again. 'Off youse go. Right now or you'll be locked inside. You have two choices: drinking or fighting. Make your minds up now.'

Through the open door, Kathleen heard a rhythmic beating and clanging and the wuther of the angry crowd. It sounded as if the Prods were approaching banging bin-lids with broom handles. Men poured from the pub onto the street. Some of the older men stayed behind clutching their pints.

'You can lock us in whenever you like, Sean,' one of them said not at all shamefaced. 'We'll take another drop with you, anytime.'

Kathleen mopped the dark-stained wood of the bar counter with a dish-cloth as she watched her Da urging men out of the pub and into the street. Everywhere was swimming in spilt beer, and she was glad of the respite to restore some order. From where she worked she couldn't see anything outside, but the noise disturbed her. It was like nothing she'd ever heard before. It was the sound of an angry mass of men, of boots on road stone, of shouts and rumbles and murmurings, a human kettle working up to the boil.

Her Da was locking the door now. She was relieved. He was a big man. She trusted him to keep them safe. She should go upstairs and make sure Niamh and her Mam were all right. She decided to finish the clearing up first. Kathleen washed and rinsed some glasses. Her Da joined her behind the bar again.

'There's going to be a terrible ruckus out there in a minute,' he said. 'You'd better get off upstairs and look to the wee one. I'll stay down here and make sure all's right.'

As he finished speaking, the noise outside rose to an angry roar. There was the sound of cracking glass and odd percussive thumps as bricks and cobbles began to be hurled. Kathleen was frozen, listening, her hand towelling the inside of a pint glass. The storm had broken before she'd had a chance to escape with Jack. She couldn't tell what ruin this might bring to their plans.

Her Da was more urgent now. 'Leave that,' he said. 'And get on out of it upstairs.'

She did as she was told. The noise of riot and affray outside became louder. The old house seemed to reverberate and shudder as if it was assailed by storm. Kathleen found her Mam and Niamh in her parents' bedroom. They were sitting on the bed, looking at a story book.

'I didn't want her to see,' Kathleen's Mam said by way of explanation.

'Why are the men fighting, Mammy?' Niamh asked.

'I don't know, my love,' Kathleen said. 'They're arguing over jobs at the shipyards.'

'But this isn't the shipyards.'

'No, it's not.'

'The truth is,' Kathleen's Mam said, 'our boys have been attacked by the Protestants.'

'Mammy, I don't want her . . .'

'She must know the truth. There's no point in lying to the

child.'

Niamh looked from one to the other on the verge of tears.

At that moment there was an awful hammering from below. Fists were banging on the front door. They were all quiet. Kathleen moved to Niamh and held her. They heard Sean McCafferty thumping up the stairs. He burst into the room.

'You'd better prepare yourselves. You might have to leave. They're after banging the door down. I don't know if it will hold.'

'Jesus, Mary and Joseph.' Kathleen's Mam crossed herself.

'Come on, Niamh, we'll get your coat on.' Kathleen was threatened by a rising tide of panic but knew she must remain calm for her daughter's sake.

'Ay, if they get in, be away out of it to Mary's place. With a bit of luck you'll be all right there. I'll stay here and see to the pub.' Kathleen's Da hurried off back downstairs, while her Ma shouted after him, 'For God's sake take care of yourself.'

With the sound of the door being battered, Kathleen urged Niamh along the corridor to her room. Fuelled by the rush of fear, her only thought was to get her daughter out of the pub to safety.

XI

Jack Young stepped outside and banged the front door behind him. It wasn't quite a slam, but enough to make a point. He was glad to be out of the close atmosphere of the back-kitchen and the enthusiasm of his Mam and Eileen for the fray.

His sisters had come home from work alight with the doings at the mill. Eileen was jubilant; Lily fearful. The workers there were all for showing solidarity with the ship-builders and throwing the Catholics out tomorrow. As Eileen trumpeted triumphalist excitement, Hughie came in breathing fire and brimstone. He wanted Jack to join him with the boys down the road. Jack had refused much to Eileen's disgust. He'd given the bold Hughie a few minutes start before setting forth himself on the excuse of looking out for his father. The old man hadn't turned up from work yet. The presumption was his tram from the city had been delayed in the rioting. In truth, Jack wanted to see what was happening up the road. He was concerned for Kathleen and Niamh. The position of the McCafferty pub might make it vulnerable.

The situation on the street was hectic now. Men strode in pairs or groups in the way they would to a football match. There was the same air of anticipation about them. But there was a crackling menace in the air as well. The improvised weapons they carried distinguished them from Saturday afternoon supporters. Some carried broom handles, others had hammers and mallets. One swung a cricket bat as he walked. A sixteen-year-old capered with a walking stick. Another group of young men had ruined a chair to make cudgels out of the arms and legs. God knows what else was concealed in pockets and down belts. It made Jack feel vulnerable. Like walking towards battle unarmed.

The scene at the junction of Donegall Pass and Cromac

Place was ominous. The soles of Jack's boots crunched on broken glass. The road was littered with stones. The fighting had evidently moved on. Jack could hear a commotion further up the road. Men began running towards the disturbance. The crowd had driven their adversaries back into Cromac Street. Jack began to jog along, the familiar sensation of fear in his guts. Adrenalin. As if he were going over the top again. He wondered if Kathleen and Niamh were still at her father's pub. He hoped they'd had the sense to get out of it before any trouble started. He would fight if he had to, unarmed or not.

The evening was warm. Sweat was running off him. No trams were coming down the road. As he turned into Cromac Street he could see why. A hundred men or more were spread across the road. Some youths wielding bats and sticks and pieces of broken furniture were systematically smashing the windows of the shops, the glass shattering in a series of bangs like grenades exploding. Others returned with interest the thrown bricks, stones, and bottles being hurled by the Catholics at the city end of the street. The chaotic rage and destruction sent familiar jolts of fear coursing through Jack's body. He wondered where the hell his Da had got to. Hoped he was not mixed up in any of this.

Jack came up to the edge of the action in time to see boys and men ransacking a spirit grocery. A frantic chain of looters passed bottles of beer and whiskey from hand to hand until the tops were knocked off and the contents swigged with crazed abandon. As the liquor kept coming, bottles were smashed to the ground and beer barrels broached, adding the smell of yeast and grain to the stink of human fury and fear. Shouts and screams to get away out of it followed, as men with crazed eyes struck matches and fire bombs made with bottles of spirits were hurled back into the place. Within minutes the shop was ablaze, acrid black smoke swirling into the street, the whoosh and crackle of the flames making a diabolical addition to the din.

The proprietor and his family ran for their lives towards the safety of their people at the top of the street. As friends and neighbours tried to help them, Jack saw men fall, beaten about the legs and chest and head by the Protestant boys fuelled by plundered booze and full of Orange pride. The crowds of men on both sides screamed abuse at each other as they hurled whatever missiles came to hand. Jack also heard away in the distance to the east the unmistakeable sound of gunfire and more explosions. Christ, if anybody started up with firearms here, there would be wholesale carnage.

As he surged forward with the rest of the crowd, he saw the next target of the rowdies was McCafferty's pub. The weight of numbers was in favour of the Prods, who were intent on looting the place despite the rain of missiles launched at them from the other side. They were going to give it the same treatment as the grocery.

A group of youths and young men were crowded round trying to force the door. Jack tried to shoulder his way through, but could make no headway. His stomach dipped and clenched as he heard the glass smashed in the door. It would be only a matter of time before the bolts were drawn and entry forced. There was nothing he could do, pressed as he was against the backs of other men wild to gain entry. He ducked as a stone came at his head. The ranks of the Catholics were advancing now. A pitched battle was in the offing.

A great cheer heralded the door going down. The crowd surged forward as men shoved their way into the pub. Jack pressed on at the back of the crowd until he could glimpse across the threshold. Inside, men were brawling, fighting with fists and anything else to hand as the attackers tried to drive out the patrons. Jack recognised old man McCafferty, a great bear of a man wielding a wooden bar stool to crown whoever came near him. He was screaming at the top of his lungs for Mother and Kathleen and the wean to get out of it as quick as they could. A man with blood coming from his ears lay motionless on the floor.

The roar of motor lorries heralded the arrival of the police. Jack watched as the vehicles drove through the Catholic ranks. Policemen spilled onto the road with batons ready to try to restore order. They were outnumbered. Jack thought they had no chance. Instead of joining the melee inside the pub, he ducked down to the house door. He arrived in time to see Kathleen, her mother and Niamh scuttling out of the place.

Some other boys made to follow him, throwing stones at the retreating women. Jack turned and faced down the assailants, feeling the fear deep in his guts as he yelled at them.

'Fuck off out of it, will you. And be men. You'll not be harming women and children, for Christ's sake. Go on, out of it. Back to the fight.'

They hesitated for a moment, uncertain whose side Jack was on. Jack moved towards them. 'Come on now lads,' he tried to sound reasonable though his voice was raised and his heart hammered. 'We don't want to get a name for harming women. We're not cowards are we?'

'Fuck off yerself,' they screamed. But then they turned back up the street towards the main game, leaving Jack to follow Kathleen, Niamh and Mrs McCafferty. They were hurrying away off into the streets behind the pub, looking nervously over their shoulders.

'Thanks Mister.' It was Kathleen's mother who addressed him over her shoulder. Kathleen was too busy struggling along with Niamh in hand to take any notice of him. He ran after them.

'I'll see you safe out of it,' he cried, as he caught up with them.

It was then Kathleen turned and saw him. Her eyes widened. 'My God,' she said. 'Jack?' She peered at him, breathless and disoriented.

'Ay, it's me all right. Come away with you. Let me carry the wean. We'll be right now.'

'Who is it Kathleen? Sure I've never seen him in my life before.'

'Never you mind now, Mammy. He's an auld friend. Come on let's get out of here.'

Jack hurried them along the street, knees bent and wobbling under the weight of his daughter. There was a fierce explosive whump behind them, and the darkness of the street was suddenly illuminated as flames burst from the downstairs windows of the pub.

'Sure they've fired the place. What will happen to my Da?'

'He'll look after himself, you'll see,' Kathleen's mother was steady. 'We need to get Niamh out of it.'

The little girl was crying as Jack carried her in his arms, her brown curls cradled in the palm of his hand. He tried to soothe her but there was little he could do. The noise of the riot and the choking smoke filling the air combined with the eerie glow from the leaping flames made the scene they were running from like some medieval vision of hell. Jack's only thought was to get to safety as quickly as possible.

As he hurried along, he hoped his Da was safe stuck in the city waiting for things to quieten down. He wasn't much concerned with Hughie. That boy could look after himself. Maybe a taste of real violence might calm him down a bit. Teach him a thing or two. Or not. It was hard to know what might change a man. Or if a man might change at all.

His father would consider him a traitor for what he was doing. His father would never change. Not now. But Jack didn't care. Kathleen and Niamh had to be made safe. That's all he knew, as they half-ran, half-walked as fast as they could away from the scene of the disaster and heard the evil cackle of machine gunfire from Ballymacarrett stain the night.

As soon as they were clear of the rioting, Jack set Niamh

on her feet. He knelt to her for a moment and wiped the snot and tears from her face with his handkerchief. Kathleen and her mother stood by watching impatiently.

Jack gave Niamh a hug and whispered to her. 'You'll be all right now. Safe as houses if we trot along here together. You trust me, don't you?'

Niamh nodded solemnly. 'I've been waiting for you to come.'

'Well here I am, right as rain.'

The little girl sniffed. 'Where's Grand-Da?'

'He'll be along in a minute, I'm sure. We need to get on with your Mammy now.'

Niamh turned away from Jack and took her mother's outstretched hand. Jack walked on the other side, so the little girl was between them. Mrs McCafferty walked in front, casting dubious glances over her shoulder, first at him, then at her daughter.

'We're for Aunt Mary's in the Falls,' Kathleen said to Jack. 'Where in the name of God did you come from?'

'I walked up the road to see what was happening. I was frightened for you.'

'You'll have to get out of it sharpish once we get over there.'

'Ay well. Let's get there first.'

It was a long and anxious walk. Behind them the twilight sky was lit with flames and smoke from burning buildings. Gunfire sounded sporadically from that direction and from Cromac Street to the south. Jack and his little party were not the only ones trekking away from the violence. There was a stream of people coming over from East Belfast, driven out by the rioting, heading towards relatives and friends in the Falls.

There was no chance of words with Kathleen. The presence of her mother was deterrent enough and Kathleen was busy encouraging Niamh, who began to complain of being tired. Jack offered to carry her again. This time he took her piggy-back, hoping this would be easier on his damaged shoulder, which was still aching from the previous haul.

As they tramped the length of Grosvenor Street, they were alarmed as several trucks bearing soldiers with rifles at the ready sped past in the direction they were walking. Kathleen glanced round and said, 'Trouble in front as well as behind by the looks of it.'

When they arrived at the junction with the Falls Road, they could hear shots and shouting in the streets to their left, but they were relieved to find the way to Kathleen's aunt's house was clear. Jack glanced over his shoulder to check on Niamh. She had put her hands over her ears. That kids should be witness to all this made Jack feel sick with anger. Warfare in the fields of France and Flanders was one thing– the wanton destruction of natural beauty part of the abomination. But to have battle joined on city streets putting women and children at risk made Jack feel ashamed, as if he were personally responsible. He was mortified that Niamh had to witness such scenes.

Mrs McCafferty strode ahead, then beat on the door, shouting to her sister-in-law to 'Open up quick.' Jack knelt to the pavement to let Niamh clamber from his back. The door opened. Jack glimpsed Kathleen's aunt, thin faced, severe hair like an iron basin, shrewd eyes peering from behind ancient eye-glasses. Mrs Mac wasted no time, bustling in explaining the situation as she went. Jack ushered Niamh past Kathleen and inside the house. 'Off you go, now,' he said. 'You're safe and sound now. I'll see you soon.'

'Bye Jack,' the little girl said. 'See you soon. We'll go to the park, won't we?'

'Ay, of course we will. Be good now and run inside.'

Niamh did as she was told. Kathleen said, 'You'd best get off, before there's more trouble. I don't want my Da to find you here.'

Before Jack could reply, Kathleen's mother reappeared on the door-step. 'I heard what young Niamh said. I know who you are and you'd best take heed. Sean will not take kindly to you hanging about. If he sees you, he'll take steps. I know he will. I'm grateful for your help tonight, but you must get away out of it and stay away, if you know what's good for you. And you,' she addressed herself to her daughter, 'need to get yourself inside as soon as you like.'

Jack nodded towards the auld woman in acknowledgement. He wasn't going to get involved in any wrangle with her. Instead, he looked to Kathleen. 'This mustn't change anything,' he said speaking low so Mrs McCafferty couldn't hear.

'Now's not the time, Jack. You must go. Get yourself home safe.'

'I'll go as soon as you tell me that what we said earlier still stands.'

A volley of shots rang out in the streets to the west of them between the Falls and the Shankill.

Kathleen shivered. 'Speak sense, man. We'll have to wait till all this trouble dies down.'

'What if it doesn't die down? We need to get Niamh out of it. As quick as we can.'

'I can't do this now, Jack. Will you get off home?'

The conversation was brought to an end by another intervention from Mrs McCafferty. 'Will you get yourself in here now,' she shouted at Kathleen, 'before I lock the door on you.'

Kathleen shrugged her shoulders at Jack, as if to say 'see what I mean?' She mouthed a word of thanks as she stepped past him and into the house. She looked back at him with troubled eyes, as Mrs McCafferty slammed the door shut in his face.

It was well after 10 before Jack got home. His parents and sisters were all still up, sitting drinking cups of tea in the kitchen. A bottle of whiskey stood on the kitchen table from which a few measures had been taken.

‘Thank God you’re here, man,’ Jack’s Mam said. And Lily came to hug him and give him a kiss. There were tears in her eyes.

‘Don’t be so daft,’ he said. ‘Da how are you? Did you get home all right?’ His father was in his usual chair by the range.

‘I had to walk from the city. All the way round to avoid Cromac Street. I couldn’t get through the Fenian mob there. They are not civilised people.’

‘And our boys are, I suppose,’ said Jack.

‘They’re fighting for what’s ours.’

Jack saw his sisters exchange glances.

‘I’m not arguing tonight Da.’

‘Have a drink of this whiskey, lad’ his Mam said. ‘Hughie brought us it in, though he was dripping in blood.’

‘I will,’ said Jack. And a cup of tea would do me as well. What’s that Hughie been up to, then? I didn’t see him.’

‘We’ve patched him up and sent him home,’ said Eileen, ‘since there’s no room for him here.’ She sounded aggrieved. ‘He got hit by a rivet. It wasn’t too bad though thank God. He said they were throwing all sorts.’

‘Ay, I noticed that myself.’

‘So where in the world have you been all this time?’ It was his Mam who asked.

Jack took the glass of whiskey and watched his hand shake as he brought it to his mouth. ‘I saw some women and children in trouble. I tried to help them. Get them out of harm’s way.’

‘Hughie said he thought he’d seen you helping some Fenians.’ It was Eileen who spoke.

‘I was helping women and children.’ Jack said.

‘I hope you’re not after bringing disgrace to this house again,’ his Da spoke quietly, deliberately, enunciating each word, as if Jack might not understand them.

‘I’m drinking my whiskey and having a cup of tea. And here we all are safe and sound. Can’t that be enough for one night, Da?'

'That's up to you.'

Jack shrugged. Standing there drinking his whiskey in the middle of the kitchen. He surveyed the faces of his family. His Mam tight-lipped and looking at the floor. Eileen angry and indignant. Lily fettling his cup of tea, glancing anxiously at him. The baby of the family, the only one who understood.

'You'll not be after seeing that woman,' his Mam said quietly. 'We've been so glad to see you home.'

Jack sipped the whiskey, felt its warmth in the pit of his stomach. 'I'm a grown man. I'll see who I want.'

'You can see who you want but if it's Catholics you're after helping you'll not be staying under this roof.' His father was thin-lipped, grim.

'Ay, well. Mebbe I won't stop for your hospitality much longer. In the meantime, good health to you.' He raised his glass to his father and took another drink.

The old man jumped to his feet finger raised towards Jack. 'I'll have none of your impertinence and none of your goings on in this house. You're gone nigh on seven year and come back bringing trouble with you. You are a disgrace to this family, that's what you are.'

'Father, that's enough,' Jack's Mam tried to intercede.

'Be quiet woman. I won't have any of his nonsense here.'

'Nonsense is it?' Jack said evenly. 'I'll tell you what's nonsense. All this fighting between Irishmen. We fought and died side by side in Belgium and France, Protestant and Catholic alike and no bother. I've seen the Ulster boys cheer as the Dubliners marched past playing their rebel tunes on the pipes. There were grins all round. I've seen Catholic boys die game and when I was lying wounded a Catholic priest gave me a smoke and a blessing. I will not raise my hand against a fellow Irishman again. It's plain madness what's happening here.'

A silence greeted Jack's speech. His father still standing

glared at him across the room. Lily put a cup of tea for him on the table and touched his arm, retreated to stand by the door into the hall with Eileen. His Mam with the handkerchief out now and the martyred expression slumped at the kitchen table.

It didn't take long for his father to wind up again. He raised his finger again, jabbing the air as if to poke home his points. 'That auld war has made you soft in the head. I'm sorry to say it. You are naïve. What do you think the Catholics were fighting for in France and Belgium? Why do you think Redmond told them to go? For the sake of the freedom of small nations. Small Catholic nations. They were for protecting the Belgian and French Catholics and wanting to make sure of Home Rule for Ireland after the war. You can be on the same side and fighting for different things. That's what you fail to understand.'

'I'm not for arguing with you any longer. I'll just say again I've done with your auld religious foolishness. Should we only have been fighting Catholic Germans, then? Most of the Fritzies are Protestants aren't they? And I'll tell yourself something else for nothing. The German boys we killed were human beings as well with mothers and fathers and brothers and sisters. It's the fighting and killing that's the insanity—making violence into the meaning of life.' Jack paused.

'You're soft in the head,' his father repeated. 'How do you think we'll be treated if we're a minority in a Papist nation? What do you think will happen to everything we've worked for?'

Jack shook his head. 'Mebbe we'd learn that there's not as much to fear from other folk as we think. Mebbe we'd learn there's good and bad in everybody.'

'You are a stubborn wee fool,' his father spluttered.

Before he could go on, Jack said, 'I'm for my bed.' He swigged his whiskey, then swallowed his tea, cool now, in one go. 'I'll bid you all good-night.'

Lily kissed his cheek as he passed by. Walking up the stairs, he heard the sharp crack of gunfire up the street. He thought the front line was far too close to his billet for comfort.

XII

As Jack struggled through nets of dream and surfaced into the light, he knew exactly what he must do. He was not even properly awake before his course of action became clear to him. He lay there watching rays of sun penetrating the thin curtains—shafts of hope. Somewhere a blackbird sang. He could hear traffic on the Ormeau Road. His sisters clattered down the stairs and there was the sound of kettle and crockery from the kitchen. His Mam on breakfast duty.

Jack decided to stay where he was until his Da and the girls left for work. It was luxurious lying there in the warmth, stretching like a cat, enjoying ease before the resumption of action. He savoured the opportunity to gather himself and summon energy, will and nerve. He would not let circumstances defeat him. No matter that last night Kathleen seemed to be wavering. The outbreak of violence between their communities made it even more imperative that they get away out of it. Jack didn't want Niamh growing up in an atmosphere which encouraged fighting as a way of life. He had to persuade Kathleen to go through with his plan.

After successive bangings of the front door, Jack ventured downstairs to face the music. He entered the kitchen in his vest, braces dangling, to have his wash and shave. His Mam greeted him with a grunt followed by pointed silence. No offer of a cooked breakfast today then. Jack gave his face a scrape while his Mam banged pots about the range and began clearing the breakfast table. The look on her face would turn milk sour, her lips compressed to a neat cat's arse. Jack ignored her and whistled as he wiped the shaving soap from his face and made his way back upstairs.

His second entry to the kitchen was more dignified. He had his shirt and collar on now.

'Cup of tea. Bread and butter.' His mother banged cup and

plate down on the table, stone-faced.

'Thank you.' Jack took his place. Obedient. Deferential. He hoped he was going to be left alone to eat and drink. It was soon made clear he had no chance. His Mam sat down opposite him and folded her arms on the table in front of her. It was evident she meant business. She stared at him belligerently before she began.

'I don't suppose there's any point in asking what you have in mind for today?'

'Not if you don't really want to know.'

'I do want to know. I most certainly do. I want to know you're not going to be running after that McCafferty woman again. Tell me you bumped into her by accident. Tell me you're going to leave her alone now. I can't understand you at all. What do you want to come back for, if it's only to make trouble and upset people?'

'I'm not after making trouble, Mam. I'm after putting things to rights.'

'How can seeing her again be putting things to rights. I'm telling you, Jack, if you go back to her, it'll be the end of your Da. He's that upset. And so is Eileen. I can't believe you're after bringing trouble down on us again after all that's happened in the past.'

Jack fought for coolness under fire. Anger clawed his guts. But still he kept his voice steady. He wouldn't be cowed by the auld witch. 'It's me making trouble is it? There'd be no trouble if you weren't so dead set against a body you don't know at all. Anyway, Mam, I'm not for arguing. I don't want to quarrel with you and Da or Eileen for that matter. Hughie might be a different story, but we'll not bother about that now. If it hadn't been for his tittle-tattling you'd know nothing about what happened last night. But now you do know, you might as well get used to the idea of me and Kathleen together. She's the mother of my little girl. Doesn't that mean anything to you? I want to make a life with them. I want to take them over the water with me. Make a new start. Can't you see how it makes me feel to have abandoned them in the first place?'

'She snared you.'

'She did not snare me. I chased her for her loveliness. We were like any young lad and lass, for God's sake.'

Jack stood up from the table.

'Jack, lad, please. I'm pleading with you. Don't do this. Don't break your poor auld Mammy's heart.' She looked at him, beseeching.

'It need not break your heart Mammy. It's a self-inflicted wound you're suffering. If you'd consent to meet her and be nice with her we could all be friends.'

'You know that can never be. And you know why.' His Mam's eyes hardened again. 'I can see there's no doing any good with you. I told father I'd try to talk some sense into you. And I've done my best. He'll be for throwing you out.'

'He won't have to throw me, Mam. If you give me a day or two to sort myself out, I'll be gone out of it. I'm sorry it has to be like this, but I can see no help for it.'

'I wish I'd had three daughters, so I do. You've brought me nothing but sorrow.'

Jack didn't wait for any more. He was on his way. His last view of his mother was of her face crumpled like the handkerchief she was reaching for to mop her grief.

Jack rode the tram into the city. It took him a wee while to calm down. His Mam and Da filled him with anger and sorrow. He was condemned to love them whether he liked it or not. He did not want to inflict this hurt on them. But he could see no other way. He was not going to sacrifice his love for Kathleen and Niamh on the altar of their prejudice. Their prejudice was their problem. From the tram window, Jack viewed the fruits of the sectarian blindness.

The army had erected sandbag walls and barbed wire barricades at either end of Cromac Street. The shops had boards at their windows or were burnt out shells. The McCaffertys' pub was a hollow blackened ruin from which stray strands of smoke still smouldered. There were soldiers on the street and policemen patrolling in threes and fours. The images matched the conflict that battered him. The words 'civil war' reverberated in Jack's head. His angry words with his Mam and Da were not civil. There was nothing civil about war. Or maybe that was wrong. Maybe every war was civil. The human animal fighting itself. The enemy always within.

As he watched men sweeping broken glass and masonry from the pavements, he wished he too could clear everything up. He remembered the filth and untidiness of the battlefield near Passchendaele and the idea he'd had then of God the cleanser. Though he wasn't sure about God, he saw his work in the cemeteries as a contribution—a setting of things to rights. Now, he felt moved by the idea of more cleaning up after himself. He couldn't square things with his Mam and Da, but at least he had a chance with Kathleen and Niamh. He patted the wallet in his inside breast pocket. The money was all there. His savings. Enough for all their travel. To get them to Belgium. And a new life. He would buy the tickets. Show his commitment.

That night the city was in flames again. Jack ventured into the strife alone. Though the sounds of urban battle reverberated in the north, east and west, he was glad to be out of the house. It had been another tense evening round the tea table—Eileen alight with enthusiasm for the way the boys at the mill had thrown the Catholics out. Lily said nothing eyes on her plate, as her sister shared with their Da a sense of righteous vindication. Apparently, the ousted workers had waited outside till knock-off time, then attacked the homeward bound Protestants with stones, bottles and all sorts. Jack had hardly had time to say, 'what do you expect?' before Hughie made an entrance full of the shootings down by the Falls and hot against the IRA. Protestants had been killed as well as Sinn Feiners. There were rumours abroad that a special Police Force was to be formed to protect the community and Hughie was keen to volunteer. 'If I were twenty year younger I'd do the same,' was the Da's comment. He looked Jack in the eye as he said so.

Jack voted with his feet. He'd walked out despite the protests of his Mam and Lily. Though he was risking a confrontation with Kathleen's father, he couldn't sit at home and do nothing, thinking of what might be happening in the Falls Road. Jack was anxious to make sure Kathleen and Niamh were safe.

In front of him, up towards Cromac Street, Jack heard gunfire ripping the night. Though he was too far away to see what was happening, there was an unnatural glow in the sky, black smoke, the smell of petrol and Christ knows what else burning. He didn't want to know. The word was more houses had been fired in the Short Strand and Catholic Churches attacked. A nunnery even. A 'carnival of bigotry' the newspaper said. This is not what he had fought for in France and Flanders. He thought of all the tales of German atrocities against the Belgians. What excuse was there for attacking a convent?

He took to the side streets, determined to fiddle his way through to Grosvenor Road and thence to the Falls. It was an eerie and unnerving experience, hurrying through the darkening avenues of terraced houses, the streets deserted, the people hiding behind closed doors and curtains, their men perhaps taking to the barricades on the main roads and points of conflict. It reminded Jack of scurrying down communication trenches behind the front lines, where you could hear the gunfire and shelling but not see. He almost expected a Very Light to go up. His heart was pumping.

Sweat ran off him. He went forward aroused, tense and alert, feeling the lack of a weapon, his eyes everywhere, looking for movement, danger.

When he hit Grosvenor Road, he was amazed. He joined a procession of people fleeing from East Belfast. The grim, fearful faces and the tales told to sympathisers along the way were of burnings and violent evictions. These people pushed hand carts and prams piled with their belongings. Small children hauled cardboard suitcases too big for them. Many wept. Some had the same long blank stare Jack had seen on troops coming out of the line. Jack was walking with refugees. Refugees from the violence and hatred of his own people. It was bewildering. They were hoping to find shelter with friends or family in the Falls.

Jack walked alone. But then came up to a large family struggling along. He took a case from the hand of a girl, maybe eleven years old. 'Thank you, Mister,' all that was said. He trudged on till they came to the cross-roads, where he relinquished his burden. A Catholic priest and what looked like seminarians from the nearby monastery were helping people. If families had no friends and relatives in the district, they were being directed to the shelter of nearby Church halls.

Jack peeled off up the road. Rifle shots echoed down the streets to his left. Women and children were running from the violence, spilling onto the Falls Road frantic and hysterical. A banging of bin lids was followed by another volley of shots. Two trucks full of soldiers roared past. Reinforcements. Jack overheard one of the young men from the monastery say the army were shooting into the crowds on both sides.

All along the road, groups of men and youths were congregating. Some carried cudgels roughly made from pick and broom handles, others were armed with mallets and bottles. Jack saw two men with what looked like Lee-Enfield rifles slung. The residents were clearly intent on protecting properties along the Falls from attack.

The rattle of small arms fire continued in the nearby streets, making Jack duck instinctively as he hurried, running now towards Kathleen's door. It was clear that as yet her place was not under direct attack. But the storms of riot and affray were all around. He pounded on her door like a man possessed. There was no response.

He banged again. Nothing from inside. He stood back from the door and shouted at the upstairs window. 'It's me, Jack. Are you all right in there?' He saw a curtain twitch, heard voices and then shoes banging down the stairs.

Kathleen opened the door, her face a mask of fear. 'What in the name of Jesus are you doing here? Do you want to get murdered now? You'd better come inside. We'll have to lie about who you are if anybody comes.'

'I had to know you were all right.' Jack walked in and Kathleen slammed shut the door. 'Are your Mam and Da here?'

'They are not. I wouldn't be for letting you in if they were. They're staying with my Uncle Mike over in Short Strand.' She paused, shaking her head, her bewildered eyes on him. 'My God, man. You're game walking down here with all this going on. I wasn't for opening the door. If the Proddies get down here, we'll all be murdered.'

A volley of rifle fire close by interrupted them. They stared at each other, until the noise died down again, and was replaced by the sound of crying from upstairs.

'I'll have to see to Niamh.'

'I've got the tickets. See here.' Jack reached inside his jacket pocket. 'I've been in today and bought them. For ten days' time.'

Kathleen stared at him. Then at the tickets. She shook her head. 'I don't know, Jack. I can't think straight with all this going on.'

'We have to get Niamh out of it, surely,' Jack said. 'This

isn't going to blow over in a day or two.'

Before Kathleen could reply, Niamh shouted from upstairs. 'Is that Jack with you, Mammy?'

'Ay, it's me,' Jack shouted back.

Aunt Mary appeared on the landing. She wore a long black skirt, black blouse buttoned to the neck, and grey knitted cardigan, the stitches coarser than they might have been. She peered at Jack with small suspicious eyes.

As she came down, she hissed, 'What in the name of God are you doing here again?' And to Kathleen, 'Will you not get him away out of it before he brings down violence on us all.'

Before Kathleen could respond, Jack brushed past the auld woman and bounded up the stairs. Niamh was sharing the back bedroom with her mother. Jack found the little girl propped up in the double bed, her eyes wide, hair dishevelled, the marks of recent tears on her cheeks. She clutched a rag doll to her. It had evidently seen good service, judging by the colour of its face and hands.

'Well hello there,' said Jack. 'Who have you got there? Aren't you going to introduce me?' He went and sat by her on the bed. She leaned into him.

'This is Rosie,' she said, her voice a whisper.

A crackle of gunfire sounded down the street. Niamh shivered. Jack put his arm round her and hugged her close.

'It's all right,' he said. 'You're safe here.'

'I don't like the noise.' She began to cry again.

'Whisht, whisht. It's only like fireworks. They can't get at you here.' He mouthed the words, not knowing if they were true, but at a loss what else to say.

'My Grand-Da says the Proddies are after getting rid of us all and we have to fight them.' Her eyes were wide.

Jack felt hollowed by dismay. He searched his mind frantically for the right words. After a minute or two, he spoke tentatively, 'That's how your Grand-Da looks at things. Not everyone thinks the same. It's an auld quarrel and there's good and bad on both sides. Not everyone wants to settle it by fighting. I'm a Proddie and I'm not after getting rid of you, am I? I've been a good friend of your Mammy for years. I'm your friend too, aren't I?'

Niamh looked at Jack doubtfully, her brow furrowed. 'But you're a Proddie? You're on the other side?' she whispered.

'I'm on nobody's side but yours, little darlin',' Jack said, giving her shoulder a squeeze. 'And Rosie's as well, of course.'

'Rosie's a Catholic,' Niamh whispered.

'Well, here's to holy Rosie. As long as she's a good girl, that's what counts, hey?'

Niamh nodded, thoughtful now, not quite convinced.

Kathleen put her head round the door. 'It's time we had lights out and Niamh was asleep. You'd best get down to the kitchen Jack, while I settle her.'

Jack kissed the little girl on the top of her head, feeling the fineness of her hair against his lips. He wanted to hold on to her and not let go. Instead, he said to her, 'You have to persuade your Mammy to come to the park on Sunday afternoon. And best not mention it to your Grand-Da. Let it be our little secret, eh?'

Kathleen frowned at him as he stood up, but said nothing.

Niamh glanced at her Mam, and then back to Jack, her eyes alight with enthusiasm. 'Will we fly the kite?'

'If the day is fine and there's any breeze, that's what we'll do.'

'That's enough for tonight, Jack,' Kathleen insisted.

Jack blew Niamh another kiss. 'I'll see you soon,' he said and left the room.

He clattered down the stairs and went down the passage towards the kitchen. He didn't relish the prospect of being in Aunt Mary's company but he was determined to stay and speak with Kathleen—try to get her assurance she would stick by their plan. He had to persuade her to get Niamh out of Belfast away from the madness.

Aunt Mary was hunched in a rocking chair by the range. She looked up as Jack entered the kitchen and gazed at him severely, her nose up-turned as if inspecting a specimen of an alien species. He stood feeling awkward. He didn't know what to do with himself.

At length the woman spoke. 'I tell you plainly, you are not welcome in this house. We're all after being murdered in our beds. I don't know what Kathleen's thinking of.'

'I'm only trying to help.' Jack said. 'Nothing more or less.'

'She needs no help from the likes of you. Youse better tread gently, or I'll be telling her father what's what, so I will.'

Jack decided any reply would be futile. He paced up and down the flags for a minute or two, all his senses alert to the noises within and without. He could hear nothing from upstairs, but the intermittent percussion combined with yells and screams from outside didn't promise much for a tranquil night. Jack hoped Kathleen would manage to pacify Niamh and lull her to sleep.

When he tired of pacing, Jack flung himself into a chair at the kitchen table. He was gripped by a terrible impatience. He wanted to be up and doing, not skulking here while the fight went on outside. It was like sitting still under shellfire with every nerve in his body urging him to fight or run. A terrible jamming of the instincts. The obligation to sit still. Do nothing. Wait for what might befall.

The minutes dragged by. He began to wonder if he'd made a mistake in coming. He reassured himself. At least this way, he knew Kathleen and Niamh were safe. He could help out if things got rough.

Footsteps on the stairs. Kathleen came in to the kitchen. Her agitation was plain. Jack got up as she came over and stood opposite him, her hands on her hips.

'Is she asleep?' Jack asked.

'Ay, for now, though God knows how long it will last with this racket going on.'

They stood looking at each other in silence. Kathleen glanced over at her Aunt Mary, and made a small gesture of her head. The older woman gave a grunt and hauled herself to her feet. 'I'll take myself off, then,' she said, 'and look to the wean. I don't think you should be giving him house room for long, mind.' She gestured dismissively at Jack as she left the room.

'I didn't want to cause more bother,' he said. 'But I couldn't think of you here alone. I had to know you were all right.'

'I'm hardly alone.'

'You know what I mean.'

'If the boys in the neighbourhood can't protect us, nobody can.'

'The army's up the road.'

'Shooting anybody and everybody, so I've heard.'

'They might keep the hard men busy.'

She brushed her hand over her forehead. She looked tired. There were shadows beneath her eyes. 'They killed a fifty year old woman last night, amongst others.' Her voice strained and weary.

'All the more reason we should get out of it. You will come with me, won't you?'

'I don't know, Jack. My Mam and Da are in such trouble now, losing the pub and all.'

Jack moved to her and took her in his arms. Kathleen was unresisting. He held her and stroked her hair. 'Your Mam and Da will be fine. We have to think of us, of our future together with Niamh. Wait till you see the little cottage I've rented. It's a darling little place. Niamh will have her own room. They're going to start a British school for the gardeners' kids and there will be health care and everything provided. And I'm learning all the time. One of these days, mebbe I can start up my own business. We can have a lovely life away from this strife. A new start. It will be grand. You have to make up your mind and come with me, Kathleen.'

She didn't speak but held him closer. It was as if she was trying to absorb his belief from the strength of his body.

They were interrupted by a violent banging at the door. They looked at each other. Kathleen's eyes wide with terror.

'I'll get it,' Jack said.

'Don't. Let me see who it is first.'

There was a thundering at the door again. Aunt Mary shouted down. 'For God's sake open the door. It's your Mam and Da.'

Jack's eyes met Kathleen's wide with shock. She didn't move.

'I'll let them in,' Jack said.

'No,' she shouted. 'Get out the back way.'

'I will not.' He moved to answer the door. He'd had enough. He'd faced and fought the Germans at Mamtez and Beaumont Hamel. He had gone forward to face them again in the mud bath near Passchendaele. He wasn't for taking a backward step now.

'Don't, Jack.' He heard her voice fall away. But he was determined. He threw the door open.

'You'd best get yourselves inside,' he said.

'Who the hell are you?' Kathleen's Da ushered his wife inside. 'Come on, mother. Get inside with you.' The old woman glanced at Jack but showed no signs of recognition. Her face was a mask of shock and grief. Her husband followed, brushing past Jack.

'Mammy, Da, what's happened now?' Kathleen appeared in the hall.

'We're completely bolloxed.' It was her father who spoke. 'They've thrown us out that's what. They came mob-handed. We hadn't a fucking chance. Proddy bastards. Taken back the house. Said they were having the place back to themselves. Told us to fuck off down south out of it. If I'd had me rifle I'd have had them. Mary.' He shouted the last name. 'Get me the gun. You know where it is.'

He paused for breath. Kathleen was hugging her mother, who seemed on the verge of collapse.

'I'll put the kettle on,' said Jack.

'Who the fuck are you?' Her father again.

'He's a friend, Da,' Kathleen said. 'Calm down will you. He helped us out last night.'

'Is that who it is?' her Mam said. But her husband ignored her.

'Will you listen to her, mother? Calm down she says. Calm down. I've only been thrown out of a second place the night after my pub's been burnt out. I'll have at the fucking cunting bastards before I've done. Where's that gun, Mary? For fuck's sake.' He paused for breath, staring round the kitchen, red-faced and belligerent. His eyes lit upon Jack again. 'I'll only ask you one more time. Who are you?'

Jack raised his hand to stop Kathleen from speaking. 'Jack Young.' He approached the big man, intending to offer his hand.

Sean McCafferty stood and stared, his hands hanging loosely, his biceps so large that his arms seemed to curve away from his torso. He looked genuinely shocked. He blew out a stream of air. As Jack moved towards him, he flung his hand out dismissing Jack's approach.

'Jack Young is it indeed. I'll be fucked. I'll give you this much. You've got some brass plated bollocks turning up here at this particular time. So you have.' He spoke low and threatening. 'I know all about you. I made it my business to know all those years ago when you spoiled our Kathleen and then fucked off over the water. You're a very lucky fella, you are. If I'd caught you before you left, you wouldn't have walked onto the boat. I would have ripped your fucking legs off. You could have used them for paddles.' The big man took a breath.

'Will you listen to me a minute.'

'You're a cheeky wee eejit. I will not fucking listen to you at all.'

'Da, please.'

'You.' he turned to his daughter. 'You shut your mouth and stay out of it. Your man's going to be lucky again.' Sean McCafferty turned his attention back to Jack. He eyeballed him for a moment before he spoke again. 'I'm not going to kill you here and now in front of the women. I'm going to kick your arse out of that door and you can fuck off out of it and never, do you understand me, never come back. And while you're in Belfast, I'd advise you to keep an eye out. I'll have you one of these days. Or Kevin will. I only need to whisper in her husband's ear.' He raised his forefinger and thumb and levelled them at Jack. A cocked pistol gesture. 'If I see you near my daughter again, you're a dead man. Do you understand me?'

'I'm only after helping Kathleen and my daughter.'

'They don't need any help from Proddy scum like you. Now fuck off out of it before I lose my temper. Go on. Get out.'

Jack's eyes sought Kathleen. She looked stricken. Gave a little shake of the head. He decided to go. There was no point in fighting now. In front of the women with Niamh upstairs. Before he left, he said to Kathleen, 'Think on about what I said. Everything's in place.'

'What's in fucking place? Get the hell out of it will you, before I brain you.'

As Jack walked through the hall to the front door, he heard Aunt Mary on the stairs. He looked over his shoulder and saw the brittle woman. She was carrying a rifle in her arms.

XIII

The next day was Friday. Jack hung about the house not knowing what to do with himself. Everybody else went to work, despite the mayhem in the city. Even his Mam went to her cleaning for Mrs Armstrong in Castlereagh. It suited Jack to be alone, though the hours were long and passed in a welter of impatience and anxiety. He couldn't see what was to be done until the possible meeting with Kathleen and Niamh in Ormeau Park on Sunday. There was no point risking the Falls Road again unless he was forced into it. If Kathleen didn't show on Sunday, then maybe. But desperate measures weren't needed yet. Lying low seemed the best option. Apart from nipping down to the corner for a paper and some fags, he spent the day lying on his bed staring at the ceiling. Sometimes the circular patterns of damp stain that discoloured the paint made him think of the newly renovated cottage in Ypres and all the hopes he had invested there. In other moments he read in the ragged brown rings a portent of entrapment in Belfast. The occasional sound of gunfire from the west and north east spelled out the ominous message that peace would be a long time coming.

At tea-time Jack was treated to the full force of parental disapproval. He endured an agony of bristling silence punctuated by venomous tirades against the Fenians. Though his father had not insisted on throwing him out, the old man's bare and icy civility cast a grim pall, which his Mam made no attempt to thaw. Instead, she added her lemon-lipped bitterness to the odd remark cast his way. Neither of the girls were of a mind to test their father's displeasure. They took their cues from him and didn't venture unbidden conversation. The only enthusiasm was reserved for Hughie's entrance. The young man's excitement made him brutally insensitive to the tension at the Young's table. He came in full of the shootings round the Falls and how many Sinn Feiners had been killed and how many Prods. There was more talk of the Special Police Force to be formed and his willingness to join up as soon as he could. All this was met with impassioned approval from Jack's Da and Eileen. Jack caught Lily's troubled eye. Hers was the only sympathy he felt.

Saturday was harder still to bear than Friday. Jack's Mam and Da were about all day. The girls went to the mill in the morning but were back in the afternoon. Jack kept to his room apart from meal times, reading the accounts of the violence in the papers. It was the sitting still and doing nothing that was the worst. It reminded him of those times in the trenches waiting and watching, nerves filed to a keen edge with no help but the presence of comrades in the same boat.

The monotony of the day was broken when Lily came in to him bringing a cup of tea with her. Jack confided his troubles and how all his hopes were pinned on seeing Kathleen the following day and persuading her to leave with him. If she didn't show, he had no idea what he was going to do. There was a comfort in the companionship of his little sister, but she had no answers to his dilemmas. And at the frigid meal times they were outnumbered. Silence was their only option in the face of the aggressive mouthings of their Mam and Da, Eileen and Hughie, who seemed disappointed by the news delivered with the *Evening Telegraph* that it had been a quieter day with less violence and no rioting. The major story was of Catholic funerals in the Falls. Six victims of the troubles were buried and all the Falls had turned out to watch. The dead were treated as martyrs and the massed observance of respect was a sure sign the Catholic community refused to be cowed. Jack could only see in the reports the seeds of further conflict. But a lull in the fighting seemed good for his immediate purposes. He went to bed hoping that the uneasy truce might linger through Sunday, both sides licking their wounds and concentrating on their religious observances.

Jack spent a restless night harried by dreams in which he floundered through a labyrinth of mud and trench and wire from which he could find no escape or relief. He was entirely alone and had no idea which direction meant safety and which led to battle. It didn't matter where he ran, he was trapped. Fear was his only companion. He awoke momentarily when he tripped over a corpse, which sat up and screamed at him. He was covered in sweat and heard the unearthly cries of cats coupling in the street. When he fell back to sleep, he fell back to the same blasted landscape, through which he clambered unarmed and without bearings.

It was an immense relief when dawn shoved bright fingers through the curtains and tickled his eyelids open. He lay there blinking with the warmth on his face, realising today was the day. He might see Kathleen and Niamh. But first he had to offend his Mam and Da by refusing Church. His sisters went of course. Jack offered no excuse. He simply said he wasn't going. Offered the observation that he saw more of God in a garden than in a Church and that he was for a walk in Ormeau Park.

He was glad when at last he escaped the house into the quiet streets. He would be far too early, but he didn't care. He guessed Kathleen and Niamh would go to Mass so as not to arouse suspicion or cause any trouble. If she got away at all it would be this afternoon. But with the day being fine and having been cooped up for the last forty eight hours Jack relished the thought of a walk and a sit in the park. He thought he would be safe from the attentions of Sean McCafferty and his pals. They would all be at Mass as well. Praying no doubt for political ascendancy. It made Jack laugh to himself in a bitter kind of a way to think how men brought God down to their own size and gave Him their own petty interests. If there was some power—a Great Creator—Jack was sure it or he was beyond such trifling. He liked to think of his God as the Great Gardener who had painted the delicacy of spring flowers and given the rosebuds their perfect whorls.

The day was fine and warm, the sky milky blue with whisps of high white cloud. Jack spent the morning in a long walk, before approaching the rotunda towards lunch time. There weren't many people about. A few courting couples. An old man walking his dog. A young woman wheeling a pram, driven perhaps to do so by the child's crying. But there weren't many kids or families about. Everyone too scared to risk moving far from home, or too exhausted by the events of recent days to consider a Sunday afternoon promenade.

He took up his customary station in the rotunda. Walked round the wooden boards a couple of times, then stood, bent at the waist, elbows on the balustrade, which had been freshly painted in cream for the summer. Nothing happened. Jack straightened and rolled a smoke. He was feeling hungry and regretting setting out without a snack in his pocket. He doubted if any of the kiosks in the park would be open on a Sunday. And anyway, Kathleen wouldn't want to go anywhere she might be seen with him. He would have to rely on tobacco to still his rumbling stomach. Just like the trenches. However awful the experience, Jack reflected, the war had taught him a lot about his ability to survive. The ability to 'hurry up and wait' as well. It looked as if that would be the form for the afternoon.

Jack soon tired of standing and prowling. On the principle that a watched pot never boiled, he took a seat on the steps of the rotunda, and let the sunshine soak into him. He began to convince himself they weren't coming and wondered fruitlessly what his next manoeuvre might be. His reverie was interrupted when a young man appeared from round the side of the rotunda. From his large hands and boots he looked like a working man in his Sunday best suit complete with tie. He looked a little startled to see Jack and then relieved. He stood for a moment, his body relaxing, before he said, 'No music today then.'

'No,' said Jack, climbing to his feet. 'No music today.'

'Sure, it's a warm one though.'

'It is.' Jack glanced to his right, having sensed movement in his peripheral vision. He saw Kathleen walking over the grass towards them.

'If you'll excuse me,' he said to the stranger. And hurried off to meet Kathleen. There was no Niamh. He wondered at this as he approached, his spirits soaring nevertheless at the sight of her. She wore a white cotton frock with a design of roses. On her feet she had cream shoes with a low heel. Though she looked tired, nothing could extinguish her beauty. As they met he took her in his arms, feeling the release of all the waiting tension, the relief of her presence. Her hair smelled of apples and the heat of her body was a gentle flame.

'Kathleen, Kathleen, he murmured, 'I'm that glad to see you. Are you all right? How's Niamh? Where is she?'

Kathleen stepped back from his arms. 'I haven't got long Jack. I've left Niamh with Mammy at Aunt Mary's. I didn't want to risk her on the streets. I didn't know if it was safe. My Da's out looking to the pub. I told Mammy I was having a cup of tea with a girlfriend. I'm not sure she believed me. Auld Mary gave me a narrow look. I can't stay long but I wanted to see you, Jack. I wanted to touch you. Make sure you were real. That I wasn't only dreaming. About a life with you. About leaving with you, maybe.' She paused, as if exhausted by the rush of speech, the tide of emotion.

'I'm real right enough.' Jack said. 'So are the tickets. We just have to get through a few more days, then we can be on our way.'

'I'm scared Jack. Scared of leaving. But Christ I'm scared of staying as well. It's no good for Niamh. You should have heard my Da in front of her yesterday. Losing the pub has sent him mad. There were all these funerals. The whole street came out to watch. People were on the pavements five and six deep. I couldn't keep our Niamh away from it. She was at the window. She wanted to see and understand. And my Da is telling her they're martyrs for a United Ireland and telling her how the bastard Prods and the bastard English have to be beaten and all the rest of it. I says that auld Mrs McGready getting caught in the crossfire while she was going next door for a cup of sugar was martyr to nothing but her sweet tooth. Da told me to shut up. He went on and on. He was teaching Niamh her heritage, and what was I after, insulting people who'd given their lives for their religion and the cause. There wasn't anything I could do or say to stop him. I don't want her growing up to hate, Jack. I don't want that.'

'There's no need to be scared. If we hold our nerve we'll be right as rain.'

Kathleen withdrew her hands from his. 'Have you got a smoke? I mustn't stay much longer. I don't want my Da getting back and asking questions about where I am.'

Jack gave her a cigarette. She put her hand on his to steady the match he held. It was a curiously intimate gesture and one that excited Jack, making his fingers tremble.

Kathleen took a long drag on the cigarette. 'What I want to know,' she said, exhaling a stream of smoke, 'is, if I am to come with you, how in God's name I'm to get out of that house with all our things without anybody stopping me? My Mam and Da are sleeping on the parlour floor. And there's Mary to consider. I don't see how it's to be done.'

'I've been thinking about that. You've no need to worry. Particularly if this violence keeps on. It's the school holidays coming up, right? You tell your people you're for taking Niamh on a trip to the sea-side to get her out of it for a while. Tell them you're off to Bangor for a few days. You pack as much as you can into a couple of suitcases and take a cab to the train station. I meet you there and we go on to the boat. No bother.'

Kathleen looked at him doubtfully. 'Where's the money coming from for a holiday in Bangor? How will I make them believe me?'

'I'll give you the money. You can say you've been saving from your allowance and your tips from behind the bar.'

'There's precious few of them.'

'Never mind. You just have to deliver the story with conviction. Get Niamh excited about it.'

'You mean lie to her?'

'You don't have to lie. Just tell her you're going on a trip. And that it will be fun.'

Kathleen looked unconvinced, her brow furrowed, her lips a thin line. 'I'll have to see what I can do,' she said. 'I'd best be getting back. I can't stay.'

'I'll walk you back to the tram.'

They walked through the park together side-by-side in silence under the dappled shade of the trees. Kathleen held out her hand. Jack took it and squeezed her fingers.

'It's going to be fine,' he said. 'We need to stay steady and believe.'

'Easier said than done.' Kathleen stopped. 'Will you hold me for a minute, Jack? While there's no one about.'

Jack took her in his arms and kissed her on the lips. Then he kissed her again and felt her lips part. Their tongues twined and they pressed closer, their bodies responding. It was only when Jack moved his hand to her breast that Kathleen broke away.

They stared at each other, breathless and enflamed.

'I wish I could lie down with you, Jack.' Kathleen said, her voice low and breathy. 'I want to feel you inside me. I have such memories of us together.'

'I love you Kathleen. I want you so much. We were grand together. We are grand together. We didn't know then, how good we were did we? Took it for granted. We won't make the same mistake again, eh?'

'I hope not.'

'We'd best get on. We can't make love here.'

Kathleen giggled. 'It would give the Sunday strollers a grand auld sight.'

'It would that. It might do them some good. Particularly if they knew we were Catholic and Proddy mixed.'

Though she nodded in agreement, a shadow seemed to cross Kathleen's face at this reminder. Jack was sorry to have changed the mood. He wanted to cheer her.

'Come on with you. Just think of having our own bedroom with its nice double bed. Whenever you feel a doubt coming on, just imagine that. Have you considered. Mebbe we could have another wean? A brother or sister for Niamh. Wouldn't that be grand?'

Kathleen smiled. Jack saw the light in her eye at the thought of another child. They walked on, arguing over names for boys and girls. Jack was not having Sean; Kathleen wouldn't hear of Margaret. They found they could agree on Thomas and Siobhan.

When they got to the road, Jack looked to his left to see if there was a tram coming. The road was empty save for a car idling a hundred yards away. The man Jack had spoken to at the rotunda was getting in the near-side rear door, as if he was being chauffeur driven, though the chauffeur had not got out to hold the door. Jack thought no more about it. His mind was running on arrangements for keeping in touch with Kathleen over the next few days.

There was nobody else at the tram stop. Jack wondered if they'd just missed one. He hoped so. It meant more time with Kathleen, more time to reassure her that all would be well. He wanted to suggest that perhaps they could try another rendezvous in the park with Niamh next week sometime. He made to speak, but before he could say anything, both he and Kathleen were distracted by the sound of a car approaching. It was the same vehicle Jack had seen earlier. It came close to them now, and swerved into the kerb beside them.

Thinking the driver might need directions, Jack stepped towards the near side front window. But as he did so both near-side doors burst open. Before he could do anything, he was grabbed by the arms. He felt rough fingers claw into his biceps. He heard Kathleen scream, as he was bundled towards the back of the car. Though he tried to resist, the two men who had hold of him were too strong for him, and with his weakened shoulder he had no chance. They forced him into the back seat. He could smell the warm leather of the upholstery, the tang of petrol. A third man shoved a flour bag over his head. The earthy tang of hessian invaded his nostrils, as the world turned close and black. He could still hear Kathleen screaming and shouting, but the other man was in beside him now so he was hemmed in and the car was roaring off and away.

'You just sit tight there, and keep your mouth shut, or you're a dead man,' a low voice advised.

'He's a dead man anyway,' another voice chuckled from the front seat. 'And good riddance.'

XIV

Kathleen saw the car disappear in a cloud of dust and exhaust. Her hopes went with it. She was hoarse with shouting, but there was no one about and the whole incident was over in seconds. She felt panic threaten to drown her. She clutched her stomach with both hands and fought for calm. She tried to think of what she might do, but her mind wouldn't work. It seemed locked into an endless loop in which Jack's abduction re-played over and over again. She stared up and down the street, hoping for help. But it remained quiet and empty. Only the retreating sound of the motor could be heard fading into the distance. Thank God Niamh wasn't with her. She thought the man in the back seat, the one who hadn't got out, might be Kevin. She hadn't recognised the other two. She wondered about the police, but had no idea where the nearest station might be. She thought about her Da. Would he still be at the pub, sifting through the wreckage or would he be home by now? Would he lift a finger to help anyway? Maybe he'd instigated the whole thing. She didn't know what to do. She felt paralysed. With every moment, Jack was being driven further away. She imagined them taking him into the countryside and executing him in some lonely place where he was far beyond help. She had to do something.

The Young's place wasn't too far away. It seemed a mad idea, but at least she could raise the alarm there. They might know how to alert the police. It would be a start. It would be something. The idea of encountering Jack's family made her feel sick with apprehension. But the idea she was powerless and could do nothing was equally awful. A life was at stake. Kathleen's mind cleared. This was no time to consider her own sensitivities. To get help was the only thing that mattered. She hurried up the street and crossed the bridge over the Lagan. As she went, she tried to remember the number of the Young's house. She broke into a jog, but her shoes made it difficult. She bent and took them off and carrying them in her hand she hurried along, the pavement hard and hot beneath her feet.

When she came to the row of houses where she thought Jack's people lived, she became confused. She wasn't sure of the number. There was no time to hesitate. Kathleen took a gamble and banged on the brown door of a house that looked meticulous enough to belong to the Young's. Jack had talked to her often about how particular his Mam and Dad were. She bent to put her shoes back on while she waited for a response.

A large florid man in shirt-sleeves and braces answered the door. He looked at Kathleen in amazement. 'What are you at Missy, near knocking my door down on a Sunday afternoon?'

'Mr Young?' Kathleen said, already doubting if it was. He looked nothing like Jack.

'Two doors down,' the big man replied frowning. 'I'll give you a tip. He won't like you thumping like that on his door any more than I do.'

'I'm sorry to have troubled you.'

Kathleen hurried away, feeling the bloke's piggy eyes following her. She tried to be less vigorous in her approach to the Young's door knocker. She noticed the polished doorstep while she waited. It had been well donkey-stoned, and recently. The door was opened by a short square woman with a broad face and whispy blues eyes. Her hair was iron grey cut short to just below her ears and side parted. She wore a grey skirt and white blouse. Sunday best presumably. She looked severe and unwelcoming. She stared at Kathleen in wonder.

'Mrs Young, I've come about Jack. He's in trouble. He needs help.'

'Who in the name of God are you? What do you mean

about our Jack?'

'I'm Kathleen McCafferty. I was with him here just now. He's been taken. Some men shoved him into a car. I'm afraid for him. I didn't know what to do.'

Mrs Young stared at her non-plussed.

'Who is it mother? What's going on?' A male voice from the depths of the house.

'You have a brass-faced nerve coming here,' the auld woman hissed. 'What are you saying about our Jack. I don't understand you?'

'I'm telling you he's been taken. By force. I'm afraid they're going to kill him.'

The owner of the cantankerous voice appeared. 'For God's sake, why don't you answer me woman. Who is it?' His face was all angles under a shock of grey hair. Jack's Dad to be sure.

'It's that McCafferty woman our Jack's been messing with. I can't understand what she's saying.'

'Mr Young, I'm trying to explain. Jack's been taken by some men. IRA maybe. I think they'll harm him. I don't know what to do. Help me, for God's sake. I think perhaps the police?'

'Which men? Why? He can't be mixed up in anything. He's only been back in Belfast a minute or two.'

'They know he was a gun runner in 1913. That might be enough for them.'

'How would they know that?' shrilled Jack's mam. 'Have you betrayed him is that it? First you seduce him. Then betray him. Then come here, pretending to care. Is that it?' She turned to her husband. 'I wish Hughie was here. He'd know what to do.'

'Be quiet woman. What could Hughie do? What can anybody do? If it's the IRA have him, I don't know what's to be done.'

'It's all this woman's fault.' Jack's Mam took a step forward as if she might hit Kathleen. 'She's ruined our boy, she has. Taken him away from us and turned him mad. What are we going to do, father? What are we going to do?'

Jack's Da ignored his wife. Pushed past her and spoke to Kathleen, his jaw thrust out, his tone belligerent. 'Do you know who these men are who have him? Do you?'

'No.' Kathleen hesitated. 'At least I don't think so.'

'She's lying, father. Listen to her. These people can't lie straight in bed.'

'I don't know the two men who grabbed him. There was a third. I didn't get a proper look at him. I thought it might be my husband. Kevin O'Donnell. But I can't be sure. I can't say for certain.'

'Listen to her,' the auld woman railed. 'Married but it doesn't stop her messing about with Jack. On a Sunday as well. She isn't decent. I always said she wasn't decent. You're a whore that's what you are.'

'You'd best go.' Jack's Da interrupted. Go on. Away out of it. I'll go to the police. Though I can't see what good it will do.'

'Yes, go on. Get out of it. If my boy's dead, it will be on your head. Fenian whore.'

Just before they slammed the door in her face, Kathleen heard someone pounding down the stairs and saw a young woman come into view. One of Jack's sisters, she guessed. She turned away, feeling her face burn with anger and shame. She found she was trembling as she walked up the road, hoping for a tram. She would go to the pub to see if her Da was still there. See if he would help. In her distress, she had no other idea. Deep in her stomach the granite stone of fear weighed heavily on her. Maybe Jack's Mam was right. If they killed him, it would be her fault. She didn't know what she could do to prevent them.

The rumbling of a tram approaching made Kathleen pick up her pace. Her only hope was help from her Da. She prayed she might catch him at the pub. Breathless and feeling the sweat uncomfortable at her hairline and neck, she reached the stop with time to spare. She looked back down the road and saw a woman running from the Young's place full tilt towards her, waving her arm. It was the girl she'd seen on the stairs. It must be Lily, Jack's younger sister. The tram eased to a stop. Kathleen made to board.

'Wait,' the girl cried.

Kathleen stood poised one foot on the step. The tram driver urged her to get on.

'Can you not see there's someone running?'

'I can't wait all day. Are you coming or not?'

Kathleen delayed as long as she could then stepped aboard as Lily came up.

'I'm coming with you,' Lily gasped as she leapt onto the tram.

The conductor hit the bell, and they were away.

XV

Jack sat still and said nothing. He could feel the arms and thighs of the men next to him, squashed as he was between them on the back seat of the car. It was another reason to sit as still as he could. He hated their proximity. The smell of their sweat. His heart rate had subsided a little but he was still aware of the ragged thump in his chest. He wondered how much longer he had. There was no doubt these people meant to kill him. He would struggle. He would not go willingly or give in. But he knew he had no chance against the three of them. He felt the bile rise from his stomach on a wave of acid anger. He kept it down, but only just. Too many cigarettes and too little food together with his outrage left him with a mouth full of bitterness. The thought of losing Kathleen and Niamh before he'd had a chance to be a proper husband and father to them was foremost in his mind. The sour irony that he had survived the war only to meet his end at the hands of his own countrymen was as vile as the thought that if these Catholic boys killed him it would harden his parents' hearts even further. He imagined Hughie plotting a tit-for-tat revenge killing with his fellow Volunteers. Lovely.

Though he hadn't recognised the men who had taken him, Jack was sure they must be connected to Kathleen's people. The threats her father had made against him hadn't been idle. Maybe they had somehow guessed his plans with Kathleen. They would use the idea that he'd been a gun-runner to justify his execution. Persuade themselves he was a legitimate target. Tell themselves a story. Like the story he'd told himself when he agreed to help with the guns in 1913. To be a man. To be part of something bigger than himself. To do something adventurous and heroic. He had learnt nothing from it. He'd told himself the same stories in 1914. To go to war. To serve. To enter into a test of himself. To risk death for a cause. To sacrifice himself. To kill. So maybe he deserved to die like this. He'd played the same game. He had been slow to learn love. It was only in the trenches that the penny dropped. When killing and being killed became more than an idea. And all he and his mates had wanted to do was come home to their families. A slow learner is what he'd been.

Jack's bleak reflections were brought to an abrupt halt as the car came to a standstill. They had only been travelling a few minutes. Jack had presumed they would drive him out of the city and shoot him in the middle of a field or in some wild country lane and leave him to rot. But no. The doors were opening.

'Out you get,' was the terse command. He was manhandled out of the car. He wondered about the possibility of escape as he reached for the pavement with his feet. But as he stood, the driver was ready for him, so that both arms were held. With the bag still over his head, there was nothing he could do.

He was marched only a few yards before he was shoved through a door. His feet scrunched on broken glass. The acrid smell of burnt wood invaded his hessian mask. The floor felt wet in places. He was in some burnt out building. He was escorted down a passage. They turned right and then left. There was another smell mixing with the smoke and damp. It was yeasty. The scent of drunks. A pub. That's where he was. The McCafferty pub.

As he was pushed forward into what felt like a smaller space, his realisation was confirmed.

'What the fuck?' Sean McCafferty's voice was loud and clear.

'Hello there, Sean. I've brought you a wee gift. We'll tie him to that chair lads.'

'I don't want him in here.'

'Don't be an auld spoil sport, Sean. I thought you could finish him off.'

Jack was forced onto the wooden seat of a straight-backed chair. They had evidently brought rope with them. Two of them held him while the third secured his arms over the back of the chair.

Sean McCafferty still wasn't impressed. 'What kind of a fool are you, bringing him here?'

'A wise one, Sean, I reckon. Did you think I'd do all your dirty work for you? I'm tired of sorting out your mess. Didn't I marry your daughter to solve your problem for you? And much thanks I've had for that. Not much joy either. So I reckon the least you can do is kill her Proddy lover boy here. I mean that's what you want isn't it? That's why you told me he was about. Thought I'd do the job for you, didn't you? Well you've got another thing coming. It's down to you to do him now.'

They were binding Jack's legs. The rope bit into the flesh round his wrists and ankles. Jack realised it was O'Donnell binding him tight, taking pleasure in his work.

'I can't kill him here. What will we do with the body?' Sean McCafferty sounded panicky.

'Wrap him up in the cellar. When the builders come in, we can carry him out with all the other auld rubbish. Nobody will be the wiser. I'll even lend you the gun and get rid of it for you. I can't say fairer.'

O'Donnell finished tying Jack up. Jack sensed him straighten before he spoke again. This time to his henchmen.

'Youse two can fuck off out of it now. I don't want the car sitting outside all night. I'll see you later. You've done well today.'

Grunts of assent were followed by the sound of boots retreating. Jack felt O'Donnell's proprietorial hand resting lightly on his shoulder. A hateful touch. McCafferty seemed to be pouring a drink. Jack heard the chink of glasses, the cap come off a bottle, the pouring of liquid. Outside, the car started up and drove off. O'Donnell semed to lean and stretch, taking a glass from McCafferty. Jack heard the men drink.

'You need some courage then, Sean?' O'Donnell sounded as if he was taunting the older man.

There was no reply. O'Donnell squeezed Jack's shoulder as he spoke again. 'We'll have a little sport before you kill him. See if he knows anything about what the Prods are up to.'

He pulled the sack from Jack's head. Jack blinked in the mid-afternoon light which angled through the door into the small office space. The wooden roof-beams were charred and the walls smoke damaged but the desk and chairs had survived. McCafferty had been busy trying to salvage his ledgers, sodden as they were by the attentions of the fire brigade. By the way the sunshine illuminated the room, Jack guessed that some of the roof had gone over the bar area. O'Donnell and McCafferty each had a glass of whiskey. Jack looked McCafferty in the face.

'What the fuck are you looking at?' McCafferty took another swig of whiskey and switched his gaze to O'Donnell. The younger man removed his hand from Jack's shoulder, and placed his whiskey on the desk. He grasped the chair and pulled it backwards a little, so there was more space in front of Jack.

'Now then, we can get at you,' O'Donnell said, walking round and crouching so he was at eye level. 'The question is,' he purred, 'What do you know about the UVF re-forming and who do you know that's involved?'

'I don't know anything or anybody. I'm not involved.'

'You're not involved. Will you listen to him, Sean? He's not involved. You were fucking involved in 1913. A leopard doesn't change its spots. Orange and fucking black you were then, orange and black you remain. I'm only going to ask you once more.'

'Ask away. I can't tell you what I don't know. Unless you want me to tell you stories.'

O'Donnell straightened and leant over Jack, placing his

left arm on the chair back above Jack's shoulder. He brought his face close so Jack could smell the whiskey sour on his breath and see the stubble black on his cheek. For a strange moment, Jack thought O'Donnell was going to kiss him. Instead, there were words in a vicious whisper. 'Don't get smart with me.'

Jack saw O'Donnell's right arm move back and braced himself but there was nothing he could do as he was fisted in the balls with a brutal jab. A black balloon of agony inflated and rose through Jack's groin and into his stomach. He gave an involuntary cry. He thought he would be sick and fought for breath.

'That's just for starters,' O'Donnell said. 'For telling your lies and for messing with my missis. We'll talk again when you have your breath back. He leaned up and took his whiskey from the desk and drank. He looked at Sean McCafferty, who stood glass in hand watching with a frown on his face.

'What's the matter with you?' O'Donnell asked McCafferty. 'You look like a love sick girl, so you do. It's going to be interesting watching you pull the trigger.'

'Beating defenceless men isn't my idea of fun.'

'Not even traitorous Proddy scum like this. He spoiled your daughter remember? And he's after fucking her again. What kind of a man are you?'

'A better one than you. You forget. I've seen you strike Kathleen. You're a coward, Kevin, that's what you are. I only put up with you these days for the sake of the cause.'

O'Donnell laughed. 'We'll see who's a coward in a minute. Are you going to shoot him for the cause? That's the question. Or am I going to have to do both of you?'

Jack listened to them wrangle through a fog of pain. O'Donnell turned to him.

'Now then, you're looking a bit pale. Are you ready to tell me what you know?'

'I am.' Jack spoke as loud as he could, though his throat

was dry and constricted.

'There. A little friendly persuasion always works wonders. Out with it, then.' O'Donnell's lips stretched in a sneering grin.

Jack glanced at McCafferty before fixing his eyes on O'Donnell. 'I know nothing.'

O'Donnell took a step forward and took a wide swipe at Jack, hitting him hard across one cheek with his open palm and back-handing the other, so Jack's head was jerked violently to left and right. 'I'll give you nothing, so I will. You're after making a fool of me with Kathleen are you?' O'Donnell reached into his belt beneath his jacket and drew out a revolver. The blue-grey gun-metal shone in the light. The barrel looked long to Jack, as O'Donnell waved it around.

'Shall I shoot your knee caps off? That makes a man scream.'

'For God's sake.' Sean McCafferty protested.

'All you have to do is to think of this jockey sticking his wee Proddy prick in your daughter and riding her. Then you won't look so delicate.'

'You have a dirty mouth on you and a dirty mind. I made a mistake when I gave Kathleen to you.'

'A mistake was it? You were grateful at the time, as I remember.'

'I was grateful till I caught you brutalising her.'

'You should know better than to come between a man and his wife, Sean. It isn't right. If she wasn't such a frigid bitch there'd be no problem at all.'

'If she's so frigid, what's she doing with yon Proddy boy there? What's he got that you haven't?'

'Fuck you, old man. You need to be careful. Watch and learn.'

O'Donnell turned to Jack, thrusting the gun into his face and said, 'Here y'are. Kiss this.' Jack felt the barrel roughly pressed against his closed lips, bruising them against his teeth.

'Open wide, you wee fucker. I'm going to make you swallow lead whether you like it or not. I'll knock your teeth out first if I have to.'

An odd calm came over Jack. He had faced guns before. He thought of going over the top in Flanders. Like stepping off a precipice. He'd been lucky so often. This time, it seemed his number was up. He parted his lips, not wanting the pain of shattered teeth. He felt the round of the barrel in his mouth, tasted the metal against his tongue. He waited for the end of his world. The beginning of peace. Instead he heard Sean McCafferty.

'I thought I was supposed to kill him.'

'I didn't think you had the stomach for it.'

'Ay, well you shouldn't judge everybody by your own standards. I'm no coward.'

'Are you not, Sean? Well that is gratifying. Christ but I'd like to blow his brains out. It's a pleasure you'd rob me of.'

'It was your idea.'

O'Donnell withdrew the barrel from Jack's mouth. He placed the gun on the table. He reached for the bottle and poured himself another slug of whiskey. He drank. Then he stooped down and from the top of his boot withdrew another smaller snub-nosed pistol. He gestured to the revolver on the desk.

'There you go, then, Sean. It's all yours. Let's get on with it. You'd better come round this side. I'll just be watching you with this, so's we make sure the job gets done right.'

O'Donnell moved behind Jack. Sean McCafferty walked slowly round the desk. He wore a look of intense concentration. He didn't look at Jack but kept his eyes on O'Donnell. The revolver was still on the desk. McCafferty picked it up. Weighed it in his hand. He levelled it at Jack's forehead. Their eyes met. Jack saw a slight tremor in the older man's hand.

'For the love of God, will you get on with it now.' O'Donnell sounded impatient. As if he still didn't believe McCafferty would shoot.

Jack saw the finger curl round the trigger. He looked into McCafferty's eyes. A last desperate appeal. 'I love Kathleen,' he said. 'I'm the father of your grand-daughter. I love her as well.'

Sean McCafferty said nothing, though Jack thought he saw him nod. Then the gun moved and a shot rang out. In that small space it was like the world exploding.

Kathleen with Lily by her side heard one bang closely followed by another as they approached the front door of the pub. A car had just gone past. They looked at each other in alarm.

'Backfire?' Lily said.

Kathleen didn't reply. She was too distressed. She led the way into the wrecked pub. They trod through ash on blackened ruined boards.

'Da, are you there?' Kathleen shouted.

There was no reply. They walked towards the back office through thick debris and broken glass. The bar was a blackened ruin.

'In here. We're in here,' a hoarse voice croaked. Kathleen didn't recognise the speaker.

When she reached the office with Lily at her shoulder, Kathleen stopped in the doorway and stared. She saw Jack, still tied to the chair, his chin down on his chest. He looked up at her, a wide stare on his livid face, a bruise just beginning to blossom on his cheek-bone. Her father stood behind Jack, a gun hanging from his hand at his side. He was looking down at the body of Kevin O'Donnell. The smell of cordite was in the air. And the smell of death.

Lily was the first to move. She brushed past Kathleen and went to Jack. She knelt and began to untie the ropes round his ankle while she murmured, 'Jack, Jack, you're all right,

Thank God.'

Sean McCafferty turned to his daughter, an awful look on his face of sorrow and anger mixed. 'Have you seen what you've brought me to? Come here and have a good look. It is your husband I've killed.'

It seemed to Kathleen he might weep. Jack looked up at her and their eyes met. There was no need of words. She moved to her father's side and made herself look down. O'Donnell's unseeing eyes stared up at her. He still held a gun in his hand. He looked surprised to have a hole drilled between his eyes and a wide dark stain of blood discolouring the front of his Sunday white shirt. Her Da had taken no chances. She felt her gorge rise and stumbled towards the door, breathing deeply and struggling not to vomit.

In a moment or two, she recovered sufficiently to turn back to the room. She knew she would never forget the sight of Kevin's body, lifeless pale and bleeding, the eyes accusing her. Her father hadn't moved, but still stood staring at his handiwork as if he couldn't believe what he had done. Jack, rose unsteadily to his feet, and moved to embrace Kathleen. It was then she wept. 'I thought they would kill you, Jack. But you're all right. You're all right. Thank God.'

'I hope you two know what you've done.' Kathleen's Da turned to them and shouted. 'What you have made me do. Of all the fella's in Belfast, why the fuck you had to fall for a Proddy bastard I don't know.'

'This is none of our doing Da. It's the auld hatred that is to blame. All we ever wanted was to be left alone to love each other.'

'I've paid the price for your love. I have killed a man.'

There was a silence in the room which stretched.

Lily looked around at them before speaking. 'We need to do something. Get away out of it before we're found.'

'She's right,' Kathleen said.

'I need to get rid of the gun,' her Da still sounded dazed

and shaky.

'I'll do that,' Jack said. 'You saved my life. I know it was for Kathleen and not for me. I thank you all the same. It was brave of you. He might have shot you.'

'He didn't think I had the balls for it. He didn't think I was going to shoot anybody. He had his gun pointed at the back of your head.' Kathleen's Da handed Jack the gun. 'We should go out the side door, hope not too many see us.'

'Will we not move him?' Jack asked.

'Let him lie. I'll discover him tomorrow.' The police won't care. They'll know who he is and presume some Proddies have had him. No further questions needed. Case closed.' Kathleen's Da spoke with bitter certainty before he looked at Jack and Kathleen. 'I don't know what you two are going to do.'

'Ay, well Da, Kathleen said. I'll talk to Mammy and yourself about that later on. Let's get out of here now, before there's any more trouble.'

They scuttled out of the side door. Kathleen and her Da walking off one way. Jack and Lily the other.

XVI

It was, Jack thought, better than a wedding day. He was standing by the rail on the boat-deck with Kathleen and Niamh, waiting for their journey to Ypres to begin. Fitful sunshine was showing through cloud. The morning had begun with light showers and a cool breeze, but now a pallid lemon light revealed the world rinsed clean and full of promise. The lough had a sparkle to it, and the cry of the gulls was the cry of freedom. Or so it seemed to Jack. Unlike a wedding there were no unwanted guests or warring parents, or nervous speeches or pious mouthings. There was only the silent communion between Jack and Kathleen and Niamh as they focused their attention on Kathleen's Mam and Da, who stood next to Lily on the quay amongst the other well-wishers seeing off family and friends.

Jack had endured an excruciating parting from his parents and Eileen earlier in the morning that put him in mind of his first departure all those years ago. In the face of his father's intransigence, his Mam had convinced herself she was saying goodbye for good. In the depths of her sorrow, she'd forgotten recriminations. Eileen was in a similar state. Only his Da remained stolid and flint-faced. 'You have betrayed everything I stand for,' the old man said, refusing to shake Jack's hand. 'You have no loyalty.' Jack had given the only reply he could. 'My loyalty is to Kathleen and Niamh. It always should have been. I'm putting things to rights.'

Now, Jack saw Lily's eyes locked on him. She held a handkerchief bunched in her palm. He waved to her again and blew her a kiss. She had insisted on coming to the quay. Though Jack felt it made the parting harder, there was something comforting and appropriate in her presence. She was the only one of his family who knew about O'Donnell's violent end. Her intelligence and courage had helped to ensure there were no repercussions from the police in the aftermath. It was Lily who had kept him steady that Sunday afternoon and walked with him to dispose of the pistol. They went back to Ormeau Park and Lily kept watch while he threw it in the Lagan. On the way home she had helped him invent a story to account for his abduction and release. It wouldn't do to tell his parents the truth for fear they would betray Kathleen's Da. The police had to be kept out of it altogether. Between them, Jack and Lily came up with the idea that Jack had been the victim of a serious prank. Some Proddies warning him off association with Kathleen. Nobody he knew or recognised. A stunt to frighten him—that's all.

His parents had been so grateful to see him alive, they accepted the story immediately. Hughie looked sceptical and said in case anyone was wondering he'd had nothing to do with it and knew nobody who had. The police reluctantly accepted the tale as well. Lily convinced them that she and Kathleen had bumped into Jack on the Ormeau Road after he'd been released. They'd seen no one and knew no one involved. Since Jack was unharmed there was nothing more for the police to do. All was well.

The unforseen consequence of their invention, though, was that Jack's Mam and Da took the idea of a warning from the Proddy boys as vindication of their own attitudes. Another reason for him to give up Kathleen. Jack told them he wouldn't be coerced. He shared with them his plans to leave with Kathleen and Niamh. They had no problem with the fiction of his abduction but they couldn't deal with the truth. They tried everything from blunt aggression to emotional blackmail to persuade him to change his mind. Since they wouldn't listen to his protestations of love for Kathleen and his daughter, he didn't labour the point. Instead, he resorted to the fact he had to leave anyway to go back to his job. It was the only way to quieten their bludgeoning arguments.

Saying goodbye to them, he felt a weight lift from his shoulders. Now, the smell of hot oil and smoke, the vibration of the deck beneath his feet spoke more of the excitement of new beginnings rather than the sadness of parting, despite Lily's tearful presence on the quay. Jack was impatient for the ship to move, to be on their way and for the tension of this last wait to be over. He had suggested to Lily maybe she could come and visit them sometime. Even think about joining them over the water. She said she would think about it. She wanted to make her own way and had to work out which way that was.

Jack glanced at Kathleen and down at Niamh, who stood holding her mother's hand. Kathleen gave him a thin smile. Her eyes were troubled. The little girl stared out at the quay, a look of stunned bewilderment on her face. Jack felt for them both. It was harder for them to leave than him.

In the wake of Kevin's death, there had been fraught discussions with Kathleen's parents about the future. Jack had tried to persuade them to leave as well. He thought Sean McCafferty could run an estaminet in Ypres as easily as a pub in Belfast. It would be good for Kathleen and Niamh to have her parents on hand and it would put some distance between them and Kevin O'Donnell's death. Kathleen and her Da, he knew, carried a burden of guilt and sadness about Kevin that he couldn't share. He'd seen better men than O'Donnell come to worse ends in the war. That didn't stop him feeling for their distress and wanting to help alleviate it in any way he could.

But Kathleen's parents didn't want to be hurried into a decision. They didn't fancy Belgium, where people spoke foreign. If they were going to leave Ireland, they would rather think of emigrating to America or Australia. But for now Sean McCafferty said he would try to resurrect the pub in Cromac Street, despite everything that had happened there. He wasn't under suspicion for O'Donnell's death. He reported finding the body the morning after the shooting and the police had made the presumptions McCafferty expected. they didn't care enough to investigate too hard.

Kathleen was torn. Jack knew she hated the thought of leaving and maybe she still had doubts about him. It was only the outbreak of more violence on the streets that had swayed her—the clinching argument of keeping Niamh from harm. It was Jack's hope and belief that once they were settled, Kathleen would see the benefits of living away from Belfast in a place where their love could blossom without scrutiny.

Jack had shaken Sean McCafferty's hand before boarding the ship. The first time he had ever done so. The older man repeated his opinion that Jack had some brass plated bollocks on him. Jack had returned the compliment. 'We'll have a Guinness together one of these days,' Sean McCafferty said, while his wife wept and made Jack promise to keep her daughter and grand-daughter safe and well.

The siren sounded its deep mourning note. Jack saw the deck-hands busy with the mooring ropes. The thrum of the engines became louder and the vibrations deeper beneath their feet. Jack bent to Niamh and lifted her, so she could better see her grand-parents and the bustle on the quay. The gangways were cleared and rolled off. The ropes flung inboard. The siren sounded again. The ship shuddered and began to move. There was a frenzy of waving and calls of farewell as the screws churned and they moved into the middle of the stream. Jack swung Niamh off his hip and held her under her arms above his head, so she was dangling in mid-air looking down at him.

'Here we go,' he cried. 'It's a new start little darlin'.'

She looked at him with wide eyes. 'Are you my Da now?' she asked breathlessly, a frown on her face.

He brought her down and hugged her. Then he set her on

her feet. 'Watch this,' he said.

The ship was steaming slowly down the lough, and the quay was receding. Kathleen gave a last tearful wave towards her Mam and Da, who grew indistinct amongst the other faces left behind. Jack kissed his hand and sent a last salute to Lily. His sorrow at parting from her was mitigated by the gladness he felt that they had become close during his visit. He felt a connection had been forged that would never be broken now however far apart they might live. Kathleen turned to him, her eyes still brimming. He took out his handkerchief and mopped them for her.

'Dry up now, will you,' he said. 'I have something here for you.' He fished in his trouser pocket. 'Come in close, Niamh. I want you to see this.' He put his arm round the little girl bringing her into a circle with him and Kathleen.

'Give us your hand.' He reached for Kathleen's left hand with his right. He held it for a moment feeling the warmth, squeezing her fingers, before, like a conjurer, he produced in his left hand a plain brass ring. He slipped it onto Kathleen's wedding finger.

Taken by surprise, Kathleen looked at him for a long moment. In the depths of her green eyes he saw both sadness and uncertainty. He took her to be thinking about Kevin; the sorrows of her marriage and the manner of its end. There was nothing he could do but trust to time's healing.

She took a step and leaned into him, whispering so Niamh couldn't hear. 'I know I must wear the band for the look of things, for Niamh's sake. But I wish to God we could do without it as we did when we first met. Do you remember? How natural we were together? That was freedom. I don't want to be trapped again.'

'I do remember. I always have. That's why I'm here, putting the ring on your finger. Surely, we can make a go of it?'

'I'll do my best. That's my promise to you.'

'If you're unhappy with me in Belgium, I'll let you go. I

won't fight or stand in your way. I won't be your gaoler. That's my promise to you.'

'Come here with you.' She said this louder, so Niamh could hear and opened her arms to him. They embraced and their lips met, lingering for a moment with the promise of their future loving, before they drew apart and Jack spoke again to the little girl who was watching with serious eyes.

'Now we're wed,' Jack announced with a wide smile. 'And I'm your Da right enough. Now and always. We're to be the best of friends. Now give us a kiss.'

Niamh kissed Jack first and then her Mam. But she did so without smiling.

'What's the matter, sweetheart?' Kathleen asked.

Niamh looked up first at her Mam, then at Jack. 'Do you not need a Church and a priest for a proper wedding?'

Jack looked at Kathleen before he answered. 'You do not. What you need is love and a promise of love.'

'Is that what you were whispering about? I didn't hear you say anything.'

'It was to be sure,' Jack said, glancing at Kathleen, defying her to contradict him.

They turned then to watch the gantries and the shipyards and the rooves of Belfast slip behind them.

'Let's give the auld town a last wave,' Jack said.

'Mebbe we can come back when the fighting's done,' Kathleen said, wistful still.

'Ay, mebbe,' Jack replied. 'When the fighting's done. That would be grand.'

They stood and watched the coastline and the hills around Belfast grow further away, the contours losing their sharpness in the summer haze.

'We mustn't keep looking backwards,' Jack said after some time. 'We must look to the future.'

Kathleen and Niamh followed his example and turned to stare out over the ocean. The breeze was in their face now.

Along with the ozone, it provided a brisk invigoration.

'There's nothing there,' Niamh said.

'Yes there is,' Jack said. He looked first at Katheen and then at Niamh again. 'Can't you feel the loveliness of it? Doesn't the sky seem higher and the world wider. It's like stepping out of a narrow stuffy room into the fresh air. And look there.' He pointed into the distance.

'I can't see anything,' Niamh complained.

'Yes you can. That's the horizon. Is it not exciting? We have all this long journey to look forward to on boat and train and boat again. And then we'll come to our new house where you'll have your own room and mebbe we can have a dog or a cat for a pet and there'll be no more mithering and no more fighting.'

Niamh giggled. 'And we'll all live happily ever after. Like in a story.'

'Jack's good at stories,' Kathleen chimed in.

'Am I?'

'Sure you are. Full of blarney, like I've always said.'

'The thing about stories,' Jack said, 'is that it's best to make your own. You don't want to be living someone else's. Choose your own tale.'

'Not chase it?' Kathleen laughed.

'Chase it as well,' Jack laughed back.

Niamh looked at her Mam and her new Da. She didn't know what they meant.

'You're funny, Jack,' she said. 'I'm glad you're my Da.'

'I'm glad too, little lovely.' The ship rolled a little as it broached the swell of the Irish Sea. Jack put out a hand to steady Niamh. 'I reckon we should go below, find a seat and have a cup of tea. It's never plain sailing on the crossing. Specially by the Isle of Man.'

Kathleen said, 'We've never had plain sailing, Jack Young. We wouldn't know what to do with it.' She looked apprehensive again, her eyes full of disquiet.

'Ay, well. I'm looking forward to that changing. With a bit of practice, we'll get used to it. Come on with you now. A cup of tea to toast a new beginning.'

Acknowledgements

The Blessing is a work of fiction and takes place in landscapes and cities of the imagination. Nevertheless, the following titles have been helpful in enabling my imagination of events in times past: Alan F. Parkinson, *Belfast's Unholy War: The Troubles of the 1920s*, Four Courts Press, 2004; R.G. Adgey, *Arming the Ulster Volunteers*, Aiken McLelland, 1955; Fearghal McGarry, *The Rising, Ireland: Easter 1916*,Oxford University Press, 2010; Michael T. Foy and Brian Barton, *The Easter Rising*, The History Press, 2011; Fabian Ware, *The Immortal Heritage: An Account of the work and policy of the Imperial War Graves Commission during twenty years, 1917–1937*, Cambridge University Press, 1937; Richard Holmes, *Tommy: The British Soldier on the Western Front 1914–1918*, Harper Collins, 2004; Robin Prior and Trevor Wilson, *Passchendaele: The Untold Story*, Yale University Press, 2002. The quotation on p.80 is from *Scott's Last Expedition*, John Murray, 1923.

On a more personal note, I'd like to thank several friends and colleagues who have contributed to the development of the novel. Bryony Cosgrove kindly gave me useful suggestions about an earlier version. Tom Healy likewise offered helpful comments when the book was in its later stages. Alex Miller and Stephanie Miller have been great friends and supporters of my work over many years and kept me writing when the going was tough. I am grateful to Nick Walker and the team at Arcadia for their enthusiasm and commitment to the project and I'd like to thank Michael Wilding for his part in bringing the book to publication. Lastly, but not least, my family have provided me with a constant source of inspiration, support and forbearance. In particular, I'd like to thank my daughter, Ellen, for describing to me her experiences of childbirth. Not only was this a privilege beyond words but it also enabled me to more intensely imagine Kathleen's experience. My wife, Claire, has shared every step of the journey with me, reading innumerable drafts, making suggestions, and enabling my work in many ways. Her strength and generosity are my touchstones. Thank you. It perhaps goes without saying that any deficiencies in the work are all mine.

www.ingramcontent.com/pod-product-compliance
Ingram Content Group Australia Pty Ltd
76 Discovery Rd, Dandenong South VIC 3175, AU
AUHW020138130726
429791AU00003B/68

9 781925 333183